THE PRINCESS AND THE REBEL BILLIONAIRE

SOPHIE PEMBROKE

COWBOY IN DISGUISE

ALLISON LEIGH

MILLS & BOON

First Published in Great Britain 2021
by Mills & Boon, an imprint of HarperCollins*Publishers* Ltd
1 London Bridge Street, London, SE1 9GF

www.harpercollins.co.uk

HarperCollins*Publishers*
1st Floor, Watermarque Building,
Ringsend Road, Dublin 4, Ireland

The Princess and the Rebel Billionaire © 2021 Harlequin Books S.A.
Cowboy in Disguise © 2021 Harlequin Books S.A.

Special thanks and acknowledgement are given to Sophie Pembroke for her contribution to *the Billion-Dollar Matches* series and Allison Leigh for her contribution to *The Fortunes of Texas: The Hotel Fortune* series.

ISBN:978-0-263-29976-2

0521

MIX
Paper from
responsible sources
FSC® C007454

This book is produced from independently certified FSC™ paper to ensure responsible forest management.

For more information visit: www.harpercollins.co.uk/green

Printed and bound in Spain
by CPI, Barcelona

THE PRINCESS AND THE REBEL BILLIONAIRE

SOPHIE PEMBROKE

To Rachael Stewart, Andrea Bolter
and Jessica Gilmore—my perfect matches!
I've loved working with all of you on this series.
Thank you for making it so much fun!

CHAPTER ONE

PRINCESS ISABELLA OF AUGUSTA turned her back on the huge, glass-fronted villa, eschewed the view from the decked terrace out over the beautiful Lake Geneva towards the Alps, and glared at her assistant, Gianna, instead.

'This is a bad idea.' Unthinkably bad. This was breaking rules that had been drummed into Isabella before she could even walk.

Gianna tossed her highlighted caramel hair over her shoulder. 'I don't have bad ideas.'

That was a blatant lie, as Isabella had met some of Gianna's ex-boyfriends when she'd brought them to the palace.

'You told me you were taking me to see Sofia.' Isabella's cousin, Sofia, would never dream of doing something so risky and ridiculous as this. Sofia followed The Rules.

Of course, The Rules had led to Sofia marrying the love of her life and living in the lap of luxury in Lake Geneva with her husband and three adorable children, while also running her charity foundation for injured donkeys. The Rules hadn't been quite so kind to Isabella, but they had at least kept her safe and out of trouble.

This plan, she sensed, was a *lot* of trouble. Especially if her parents found out.

'This is better than another visit to Sofia,' Gianna said persuasively. 'This is a whole week of freedom, Your Highness. One week where you can be Bella for a change.'

'I'm always Bella with Sofia,' Isabella pointed out mulishly. She pushed away any thoughts of the one other person outside the royal family who'd been close enough to call her Bella, for a time. It would only make her miserable.

'*Sofia* thought it was a brilliant idea,' Gianna countered.

Isabella paused, blinked, and regrouped. 'Sofia *knows* about this plan?'

'Of course! Who do you think is covering for you if the King and Queen start asking any questions?'

It wouldn't be her parents, Their Royal Majesties King Leonardo and Queen Gabriela of Augusta, who'd be asking the questions, though, Isabella knew. It would be their private secretaries, or another member of household staff. Someone like Ferdinand, her father's right-hand man, whose job depended on all the royal children and cousins following The Rules.

His previous right-hand man had been fired after the last time Isabella thought there was a chance to break them. She'd been wrong, of course.

Just as Gianna was wrong now.

Isabella shook her head. 'Someone will find out.'

'They won't.' Pulling a folder from her laptop bag, Gianna spread out the papers on the high-gloss table in the middle of the terrace. She motioned for the Princess to take a seat and, dubiously, she did.

'Look.' Gianna pushed the top page towards her, and

Isabella took in the stylised M of the logo, and the words 'discretion guaranteed' underneath. 'This isn't your usual dating agency, Your Highness. M only works with the rich and famous, and it offers them something they can't find anywhere else.'

'A villa on Lake Geneva?' Isabella said, knowing she was being facetious.

Gianna rolled her eyes, probably hoping her employer wasn't looking. '*Privacy.* They offer you one week with your perfect match in an ultra-exclusive, completely private and secluded location—they even arrange security, at a discreet distance.'

They were, Isabella had to admit, very much secluded. While the shores of Lake Geneva boasted many small towns and villages—as well as the city of Geneva itself—on both the Swiss and French sides of the border, it was large enough that villas, like the one Gianna had driven her to from the small private airfield where they'd landed, were miles away from any other signs of human habitation. Their nearest neighbour, as far as Isabella could see, was across the lake—far enough away that she could only make out the winking of sunlight on the windows of the building.

As for the rest of it…

'How could this agency possibly know my perfect match? Some sort of algorithm, I suppose, based on my star sign or my photograph?'

'No, not at all,' Gianna said patiently. 'You fill in an incredibly detailed personality test—'

'Which I didn't do,' Isabella pointed out.

'I did it for you.'

'Doesn't that rather defeat the point?'

Gianna gave her a long, steady look. 'Your Highness, I've been part of the palace since I was a child. I was your friend long before I was on your staff. I've seen you grow up, stifled by the court and their rules. I've seen *you*, all these years. Seen you cry. Seen you laugh. Seen you—'

She broke off there, but Isabella knew, instinctively, what her friend would have said. *Love*.

Gianna had been there the last time Isabella broke The Rules. She knew exactly what that had done to her.

If she wanted her to risk it again…there had to be a good reason.

'The point is, I know you,' Gianna went on. 'I know your hopes and your dreams, your loves and your hates. And I was willing to be honest about them on the form, which I know you wouldn't have been. You'd have been thinking about what the palace expected from you, what your parents wanted, what The Rules said. Anything except how you actually felt or what *you* wanted.'

'You're right,' Isabella admitted softly. 'I would have done that.' She pulled the brochure from M closer. 'It says here there's a video interview required, too? I didn't do one of those.'

'Yes, you did.' Gianna smiled wickedly. 'Remember that Internet chat you did with that website? The one for young women, seeking their place in the world?'

Isabella frowned. She didn't do many interviews or royal events these days, if she could possibly avoid it. But Gianna had been insistent about doing that particular one…

'The one with that woman? The pretty one, from America? Morgan? No, Madison. Madison Morgan, right?' She'd liked that interview. Madison Morgan had asked her all sorts of interesting questions—much better than the usual stuff she got asked in interviews like that. As the third child of the King and Queen of Augusta she was a princess, but she'd never rule the country—that was down to her brother, Leo, named for their father. She'd never had any real role beyond doing what she was told. So all anyone really asked her was who had designed her dress, and which parties she'd be attending. The answer to the first was usually, 'Ask Gianna,' and the second, 'None if I can possibly avoid it.'

Morgan had asked her things about her*self.* Who she was, who she wanted to be. What mattered to her most. What her ideal date looked like… *How did I not see it?*

In fact, there *had* been a couple of moments that had struck her as odd during the interview—questions that didn't quite make sense, comments she didn't understand. At the time, Isabella had put it down to cultural differences, or her being out of practice at interviews, or even the language barrier. Her English was fluent, and she was usually good at picking up idioms, but still, it wasn't her native tongue and that could cause problems sometimes. And there hadn't been anything to set alarm bells ringing—besides, Gianna had been there the whole time.

Of course, she had. Because she'd set this whole thing up.

'Why, Gianna?' Isabella asked now. 'Why did you do this?'

'Why did I risk my career and my future to find you a week of freedom and bliss with a man who might be your perfect match?' Gianna smiled, softly. 'Because you deserve it, Bella.'

How long since her best friend had last called her by that nickname? Too long. They'd become employer and employee, not friends, the moment Isabella reached adulthood.

Gianna took her hand. 'I've seen you, fake smiling through every date your family has arranged with a "suitable suitor". Every boring Augustian duke or lord, even the ones twenty years older than you. I've seen you miserable and lonely, because not everyone gets as lucky as Sofia did, and finds their perfect match in the palace. I've seen you trying to find a moment to just be you, away from the bodyguards or the cameras or the men who want to marry into the royal family. I've seen you withering away in that palace ever since Nathanial—'

'Don't.' Isabella shook her head violently. 'Not…just, don't.'

'Okay. Okay.' Gianna ran her fingers soothingly over the Princess's arm. 'But you were miserable, Your Highness. And I saw something I could do about that…so I did it.'

'Do you really think this will change anything?' Isabella met her friend's gaze with her own, and found nothing but compassion there. 'One week with some guy? It's not like he's going to magically turn out to be a mysterious aristocrat or something. He won't be someone my parents would let me marry—I've already met every single guy they consider suitable. So it can't ever be more than this—just one week with someone I *might* be… compatible with.'

She felt a slight heat rise in her cheeks as she said the words. She hadn't been *compatible* with anyone for a very long time. Just once, in fact. With Na— No. She wasn't even going to think his name.

Did Gianna really think that a week with a man some agency thought was her perfect match would fix everything that was wrong with Isabella?

'Maybe it won't change *everything*,' Gianna admitted. 'But it might help. At worst, it's a week of fun and freedom—no bodyguards, except Tessa from your staff, and the small security team the agency sent to guard the perimeter, and they'll all be at the cabin on the edge of the estate. No royal obligations, no expectations. Just a guy that you might like…and the chance to have some fun, if you want it.'

'I'm not looking for that, either,' Isabella said flatly. How could she? *That* was definitely against The Rules.

Gianna sighed. 'Bella, this isn't some sort of hook-up agency I went to here. It's M. The premier, most expensive and exclusive dating agency in the business. Whoever they've sent to meet you, he's not here for sex. He's here to get to know you.'

The knot in Isabella's stomach started to loosen, just a little. 'You're sure?' Maybe she could come out of this having made a friend. A friend would be nice. A lover would be…trouble. Lots of trouble.

'Sure.' Gianna glanced over Isabella's shoulder, then gave her a mischievous grin. 'But looking at your Perfect Match, you might want to consider just a *little* romance this week.'

Isabella's heart thudded in her chest as she realised she *wanted* that. She wanted to find someone to talk with, relax with, laugh with, even love with, in a way she'd hadn't in so long. In a way she'd stopped hoping for.

But what was the point, if it was only for one week?

She shook her head. 'No, Gianna. A friend is one thing. Anything else is—'

'Against The Rules,' her friend finished for her, rolling her eyes.

'Yes.' But it wasn't just The Rules, Isabella realised. It was the risk. To her reputation, her family…her heart. She'd risked it all for love once before. It wasn't a mistake she intended to make again.

Gianna was still staring blatantly at the glass-fronted villa where Isabella's perfect match was waiting. If she wanted this week away from reality, Isabella knew she had to turn now. Had to see what sort of person M had decided was right for her. Had to open up her mind and her heart to the possibility of a friendship beyond The Rules.

Sucking in a deep breath, Isabella turned slowly to face the villa on the lake, and stared up through the glass to the man standing, one hand on his hip, the other holding a phone to his ear, looking down at them from what had to be the bedroom.

Was he really so tall, or was it just because she was looking up at him? Either way, the glass and the distance between them couldn't hide his admirable figure—the breadth of his shoulders, the muscles showing through the tight T-shirt he wore, or the long legs with their thick thighs... His black hair was cropped short, his skin as tanned and warm as her own Mediterranean complexion.

He was, she had to admit, the best-looking man she'd ever been set up on a date with. But then, the bar for that had never been particularly high.

Most of all, though, he looked like trouble.

He looked down, and her breath caught in her chest as his gaze met hers.

Maybe Madison knows what she's doing, she thought as the funny feeling in her chest moved lower, turning warmer. Maybe this guy wasn't her perfect match, but she couldn't deny the heat she felt at the idea of a week alone with him.

She pushed it aside. A new friend, that was what she was looking for here.

Even if that new friend looked like sin and risk and everything she'd spent every moment since Nathanial avoiding. She couldn't imagine what M thought they'd have in common, but she supposed there must be something. As Gianna said, they'd been matched on their personalities, first and foremost.

'So, you're going in?' Gianna asked, a giggle in her voice.

Isabella swallowed. 'Well, I've come this far.' She'd already left all but one of her security staff at the airport, lied to her parents about where she was, and apparently dragged Sofia in on the deception. 'What's one week?'

One small risk—a week away, getting to know a new friend. After that, she'd go back to The Rules. She'd be Princess Isabella again, and everything that entailed.

But first, she'd have this one week of freedom.

With him.

Matteo Rossi stared out over Lake Geneva through the huge panes of glass that spanned the whole front of the villa. It was quite the view, he had to admit that. The lake glistening in the late-afternoon sun, the snow-peaked mountains in the distance, even in June. And it was definitely in the middle of nowhere—which he was pretty sure his management team had insisted on. Nowhere for him to get into trouble, and wasn't that the whole point of this week?

'So, it's nice?' his manager, Gabe, asked on the other end of the phone line, probably happily ensconced in his office in Rome, preparing for the next race. A race where Matteo pointedly *wasn't* driving, even though his broken leg had healed perfectly well already. 'Madison promised it would be nice.'

Ah, yes, the famous Madison Morgan. Former child actress and now the owner of the M dating agency, the latest strategy Gabe and the others had hit on to slow him down, and the reason he was now stuck in Switzerland and not on the racetrack where he belonged.

'It's fine,' Matteo said dismissively. He'd stayed in some of the finest hotels in the world, from Abu Dhabi to Las Vegas and home to Rome. This villa was just a building, impressive though it was.

'And is *she* there yet?' There was a knowing lilt in Gabe's voice, a teasing note. Because Gabe wasn't talking about Madison, of course.

He was talking about Matteo's Perfect Match.

Matteo rolled his eyes just thinking the words.

'No, she's not here yet.' But then he looked down at the terrace outside the villa and saw two women talking. One—with caramel hair and a skirt suit—was obviously talking a mile a minute, if the way her hands were waving around was anything to go by. She was pretty, Matteo conceded. But his attention was already held by the other woman, the one with her back to him.

Dark curls tumbled down her back, loose and wild, falling almost to where her waist nipped in before curving out over generous hips. From what he could tell from behind, she had her arms folded in front of her, one hip tilted out as she stood, as if she was listening to what her companion had to say but didn't really believe it.

Her. He felt the word run through his body more than he consciously thought it, but he knew in an instant it was true. If she wasn't the woman Madison had picked for his perfect match, then the woman was doing her job wrong.

Suddenly, the idea of this week in exile wasn't looking quite so bad.

Except, no. Because whichever woman was here to meet him, she'd be expecting something he couldn't give. The M agency didn't do booty calls; his perfect match was expecting true love. Commitment. Forever.

Matteo had far too many adventures in his future to even *think* about settling down with someone. Which meant he couldn't give the woman the wrong idea.

Still, they'd been matched on personality, so hopefully

hanging out with her for a week wouldn't be too bad. They could blow this place and go explore the region. There had to be *some* interesting things to do around here, and, if she was his perfect match, she'd be up for an adventure.

Just as long as he made it clear she couldn't expect anything more.

'Are you looking forward to meeting her?' Gabe asked. Was it just guilt keeping his manager on the line so long? He'd sent Matteo here, away from his team, away from racing. They'd told him it was for his own good—a treat, even. But Matteo knew the truth.

This was a last-ditch attempt to repair his reputation—and his sponsorship deals. Apparently some of his most recent adventures had cut a bit too close to the line. Were they hoping that the lure of true love would tame him? Stop him chasing after the next adventure, taking bigger risk after bigger risk?

If they were, they were going to be disappointed.

'I guess,' he replied. After all, he wanted to save those sponsorship deals, too. Not to mention his career. He'd already made more money than he could spend in a lifetime, on and off the track. But if he didn't have racing, his dream career, what would he do?

Whose dream career? The whispered question in the back of his mind surprised him.

See, this was what happened when he slowed down. He started thinking. And unless he was thinking about speed and angles and winning, what was the point? As a rule, Matteo getting all introspective wasn't good for anybody. He acted, that was who he was. Who he'd always been.

Only since Giovanni died.

That voice. Matteo shook it away and turned his attention back to the women by the lake instead. Women, he understood. The thoughts that came to him late at night, or when he wasn't distracted by something fun…those he didn't *want* to understand.

But as he looked down, he realised the woman with the dark hair, his possible perfect match, had turned around to face him. Even through the glass, and over the distance between them, he felt it the moment her gaze met his. A feeling that hit his chest and spread through his body. And he wasn't entirely sure he understood that, either.

It was just her curves, he told himself. The way her folded arms highlighted her perfect breasts, the narrowness of her waist and the arch of her hips. Or her mouth, full and luscious. A purely physical reaction to a beautiful woman, nothing more. Of course, it was.

'It's just one week, Matteo,' Gabe was saying, when he finally tuned back into the phone conversation. 'Just… stay out of trouble this week. Finish healing.'

'My leg—'

'I know, I know. The doctors said it was fine, but they also said not to push it too far, too soon. And that's basically your motto in life, so…just take the week. When you get back, we'll come up with the next stage of the plan to get you back out on the racetrack. But, Matteo?'

There was something in his manager's voice that made him nervous. 'Yeah?'

'If you *did* happen to come out of this week happy, in love and ready to settle down with the love of your life… I don't think any of your sponsors would be disappointed.'

Because as much as they wanted the maverick, risky moves that won races, they needed him to appear a good role model for the younger fans, responsible enough that people trusted the things he was selling, however tangentially.

How do they expect me to be a champion and *a boring, stay-at-home guy, all at the same time?* The adrenaline was in his blood. The need to live life to the fullest, to chase every dream, tackle every challenge, beat every odd—on the track and off.

Except, the last time he'd gone adventuring, the odds had beaten him. Calling Gabe from the hospital to admit that he'd broken his leg while cliff diving, two weeks before the Dutch Grand Prix, had not been his finest moment.

Everyone wanted him to slow down—just not when he was behind the wheel.

Matteo sighed. 'Message received.' He hung up.

Down below, the terrace was empty—and he heard the electric buzz of the front door closing and locking behind whoever had just keyed in the confidential code. A code only he and the woman who was supposed to be his perfect match had.

No sign of the other woman outside, either, so he couldn't know exactly who was waiting for him downstairs—he just hoped he was right in his guess.

He didn't believe for a moment that some agency could find him his dream woman based on a questionnaire— one he'd been forced to fill in while still in the hospital— or a brief video interview, which he'd done with his leg in plaster, propped up on Gabe's coffee table.

But if the right woman was waiting downstairs—if she really was a match for his restless, reckless spirit— they might at least have found a way to stop him thinking too much. And Matteo would take that as good enough for now.

CHAPTER TWO

IT WASN'T UNTIL the door swung shut behind her, the alarm beeped, and the sound of Gianna's car driving away down that long, private driveway faded, that Isabella realised this could be a massive mistake.

She was alone in a house in the middle of nowhere with a man she'd never met. Sure, Gianna said there were security personnel in the cabin down the driveway—including Isabella's own long-term security woman, Tessa, apparently—towards the perimeter of the grounds, but what if she was wrong? What if this was a set-up? What if Gianna had been blackmailed into bringing her here? What if…?

No. Gianna never would—not for anything. One betrayal didn't mean Isabella had to keep looking for another one around every corner, and, besides, she was a very minor royal of a very minor Mediterranean country. Nobody would go to this much trouble to set her up, would they?

Isabella forced herself to breathe slowly, mindfully, as she took in her surroundings. Modern, sparse furnishings—the opposite of the palace at Augusta with all its heavy wood and dark antiques. Bright white walls, and comfortable-looking sofas loaded with cushions and blankets in various textures and shades of white, both looking out over Lake Geneva. She supposed the interior designer who furnished the place hadn't wanted anything to distract from that incredible view, through that all-glass wall out to the water.

She felt calmer already. This villa might not be like anywhere she'd stayed before—her family tended towards the traditional, even when travelling—but there was something about it. Something peaceful.

Hopeful, even.

This place gave her hope that she might be able to take this week to regroup, to find herself again after so long feeling adrift in her royal world.

Following The Rules was all well and good, and after everything with Nathanial she understood better than ever why it was important. But still, she couldn't help feeling hemmed in sometimes. As if she were pushing against tightly woven walls of cloth holding her in, stopping her from stretching, from reaching out for something more.

Maybe here, in peace and solitude, she could figure out what that something more was.

Except she wasn't alone, was she?

She heard a tread on the stairs behind her and knew it must be him. Her perfect match, if such a thing really existed.

She hoped he wasn't dreaming of too much from this week. A fairy-tale ending with a princess, for instance. Because however nice he was, that wasn't in her power to give. Friendship was all she had to offer.

Pasting on a smile, Isabella turned away from the lake to face him.

Gosh, he was even better looking up close. That cropped black hair, curling tightly against his skull. Those bright green eyes. And that body…tall, lean but obviously muscled; she'd been able to tell that even from a distance. Up close it was almost overwhelming, the sheer physicality of him.

He was staring at her, too. Good. At least she didn't have to worry about being accused of ogling. She wondered what he saw. Did he know who she was? Probably not, unless Madison had told him; she wasn't exactly highly visible outside Augusta, most of the time, and the palace had been keeping an even tighter rein than normal over her publicity since the incident five years ago.

Isabella frowned. Should she know who *he* was? He looked faintly familiar, in some way, but she couldn't put her finger on it. And it wasn't as if she were particularly well up on the rich, famous and notable of Europe—or the world—either. Since her father mostly just involved her brother Leo in international business, the only men she really got to meet were potential suitors. Especially since Nate.

And none of her suitors had *ever* looked like this man.

'Hi,' he said, finally, a wide, open smile spreading across his face. 'I'm Matteo. Matteo Rossi.'

Even the name rang a bell, but she still couldn't tell from where.

She moved forward to meet him as he descended the last few steps, and held out her hand. 'Isabella.' And then, because there was no point trying to hide these things, she continued, 'Princess Isabella of Augusta.'

Matteo's eyebrows shot up and, instead of shaking her hand as he'd clearly been about to, he twisted it and brought it to his lips. 'Should I bow?' he murmured as he kissed the backs of her fingers.

He should, really, she supposed. But the warmth that spread through her from the touch of his lips on her skin was more than an adequate substitute.

'It's probably going to get a little awkward if you have

to go around the house bowing to me all week,' she said, after pretending to consider it for a moment. 'I think we can let it go, just this once. Under the circumstances.'

Matteo straightened up and stepped back, but kept a hold of her hand, a wicked smile dancing over his lips. 'Good to know, Your Highness.'

'Isabella, please.' Maybe she didn't want to be a princess this week. Not with this man.

Maybe she wanted to be something more than just royal. Human, perhaps.

'Ah, but I'm only a humble racing-car driver, Your Highness,' he teased. 'Are you sure it would be appropriate?'

'*That's* where I've seen you before!' Isabella snapped her fingers as it came to her. Humble racing-car driver her foot. Even *she* knew that he'd made the rich list last year, his billions earned from racing and sponsorship deals ratcheting him up the rankings. 'Matteo Rossi. I watched you race in Barcelona last year. You won, of course.'

That had been a treat for her. A rare trip out of Augusta with Leo and his wife. A chance to escape the stifling air of the palace, just for a few days. She hadn't seen much of Barcelona, but watching the cars racing around the track she'd envied them their freedom. Until her sister-in-law, Princess Serena, had pointed out that they only ever went in circles, and only where someone else pointed them.

Isabella had wondered if maybe *nobody* had the kind of freedom she dreamed of sometimes, late at night, with the windows open. But looking at the man in front of her now…he didn't seem hemmed in by anybody.

She would bet he could go anywhere, any time, with anybody, whenever he chose.

And he was here in Lake Geneva with her.

A nervous excitement jolted through her at the realisation. Maybe she could learn a little freedom from this man. And she had a feeling she would enjoy the lesson.

A princess. Madison Morgan thought his dream woman was a freaking *princess*?

Matteo hadn't exactly spent time memorising the names and faces of European nobility, but he still surprised he hadn't recognised her. Hell, she'd recognised *him*, and he was nobody, really.

Well, he was the world champion, but what did that really mean to people who didn't follow the sport? What did it mean to *royalty*?

He was still holding her hand. He should stop that.

He'd been so relieved when he'd walked down the stairs to find the curvaceous, dark-haired woman standing with her back to him again, looking out over the lake. The idea that she might have left before he found out if that instant connection he'd felt when their gazes had met meant something had been unbearable to him.

Now, he wasn't sure what any of it meant. The Princess seemed...cautious. Guarded, perhaps. There was something in her eyes, even when she was joking about him bowing, that told him this was not a woman who let people in. Which was okay by him, since he didn't particularly want or need anyone getting close to him, either.

But a princess. He was pretty sure she'd never climbed Machu Picchu or been bungee jumping or travelled across America in a convertible, as he'd done over the past few years. From her tone when she talked about watching him race in Barcelona, he suspected that was the most excitement she'd had in years. Just *watching* someone else have fun.

That was what royals did, wasn't it? They hid away

in their palaces and watched over other people actually living their lives.

Which begged the question, what was a princess doing signing up to an exclusive dating service? Let alone spending a week in a secluded location with a strange man, like him. She couldn't really believe *he* could be her perfect match, could she? And if she did, he needed to disabuse her of that idea pretty quick.

More than ever, he was glad he'd already resolved that this week would be about friendship and fun, rather than romance or anything more. He liked a risk as much as the next guy, but he *definitely* wasn't Prince Charming material.

Somewhere behind him, something pinged. And then it did it again.

'Is that…some sort of security alarm?' Isabella asked, her eyebrows furrowed.

Matteo listened to the ping. 'I think it's an oven timer, actually.'

Even a place as designer and minimalist as this villa on the lake had to have a kitchen, right? And it sounded as if someone had planned dinner for them.

'Come on, Princess. Let's go investigate.'

Downstairs had seemed completely open plan—with sitting areas and a dining table and a well-stocked bar with stools, all looking out towards the incredible view. But first appearances could be deceiving, Matteo realised. Behind the white stone staircase that ran from the centre of the room up to the first floor was a hidden corridor—one that led to a state-of-the-art kitchen, and a pinging oven timer.

With a little trial and error, Matteo found the right button to stop it pinging, turned down the oven temperature and opened the door. There were oven gloves hanging right next to it, and he used them to lift out a steaming dish of lasagne. His mouth watered at the sight. This was *proper* food.

Normally, when he was training, he watched his diet carefully to keep himself at peak fitness. Everything made a difference on the track and, besides, he was usually training for something else as well—like the Machu Picchu hike, or the Paris marathon, or a cross-Channel swim.

While he'd been in recovery with his broken leg, he'd kept up the habits—keen to show the team that he was ready to get back out there the moment it was healed. But since he'd been sidelined anyway, sent to Lake Geneva to keep him out of trouble…surely a little lasagne wouldn't hurt.

He turned and placed the dish on a waiting trivet on the marble counter, and found two plates already set out with fresh salad, complete with gleaming red tomatoes, and the gloss of oil and balsamic vinegar. A marble bowl filled with crusty bread sat beside it. Matteo touched it; still warm.

'That door must lead to the housekeeper's quarters,' he guessed, nodding towards a slim white door, almost camouflaged between the kitchen cabinets. '"Discreet household staff included,"' he quoted from M's literature.

'It looks delicious.' Isabella's eyes had lit up at the sight of the food. He supposed having actual staff would just be commonplace for her, growing up in a palace. But for him, even since he'd reached the heights of his career and grown more or less accustomed to having staff and help around for the day-to-day essentials of life, it still felt like an incredible luxury.

If Giovanni could see me now. On holiday with a princess, with staff *to do all the cooking and cleaning.*

His brother wouldn't believe it. Not even in his wildest dreams. Not after their childhood in Rome, both taking on their share of the household tasks while their mother worked two jobs to keep a roof over their heads.

But Giovanni couldn't see him, and neither could his mother. Or if, as Matteo sometimes let himself hope, they could look down from above and watch him, they couldn't tell him what they thought of his lifestyle—his success, his billions in the bank, his fame.

Sometimes, he wished they could, so he could hear their advice. Other times, he thought it was just as well they couldn't. He could only imagine the bickering.

'There was a table out on the balcony upstairs,' he said impulsively as he dished up the lasagne onto the waiting plates. 'Why don't we take it up there to eat?'

Isabella nodded and, between them, they loaded up a couple of trays with the food and cutlery, as well as the carafe of wine and the glasses that had been laid out for them. Negotiating the stairs slowly, Matteo made a joke about not dropping anything on these stone floors and was gratified when Isabella laughed.

He wasn't sure what he'd expected when she'd said the word 'princess', but this pasta-loving beauty wasn't exactly it.

He heard her falter behind him, though, as he reached the bedroom. Placing his tray down on the table on the balcony, he turned back to find her staring at the bed.

'There's another bedroom next door,' he told her, quickly realising the cause of her alarm. 'I thought I could use that one, if you wanted to be in here? I think the staff have already brought up our bags.'

Her gaze flickered from the bed to the solitary suitcase beside it—her suitcase, he assumed, since he'd already put his next door. Who knew how the staff had managed that without them noticing.

The view was just as good from both rooms, he'd decided, and the balcony here stretched between the two rooms anyway, accessible from either one of the glass doors that were in place in lieu of windows or walls, over the lake.

'Oh, okay. Great.' Her stretched smile didn't look quite natural, though. Matteo tried to look reassuring as he reached over to take the wine and glasses from her.

Of course, she still thought this week was about romance and love—and sex. Whereas he'd already known that true love wasn't on the cards for him, even before the discovery that she was a princess. They were worlds apart in so many ways—but she'd come here under a false assumption. That he was looking for love.

He needed to set that straight.

Pouring a glass of wine for them both, Matteo waited for Isabella to take her seat at the small balcony table before sitting down himself. His mother had instilled *some* manners in him, at least.

Then he waited until she'd taken a large mouthful of lasagne—so she'd have time to think about her answer—then asked his question.

'So, what's a princess doing using an elite dating site? Don't you have to marry a prince or something?'

The food—delicious as it was—turned to ashes in her mouth at Matteo's question.

Don't you have to marry a prince?

He'd put his finger straight on the biggest problem with this whole set-up. She wasn't free to fall in love with whoever M decided her perfect match was. And she needed to tell him that.

'Not necessarily a prince,' she said, with a small, one-shoulder shrug. 'But a lord or a duke, yeah. Preferably Augustian, to make my father *really* happy.'

'Are there many Augustian lords and dukes your age?'

'I think my cousin married the last of them.' She didn't begrudge Sofia her happiness—or her husband. But it did narrow the acceptable dating pool quite considerably.

'Ah. So that's why you're here?' Matteo grinned. 'Because I think you already know I'm not a duke or a lord.'

No. He was a *racing-car driver,* of all things. Isabella could just imagine her brother's face if he knew where she was right now, who she was with. Leo sometimes seemed even more hidebound and determined to follow The Rules—or, at least, make Isabella follow them—than the King and Queen were.

For a man who was supposed to be her perfect match, it was hard to think of anyone less suitable. From what she knew of his reputation—which was mostly stuff she'd heard whispered in the crowd in Barcelona last year—he was a risk-taker, a daredevil. A Lothario on the racing circuit.

The absolute opposite to the stuffed-shirt lords her parents had been setting her up on dates with for the last five years.

But if he realised she wasn't really his perfect match, he didn't seem too disappointed.

Isabella reached for a piece of bread and dipped it in the waiting oil and vinegar. Her mother, if she were here, would have looked despairingly at Isabella's hips. But she wasn't here—nobody was, except Matteo—so it was safe to be a little bit rebellious, right? *Ooh, look at you, eating bread. You rebel.*

And having dinner with a racing-car driver. That probably counted more.

'I'm here because my assistant, Gianna, lied to me,' she said casually, as if things like this happened to her all the time.

Matteo sat back in his seat, eyebrows high, his arms folded across his chest. 'She told you that you were meeting a prince?'

'She told me I was going to visit my cousin for the week, like I often do at this time of year. That's what she told the palace, and my parents, too. Nobody knows I'm here except for Gianna, my cousin Sofia, Tessa—the longest serving and most trusted member of my security team, Madison Morgan—and you.' It felt dangerous, giving up that secret. Information that could hurt her, if Matteo chose to share it with the papers, or via the internet.

But it felt good, too. Freeing.

What was that quote? Publish and be damned. But she didn't think that Matteo would suddenly jump on social media and reveal her whereabouts. After all, discretion was guaranteed by the M dating agency, and she couldn't imagine Madison Morgan would be very happy with him—or give him another chance to find his one true love—if he broke that rule.

Which brought her back to her original problem. Matteo was there to find his perfect match. That was who he was expecting to meet when he walked into the villa. And instead he got her—a princess who couldn't fall in love with him even if she wanted to, and had now admitted she was only there because she was tricked into it.

She must be quite a disappointment to him.

It was probably a good job she was used to being a disappointment to people.

'I'm sorry,' she said. 'You came here to find your perfect match, and it's only the first night and I've already ruined that for you.' She got to her feet. 'This wasn't fair.

Let me call Madison and explain, and I'm sure she'll re-fund you, or find you an *actual* perfect match for your next date.'

Matteo laughed, and Isabella paused half out of her chair, unsure what was funny about the situation.

'I'm not laughing at you,' he said after a moment, ob-viously sensing her discomfort. She was a princess. She really wasn't used to people laughing at her—well, apart from her older siblings, of course. Leo and Rosa could always find *something* hilarious about her words or ac-tions—when they weren't being horrified.

He motioned for her to sit back down, and she did so cautiously. But there was still lasagne and bread left—she assumed the meal had been planned towards his cultural heritage, and wondered whether tomorrow might bring an Augustian speciality, or even a Swiss one—and she hated to leave good food uneaten.

'So why *are* you laughing?' she asked, reaching for another piece of the delicious, still-warm bread.

'Because this whole situation is hilarious.' Matteo leaned across the table, closer to her than anyone who wasn't an employee or a blood relative had been in a very long time. Then, swiping the last piece of bread from the bowl, he said, 'You see, I didn't choose to come here either.'

Isabella blinked. 'You…didn't?' He was already sit-ting back in his chair, smirking at her as he chewed his prize, but she could still feel his breath against her cheek as he spoke.

What was it about this man that affected her so? Was it just that it had been such a long time since she'd found a man attractive at all? Now, sitting across the table from Matteo Rossi, with all that lean, long muscle and that smirk... Isabella admitted to herself that it had *definitely* been too long.

Not that she could really do anything about that, unless she wanted to marry one of the stuffed shirts Leo kept setting her up with.

Back to the point. 'So, why are you here?'

This was supposed to be their perfect date, their chance to find true love—without the usual scrutiny of the press or the public. But if *neither* of them had chosen to be there at all, where did that leave them?

'Same reason as you, more or less.' With a shrug, Matteo reached over for the carafe of red wine and topped up her glass. 'My management team thought it was a good idea.'

'Why?' Isabella thought she understood why Gianna believed it was a good idea for her to be there—a chance to kick back, relax, have the freedom to be herself, and maybe even have some fun. But surely Matteo had all those things available to him in the real world, in a way that the Princess of Augusta really didn't.

'To keep me out of trouble.' One eyebrow arched up above Matteo's bright green eyes. 'Although we might be able to find just a *little* bit of trouble here this week, don't you think?'

And from the heat that pulsed through her body at his words, Isabella had to agree.

This man could be an awful lot of trouble.

CHAPTER THREE

HER EYES DARKENED at his words; he could see it, clear as day in the fading evening light.

But he couldn't do anything about it.

She's a princess, Matteo. It was his mother's voice in his head, even after all these years. *Have some respect.*

Yeah, he was pretty sure Gabe and the sponsors wouldn't have sent him here if they'd known who his perfect match was. They'd be too afraid of his causing an international incident or something.

Matteo wasn't entirely sure it wasn't a possibility himself.

He looked away, turning his attention back to the bread in his hand as if it were the most fascinating thing on the balcony, and added, 'I mean, if you're my perfect match, you must like a little adventure, right? There have to be places to explore around here...'

He trailed off as he saw her eyes widen in horror. Yeah, his first instincts hadn't been wrong. The Princess wasn't a risk-taker.

'Or we could hang out here at the villa, get to know one another,' he finished with a sigh.

Isabella visibly relaxed, her eyes lighting up. 'That sounds nice. It's not often I get the opportunity to make a new friend.'

He couldn't help but return her smile. It might not be the week he'd plan for himself, but he got the impression that the Princess needed to be gentled along in this. By the end of the week, he was sure he'd manage to talk her into *some* small adventure.

'So if you were tricked into coming here, what made you stay?' Matteo asked, curious.

Isabella looked up and met his gaze with her own, direct, brown one. And just as it had when she'd looked up at him in the window of the villa earlier, his chest tightened.

For a moment, he was almost certain she was going to say, *You.*

She didn't, and he tried not to feel disappointed at that.

'At the palace my life is rather…let's say tightly controlled.'

'You mean boring?' he guessed.

That raised half a smile from her. 'Amongst other things. And I decided that a week away from that—a week to relax and be myself, not just Princess Isabella— might be good for me. Plus,' she added, with an impish grin that lit up her whole face, 'I was pretty sure from the moment I saw you that the last thing you'd be was boring. And that was before I even realised you were a racing star!'

No, Matteo had never been accused of being boring. At least, not since Giovanni died, and he started living his life for both of them.

'So, you're looking for someone to help you relax and have a bit of fun for a change, then, rather than your true love?' That worked out nicely for him, even if her idea of adventure didn't match his.

'I guess I am.' Isabella sounded almost surprised at her own words, as if she hadn't really factored him into her plans, despite what she'd said about him not being boring. 'What about you? What are you looking for out of this week, if it's not your perfect match?'

What *was* he looking for?

'Well, like I said, my management team are just hoping to keep me out of trouble.'

Isabella raised her eyebrows at that. 'Seems kind of an extreme way of doing it—going through all the rigmarole of setting you up with the M agency. It's not exactly cheap, either, from what I understand.'

'One hundred grand deposit,' Matteo agreed with a wince. Even now that amount was a tiny drop in his investment and savings accounts, he still couldn't help but imagine his mother's horror at the casual way he spent it. 'But at least most of it goes to charity.' He'd donated his chunk to the cancer charity he'd supported ever since they'd helped Giovanni through those last weeks and days. That way, something good was coming out of his side-lining, he'd reasoned.

Isabella gave a low whistle, which seemed kind of out of keeping for a princess. But then, he was coming to suspect that she wasn't just any princess. 'You must have *really* got in a lot of trouble for them to go that far. What did you do?'

'Broke my leg cliff diving,' he admitted, and she winced.

'Ouch. It's better now?'

'Yeah. Docs all say it should be as good as new.' Even if it still ached a little, most days. He was doing his strengthening exercises, and he sure as hell wouldn't let it affect his driving. That was what mattered. 'But I was out of commission for a while. Couldn't race, couldn't work out, couldn't do anything much.'

He'd hated that—the inaction—more than anything.

That was still one of the concerns he had about this week. If she expected him to sit around doing nothing...he'd end up abseiling down from the roof out of sheer boredom.

'It wasn't just the broken leg, though,' he admitted. 'I guess the team—and Gabe, my manager, in particular— were fed up with my antics in general.' In fact, he knew they were, because those were the exact words Gabe had used at the team intervention. He'd been lying there in his hospital bed, lucky to be alive, and Gabe had been ranting about 'your antics putting everything at risk'.

He'd apologised later, although Matteo hadn't needed him to. He knew what fear and love sounded like together, and Gabe had been like an older brother to him since he'd lost his own.

'You're a bit of a daredevil, huh?' Isabella asked.

Matteo shrugged. 'You could say that. I like adventures.' It sounded easy, when he said it like that. The truth was more complicated, of course, but wasn't it always? And in his experience, girls didn't want to hear the truth. They wanted the story, the fairy tale of the wild and reckless racing-car driver. Even if behaving that way on the track would only get people killed. Matteo was always responsible behind the wheel, even if no one watching would ever see that.

And that was the problem. The public—and the sponsors—only saw him speeding around corners at work, then taking risks in his private life. His reputation was established—and it wasn't the sort of reputation that got him respect.

'And now you're stuck here with me for a week, in a luxury villa with excellent food.' Isabella polished off the last of the wine in her glass and glanced over at the desserts still sitting on the tray.

'Pudding?' Matteo suggested and she nodded enthusiastically. The Princess liked her food. Matteo made a mental note in case that came in useful some time.

He got the feeling he was going to get to know a lot about the Princess this week. And he found himself strangely thrilled at the idea.

Maybe *she* was his next adventure after all.

Isabella had expected to struggle to sleep in a strange place, but the bed in the villa was so comfortable, and the food, wine and company over dinner had been so pleasant, that she found herself sleeping in the next morning.

By the time she woke, the sun was already high above the lake, streaming through the gauzy curtains that covered the floor-to-ceiling windows—and she could hear the sound of coffee cups on the balcony.

Coffee. That sounded like something worth getting up for.

Dragging herself out of bed, she wrapped her dressing gown around her, blushing as she realised what Gianna considered appropriate nightwear for a princess on holiday wasn't exactly modest. Her pale pink silk pyjama shorts and matching camisole were barely covered by the thin, short white broderie wrap.

She paused for a second by the glass doors to the balcony. Maybe she should shower and dress before heading out. But the coffee smelled so good…

'If you don't get out here quick, I'm going to eat all the pastries,' Matteo called from outside. 'I'm starving.'

Well, that made the decision for her. There was no way she was missing out on pastries.

Matteo was already sitting at the table they'd shared the night before—at some point in the night, it must have been cleared and reset, as it was now laden with pastries and steaming hot coffee. Isabella looked around and spotted a small staircase she'd missed the previous night, leading down to where she imagined the kitchen door must be at the side of the house. Whoever their house fairies were, sent to take care of them this week, they were certainly discreet and silent.

Taking a breath, Isabella stepped forward, her princess smile in place, and took her seat opposite him. 'Good morning.'

His eyes widened as he looked up and clocked her nightwear, but he didn't say anything, which she appreciated. And he poured her coffee, which she appreciated even more.

'Have you been up long?' She took the cup and lifted it to her lips, breathing in the bitter scent and taking one cautious, hot sip.

Matteo shrugged. 'A little while. Went for an early morning run by the lake, then came back for a shower. When I came out, I found breakfast ready.'

'You still run on holiday?' Exercise for Isabella was limited to yoga classes with Gianna, and walks around the palace estates.

'It's a habit,' he replied. 'Plus I'm still strengthening my leg. The physio gave me exercises, but now it's more about rebuilding my stamina.'

'I wouldn't have thought that driving was a particularly fitness-focused sport.' Although given the way his muscles showed through his thin white T-shirt—dampened in places from the water dripping from his tight black curls—she wasn't really surprised to learn that he took his physical fitness seriously.

'I hear that a lot.' Matteo leant back in his chair, one foot propped up on his other knee, his arm sprawled across the railing on the edge of the balcony. Just looking at him made her cheeks feel warm at her suggestion.

Of course he was in peak physical condition. 'Actually, fitness is really important in racing.'

At least he didn't seem annoyed by her comment. 'How come?'

'Well, first off there's the strength needed for controlling the car at high speeds.' Matteo ticked that point off on his finger before raising another one. 'There's the heat to contend with in there, too. But most of all, it's our hearts.'

'Your heart?'

'A race can be two hours long,' Matteo explained. 'And our hearts are pumping at way above normal levels for that whole time—like we're exercising hard for a sustained period. The G-forces over a two-hour race are immense—you feel like your head weighs ten times what it normally does.'

'I hadn't thought about any of that,' Isabella admitted.

'No reason you should,' he replied, with a shrug. 'For me, the biggest thing is my brain.'

'Yeah?' She also hadn't really thought of racing as a particularly cerebral activity either, but she figured it probably wasn't a good idea to mention that.

'Racing needs split-second reactions, it needs me to be able to think ahead, to calculate risks and take them quickly. If my body is tired, my brain gets tired too and my concentration starts to lapse. I can't afford that in a race; it could cost me too much.'

Not just the winner's flag, Isabella realised. If Matteo lost focus out of the racetrack, if he wasn't up to the rigours of a two-hour race, it could cost him—or someone else—their life. She shivered, even though the morning was warm.

He seemed to sense her discomfort with the topic and moved on.

'So, what do you have planned for today?' Matteo

topped up her almost empty cup of coffee and she took it gratefully, sipping the hot liquid carefully while she considered her answer.

Planned? She didn't have anything planned. There was no Gianna standing there with her schedule for the day, reminding her of appearances she'd reluctantly agreed to make, or letters she needed to write. No member of the royal household summoning her for another awful, awkward date with a man she didn't want to marry. No rules keeping her from escaping into the city and exploring alone. No security guard trailing after her, even—although she suspected that if she tried to pass the gatehouse where the security staff were staying, she'd soon pick one up.

The point was, there was nothing she was *supposed* to be doing today. Which meant she could choose for herself.

What a luxury.

And a pity she had no idea what to do with it.

'I saw a well-stocked bookcase inside,' she said eventually. 'Maybe I'll read.'

'Sounds good,' Matteo replied, not really sounding as if he meant it.

She supposed that was a little antisocial, considering she was supposed to be getting to know her companion better. 'There were some board games too, I think?'

A wide smile spread across Matteo's face. 'Now, that sounds more like it. But I warn you—I'm very competitive.'

'Why am I not surprised?' Isabella asked, grinning in return.

By later that afternoon, Matteo was regretting almost everything about this week.

Well, that wasn't strictly true. Mostly, he was just regretting his personal promise to himself to keep his hands off the Princess.

From the moment she'd appeared that morning, dressed in those indecently short pyjamas and a wrap that was basically see-through, he'd been struggling to keep his eyes—and his libido—where they belonged.

He'd thought that playing board games would help. After all, he associated them with being a kid, playing with his brother. They were inherently unsexy, and she'd even put real clothes on to play them. It was the perfect 'new friend' activity, right?

Except it turned out that Princess Isabella had a competitive streak to rival his own, and the wicked smile that flashed across her lips every time she was winning sent heat flashing through his body.

And that wasn't the only problem.

Isabella reached past him for the dice, her warm skin pressing against his arm as she moved. The dark curls of her hair hung over her face, and he could smell roses when he breathed in.

He tensed, waiting for her to retreat again—but when she did, the softness of her breasts brushed against his shoulder, forcing him to swallow hard.

This was unbearable.

Because M knew what it was doing. The agency, or Madison Morgan herself, had picked his perfect woman—at least in one way. Isabella was beautiful, curvaceous, oozing an unconscious sex appeal that was driving him insane.

He had a whole week alone with the most beautiful woman he'd ever seen in real life, and he was going to spend it playing Monopoly.

This was why he needed to get out of the villa and *do* something. Sitting around only let him think and feel and imagine, and that wasn't good for either of them right now.

As soon as she'd passed go and collected her money, Matteo grabbed for the dice and rolled them. Isabella moved his piece for him, since it was on her side of the board, and gleefully shouted, 'Rent!'

Thank God. Handing over the remains of his pretend savings, he sprang to his feet. 'Then that's me out. You win. Uh… I need to go for a run.'

Her forehead creased adorably. *Not adorably. Just normally. Like any normal woman.*

'Didn't you already go for one this morning?'

Yes. Yes, he had. 'Gotta catch up on training, right?'

'Sure,' she replied, not sounding convinced. 'Um, I'll see you for dinner, then?'

'Definitely.'

Because even he wasn't as unchivalrous as to leave his only companion all alone for dinner. Nothing to do with the almost *orgasmic* look that crossed her face whenever she was eating the food here.

He was almost *certain* she wanted him too, not that she'd been obvious about it. It was the little things, the ones he only saw because he was looking for them. The way her eyes darkened when she smiled at him, the way she bit into her lower lip and looked away when he smiled back. The heat that seemed to sizzle between them, whenever they got too close…

In the end, he didn't bother changing into his running gear, and just walked straight out along the path that meandered down towards the edge of the lake and around it. He needed to think, not run, this time.

Identify the problem, Matteo. This was no different from a problem with a car, or a bend of the track he couldn't quite hit right. No different from any of the challenges in his life he'd overcome to get where he was now.

He'd taken trips and risks other people didn't even dream of. He'd trekked Machu Picchu, done solo sky-dives, skied mountains others just sat and looked at. He'd come from nothing and made his billions. He risked his money as easily as his life, and he *always* came out on top, whatever the concerns of his management team.

He beat the odds, every time.

And he wasn't going to be thrown off his game by a princess who was too scared to leave the house.

Maybe the problem wasn't that she was beautiful. He'd met many beautiful women in his life, and had plenty of them in his bed, come to that. But none of them had ever filled his mind the way Isabella had over the last day—to the point where even an innocent game of Monopoly had led to him imagining making love to her on top of the damned board.

Was it the princess thing? No. He'd never had any par-ticular interest in royalty, and his money and his fame had put him in plenty of aristocratic company before now without problems. Royalty were just one more type of celebrity really, weren't they? And he had enough ce-lebrity of his own.

Except…there was one aspect of the princess thing that made a difference.

The untouchable part.

Matteo groaned aloud as he realised, scaring a bird in a nearby tree into flapping off in a hurry. Lowering him-self to sit on a flat rock by the water's edge, he looked out over the huge expanse of Lake Geneva towards the distant mountains and thought his way through to the heart of the problem.

He'd promised himself, even before he'd met her, that

he'd keep this week light. That he'd focus on friendship. Because the woman he'd be spending the week with was looking for her perfect match, and he wasn't offering true love to *anyone*. He was there under false pretences, and it would be wrong to lead her on.

Except, of course, by making Isabella forbidden fruit, he only wanted her more. And the fact that she was a princess, that the royal family would never allow her to date him, let alone marry him, well…

Matteo had never done well with being told what he could and couldn't do. Even by himself.

So. He'd identified the problem. Now he just needed to figure out what to do about it. Because nothing had changed—

Wait.

Yes, it had.

He'd been assuming that Isabella was here looking for her Prince Charming. But she wasn't. She'd been manipulated into coming, just as he had.

She wasn't looking for love from him.

Matteo smiled to himself, as Lake Geneva shone in the June sunshine.

Because that opened up all sorts of possibilities.

Isabella was nowhere to be seen when he finally returned to the villa, so Matteo headed to his room and showered and changed for dinner. As he towelled off his hair, he heard movement on the balcony—but by the time he'd dressed and went to investigate, whoever had been out there had gone.

Their discreet housekeeping staff had left them another feast, though. Obviously they'd observed their preference for eating on the balcony and brought dinner straight to them this evening. Tonight's dinner, when he peeped under the silver cloche keeping it warm, appeared to be some sort of fish dish with rice that smelled amazing.

'Is it time for dinner?' Isabella appeared in her doorway. The jeans and T-shirt she'd worn during the day had been replaced by a bright red sundress, and the matching lipstick she wore made Matteo all the happier he'd figured out his issues during his walk.

She did appear subdued, though, and dinner passed relatively quietly, without any of the chatter they'd enjoyed at breakfast, or the night before.

Her eyes lit up as he unveiled the tiramisu waiting for them on the nearby trolley, though, and Matteo decided it was time the address the elephant in the room.

Except Isabella got there first.

'I think we need to talk,' she said as he reached for the serving spoon for the tiramisu.

'I agree,' he replied.

He heard her take a deep breath, as if steeling herself for something unpleasant. He added an extra spoonful of pudding into her bowl, just in case.

'The thing is…we're stuck here all week, right? Together. And since playing board games clearly isn't your cup of tea, neither of us are *actually* looking for true love, and we're both supposed to be staying out of trouble…what do you suggest we spend this week doing?' she asked.

Matteo handed her the over-full bowl of dessert and sat back in his chair, trying not to smile. She'd given him the perfect opening.

'Well, I see it as an opportunity.' He hadn't, until he'd spent the day trying to keep his hands off her. Now, it was all he could think of.

'An opportunity?' She took a spoonful of tiramisu and

slipped it between her lips, her eyes fluttering shut with pleasure as she tasted it. 'Mmm, you have got to try this.'

It wasn't the pudding he wanted to try, though. It was her. He wanted to taste her lips, and the cream still lingering there. He wanted to kiss every inch of her curves. He wanted to learn all the other things he could do to coax that satisfied, pleasured moan from her mouth.

And after a day of fighting it, he was done.

'I will,' he said, swallowing. 'And yes, an opportunity. After all, we still have everything M promised, right? A week of seclusion. The freedom to do whatever we want, without anyone watching. And we were chosen to spend the time together because we're supposed to be perfectly matched. Compatible, if you like.'

What was the point of trying to resist a temptation that had been so perfectly selected to tempt him? If she didn't expect true love from him…what was stopping them?

Her eyes were open now, wide and wondering—so wide he could almost read the thoughts passing behind them. Maybe she hadn't been thinking them before, but now he could tell that her thoughts echoed his own. She was seeing the possibilities, too.

Matteo couldn't be the only one feeling the chemistry between them. That kind of sensation only happened when it went both ways, in his experience. And M had got one thing right, at least—the chemistry between them was like nothing he'd ever felt before.

He wanted to know where that would lead. Where it could take them. And from the look in Isabella's eyes, she did too.

She wasn't saying anything, though. And he didn't want to rush her.

She was thinking about it. That was enough for tonight.

Leaning closer, over the table, Matteo dropped his

voice to a low purr—the one an ex-girlfriend had told him sounded like his engine warming up. 'I'm not a prince, Isabella. And I've got no interest in being one, either. After this week, we'll both go our own ways, right? Back to the lives we live in our own worlds. But until then… why not make the most of the freedom we've been given this week? Live a little dangerously.'

Reaching out, he swept way the morsel of cream that clung to her full lips, then sucked his finger into his own mouth to taste it, hearing her breath hitch at his movements.

'I… I don't know.' He could feel her holding herself back. Was that just her royal upbringing, or something else? Was it just because he wasn't a prince? Because the attraction between them definitely wasn't all in his imagination. He could see it in her glassy eyes, pupils blown. In the way she swallowed and her tongue darted out to wet her bottom lip and, *God*, he wanted to kiss her.

But he wouldn't. Not until she told him herself that she wanted that too.

'Think about it,' he murmured. 'And I'll see you in the morning.'

Then he turned and headed for his lonely bedroom, knowing he wasn't going to be thinking about anything but her tonight.

CHAPTER FOUR

ISABELLA DID NOT have a second restful night.

She left the dinner dishes on the balcony and retreated to the calm, cool bedroom to follow her usual bedtime routine, just as she had the night before. A bath, with the lavender oil she always travelled with, followed by her skincare regime—the one her mother said would keep her looking 'acceptable' for longer. Then, wrapped up in her pale pink silk pyjamas, she curled up on the bed with her book.

She barely read a page.

In fact, she'd gone through her whole routine on autopilot.

Think about it, Matteo had said. It seemed as though she'd be doing nothing but.

He'd barely touched her—just removed a blob of cream from her lips. A mother or nanny might have done the same, brusquely or absently. But when *he* did it…

His fingertip brushing against her lip had sent sparks firing through her body—sparks she hadn't been sure she was capable of even feeling, any more. That slight pressure had been enough for her to imagine his touch everywhere else—over every inch of her body.

There was no ambiguity in what he'd been suggesting. In fact, she was almost surprised neither of them had mentioned it before. Gianna had hinted at it, of course, but Isabella…

Isabella had suggested they play board games.

She groaned at the memory. How out of touch was she with men and romance that this idea hadn't occurred to her?

Except that was a lie, and Isabella tried hard not to lie—even to herself.

She *had* thought about it, from the moment she'd seen Matteo standing above her on the balcony and known he was supposed to be her perfect match. She'd thought about it every time he stood close enough for her to feel the heat of his skin or smell his cologne. Every time she'd brushed past him to retrieve the dice when they were playing. Every time he'd smiled at her or watched her enjoy dessert. She'd just been too scared of what that meant to even consider doing anything about the thought.

Now, snuggled down on the cool, crisp sheets, Isabella stopped trying to ignore the possibility, and let herself think about it properly.

One week. No rules, no prying eyes, no consequences.

For this one week she could cut loose. And if she wanted, she could take Matteo as a lover—bring him to her bed and let him worship her body, and explore his in return. He'd made it clear that was how he'd choose to spend this week, rather than playing Monopoly.

She supposed that was a fairly common thing for him. She was sure his daredevil attitude to life continued into his romantic entanglements, too. She hadn't followed his career particularly closely, but even she'd seen enough clips on the Internet or in papers to know that he never dated the same woman twice, but always had a beauty on his arm whenever he wanted one. Picking up a woman for a week of debauchery and seduction was probably par for the course in his downtime.

But for her…

She hadn't been with a man since Nate, and even that had been a lie. She wasn't a virgin, but she definitely wasn't experienced, either. And honestly, since Nate she hadn't really been interested in anyone all. She knew there were plenty of stories on Augustian social media about her love life, but they were all fabrications.

Her heart had been broken, and her faith in people severely dented, by her first foray into love. It was one of the reasons she'd been so unsure about the whole idea of her 'perfect match' in the first place.

Except that wasn't what she was here for, and it wasn't what Matteo was offering, either.

He was offering a week of giving in to the chemistry between them. A week of pleasure, she was sure. A week of fun, strings-free.

And she wanted it. She had to admit that much to herself.

But was she brave enough to take it? Even knowing what had happened last time she'd let go in such a way?

She wasn't sure. And by the time she fell asleep that night she still hadn't decided.

Her dreams were filled with unfamiliar images—and feelings. The water of Lake Geneva, lapping around her. The scent of the flowers that grew in the pots on the balcony, mingled with the more familiar lavender of her pillows, and a spicy, new scent that she knew was Matteo himself.

Skin on skin, slick with water and want. That was all she remembered when she awoke, unsatisfied and frustrated, from a night of dreams.

And now she had to face him again.

Great.

Isabella took her time washing and dressing, trying to scrub the dreams from her body in case Matteo could see them on her, somehow. Or smell them, perhaps, the way she dreamt she could still smell him in the air around her.

But eventually she had to admit to herself that she was just postponing the inevitable. She had the whole rest of the week here in this glorious villa, beside this beautiful lake, with Matteo. Not making the most of it would be a terrible waste.

Throwing open the doors to the shared balcony that joined their bedrooms, Isabella let the morning air rush in, and felt her own breath rush out.

Once again, Matteo was already sitting at the table on the balcony. There were shadows under his eyes that suggested his sleep might have been as disturbed as her own. But he looked up as she appeared, and a slow smile spread across his face at the sight of her, making him look instantly younger. More free.

Was he remembering that moment last night, too? The one when he'd been close enough for her to kiss, if she'd moved her head just ever so slightly? Was he thinking about the suggestion he'd made to her?

The smirk on his face suggested he probably was.

'Good morning,' he said, his voice low and warm. 'Sleep well?'

She took her seat. 'Like a baby.' It wasn't a lie. Babies were notoriously bad sleepers, weren't they?

'Me too.' The smirk hadn't gone anywhere. 'So, how are we going to spend our second day in secluded paradise? Chess? Poker?'

He was teasing her now, but she didn't rise to it. Instead, she looked out over the lake, the balcony suddenly claustrophobic, despite all the fresh air. This villa was huge, and she knew that if she asked for space Matteo would give it to her. He wasn't the kind of man to press where he wasn't wanted, she could tell that already from the way he'd backed off last night after the merest suggestion of more.

The problem was, she wasn't at all sure she wanted him to keep backing off. But she wasn't certain enough to let him in, either.

She wanted him; she wasn't lying to herself about that any more. But it was *so* against The Rules. And beyond anything she'd let herself want for so long—ever since Nate. The desire she felt for Matteo…it was overwhelming, and terrifying.

And it felt amazing, all the same.

She stared out over the water and the mountains in the distance. The June air was warm and welcoming, but the breeze from the water kept things fresh in the shady trees that surrounded the villa.

She didn't want to be trapped inside today—otherwise, this villa was no better than the palace in Augusta that she'd escaped from.

Maybe she wasn't ready to take the risk of letting Matteo in quite yet. But perhaps she could take the tiny risk of letting herself out. Just a little bit.

One small first step towards where she was almost ready to admit she really wanted to go.

To bed, with Matteo.

Isabella placed her empty coffee cup down on her saucer. 'I'm going for a walk, down by the lake,' she said, before she could change her mind. That would give her time and space to keep figuring out what she wanted from this week. Time away from the allure of Matteo's smile, or those green eyes that pulled her in whenever she caught them.

Matteo grinned. 'Great! I'll come with you.'

* * *

There was a narrow path, leading away from the villa in the opposite direction from the easier one he'd taken for yesterday's walk, down the slope of the ground to the water's edge. Matteo hopped down it easily, hands in his pockets, then looked back to find Isabella picking her way along the uneven ground more cautiously.

'Need a hand?' He stretched out his arm to offer his assistance, but Isabella shook her head.

'I'm fine.'

That was a lie if ever he'd heard one. Oh, not with the path—he was sure she was more than capable of making her way down that alone.

But Princess Isabella of Augusta was not fine.

Perhaps it was just being away from the palace and out on her own for what, he imagined, had to be the first time in a long time. But he suspected it had more to do with the ideas he'd put in her head over dinner the night before.

She was a princess, not a casual hook-up in his usual fashion, he knew that. But still…they needed to find a way to entertain themselves this week, right? And since his usual methods of adrenaline-seeking were off the table, Matteo could only think of one good one.

Not to mention the fact that the more time he spent with her, the more inevitable them falling into bed together seemed. So why put it off? Why not enjoy the hell out of it while they had the time? Now he'd made the decision, Matteo was done denying what he wanted.

But back to the Princess.

After he'd retreated to his room the night before, Matteo had done a little internet research. Only natural, really, he figured. After all, she knew who *he* was, and was presumably familiar with his reputation. It was only fair that he use the tools at his disposal to put them on an equal footing. Thank goodness for high class Wi-Fi in such a remote spot.

Augusta, he'd learned, was a tiny little country—one of those ones squeezed between the bigger, more familiar European powers. Still, its monarchy had its fans—especially the next generation. Matteo was secure enough in his own masculinity to admit that Isabella's older brother, Leo, the Crown Prince, was handsome, built, and probably the subject of teenage Augustian girl fantasies, despite the fact he'd got married a few years before. Her sister, too, was married off, as were all the cousins and second cousins—at least, the ones over twenty-one.

Isabella, at twenty-eight, was already gaining articles about her being 'on the shelf', which seemed kind of ridiculous to Matteo, who was already five years older than that and had no intention of marrying any time soon. But it was different for royals, he supposed.

There'd been a short mention of a boyfriend in one of the articles from a few years ago, but nothing much more. And he'd avoided most of the gossipy pieces; he knew from his own experience how inaccurate they could be.

'Okay?' he asked as Isabella reached the bottom of the path.

'Fine,' she said again.

He wished she'd stop saying that.

Because the thing was, Matteo had only known the Princess for less than forty-eight hours, and he already knew it was a lie. She was beautiful, witty, bright and fun to be around—and he thought that was more to do with her natural personality than her royal training. She didn't ask the 'have you travelled far?' or 'what do you do?' questions he'd been asked on being presented to other members of other royal families. She didn't keep up that screen of polite reserve, of smiling because she was supposed to smile, or listening because she was supposed to listen, not because she was happy or interested.

And yet…she was definitely holding back. He could sense it in the straightness of her back, the way she paused too long before answering his questions. The way uncertainty would flash behind her eyes whenever he got too close.

He'd seen that before—in other women, and in friends, too.

Someone had hurt her. Someone she loved.

Not that it was any of his business, he knew.

And yet…part of him wanted it to be.

She's just one more challenge, that's all, he told himself. And she wasn't even on Giovanni's list. He needed to let it go.

'Which way do you want to go?' he asked as they reached the edge of the water. The path, a little more established here, stretched out in both directions, surrounding this corner of Lake Geneva. To the right, it joined up with the path he thought he'd taken yesterday.

Matteo's geography was a little rusty, but he seemed to remember that the lake was *huge*, almost like an ocean between the countries of Switzerland and France. Driving in from the private airfield where he'd landed, he'd passed dozens of small lakeside towns and resorts, before disappearing into the trees that surrounded the villa he and Isabella were staying in.

Maybe he'd persuade Isabella to go explore some of them with him one day, once she trusted him a little more.

'That way.' She pointed to the left, seemingly randomly, but as they broke out of the tree cover Matteo decided it was a good choice, all the same. Up ahead was a small jetty, seemingly attached to their villa, since there were no other residences in sight. A speedboat, painted in white and blue, was moored up beside it practically calling his name; he would have to take that out on the water this week. Maybe he could even convince Isabella to join him in that adventure, if she wouldn't risk the towns…

There was also, he realised somewhat belatedly, another, much easier path down from this side of the villa. Oh, well; coming down the forest path had been an adventure. And wasn't that what he was known for?

'It's beautiful here, isn't it?' Isabella said.

He looked at her. The June sun beat down on her dark curls, making them shine so brightly they were almost white where the light hit. Her face was tilted up towards the sky, soaking in the warmth, her arms loose at her sides and her white cotton sundress dancing around her calves in the slight breeze.

She was beautiful. Never mind the damn lake.

Again, he felt that tug of lust down low in his belly, the one he'd been vaguely conscious of since the moment he first saw her, standing with her back to him on the terrace. 'It's gorgeous,' he replied, a beat too late.

Isabella turned to him and smiled. 'I'll race you to the jetty.'

And before he could even process her words, she was already running, racing towards the slatted wooden platform that jutted out over the water.

He could have caught her easily, if he'd started moving immediately. But instead he took a moment to watch her run, her hair flowing in the wind, her curved calves flashing under her thin white skirt.

Then he caught her.

In a few long strides, he reached her side and, as they approached the jetty, wrapped an arm around her waist to catch her, pulling her body tight against his as she laughed and he grinned against the warmth of her hair.

It was a game, a moment of lightness and fun…and then it changed.

Like a cloud passing over the sun, Matteo felt all the playfulness of the moment disappear in a shadow of an instant.

Her curves pressed against the planes of his body, soft and yielding in his arms, and for a second he almost forgot there was clothing between them at all. Her hair smelled of roses and sunshine, and it overwhelmed his senses. He heard her breath hitch in her throat and realised that he'd stopped breathing altogether.

He'd known she was beautiful. But like this, pressed against him as if the only place she belonged was in his arms…she was so much more.

She was magnificent.

He should let go. That would be the gentlemanly thing to do. But how could he when this felt so right?

'Matteo…' She twisted her head to look up at him, her tongue darting out to moisten her full lower lip in a way that made him groan with want. He was so instantly, painfully hard, pressed against her, she had to know exactly how he felt. What he wanted. How he needed her.

He'd expected to see uncertainty in her eyes. But when he met her gaze with his own he found only a reflection of his own want.

Lust surged through him as he hauled her up until his mouth met hers. He kissed her the way he'd wanted to since he first saw that lush mouth of hers—deep and hard and as if there were nothing more in the world but the two of them.

And she kissed him back, matching his passion as she turned in his arms, raking her hands up into his hair to hold him closer. God, how had he thought this siren reserved and shy? Instead, she was everything he needed to remind him he was still alive, still had adventures to find, places to explore.

Like her entire naked body. Preferably now. They'd been promised seclusion, right? He hadn't seen another villa for miles before he reached theirs. No one would see if he stripped her dress from her and made love to her here on the sun-warmed wood, right? And even if they did... Matteo was past caring.

But Isabella was not, it seemed.

As he reached for the straps holding her dress up and slowly pushed them down her arms, she wrenched her mouth away from his at last. Her eyes were still wild, her hair curling in all directions where he'd been running his hands through it. And her mouth—those gorgeous plump lips—was swollen from his kiss.

Matteo started to drop his hands from her body, but she grabbed them before he could, holding them between them, crushed against her breasts. His fingers itched to reach out and stroke the line of her neck, down past her collarbone and under the white cotton of her dress. But he made himself wait and listen.

This, he assumed, was where she told him all the reasons this was a bad idea, reminded him that she was a *princess*, so could never think of acting on the obvious attraction between them. He tried to prepare himself for the inevitable, even though his body was clearly still far more optimistic than his mind.

And then the Princess said, 'Race you to a bed.'

CHAPTER FIVE

ISABELLA DROPPED HIS HANDS, turned and started to run.

She had no real hope of being able to outrun Matteo—not that she really wanted to, for long. But if she acted fast enough, perhaps she could outrun the voice in her head reminding her of all the reasons that this was a terrible idea.

She didn't care. Not right now. And maybe that would come back to bite her later, but she'd deal with that then.

This was her week of freedom. Her week to be Isabella, not the Princess. Her week to find her own happiness, her own pleasure.

And from just one kiss, she already knew that Matteo Rossi could give her a hell of a lot more pleasure than anyone else in her life ever had.

Her blood pounded in her ears as she raced up the path towards the house—the simple, straight one, not the one through the trees they'd come down. She wasn't wasting any time getting back to the villa now she'd made her decision.

No, she hadn't decided. More…followed her instincts, for once.

From the moment Matteo had caught her, the instant she'd felt his body against hers, she'd known she was done fighting the attraction between them. Because if she left this villa at the end of the week without sampling everything he was offering, she knew that she'd regret it for the rest of her life.

She could hear Matteo's thudding footsteps on the path behind her, slow and steady, as she approached the villa. He was pacing himself, of course. He didn't want to beat her, and he wanted to save his energy for what would happen when he *did* catch her.

Isabella allowed herself a small, secret smile at the thought. God, she couldn't wait for him to catch her.

She risked a glance back over her shoulder and found him almost right behind her. Her heart was racing—was it because of the running, or the pursuit? Or because it knew what was coming next...

Finally, finally she reached her destination.

Grabbing the handle of the large, sliding glass door that opened up the whole ground floor to the outside world, she yanked it open and tripped inside. Matteo's arm was around her waist in an instant, keeping her upright, keeping her close.

'Caught you,' he murmured into her ear, and she shivered in delight.

'I don't see a bed yet,' she whispered.

In response, Matteo swept her up into his arms and strode purposefully towards the stairs. 'We can fix that.'

Isabella laughed. 'You don't need to carry me!'

'I'm not risking you running away again.'

But she wouldn't, she knew. Maybe she *had* made a decision, after all.

One to make the most of every moment of freedom she had this week. One to put aside her fears and The Rules and her trust issues and go with her feelings instead. Her body, even.

Gianna had given her this week, and now Isabella was giving herself *this*.

She wasn't going to let herself back away again. Not for anything.

They'd barely made it up the first step, though, when a sharp, ringing sound rang out through the villa.

Matteo froze, mid step.

'Alarm?' Isabella asked.

'Phone,' Matteo corrected her.

The noise repeated. And repeated.

'Right. Of course.' She knew what a phone sounded like. It was just that in her world, a noise like that was more likely to be a fox setting off one of the proximity alarms at the palace, or a sightseer getting a little too enthusiastic about their visit and pushing through an alarmed barrier to a room that was out of bounds. 'Leave it.' It was the reckless kind of thing she did this week—ignoring phone calls and alarms.

The phone was still ringing. And Matteo was still holding her, motionless on the stairs, obviously at war within himself.

Finally, he sighed and put her down. 'It could be the security team,' he said, far too reasonably for her liking. 'If we don't answer, someone will come up here and interrupt us anyway. And I'd rather take the call fully clothed than deal with a burly security guard bursting in when I'm buried deep inside you.'

His voice dropped on the last part of his sentence, and Isabella felt it resonate through her body until she was throbbing with the need to feel him there, not just talking about it.

But instead, Matteo swept across the room, picked up the receiver and barked, 'Yes?'

As she watched, his demeanour softened a little even

as his shoulders slumped in resignation. 'Madison. Hi. Yes, we both made it here okay.' He looked up and caught Isabella's gaze with his own, apology in his eyes. Then he chuckled at something the dating-agency owner had said, and he looked away. 'Getting you to check up on me, are they? Sure, sure, you always check in on day two. Well, you can tell my management team that I am staying out of trouble. The Princess and I have been for a lovely walk through the woods this morning, and around the lake to the jetty.'

Isabella smiled. The truth, if not the whole truth.

She could see the strain on Matteo's face as he tried to remain polite, to convince Madison—and presumably, by association, his team—that he was behaving. Not that she imagined they'd be complaining too much about his seducing her—or the other way around, if she was honest. After all, why send him on a dream date if they didn't want him to, well, find a little relaxation that way?

Still, this conversation was going on far too long for her liking. Isabella smiled. She had just the way to fix that.

If he'd honestly believed that this was just a courtesy call from Madison Morgan to check that they'd settled in okay, Matteo would have hung up in an instant. But he knew his team, his management. He knew Gabe.

He'd been ignoring his phone ever since Isabella had arrived, and that would have Gabe worried. So he'd found another way to check up on him. His manager had always been a little overprotective of the talent.

No, that wasn't fair. Gabe had always been overprotective of *him*. And if he'd set Madison up to make this call and Matteo didn't answer...well, those security guards would be bursting in again any moment. And he *really* didn't like being interrupted.

'Everything has been perfect,' he reassured Madison. *Everything apart from the timing of this phone call.* Because now Isabella had an excuse to overthink, to start listing all the reasons this was a bad idea. And that would lead to her changing her mind.

He could almost see the thoughts passing over her face as the occurred to her. She took a step back up the stairs, getting ready to run.

The attraction between them was undeniable, but even he had to admit the logistics weren't great. If he'd *actually* been looking for his one true love, he'd have been pretty pissed off. But as it was, this worked perfectly for him. Although he knew his team had been hoping this week might lead to a stable girlfriend for him, one who might take over responsibility for keeping his feet on the ground and the whole of him out of hospital for a while, that wasn't what Matteo wanted.

He just wanted Isabella, naked, under him, on top of him, and anywhere else she wanted, for the rest of this week. And Madison Morgan, matchmaker extraordinaire, was going to ruin that for him. The irony was actually painful.

But then, something changed, somewhere inside Isabella's mind. He'd probably never know exactly what, but he didn't really care.

A wicked smile flickered across her lips. And then, her eyes wide, she reached up and untied one of the bows at her shoulders that held up her dress.

Half of the white fabric of the bodice fell, sliding over the curve of her breast to hang under it, revealing the intricate, gossamer-thin lace of her strapless bra.

Matteo swallowed, his whole body tense with need.

God, he wanted to drop the phone, race over there and take that perfect peak in his mouth.

But he also wanted to see what Isabella did next.

He didn't have long to wait. Slowly, deliberately, she reached up and untied the other bow.

The white sundress slipped away from her skin, hanging around her hips, leaving her torso covered only by that see-through bra.

On the other end of the line, Madison was saying something about the boat at the jetty, but he wasn't listening. He was picturing his hands, his mouth, his body on those perfect curves. His gaze followed the gorgeous, undulating line of her, curving down over her shoulder, swelling over her breasts, dipping in for that narrow waist before flaring out again at her hips, where that damned sundress still hung, caught on the sheer generosity of her body.

'Right,' he said to Madison, with no idea what he was agreeing with.

Isabella smirked, as if she knew exactly how distracted he was. Maybe she did. Her eyes were almost black, and even at this distance he could tell she was breathing harder than her actions warranted.

She's turned on by this too. Thank God.

How had he thought, even for a moment, that this princess was buttoned up and boring?

'Yeah, of course,' he said, even though the words were meaningless. Matteo didn't take his eyes from Isabella for a moment.

And as he watched, she put her hands to her hips, and pushed the white cotton over them.

The dress fell to the floor, and Matteo gripped onto the edge of the telephone table hard, just in case he suddenly passed out from wanting her. It didn't seem completely impossible right now.

Had he ever been this hard, this desperate for a woman before? He didn't think so.

And he'd barely even touched her, kissed her.

God, he wanted to do so much more.

He let his gaze roam from her perfectly painted toes—her sandals abandoned by the door, he supposed—all the way up those long, shapely calves and thighs. He skirted past her wispy lace panties—because he knew there was no way he could keep control of himself if he lingered too long there—and continued along the curve of her waist, over her breasts, up to her face and met her gaze with his own.

The desire he saw there echoed the one throbbing through his body, and he knew he couldn't wait any longer. However exquisite the feeling of drawing out this pleasure had been, now he needed to act, not watch.

Isabella reached behind her back, unfastened her bra, and let it fall to the ground. Her magnificent breasts bobbed in front of him, and Matteo swore he was starting to see stars.

'Madison, I have to go.' He dropped the phone back onto its receiver and raced towards the stairs.

Definitely time to act.

Isabella laughed as she darted up the stairs before he could reach her, heading straight for her bedroom. A striptease for a man she barely knew hadn't exactly been on her to-do list for the week, but she *had* decided to go with her instincts for once...

And seeing the lust in Matteo's gaze as he'd watched her, she was glad she had. She'd felt powerful, in control of her own future for once—at least, her immediate future. The one that ended with her and Matteo in her bed. Taking control in such a way had calmed her re-emerging nerves about that part, too.

She careened around the corner into her bedroom, squealing as he caught her at last, wrapping an arm around her waist and hauling her to him, just as he'd done down by the lake.

'That was cruel,' he rasped against her ear, the desperation clear in his voice.

'I think the word you're looking for is "inspired",' she corrected him.

'That too.' He pressed a kiss to the patch of skin where her neck met her shoulders and she squirmed in his arms as pleasure fired through her nerves. 'You like that?'

'Mmm,' she agreed.

'Good.' Lifting her roughly, he dropped her down onto the bed from a just high enough height that she bounced. 'Let's find out what else you like.'

She'd thought that stripping for Matteo would be a treat for him. She hadn't anticipated how much it would turn her on, too.

She didn't do things like this—not least because, as a protected Princess of Augusta, she'd never had the chance.

Now she *had* that chance, just for the week. And she was going to take it.

Isabella moaned as Matteo kissed his way down her throat, over her collarbone, and further down, towards her breasts. With an appreciative noise from the back of his throat, he closed his mouth over her nipple, running his tongue around the sensitive nub until she writhed underneath him. God, that mouth wasn't only made for talking. She could feel him smiling against her skin before he released her with a pop, and moved across to give the other nipple the same treatment.

His hands weren't still either. As his mouth worked on her breasts, his hands brushed up and down her sides, caressing the curve of her hip. Then suddenly, they slipped underneath her, gripping her and pressing her against him.

Oh, she could feel him. He'd been keeping his weight off her, but now… She might be stripped down to her panties, but he was still fully clothed—and still, she could feel the hard length of him pressed against her bare skin, even through his jeans. Could imagine the size and the feel of him in her hand. In her mouth. Inside her…

It had been so, so long. And she'd spent too long thinking that the mistakes that came out of her last venture into lovemaking were her fault, that they meant she wasn't destined to have this in her life.

Yet here she was.

Matteo pressed one last kiss to her nipple then looked up, his green eyes bright as he met her gaze.

'You okay?' he asked.

'I will be.'

He smiled at that. 'Tell me what you need.'

You, inside me. The thought was instant, but saying the words was another matter. She bit her lip and watched his eyes darken.

'I need the words,' he said, sounding as though just talking was taking all of his self-control right now.

Maybe it was.

And yet, she knew if she said, *No, I can't, let's stop,* he would. Nate would have cajoled her, told her to stay with him a little longer and she'd change her mind.

Matteo would back off the second she said the words.

Maybe that was one of the reasons that, this time, she didn't want to.

'I want you to make love to me.' It came out a little faster, a little more desperate than she'd intended, but Matteo didn't seem to mind. Quite the opposite, in fact.

With a noise in the back of his throat that was almost a growl, he lowered his head and kissed her again, deeper and deeper. Which was wonderful, but wasn't getting him any more naked, so Isabella set about rectifying that instead, her fingers making quick work of the buttons of his shirt before she stripped it from his shoulders.

She let herself be distracted, for a moment, by all that lovely hard muscle and tanned skin, brushed with a dusting of dark hair. Closing her eyes, she ran her hands over the planes and dips of him, just as he'd done to her, memorising his body by touch alone.

But she couldn't allow herself to be *too* distracted. Opening her eyes again to find Matteo watching her, she held his gaze as she reached determinedly down to unfasten his jeans.

He helped her push his jeans and boxers down over those long, muscled legs, then stripped away her panties too, and suddenly there was nothing between them at all. Well, nothing that mattered right now.

She swallowed, as her gaze roamed down the length of him. It really had been a long time…but now she was here, she was almost dizzy with the need for him.

'Condom?' she asked breathily, as a reminder to herself that she hadn't completely lost her mind.

Matteo reached across to the small table beside the bed and pulled a strip of them from the drawer. Excellent.

'You're sure?' he asked again as he ripped open the packet.

'Very.' She took the condom from him and reached out to roll it securely in place. She wasn't taking any chances.

His breathing ragged, Matteo reached for her again, and Isabella went willingly into his arms, ready to embrace her freedom.

Making love to a princess, Matteo had decided, was probably the same as making love to any other woman.

But making love to Isabella? That was something new. Something special. Something totally unexpected—and a little unsettling. He'd thought this would be something else to tick off his list of adventures, another risk to take, even.

So why did it feel like something else?

The way she'd affected him since the moment he saw her should have been his first clue. He'd never wanted a woman the way he'd wanted Isabella. Wanted to touch her, to feel her in his arms, to smell her hair and taste her skin, to get as close to her as it was possible for two people to be.

And now that he was…he couldn't remember why he'd ever wanted to be anywhere else.

Holding himself up on his elbows, he let her guide him inside her, taking things at her pace, not his. Slowly, slowly he filled her, giving her time to adjust to him before he moved any more, watching her face carefully for every reaction.

Isabella's eyes were closed, her face clear and smooth, and for a brief, horrible moment it occurred to Matteo that she might not have done this before. That, as a princess, she might have been kept pure and chaste and…oh, God, what if he was her first?

Then her eyes flashed open and she gave him that wicked grin he'd seem when she was beating him at Monopoly. 'What are you waiting for, superstar? *Move.*'

And he did.

What had started slow and sweet and careful soon became more frantic, more desperate as they moved together, in perfect synchronicity. Isabella's hands clutched at his back, pulling her to him, driving him deeper with every thrust. Matteo had a feeling this would be over in an embarrassingly short space of time…but at least they had the rest of the week to make up for it.

Tugging her round, he flipped them so he was on his back, letting her ride him to her own pleasure. Long, loose dark curls hung down over her breasts as she moved, more languidly than he'd be capable of right now. Her chin tilted up, that aristocratic neck long and elegant, she bit down on her plump lower lip and Matteo thought he might be done for. Reaching up, he brushed the hair away from her breasts to cup them with his hands, and ran his fingers across her nipples, making her shiver above him.

Good. He needed to know this was affecting her the same way it was him.

'Isabella.' Her name came out as more of a moan than he'd intended, but it worked. Her eyes fluttered open and she looked down at him, her hips not losing their sanity-depriving rhythm for a moment.

The lust he saw in her eyes was the same one he felt coursing through his blood. And that was all it took for his baser instincts to take over.

Grabbing tight hold of her hips, he thrust up into her, gratified when she upped the speed of her own movements to match him. Not losing pace for a moment, he shifted one hand towards her core, teasing her with his fingers and driving her further and further to where he needed her to go.

And just when he thought he might lose his mind, she

gasped and tightened around him, again and again as she cried out, her hips stuttering to a stop as he thrust once, twice, three times more…and felt his world explode.

'Oh, God.' Isabella slumped against his chest, sweaty and sated and salty sweet under his kisses. 'That was a good idea.'

'Glad you agree,' Matteo murmured against her skin. Although, 'good idea' weren't exactly the words he'd have chosen.

Transcendental, perhaps. Life-changing. Magical.

He blinked, and forced the thoughts away. It was just sex, same as any other sex he'd had with many other women. Sure, he was more attracted to Isabella than any of the other women he'd met lately—maybe ever. But that was just chemistry. Physical lust didn't mean anything more than an incredible time between the sheets.

And he was just lucky he got to experience that for a week, before going back to the real world.

Isabella rolled away from him, leaving his skin cooling in the breeze from the open window as she lay beside him on the huge bed. Last night, lying in his own bed next door, he'd felt frustrated, adrift and alone. Before that, he'd felt unsettled and aroused and distracted by being around her.

Now, he only felt sated, relaxed and as if there was nowhere in the world he'd rather be.

He blinked at the thought. When had he last felt that way?

Speeding around the racetrack, it was a familiar feeling—especially as he cornered the last turn before the flag. But outside a racing car? That feeling was a lot harder to find.

On the top of a mountain, perhaps, looking out at the blue sky and great depths below. The second when he jumped from a plane, in the moments before he opened his parachute. Or when he sprang away from that cliff-side and dived towards the water—before he broke his leg, of course.

But those highs only ever lasted until he reached solid ground again. Until the race was over, the adrenaline gone.

Until now.

He'd travelled the world on one adventure after another, taking bigger and better risks, beating the odds—chasing the adrenaline high that reminded him he was alive, when so many others weren't. He'd taken chances that terrified the people around him so much that they'd sent him here, a last-ditch attempt to keep him safe and out of trouble.

And here, in Isabella's bed, he'd found that same peace he hunted for, that same high.

He just had a feeling it also came with a whole different sort of trouble.

Shifting onto his side, he watched Isabella's chest rise and fall as her breath slowly returned to normal.

'What are you thinking?' The question was out of his mouth before he had a chance to think whether he really wanted to know the answer. Because the odds of Princess Isabella of Augusta feeling the same as him right now seemed slim.

They both knew what this week was about, and it wasn't about transcendental feelings of satisfaction with the world. It wasn't about him finding a way to get his adrenaline high that didn't involve breaking any bones or taking any risks. Although he knew his team wouldn't mind if that was the case...

This wasn't a permanent solution. This was one week, that was all. Princess Isabella wasn't about to turn to him and tell him he'd so rocked her world that she loved him and wanted to make him her prince.

Which was good, because he didn't want that either.

Still, he couldn't help but smile when she turned her face towards his and said, 'Do you think there's any more food downstairs? I'm starving.'

CHAPTER SIX

ISABELLA HADN'T BEEN lying when she told Matteo she was hungry. But as he laughed and pulled on his jeans to go and raid the kitchen for her, she had to admit she hadn't been telling the whole truth, either.

She'd been thinking about taking chances. And how good it felt to take a risk for a change.

How buttoned up had her life been? Oh, maybe it wouldn't have been obvious to the casual onlooker. To someone who only knew her through her publicity photos or the palace's social media channels, she must seem the ultimate carefree princess. Never having to worry about the things that consumed so many other people's lives—like having a roof over their heads or enough money for food or keeping their family healthy and well. She'd always had a home at the palace—not to mention the 'summer house', a mansion in the hills of Augusta where the court could decamp in the hot weather—and royal property she could use throughout the country. She'd never had to prepare her own food, although since she'd been an adult her rooms had their own kitchen where she *could* cook, if she chose. Meals—no, banquets—had been the norm in the palace. The best doctors in the land—in Europe, the world—had been at their beck and call when required.

Isabella wasn't playing poor little rich girl. She knew how lucky she was.

It had just taken until now to realise what freedom truly felt like.

'I'm starting to think the staff here might be psychic.' Matteo pushed the door open with his knee, grinning as he appeared with a heavily laden tray. 'That, or we were a lot louder than I'd thought.'

Isabella pulled herself up to rest against the padded headboard, the sheets falling away from her body and leaving her bare from the waist up. 'What did they leave us?'

Matteo didn't answer immediately, apparently too busy admiring the view as his gaze roamed over her torso. Isabella didn't reach for the sheet to cover herself.

Yesterday, I would have done.

Yesterday, she'd have been embarrassed at the idea of someone listening to her having sex, and providing snacks ready for afters. Yesterday, she'd have blushed at the blatant ogling Matteo was indulging in.

Today…today she felt like a different person. Had done since that moment by the lake when she made her decision to embrace the possibilities of this week.

And she wasn't done embracing yet.

'I'm getting hungrier, here,' she teased, and Matteo gave her a shameless grin before setting the tray down on the bed and perching beside it.

'We've got coffee, cookies, some sort of gooey cake… plenty of sugar to keep our energy levels up.'

'Good.' She smiled up at him—her best princess smile. 'I think you're going to need it.'

Later, quite a lot later, when the cake was demolished to crumbs, the dregs of the coffee were cold, and Isabella's muscles were relaxed to the point of melting into the mattress, Matteo turned on his side and propped his head up on one hand.

'What changed your mind?' he asked as he studied her.

Isabella tried not to shift uncomfortably under his gaze. After all, the man had touched, tasted and loved every inch of her body over the course of the last handful of hours. Maybe longer; the sun looked a lot lower in the sky than she'd have thought...

'Changed my mind about what?'

'About me.' He raised his eyebrows. 'I mean, last night I definitely got "this is not behaviour befitting a princess" vibes from you. But today...' He left it hanging, their mutual nakedness doing all the talking for him.

'Maybe I just decided that I deserved a week off from being a princess.'

'And is that something you do often?'

'Never.' Except that was a lie, and here, beside him in her bed, Isabella found that she didn't *want* to lie to Matteo. Not even to preserve her reputation, or the monarchy of Augusta's reputation, come to that. 'Once,' she amended.

Curiosity flared behind Matteo's green eyes. 'Tell me? I mean, if you want to. Since you're just being Isabella this week, not a princess.'

'And this is something normal people do? Talk about their romantic disasters?' She wouldn't know. Her family had told her to lock it away inside her, pretend it never happened. Deny everything if Nate ever tried again to make another story out of it—although she suspected that Leo had paid him enough to make it worth his while to pretend it hadn't happened, either, after the initial flurry of press.

'This is something that normal people do,' Matteo confirmed. 'Well, some of them, anyway.'

'Not you?'

'I don't have romantic disasters.'

'Just cliff-diving ones.'

'Just those,' Matteo confirmed, with a grin.

'Although…that's not what the gossip magazines say.' Isabella shifted closer, her hands under her head as she curled towards him. 'They're forever talking about which heart you've broken now.'

Matteo rolled his eyes. 'You shouldn't pay any attention to them. They'll say anything to get people to buy a copy.'

'I don't know,' Isabella teased. 'There are a lot of photos of you…'

He reached over to brush his hand over her waist, almost light enough to tickle, before pulling her closer. 'Is this the part where I tell you none of them meant anything before you?'

It was her turn to roll her eyes, now. 'If this was a normal M dating agency week of passion, or whatever they call it, probably. But I think we both know neither of us are here for *that*. So the truth will do just fine instead, thank you very much.'

Matteo loosened his hold on her side, and flopped onto his back. 'The *truth*? No one ever seems to care about that.'

'I do.' Because she knew she couldn't trust herself to interpret the world without it. People lied, all the time, and she wasn't sophisticated enough in the way of life outside the palace to even tell when it was happening.

'Fine. I like women—I like their company, and, well, I like sex.'

'I noticed,' Isabella said, with a smirk.

She didn't add, 'So do I.' Because she hadn't known that she did, not like this. Not until today.

And that was a discovery she was still adjusting to.

'But I'm always upfront with women about what I can

offer,' Matteo went on, oblivious to her omission. 'I'm not in the market for a serious relationship, or anything more than a few nights of fun. I've got too many other things to do.'

'Like go cliff diving.'

'And win world championships.'

Isabella stretched out her legs under the thin sheets, feeling her well-used muscles protest at still being expected to move. 'But you've done both of those things now,' she pointed out. 'What else is on your list?'

There was a pause she didn't expect after her question. Not one that felt as though Matteo was trying to think of something to say, or remember what daring plans he had next. More as though he was trying to decide whether to share it with her.

She wondered how outrageous it had to be, for that.

Finally, he moved to sit up against the headboard, and reached for his phone, swiping across the screen a few times before handing it to her.

She'd expected a website or a booking email or something—perhaps for deep-sea diving in the Red Sea, or a trek into the Himalayas. Instead, she found herself looking at a photo of a handwritten list.

He had an actual list.

Except…she frowned at the carefully printed words at the top of the page in the photo.

Giovanni Rossi's Bucket List

This wasn't Matteo's list. Even though she could see that he'd carefully crossed out plenty of items on it—including cliff diving. And becoming the racing world champion.

'I don't understand,' she said, handing back the phone.

Matteo took it from her, glanced at the screen with an indecipherable look on his face, then placed it back on the table beside him. He looked…lost, somehow. She hadn't expected that from him, especially after the self-assuredness he'd shown in bed.

On impulse, she nestled closer, until he wrapped one arm around her shoulder as she rested her head on his firm chest.

'My brother,' he said, eventually. 'Giovanni. He was three years older than me.'

Isabella heard the *was* and knew that nothing that followed was going to be good.

'He was the daredevil, when we were kids,' Matteo went on, a fond smile on his face. 'Always the one getting into scrapes or trying the impossible just to prove that he could.'

He fell silent, and Isabella could feel the weight of that silence in the air around them.

'What happened to him?' she asked, when she couldn't bear it any longer.

She'd braced herself for a car accident, or some other sort of dangerous, reckless end. Which was why Matteo's reply made her gasp at the tragedy of it all.

'He was diagnosed with terminal cancer when I was sixteen.' His words were flat, emotionless, but Isabella could tell that was through practice. He said it the same way she said Nate's name, these days, and it had taken her years to perfect that emptiness between the syllables. *Nath-an-ial. Ter-min-al.* They sounded the same in her head.

'I'm so sorry, Matteo.' Isabella pressed a soft kiss to his skin and wished there were more she could do. But grief was grief, wasn't it? Whatever the cause, it was personal, and permanent.

He shrugged, and she felt the shift of his muscles under her cheek. 'It was a lot of years ago, now. Seventeen, almost.'

'Still. He was your brother.' Nathanial had been her world, and he didn't even have the good grace to be *dead*.

'Yeah.' Matteo slumped a little lower against the headboard, pulling her closer until her whole body half covered his. 'After he got sick…he made this list. All the things he'd wanted to do in his life but was never going to get the chance. I… I helped him. Because I think, even then, I thought he was going to get better. I thought it would give him something to look forward to, once the treatment was over. But instead…' She felt him swallow and wrapped her arm a little tighter around him. 'He died. And I was just left with this list. So I promised myself—promised him, really—that I'd do every single damn thing on it. Everything he didn't have time to do. Everything that was taken from him. And I am. I have.'

Become world champion. The list item floated in front of her mind's eye. Had Matteo based his whole career on his brother's dying wish list?

She couldn't ask that. She'd only known the man a couple of days, however much some algorithm somewhere said she was his perfect match.

But she could hear the grief in his voice—still there, not diminished at all by every challenge he crossed off his brother's bucket list. Unresolved.

'So what's next?' she asked instead. 'What's left on the list?' Because as far as she could tell, almost everything had been crossed off.

'Well, even Giovanni didn't envision making love to a princess,' Matteo joked, although there wasn't any real humour in his voice. 'So… I guess I'm pretty much done.

Becoming world champion…that was his big dream, and I did it. And went cliff diving to celebrate.'

Isabella half smiled at that. 'I guess that means you'll have to start writing your own list now, then, huh?'

'I guess it does.' There was a hint of amazement, disbelief even, in his tone. But it was gone before she could even be totally sure it was there at all, as he twisted them around so she was underneath him again, and all she could think about was how right his body felt against hers. As if they were two parts of the same whole.

'But the list can wait?' she guessed as he pressed her further into the mattress, his arousal obvious against her belly.

'The list can *definitely* wait,' he agreed, before kissing her.

She hadn't answered his question.

Matteo didn't realise it until he awoke to the early morning light filtering through the gauzy curtains that barely covered the glass front of the villa. In fairness, he'd been far more preoccupied with all the things she *had* been telling him—*more, now, again*—to focus on the conversation she'd sidestepped.

But lying there in the pale June dawn, with Isabella's body curled against his, he realised, and he wondered.

How had she persuaded him to tell all his secrets about Giovanni, about the list, about why he did the things he did, and still managed to evade telling him *anything* about herself? In fact, beyond the small detail of her being a princess, he wasn't sure he'd found out anything personal about her at all.

Was that part of being royal? The ability to ask polite questions and listen to the answers without ever giving anything in return? He didn't know. Isabella was the

first royal he'd ever spent real time with, beyond the polite niceties, and he had a suspicion that she wasn't exactly typical.

He looked down at her, sleeping in his arms, and considered what he *did* know about her.

She wasn't looking for true love.

She hadn't been enamoured of any of the suitable pro-
spective husbands Augusta had thrown up.

She hadn't come here through her own choice.

She wanted a break from being a princess—and she'd
done that only once before…

What had happened then? Matteo was willing to place
money that someone had hurt her. Someone had made her
this way—cautious and careful. And if she was letting that
go this week, with him… Matteo wasn't sure he could bear
to see her go back to her buttoned-up ways afterwards.

Ever since he'd admitted that the chemistry between
them was unavoidable, he'd hoped. He'd flirted and he'd
hinted and he'd hoped—but he hadn't really expected.
He'd figured a week of frustration and an inappropriate
royal crush was probably punishment from the universe
for something—maybe the broken leg, maybe the hearts
he knew he'd broken, even when he'd been trying not to.

But he hadn't imagined this. Hadn't dreamt for a moment that their second full day together would lead to a
race to the jetty and that kiss…not to mention everything that came after.

His position hadn't changed; he was the same man
who'd seen a curvaceous brunette on the terrace below
and hoped.

But Isabella…she'd become someone new overnight.
Consciously, intentionally. She'd made a decision to be
Just Isabella, rather than the Princess—but Matteo knew
without her having to say the words that it wasn't a per-

manent change. This week was a holiday from being herself. Except, having seen how free and alive she seemed... Didn't she deserve to be that way all the time?

He wondered if he could convince her. If he could show her, in the days they had left together, that she could be whoever she wanted to be—not just in Lake Geneva, but in Augusta, too.

To do that, he suspected he'd need to get her to open up and tell him the story of the last time she tossed aside her crown for a while. And perhaps that was something she needed to work up to.

So he'd start small instead. See if he could show the Princess that taking risks could be fun, sometimes. Even *outside* the bedroom.

Isabella stirred in his arms, and Matteo smiled to himself as he bent to kiss the top of her head, settling more comfortably down beside her. He wouldn't sleep any more, he knew, not now he had adventures to plan. But she was going to need her rest.

She wanted a week off from being a princess? Well, then... Matteo was going to give her the best week's holiday she could imagine.

And maybe by the end of it, she wouldn't want to stop.

'So, what are we going to do today?' Isabella asked, some time later that morning, as they shared coffee and a late breakfast on the balcony outside their rooms.

Matteo raised his eyebrows in what he'd been told was an expressive manner, and she rolled her eyes.

'Is your plan to spend the *whole* week here in bed?' It wasn't, of course. But he couldn't quite tell if she was actually disapproving of that idea, or just felt some princessy need to pretend she was.

'Would that be such a terrible plan?'

When she smiled, her dimples popped into existence, and it made Matteo smile back, every time. They didn't show up, he'd noticed, in her official Princess Isabella smile, the one she'd given him that first night they'd met—the smile she was displaying in every single photo of her that seemed to be in the public domain, at least the ones that he'd been able to find online.

The dimples only appeared when she was truly smiling with happiness or amusement. Matteo had started counting the number of times he got to see them, and the total was already gratifyingly high.

'Maybe not *terrible*, exactly,' she said, her voice a soft purr. 'But I figure we might need a small break. Sometimes.'

Matteo sighed dramatically. 'Oh, I suppose you're right.'

She tossed a small piece of bread at him, then giggled and ducked when he tried to throw one back.

'Actually, I had thought we might go on a small adventure today,' he said, once the mini food fight had died down.

Across the table, Isabella stilled with what he knew instinctively was apprehension. Fear, even. Fear that felt more than just a general nervousness of the unknown, somehow.

'What sort of an adventure?' Her tone was cautious. Matteo supposed he didn't blame her. After all, he *was* famous for choosing the more extreme sort of adventures.

'I'm not going to force you to go skydiving or anything,' he said to reassure her. She didn't look particularly reassured. 'I thought we might take the boat out on the lake.'

She blinked. 'Boat?'

'The one that was tied up by the jetty. We saw it yesterday?'

Her cheeks turned pink. 'Oh, yes. Of course.'

'You did *see* the boat, right, Isabella?' he teased. 'I mean, you weren't so distracted by something that you failed to even notice the big boat tied up right next to you?' Okay, so it was quite a small boat in reality, but the point still held. She'd been so focused on his kisses, his touch, she'd lost all track of her surroundings.

The thought made his body start to tighten, and he was reconsidering the whole boat-trip idea when she tossed another piece of bread at him—this time, covered in jam.

'I saw the boat,' she said shortly, and he was fairly sure it was a lie. 'But do you really think we should take it out? I mean, I don't know anything about boats. Would we need to take one of the security team with us?'

'It's a fairly basic boat; I've driven them before. And there are life jackets here somewhere, I'm sure. We'll be fine. We won't even go too far from the villa, if you don't want to.' It was the smallest step he could think of for her to take, after she'd already taken the much bigger one of allowing him into her bed.

But it could be the first step to a new mindset for her. One where she didn't always automatically say no to things, until she was compelled to change her mind by events—or, in their case, sheer physical chemistry.

She looked down at her hands, suddenly the reserved, unsure Princess she'd been on arrival again—rather than the mischievous Isabella who tossed bread at him and made him come completely undone in bed. He watched as she came to a decision, lifted her chin and, with a determination he didn't really feel the suggestion warranted, said, 'Okay, then. We'll go out on the lake.'

Matteo smiled to himself. Stage one of his plan was complete.

CHAPTER SEVEN

ISABELLA WAS NOT at all sure that this was a good idea.

On the face of it, a short trip out on a boat on a lake, still miles away from anywhere, wasn't exactly a dangerous threat. But she was compiling a mental list of reasons this could be a disaster anyway.

1) They could capsize and drown, despite their life jackets.
2) Some paparazzi on a boat might find them and take photos through those ridiculous long lenses they had, and then her parents would know she wasn't with Sofia and it would be like Nathanial all over again.
3)...

Okay, that was all she had for now. But surely they were reason enough not to risk it?

She sat, tucked up in her life jacket, at the far end of the small boat from where Matteo was starting the engine. Despite the life jacket he wore—at her insistence—she could still enjoy the sight of his arm muscles as he worked to untie them from the jetty, the thick muscles of his thighs as he braced himself against the movement of the boat. She swallowed as she watched a bead of sweat work its way down his neck in the bright June sunlight…

Right.

3) They might not be able to keep their hands off each other, even on a damn boat, and then they'd take their life jackets off and cause the boat to capsize and then they'd definitely drown. Probably while paparazzi took photos of her naked, and it would be even worse than everything with Nathanial had been.

'You're catastrophising,' Matteo said mildly as the boat chugged away from the jetty.

Isabella blinked. 'I'm what?'

'You're thinking about all the things that could possibly go wrong out here on the water.'

'No, I'm…' He gave her a look, and she sighed. 'Fine, I'm catastrophising. But that's what keeps me safe—thinking about all the things that could go wrong *before* they happen.'

It was a lesson her father and mother had drilled into her after Nate. That she was not somebody who could just take chances, or jump at opportunities and see where they led, or—and this one was said with a certain amount of disgusted disbelief—*follow her heart.*

She was a Princess of Augusta, and with that privilege came expectations, amongst them the always unstated rule that she would not cause any sort of scandal to fall upon the royal house.

Well, unstated until that horrible week after Nate had left, at which point it was stated quite firmly and repeatedly, as if she had somehow missed it in the undercurrents of her upbringing.

She hadn't, of course. She'd just believed that love

trumped duty somehow. She'd believed in happy endings, and in everything working out for the best.

She knew better than that now.

She knew better than to be on this boat. To be in Lake Geneva at all. To be spending the week in the bed of a *most* unsuitable man.

But she was doing those things anyway, even though she knew what her parents, her brother would say.

You're making the same mistakes all over again.

Except Matteo wasn't Nate, and they weren't in Augusta, where her every move was tracked and recorded and reported. There was a privacy agreement in place with the M agency; she'd checked.

They were alone in this part of the lake; the sun was shining down and it was a beautiful day. She should relax and enjoy it.

Except she couldn't.

Matteo settled himself opposite her in the small boat, where he could watch her *and* where they were going, which she appreciated.

'Can you trust *me* to keep you safe?' he asked softly. 'Just for today?'

On the face of it, it was a ridiculous question. He was a risk-taking daredevil, known for his chequered history with women and famous for driving too fast around racetracks. He was the *last* person anyone should trust to keep them safe, right?

But once again, Isabella's heart spoke louder than her head. 'Yes,' she said gently. 'I trust you.'

Matteo smiled, as warm as the June sun. 'Good. Then sit back and enjoy the trip.'

The lake was surprisingly peaceful, once she'd stopped catastrophising. Isabella leaned back against the edge of the boat and tipped her chin so the sun streamed down on her face as the air brushed past her, raising the ends of her shorter curls around her shoulders.

'You are very distracting up there, you know,' Matteo said, and when she looked up, he was watching her intently.

'If you try and seduce me here we'll capsize the boat.' That wasn't catastrophising. That was physics. She knew how…vigorous their lovemaking could get.

'More's the pity.' Shutting off the small engine, he let the boat drift a little on the water. 'Well, if seduction is off the table, how about lunch?'

Isabella sat up with interest. 'We have lunch?'

'Of course, we have lunch.' Matteo grinned. 'I found it ready for us in the kitchen before we left, all packed up in a cool bag.'

'The invisible servants really do know their stuff.' Had they heard them talking about going out on the boat, or just guessed when Matteo went searching for life jackets? Either way, they were as good at anticipating their needs as any of the staff at the royal palace. Leo or her father would probably want to steal them if they knew about their existence.

Which they wouldn't. Because once this week was over, Isabella would never speak of it again, and she and Matteo would be the only people in the world who ever knew it happened.

She'd never speak to Matteo again either, probably. Certainly never make love to him again.

'Hey.' Matteo frowned as he paused in pulling out the food from the bag. 'What just happened? You look like the sun just disappeared.'

Isabella forced a smile, shaking her head to rid it of the thoughts. They wouldn't go. 'It's nothing,' she said, when it was clear that her smile wasn't enough to convince him. 'I was just thinking about what happens after this week is over.'

He stilled for a moment, then placed the container of strawberries he was holding on the seat between them that was serving as a table.

'You mean between us? Or for you?'

'Both, I suppose.'

'Well, I expect that depends on you, really, doesn't it?' he said, his tone careful.

He really was from a different world if he believed that. 'Not exactly.'

'Because of the princess thing?'

Her whole life reduced to a 'princess thing'.

'Because there are expectations placed on me.'

'Stay out of trouble and marry a duke? Isn't that about the size of it?' He made it sound like nothing. 'Because the thing is, Isabella, I kind of had the feeling that princesses were people too. Real flesh and blood people, who felt things and wanted things and deserved to live their lives the way they wanted.'

She could feel his words in her veins, filling her body with the hope of them. Reaching across the seat between them, he ran his fingers up her hand, before circling her wrist with them, the pads of his fingertips resting on her pulse point, feeling the beat of her heart as it thrummed through her.

'See?' he whispered. 'Not just a princess.'

Isabella pulled her hand away. 'Maybe not. But I *am* a Princess of Augusta, and that means something. Maybe not to you, but to my family, my country. And to me.'

How had this conversation got so deep, so fast? She wanted to go back to tossing jammy bread at him or sinking her body down on top of his.

They should have just stayed in bed today after all. This whole thing was much easier to navigate between the sheets than out of them.

He sat back, studying her so keenly that she had to force herself not to fidget under his gaze. 'Wouldn't your family just want you to be happy?'

She almost laughed, the idea was so absurd. 'Have you *met* many kings and queens?'

'A few,' he replied, with a shrug. 'But I'll admit I never had time to discuss their daughters' sex lives with them.'

That did make her laugh, despite herself. How did he do that? Always lighten the moment, just when she was getting down?

'So what would the obedient Princess of Augusta do next?' he asked.

That one was easy. 'She'd go home to the palace and continue life as always. Public engagements, charity events, hospital visits, that sort of thing.' When she couldn't get out of them.

'And blind dates with aristocrats you already know you don't want to marry.'

'That, too.' But in some ways, Isabella had come to realise, that was better than the alternative. Because at least when she went into something knowing it wasn't for ever, that it wasn't even what she wanted, her heart couldn't be broken at the end of it. Not this time.

'Okay.' He leant forward, his forearms resting on those muscled thighs as he held her gaze. 'And what does *Isabella* want to happen next?'

Something else. She had no idea what, but there had to be more than just that, didn't there?

Except last time she'd tried to reach for it, her whole world had almost come crashing down.

'The same thing,' she said coldly. 'I *am* the Princess, after all.'

'Of course.' His eyes were sad. 'And I don't suppose the Princess would be allowed to socialise with a reckless, common-born racing-car driver, either.'

'I don't suppose she would.' Isabella ignored the sharp, short pain in her chest at the thought.

Matteo turned away, his attention apparently back on steering the boat again, even though they weren't moving. 'Then it's just as well we agreed at the outset that this was just for the week. We can have all the fun we want together, then go back to our real lives as if it never happened.'

'Just as well,' she echoed, and wondered how to convince herself that she wasn't lying.

Their boat trip hadn't exactly given him the information he'd hoped for from Isabella, but Matteo had to admit it had crystallised exactly where they both stood in their current situations.

They'd agreed that first night that this could only be for the week, and it wasn't as if he was even looking to change that. But the idea of Isabella being stuck in a life that was so obviously suffocating her...that unsettled him. A lot.

Still, she was a princess. Maybe that royal status— and the money, prestige and luxury that went with it— was more important to her than happiness, or freedom. It would be for a lot of people, he knew. Money might not buy happiness, but it could buy a hell of a lot of other things, as he'd discovered as his career had progressed, and the prize pots and sponsorship deals got bigger.

Matteo wouldn't judge. Well, he wouldn't judge *much*. But he might feel a little bit of pity.

They'd separated and gone to their own rooms after their outing on the lake, both intuiting the need for a break from the unrelenting closeness of the past day or two. But it was already Thursday, and Matteo knew that their time together was limited; he didn't want to waste any more of it. Four days down and three more to go...

He knew he should just relax and enjoy Isabella's company while he had it. But somehow, that wasn't enough. He needed...what, exactly? To help her? To change her?

Or just to know that he'd had an impact on her life. That this week had meant something to her.

Because he was starting to feel as if seven days with Princess Isabella of Augusta might have more of an impact on his life than he'd ever imagined it could.

At the end of it, he'd walk away with a smile and a kiss and a thank you, the way he did with all of his love affairs. And he was perfectly happy with that plan.

He just didn't try to fool himself any more that forgetting Isabella would be as easy as forgetting any of the women who had come before her.

M knew what it was doing, after all. The dating agency had found him someone who, in another world, could have been his perfect match. He'd thought that meant someone like him—someone to take adventures and risks with, because she had the same adventurer's spirit as him.

Instead, they'd given him someone who needed him. Someone who he could ease out of her comfort zone, even while she calmed him. Not to the point of being a different person—he was still hankering for his next adventure. But when he was with her...it was as if she soothed his restless edges. As if he could rest for a while, between risks.

Being needed reminded him of his brother. Being

soothed reminded him of his mother. The two people he'd loved most in the world, both of them gone, now.

And Isabella…she could be…

No.

He didn't want that kind of love again—not when he knew how easily it could be taken from him, the way his brother and his mother had been. And he didn't want the obligations love forced on him, either. He'd seen it with other drivers on his team, and in races. They fell in love, they got married, started families even—and that was when they lost their edge. Because taking risks for themselves was easy; taking risks for people they loved was another game entirely. One that not many were made to play.

He needed those restless, reckless edges of his. He couldn't let Isabella smooth them down too much, whatever Gabe and the others hoped.

Even if he had wanted to follow up on this dream date matching, once the week was over, it wasn't what Isabella wanted either. She wanted to go back to a life he could never be a part of. Her stifling, royal life.

So really, there was no point thinking about what happened after this week until it was over. There'd be another adventure waiting for him and he'd take it, as he always did. Giovanni's list might be finished, but there were more adventures that his brother had never even dreamed of. Not to mention a racing career to get back to. He still had two lives to live, to make the most of, for Giovanni's sake.

All the same, when he heard movement out on the balcony that linked his bedroom to Isabella's, he couldn't help but head straight for the door.

Three days.

He couldn't afford to waste any of them.

'When do you think they put this out here?' Isabella didn't turn around as she asked the question, her back still towards him. Apparently she was as attuned to his movements as he was to hers.

He turned his gaze from the way her curls were swept over one bare shoulder, above a thin, strapless sundress that clung to her curves down over her hips, then flared out to swirl around her legs to mid-calf. On the table in the centre of the balcony was another feast, ready for their evening meal. How had the servants got that there without him noticing? Okay, he'd been preoccupied with his thoughts of Isabella, but still…

'The staff here are starting to get a little creepy now.' He took his seat, grinning up at her as she laughed.

'Well, as long as they keep the food coming.'

'True.' She sat down opposite him, the evening sunlight sinking into her midnight hair, the most beautiful woman he'd ever seen in real life—and the most unattainable.

Yeah, there was no way he was going to be forgetting Isabella of Augusta any time soon.

Which meant he had to make sure she didn't forget him, either.

They'd do this on the terms they'd agreed—one week, then it never happened. But while the rest of the world might never know about their week, he needed to be sure that *Isabella* would keep it with her. Maybe even let it loosen her up a bit.

It was the one thing he *could* give her. A parting gift, say.

They ate their meal in companionable silence, their only conversation comments on the food, or the wine. But under their sparse words, Matteo could feel all the things they weren't saying.

Would they really make it the whole week without any of them coming out? He doubted it.

'I was thinking about tomorrow,' he said as Isabella finished off her chocolate dessert.

He loved watching her eat, loved the secret smile as her mouth curved around her dessert spoon and she savoured the taste. He knew now that she looked the same way when she wrapped her mouth around him, and he knew also that he'd never forget that. The image of her sinking down to her knees in front of him, hands on his thighs as she eyed him up, was burnt into his memory for ever. Thankfully.

She swallowed her dessert, and he swallowed his thoughts.

'What about tomorrow?' she asked.

'How would you feel about another little adventure?' *Before you go back to locking yourself up in that palace again.*

She froze, just for a moment, her eyes darting to one side as she formed her response. 'An adventure? What sort of an adventure?'

He was pushing her, faster than she wanted to go. But they had so little time left…

'I thought we could slip away from here, take my car out to the nearest town, have a look around?' How could they come all the way to Lake Geneva and not see anything more than a villa and the water and the views? 'You know I'm not one for sitting around, doing nothing. And as you so rightly pointed out, we can't spend *all* week in bed. So we need to find some other things to do. Right?'

Isabella wasn't looking so sure, however.

'What about our security detail?' That wasn't a no. He'd take it.

He flashed her his most wicked grin. '*Cara*, I'm a

racing-car driver. If you think I can't lose two guys in a big black car on these roads, you really haven't been paying attention.'

Isabella clamped her sun hat to her head with one hand and grabbed hold of the car seat beneath her with the other. Oh, how on earth had he got her to agree to this?

Actually, she admitted to herself, she knew *exactly* how. He'd fed her the remains of his chocolate pudding, then moved the table aside to kiss her—first her mouth, then her neck, then down to her breasts, pulling the elasticated top of her strapless dress to her waist, effortlessly. Just as she'd imagined him doing when she'd put it on that evening.

And then he'd pulled the whole thing down her body, nudging her to lift her hips from the chair so he could drag the fabric down her legs, slow enough to drive her crazy as he followed it with his kisses...

Isabella blushed at the memory, but she had to admit it *had* been convincing. She'd agreed to today's day trip easily, breathlessly, by the time he was done. She'd let him make love to her out there on the balcony, in full view of anyone who cared to be looking—which she hoped was nobody, but you never really knew with those long lenses, did you? Plus there was the mysterious villa staff, and the security team—

The security team Matteo had effectively out-driven and lost ten minutes ago, with a driving manoeuvre she'd never seen anyone pull on an actual road before. She was fairly sure it would have got him disqualified on a racetrack, too.

'Where did you learn to drive like that?' she asked as they took another corner at speed. The road they were on now followed the line of Lake Geneva, past more villas and wooded areas. Hopefully the security team were still circling the lake in the opposite direction, unaware of Matteo's clever double-back.

'I took a police driving course,' Matteo said, driving with one hand on the wheel, the other on her thigh. 'Made friends with one of the instructors, and even got to go out with the *polizia* a couple of times.'

'Of course, you did.' Because there was excitement, risk there that he couldn't find in everyday life. That was what Matteo Rossi lived for, right?

And now she was living it with him—ditching her security team, heading out to some town she'd never heard of with a man she'd only known a few days… God, she'd been here before when she was young and stupid, and she'd sworn she'd never do anything like this again.

But then Matteo had stripped her naked on the balcony and made love to her on a blanket until she'd seen metaphorical stars as well as the ones in the sky above her. And suddenly she couldn't say no to him.

It really was a good thing that they only had a week together. Any longer and who knew what he'd talk her into? Selling the Crown Jewels of Augusta on eBay to finance a cave-diving trip, or something, probably.

One week of taking risks with Matteo. She had to admit, it wasn't what she'd expected from her early summer break.

Her phone buzzed in the pocket of her sundress, and she pulled it out, not surprised to see Gianna's number on the screen.

'Tell them you're fine and you'll be back later tonight,' Matteo said as she stared at the ringing phone. 'It's easy.'

Biting her lip, Isabella pressed answer.

'Your Highness? Oh, thank goodness. Is everything okay? The security team at the villa—'

'Everything is fine, Gianna,' she interrupted, keeping her voice as calm as possible, and hoping Gianna couldn't tell how far over the speed limit Matteo had been going. He'd slowed down a little now they were away from the villa, enough that she could just about hear Gianna over the rushing air racing over the convertible. 'You can tell the security team not to worry. We'll be back tonight.'

'Are you sure?' Despite the wind, Isabella could still hear the worry in her friend's voice.

She looked over at Matteo behind the wheel, sunglasses in place, smiling as he drove through the Swiss countryside.

'Yes,' she said. 'I'm sure.'

Because it might only be for a week, but she wasn't ready to start saying 'no' to Matteo Rossi just yet.

Isabella lost track of how long they'd been driving, focused instead on Matteo's hand on her thigh, and the secret smile on his face under his sunglasses. Was this how normal women felt? Out for a drive with their…no, she wasn't sure there *was* a word for what she and Matteo were. Lovers, she supposed, was closest. But somehow it didn't feel right. It wasn't…enough, somehow. Which was ridiculous, given that she'd known him all of four and a half days and they'd spent most of that time in bed.

She focused on his driving instead. She'd never taken lessons, or a test, or even sat behind the wheel of a car. She was always in the back, being driven places, never driving there. Never choosing her destination or even her direction herself.

She wasn't now, either, she reminded herself. She had no idea where they were even going. She just hoped that Matteo did.

'There it is,' he said eventually, and Isabella forced

herself to pay attention to her surroundings again, rather than just her thoughts. Here she was, in this most beautiful of locations, and she was—

'Wow!' She interrupted her own thoughts as she finally took in where they were headed.

There, jutting out over the water of Lake Geneva, was a castle—a proper, fairy-tale castle.

'I thought it might be rather old hat to you, living in a palace like you do,' Matteo said, with a grin.

She smiled back. 'Not one like this, though.'

The palace at Augusta was very grand, filled with tapestries and red brocade and family portraits and all the other things royals seemed to need to prove their place in the world. But the truth was the original palace had burnt almost to the ground in the late nineteenth century, and the rebuilt version, while beautiful, didn't have the history of a place like this. Or the magic.

'What's it called?' she asked, still wondering at the sight.

'Château de Chillon,' Matteo replied. 'Chillon Castle.'

Fat round turrets climbed towards the bright blue sky, joined by boxier square ones, many of them topped by flags that fluttered in the light summer breeze. She could imagine Rapunzel sitting at the top of one of them, her hair hanging out of the window just waiting for a prince to scamper up it and set her free.

'Do you want to go inside?' Matteo asked.

'Can we?' She felt her eyes widen. Only strictly arranged visits were allowed at the castle in Augusta, and Isabella had spent the last few years carefully avoiding any of them.

Matteo just smiled.

It turned out that tourists were welcome at the Château de Chillon, and nobody seemed to notice that one of the tourists was actually a visiting member of another royal family. Isabella kept her sunglasses on to hide her face, but, honestly, she didn't think anyone was looking at her anyway. The castle was full of enough treasures to draw attention away. From the open courtyards to the friezes painted on the walls—not to mention the views out over the lake and the mountains, or towards the vineyards.

'Besides,' Matteo murmured in her ear as they took in one of the displays of armour, 'who would honestly expect a real princess to be walking around with the rest of the tourists?'

After they'd toured the rooms of the castle that were open to them, they climbed to the top of the keep in the centre of the castle and took in the view all around them. Standing close behind her, Matteo whispered information about what they were looking at into her ear as he turned her to face different directions.

'And that, down there, is where I'm taking you tomorrow,' he said finally.

Isabella squinted to see where he was pointing. 'The Château café?'

Matteo shook his head. 'The town of Montreux.'

CHAPTER EIGHT

MATTEO WAS STILL grinning to himself as he showered the day off him and changed into loose trousers and a shirt for dinner on the balcony that evening. The trip to Château du Chillon had been a success, and Isabella had already all but agreed to another outing tomorrow.

'I'd never have seen this, if I hadn't met you,' she'd whispered to him, as they'd stood atop the keep tower, looking out over water and mountains and towns and fields. 'Thank you.'

He'd known then that he couldn't stop yet.

As much as he wanted to take Isabella to bed and keep her there for the rest of their stay at the villa, there was a certain joy in exploring their surroundings with her too. His favourite part was watching Isabella get to pretend to be a normal, ordinary person, rather than a princess. The pleasure she took from fading into the background and watching others—even when they were just sitting in the café together sipping coffee— was palpable.

I gave that to her. She'll remember that.

It was something, at least.

And, he thought as he headed out to meet her on the balcony, he was almost certain that their day trips into tourist life wouldn't be the only things she remembered.

She'd remember the nights they had together, too—the same way he would.

Those nights were seared into his memory for ever, he knew that already.

'What's on the menu tonight?' Matteo's blood warmed at the sight of Isabella in another one of her sundresses. This one, he noted, tied around the neck, covering her high to her throat and down to her ankles. While it showed off her beautiful shoulders, it was definitely more modest than many of the others she'd worn.

Then she turned to get to what had become, over the past few days, her chair, and he saw that the whole back was missing, the fabric draping down over the swell of her bottom, so low that he was pretty sure there was no way she was wearing anything at all under the dress.

God, he hoped not. Even if he wasn't entirely sure how to get through dinner without knowing for sure.

Isabella lifted the metal cloche covering their plates and revealed a chicken dish with a creamy mushroom and leek sauce, plus a side dish of potatoes, and licked her lips in anticipation. Matteo's body tightened at the sight. He wanted her to look at him that way, and soon.

'I've been looking forward to this all day, haven't you?' she said. 'I'm starving. Not that the sandwich in the Château café wasn't lovely too...'

How were they still talking about food? When she looked like that and he hadn't touched her for *hours*.

Had he totally regressed to being a teenager, unable to think about anything but sex? Apparently so.

Then she looked up and met his gaze, and he watched her pupils widen further. Was she having the same thoughts that he was? It looked likely. And yet, decorum dictated that they eat dinner before anything else.

Matteo hated decorum. But despite all his efforts, Isabella was still ruled by it.

That, or she was just tormenting him for fun.

Dinner was an excruciatingly pleasurable torture. Every mouthful she took made him want to kiss her more. Each time she reached for her wine glass that damn dress shifted around what he was now certain were her bare breasts, and he ached to touch her.

Isabella kept up a light conversation about the château and the sights they'd enjoyed that day, seemingly unaware of his distraction, until she'd finished the last mouthful of her lemon mousse.

Then she smiled at him, warm and wicked, and he knew that every moment of the meal had been intentional.

'What shall we do with the rest of our evening, I wonder?' she said, her voice too innocent to be real. 'It's been such a lovely day, and we only have such a limited time here, it seems a shame to waste the later hours. We could walk by the lake, perhaps, or in the gardens. Or maybe there's another board game around here somewhere we could play…'

She started to stand, and Matteo's hand shot out to circle her wrist with firm fingers. 'Or I could take you to bed right now and see how loudly I can make you scream using only my tongue.'

Her pulse kicked up a gear under his fingertips, and he knew they weren't going to be playing Monopoly again any time soon.

'Or we could do that.' Isabella's eyes were nearly black as she slid into his lap, warm and wanting.

Matteo slid his hands up under the fabric of her skirt, palms against the smooth skin of her thighs. 'Was this whole meal just a plan to torture me?'

'Well, I was genuinely hungry.' She kissed his neck, and he shivered with need. 'But honestly? Yes.'

'Why?'

She shrugged, and everything moved under her dress in a way that made his everything stand even more firmly to attention. Any moment now, he was going to untie that tiny ribbon bow that held the dress up and let it fall away completely. Then he'd know for sure what was under it.

God, he hoped it was nothing but Isabella's bare skin.

'Because…you were in charge today,' she said. 'You drove, decided where we went, how long we stayed. And I loved our day out, I really did—and I wouldn't have had the courage to take us there myself, even if I *could* drive. But…'

'You wanted to be in charge of something too,' he guessed. 'In control.'

'I suppose so.' She shrugged again and he nearly lost his mind. 'Silly, really.'

'Not at all.' How often did a princess get to decide anything about her life? Not nearly often enough, was Matteo's guess. 'So, do you want to choose our activities for the rest of the week?'

She tilted her head a little as she studied him, and he realised he could look right down the side of her dress. *Definitely* no bra.

He'd let her decide everything if she'd just let him confirm the 'no underwear' part of his hypothesis.

'No,' she said finally. 'Not all of them. Just some of them.'

'That sounds fair.' He swallowed. 'So, do you want to play Monopoly, or…?'

Isabella reached up behind her neck and unfastened the bow that had been driving him crazy for the last hour. Then she stood up, let the dress fall to the floor of the balcony, and stalked naked back into her bedroom.

'We're definitely going with your plan for this evening,' she called back over one bare shoulder. 'What are you waiting for?'

Matteo hurried to his feet and after her.

They only had two more days, after all. He didn't want to waste a moment.

At the palace in Augusta, a week could feel like a year if there wasn't anything interesting going on—or, as often happened, if she was avoiding getting caught up in official royal engagements where her only purpose was to smile and stay quiet. Here on Lake Geneva, Isabella's week with Matteo seemed to have passed in a flash.

Which wasn't to say they hadn't made the most of their time together. Quite apart from the hours spent exploring each other's bodies, or whispering thoughts and histories to each other in the dark, Matteo had taken her on the sort of everyday adventures she'd never been allowed to have before.

He hadn't pushed her too far, ever, but just slipping away from their security detail—who'd been surprisingly sanguine about it after the first time, so she suspected Gianna had had a word and told them to let them go—felt like a rebellion. Putting on a floppy straw hat and wandering incognito around the resort town of Montreux, eating lunch in a side-street café where no one knew who she was, or even who Matteo was, had felt liberating. Swimming in the waters of Lake Geneva, with Matteo's arms around her as he stole wet kisses, had been something entirely new.

And then there were the nights.

After Nate, she'd never really expected to feel such

passion again—or to trust it if she did. But with Matteo, everything seemed so natural. Whatever her body needed, he was always there to give it to her. And she felt no embarrassment in needing to learn what he liked, what he wanted, what made him moan and flip them over and thrust into her until they both fell over the edge of pleasure together.

Being with Matteo had felt nothing like her time with Nate. Nothing like anything she'd ever experienced before.

And now, too soon, it was time to say goodbye to it and head back to the real world.

They'd elected to spend their last day together at the villa—mostly in bed, which was fine by Isabella. The morning had been a haze of pleasure and the occasional pastry and coffee, when they needed to build up their energy reserves again. They'd managed a small walk down to the water's edge and along the path after lunch, but the temptation to touch and kiss and more had been too great, and it wasn't long before they were back in bed.

Maybe they were just reassuring each other that they were still there. For now. Isabella wasn't sure. She was trying to ignore the fact that, after tomorrow, she'd be on her own again.

'What are you thinking about?' Matteo murmured against her shoulder.

She twisted under the light sheets until she could rest her cheek against his chest. 'Tomorrow, I guess.'

Matteo was silent for a moment. 'Back to the real world, huh? You going to miss me?' He grinned as he said it, and she knew it was just a joke, a request from his perfectly healthy ego.

'I'll miss *this*.' She pressed a kiss to his skin, then lifted her face to kiss his lips, too. 'This week…it's like

I've been a different person. It's strange to think I have to say goodbye to her tomorrow morning.'

And to you.

'You've been able to be Isabella. Not just the Princess.'

'Yeah.' And now she wasn't sure she wanted to go back to being the Princess at all. But what choice did she have? It was who she was. Who her family expected her to be.

She'd always known that her place in the family, the love of the King, Queen and all their subjects, were contingent on following The Rules. Ever since she'd heard the whispered stories about her Aunt Josephine, and her banishment from the palace after she fell in love with the man who looked after her horses—old gossip by the time it had reached ten-year-old Isabella's ears, but still shocking. Aunt Josephine had refused to give him up, and that was why Isabella had never met her.

Everything that had happened with Nate had only reinforced the lesson and confirmed to her that nothing had changed. Augusta was still as rule-bound, stuffy and unforgiving as always.

Beside her, Matteo shifted, lying flat beside her on his side so he could meet her gaze. 'You told me that you'd taken time off from being a princess once before. But you never told me what happened.'

'No, I didn't.' And that had been intentional. She'd distracted him, got him to tell her his secrets instead. He'd shared about his brother's death, his bucket list, everything.

And she'd kept her secrets close, locked inside, as always.

'No one can ever know, Isabella.' Her father's words. And, always remembering Aunt Josephine, she'd lived by them.

'Will you tell me now?' Matteo asked.

Isabella bit her lip as she considered. Matteo wouldn't spill her secrets—if he was going to, he had far juicier stuff to share now after their week together. Plus, there was that non-disclosure agreement he must have signed before coming to Lake Geneva in the first place.

Besides, she knew in her heart that Matteo wouldn't betray her that way.

Except I thought the same thing about Nate, too.

Was that why she didn't want to tell him? No, she admitted to herself. It wasn't fear that was stopping her telling him the truth. It was shame, or at least embarrassment. That she'd ever been that naive, trusting girl.

That, in some ways, she still was.

'If you don't want to—' Matteo started, but she cut him off.

'No. I mean, yes, I don't. But not because of you. Because of me. Because it's just so…stupid.'

This wasn't like the secrets he'd shared with her. Nothing so tragic as a dead brother, or as noble as fulfilling his lost dreams. This was just…humiliating.

'Okay.' Matteo looked confused. She didn't really blame him.

With a sigh, she sat up, drawing the sheets up to cover her bare breasts. 'I'll tell you. But bring me some of those chocolates first, okay?' She was going to need something sweet to counteract the bitterness of the memory.

He flashed her an indulgent smile, then retrieved the box of truffles from the table in the corner, placing them on the bed between them as he settled back down next to her.

Isabella took one and stuffed it in her mouth as she figured out how best to begin.

'I've never told this story to anyone,' she said. 'The

only people who know are the ones who lived it with me. So if I don't tell it well, that's why. Okay?'

'Okay.' Matteo wrapped an arm around her shoulders, pulling her closer. 'And if you want to stop, if you decide you don't want me to know, that's fine too, okay? I won't push.'

Another difference between him and Nate. Nate had *always* pushed. He'd had to, hadn't he? It was his job.

'When I was twenty-two, I met a guy.' God, how many tragic stories started that way? Too many, Isabella was sure. 'Nathanial was Augustan and from a decent enough family to be invited to an event at the palace, but not aristocracy, so not a suitable courtship partner for me in the eyes of my family. But I thought I was in love, of course. At his urging, I'd throw off my princess persona and escape the castle to be with him. He was my first love, my first everything really. Being with him was the first time since puberty that I felt like myself, like Isabella, not just a princess.'

'So, what went wrong?' Matteo asked. 'Your parents found out?'

'They did,' Isabella admitted. 'But not until it showed up in the papers. It turned out that Nate was an aspiring reporter, and he'd used his flirtation with me to get photos, quotes about my family, insider gossip from the palace, everything. He sold it to the *Augustan Times* in return for a job there.'

Matteo swore. 'Bella, I'm… That's awful. I'm so sorry.'

'It was a long time ago. Five years—no, nearly six since it started.' And in that whole time she'd kept her distance from everyone, kept herself safe behind the title of Princess, using it as a barrier. Until this week.

'What happened next?'

'Isn't that enough?' She flashed him a grin, but she could see from his eyes that he knew the aftermath mattered almost as much as the event itself. She sighed and went on. 'The palace put out a statement denying most of it—saying he was a desperate young man who had made up these quotes and stories to find fame. But there were photos of us together, and too many of the stories rang true with other gossip, so I don't think anyone believed it. It was easy enough to see what had really happened. I'd been a fool.'

Matteo shook his head. 'You were taken advantage of. You were in love.'

'I'm not even sure I was, now. Not really. Love…you think you know what it is when it happens for the first time, don't you? But now, I'm not sure I'd recognise it if it jumped up and down throwing heart confetti at me. I just… I don't know how anyone trusts anyone else that much. Not without a non-disclosure agreement, anyway.' She laughed at her joke, but he didn't.

'Isabella.' His bright green eyes were serious. 'You know I wouldn't tell anyone about all we've shared here this week, non-disclosure agreement or not.'

'I do.' She couldn't have explained how she knew she could trust him, but there was no doubt inside her that she did. She'd trusted him with her body all week. She could trust him with her secrets, too.

'Anyway, my parents—and my older brother, Leo—were all horrified at the peril I'd placed the palace in. Those are their exact words, incidentally.' She almost smiled at the memory, except to this day the sight of the King and Queen and the Crown Prince of Augusta all staring at her in disapproving disbelief was still the thing that gave her the most nightmares. 'They couldn't believe I hadn't seen what was happening. In fact… I wondered if they actually thought I'd done it on purpose, as some sort of rebellion.'

'Did you ever ask them that?'

Isabella shook her head. 'No. We…after all the initial lectures and lessons about how to guard my royal privacy—or, more pertinently, theirs—we never talked about it again. His name is never mentioned in the palace, neither is that whole period of my life. It's as if it never happened.' As if she'd never been anyone but Princess Isabella at all. Just as Aunt Josephine had been written out of the family history.

Matteo was silent for a long moment, his lips pressed against her hair. She could almost hear him thinking.

'Do you think…this week…?' he said, finally. 'Has it given you anything?'

She didn't have to think about the answer. 'It's given me everything.'

The chance to be herself, for once, not her title. The ability to explore all the things she'd never thought she'd have again. To take a few risks, to live a little.

But most of all, it had enabled her to trust her own judgement again. To believe that Isabella was a person worth being, princess or not.

She couldn't put all that emotion into words, though. Not without ugly crying, and ruining their last, perfect night together. So instead, she reached up and wound a hand around the back of Matteo's neck, pulling his mouth to hers, putting all of her feelings into her kisses instead.

And as he responded she knew that this was the perfect way to spend their final hours together. Lost in each other, bodies so close they were almost the same person, without any more secrets between them. Just enjoying this space out of time, where they could be themselves.

This is perfect, Isabella thought as Matteo made love

to her, the intensity of their coupling somehow so much more than the other nights they'd spent together.

So close, as her body tightened and her release swelled within her, and Matteo began to move faster as she fought to match his pace.

So perfect, as her orgasm crashed over her, and every muscle in her body seemed to tense then relax, drifting away on a contented cloud of daydreams.

In fact, everything was perfect, until Matteo jumped up and swore, loudly and proficiently.

'What is it?' she asked, forcing her trembling body to sit up.

He met her gaze with grave eyes. 'The condom broke.'

CHAPTER NINE

THE NEXT MORNING—the last morning—Matteo sat on the balcony with his morning coffee and watched Isabella leave.

Except in reality she'd already left him, hours ago. The moment the damn condom broke, she'd shot out of his bed and his life.

He'd tried to talk to her, of course. Offered to find the nearest all-night chemist that might provide a morning-after pill or something, but she'd refused to listen. Told him she'd handle it herself.

Which he expected meant she'd be asking one of her royal advisors to handle it, since he couldn't exactly see her walking into a pharmacy herself to do it.

But after all the walls they'd broken down between them over the past week, it frustrated the hell out of him that this had put them all back up again.

She hadn't even joined him for breakfast that morning—which meant she hadn't eaten anything at all. Behaviour so unlike the Isabella he'd come to know this week, he'd really started to worry.

She had come to say goodbye, though. He supposed that much politeness at least was bred into princesses.

'My assistant will be here with my car any moment,' she'd said, lingering in the doorway to the balcony. 'I'm going to go and wait downstairs. So… I guess this is goodbye.'

'I'll take your bag down for you,' he'd offered, but she'd shaken her head.

'Even princesses can carry a bag, Matteo.' It had been a joke, he supposed, but he hadn't laughed.

Because that was what she was again, wasn't it? Princess Isabella, a world away from him.

And because of a stupid piece of latex, he hadn't even been able to enjoy their last night together.

'It's too much, Matteo,' she'd whispered through the door, after she'd shut it on him. *'Too much risk. This whole week… It's too much.'*

She wasn't wrong. He'd spent a sleepless night trying to deal with just how much it all was. And how saying goodbye suddenly seemed so much bigger than it had in his head, now he really had to do it.

He wasn't a fool. He hadn't expected this week to end with hearts and flowers and a royal wedding, even before she'd told him about her experiences with the idiot reporter. And he hadn't wanted it to, either.

Matteo Rossi wasn't the settling-down type, and he definitely wasn't anybody's idea of a prince.

But the idea of never seeing Isabella again—never touching her, never kissing her, never making love to her again—that made his whole chest ache in a way he hadn't anticipated when he'd stood on this balcony a week ago and looked down to see her standing on the terrace.

Maybe M knew what it was doing after all. Because he'd never met a woman so perfect for him.

If only she weren't the most impossible person for him to love, all at the same time.

This was for the best. He had to remember that. He needed to live his own life, a life he couldn't live if he was worrying about her—or even if he knew she was somewhere, worrying about him. Love, like the love he'd felt for his mother and brother, came with limits, and it came with loss and pain.

He didn't have space for any of those things in the life he was living for himself, and for Giovanni.

A car pulled around the corner of the driveway, out from the trees that shielded the villa from the passing roads, and halted beside the terrace. Tinted windows, probably bullet-proof glass, and high wheels that put the driver and passengers above many of the other cars on the road.

A carriage fit for a princess—a modern-day one, anyway. Even if Augusta seemed to be stuck in the past when it came to the rules it expected its princesses to follow.

The honey-blonde woman Isabella had been arguing with the day he first saw her—Gianna, his memory filled in—stepped out from the back seat and hurried across to the terrace. Just like that first day, he was too far away to make out their conversation, but the concern on Gianna's face was evident even at a distance. What did she see in Isabella's face that made her look like that?

He wished he knew. That he could see. That he could take the Princess in his arms and kiss her better.

Was Isabella feeling as torn up as he was right now? Or was she just telling her friend about last night's accident and begging her to help make it go away.

His child…

No. That was stupid. It was one broken condom; the chances of Isabella being pregnant were low, surely?

Just imagining it was another way to hold onto her, beyond the end of this week. And that wasn't something he could do; they'd both been clear enough about that from the start. Nothing had changed in either of their worlds outside this place.

Even if he felt like a different person inside, all of a sudden.

Down on the terrace, Gianna put her arm around Isabella and led her towards the car, carrying her case in her other hand. Matteo watched intently from the balcony. Would she turn around? Would she wave goodbye? Did he even want her to? He wasn't sure.

Isabella reached the car door, and he braced himself for her disappearing behind those tinted windows, and the prison of her position as Princess. But, at the last minute, she paused and looked back up at him.

He drank in that last glimpse of her. That creamy skin, the dark curls that bounced past her shoulders. The curves he'd held close. The lips he'd kissed.

She raised her hand, a last royal wave. He huffed a laugh he knew she'd never hear and blew her a kiss instead.

And then, with the closing of a door and the purr of an engine, Princess Isabella of Augusta drove out of his life for good.

'Are you really sure you're okay?' Gianna asked as the car door shut behind her, and the driver started the engine again. 'I thought you were having fun! When you texted, you said it was good, that he was nice.'

Her head was buzzing with all the things she'd never said to him. With the memory of that awful moment last night. With the fear and the risk that had sent her running from his arms.

'I'm fine,' Isabella lied. 'Really.'

Gianna clearly didn't believe her. She reached across the seat between them and took the Princess's hand in her own. 'If he did something, said something, you need to tell me now, Your Highness. He signed a non-disclosure agreement, so we can sue him to high heaven if he tries to sell his story, but if there's anything more—'

Isabella sobbed a laugh. 'No! No, honestly, Gianna. It's nothing like that. He was…he was wonderful.'

And she'd run out on him, too afraid to face the risks she'd been taking.

No birth control was one hundred per cent effective, she knew that. There was always the risk of pregnancy, from the moment she'd decided to take him to bed.

She'd told herself that it was Matteo making her take more risks—ditching the security detail, swimming in the lake, pretending to be a normal tourist—but she'd taken the biggest one all by herself. She'd let him into her bed, into her body.

Even *that* wasn't the biggest risk she'd taken this week, even if the magnitude of what she'd done was only now crashing down on her as she drove away.

She'd let him into her *heart*.

And now she wasn't entirely sure how to get him back out again. If that was even possible.

Was this how Aunt Josephine felt?

Gianna's expression had gone from concerned to horrified. 'I should never have sent you. Oh, Your Highness, I'm so sorry! It was meant to be fun, a chance for you to relax…'

'It was all those things,' Isabella sobbed. 'Honestly, I'm glad you set it up.' Even if now she couldn't stop crying.

'Isabella, what *happened*?' Gianna asked, desperately, and Isabella knew her friend had to be worried because she'd used her name, not her title.

'I don't know,' Isabella replied. There were still tears

dripping down her face; she could feel them plopping off her chin and nose and into her lap. God, she was a mess. 'I don't know.'

I'm very afraid I might have started to fall in love. And I might be pregnant. And both of these things are impossible, and no one can ever know.

Matteo hadn't wanted a perfect-match love affair any more than she had at the start of the week, and she had no reason to believe his feelings on that had changed. They were from two different worlds, and they both wanted to stay in them. Love was off the table.

She should ask Gianna to take them by a pharmacy, or to call the royal family doctor, or something. She needed to do something about that burst condom.

This wasn't just an ill-advised affair. This wasn't an immature fling gone wrong. It wasn't some photos and embarrassing quotes in the paper.

A princess, pregnant out of wedlock? A single-mother princess?

Augusta was a conservative country, and its monarchs were the most conservative of all. Her parents might never get over the shock. They'd forgiven her once, for being young and stupid. They'd blamed her naivety, given her the benefit of the doubt and helped her cover it up. Hammered home The Rules to make sure she couldn't make the same mistake twice.

But she wasn't so young now, and she didn't feel stupid, or as if her time with Matteo was a mistake. Would they forgive her again? Or would this be one transgression too far?

She should make sure she didn't put them in the position of having to decide.

She should.

But instead, she hugged herself and cried. For the life

she'd had a glimpse of, the possibilities she'd walked away from, and the future she knew could never be hers.

He wasn't back on the team.

Matteo had left Lake Geneva for Rome, ready to throw himself back into his normal life, only to discover that his normal life wasn't ready for him yet.

'That leg needs another few weeks of physio,' Gabe told him on his return. 'Doctor's orders—don't blame me.'

He did, of course. He blamed everybody there for messing with his career, his head, his future.

For showing him something he couldn't have. Something he'd never even imagined he might want, until now.

So now he was sitting in Gabe's office—feet on the desk, of course—figuring out his next move.

'You do realise you don't have to be here, don't you?' Gabe said as he walked in, a sheaf of papers in his hands.

'I'm still part of the team, aren't I?' Matteo said obstinately. 'Even if I'm not allowed to race.'

Gabe rolled his eyes. 'You're on medical leave, Matteo.' He moved to push Matteo's feet from the desk before obviously remembering about his still-healing leg and resisting the urge.

Matteo kept his feet exactly where they were.

'My leg is fine,' he grumbled.

'Then you can get it off my desk.'

Rolling his eyes, Matteo stomped his feet onto the ground. 'Look, if I was well enough to be shipped off to Lake Geneva to show some random woman the sights, I'm well enough to drive, yeah?'

Taking his own seat on the other side of the desk, Gabe looked at him with interest. 'I've been waiting to hear all about your Swiss exploits. Are you ready to share with Uncle Gabe yet?'

Matteo shrugged. 'What's to share? It was a week in Lake Geneva taking in the tourist attractions and eating too much good food.'

'With a woman that M dating agency swears is your perfect match.' From the smirk on Gabe's face, he could tell that his manager wasn't taking that claim any more seriously than Matteo had, when he'd arrived at the villa.

Before he'd met Isabella.

'So, are you going to tell me about her?' Gabe pushed.

'What do you want to know?' Suddenly, he was strangely reluctant to share any details of his week. To give up any of the perfect, private experience that had been his week with Isabella.

The memories were his, and they were hers, and they didn't belong to anyone else.

Even when Madison Morgan herself had called to check in, post-date-week, and ask how it had gone, Matteo had kept his responses to a minimum. He'd confirmed that they'd had a great time, that the villa was perfect and they'd got on well, but left it at that. Madison had sounded faintly disappointed, but she was a professional, and she hadn't pushed him for gossip or sordid details.

Gabe, Matteo knew from experience, would *definitely* push him for both of those things.

'Was she as perfect for you as the agency promised?' Gabe asked, surprising him.

'Yes.' The word was out before he could stop it. 'In lots of ways, she was.'

Gabe beamed like a proud father. 'So, you'll be seeing her again?'

Matteo shook his head. 'I don't imagine so.'

'Why not?'

Gabe, Matteo knew, had been married to the love of his life since he was twenty-two, and never looked at another woman. He lived vicariously through his drivers, instead. For him, love was simple: you found it, you grabbed it, and you made damn sure never to let go.

He wouldn't understand that Isabella wasn't meant for him to hold onto, even if he wanted to.

What Isabella needed most in the world was to fly free; but what her position demanded of her was the opposite. That wasn't a fight Matteo intended to get in the middle of—not when she'd so clearly already made her choice.

'It wouldn't work between us,' Matteo said eventually. It had the benefit of being true, at least.

'How can you know if you don't try?'

When he didn't answer, Gabe sighed, and tossed the paperwork he clearly wasn't reading aside on his desk. Matteo wondered if he had enough time to run before the inevitable lecture Gabe was obviously building up to.

'Matteo…' Apparently not. 'You know I love you like a younger brother. A son, even.'

'Right down to the parental lectures and interfering in my love life, apparently.'

'You haven't *had* a love life until now,' Gabe pointed out. 'A sex life, sure. A dating life, for definite. But love?'

'I'm not looking for love,' Matteo pointed out.

'Why not?'

Because if I can't have Isabella, what's the point?

'Because love would slow me down.' That was a more acceptable, Matteo Rossi answer, right? 'You know how it goes. You fall in love and suddenly you have to change your whole life for them. Be more careful—on the track and off. Stop doing fun stuff.'

'*Dangerous* stuff,' Gabe countered.

'The stuff that makes me feel like I'm *living*.' Except he'd felt alive with Isabella. Calm, at peace—but alive. And now he'd crossed off everything on Giovanni's list, what was he going to do next, anyway? What risks were still out there to take? What heart-pulsing, blood-pumping things could he do to make the most of his life?

Possibly getting a princess pregnant is probably pretty risky, his mind added unhelpfully. *Her parents could probably have me assassinated.*

Okay, he wasn't thinking about that any more. Wasn't thinking about Isabella, either. Because whatever he thought he might have to give up for a chance of a relationship with her, it was nothing to what she would definitely have to sacrifice. Augustan princesses couldn't fall in love with Italian racing-car drivers. It was aristocracy or nothing.

He'd done a little research since he left Lake Geneva—and not just to look at photos of Isabella online, and curse the fact that he hadn't had the foresight to take any of her while they were together, if she'd have even let him. He'd found, buried in the depths of the Internet, the original coverage of the debacle she'd told him about with the reporter. And, with it, an interesting sidebar about the traditions of royal marriage in Augusta.

She'd have to give up her title, her place in the line of succession, not to mention probably a lot of money, to marry someone her family didn't approve of. Apparently her aunt had made the sacrifice before Isabella was even born. Augustan royalty took the rules seriously.

No wonder she didn't want to chance getting close to anyone that might make her want to risk it.

Across the desk, Gabe was watching him silently, as if he could see Matteo's thoughts ticking across his brain.

Matteo sincerely hoped that he couldn't, for any number of reasons.

'I'm not going to tell you that life without love isn't worth living,' he said slowly. 'But I would like you to think about one thing, Matteo. Will you do that for me?'

'Of course.' Gabe had been his mentor as much as his manager for most of his adult life. He always thought about the things Gabe told him—even though most often they were to do with how he took a corner, or the right mindset for an upcoming race.

'All the things you've done—the places you've been, the adventures you've had—you've done them alone. Ever since Giovanni died, it's just been you against the world, and every challenge it can throw at you.' Gabe got to his feet, the papers he'd walked in with long forgotten. 'Wouldn't it be nice to have someone to face those challenges with, again?'

He left before Matteo could marshal any arguments against his words, or point out that no one would ever be able to take his brother's place in his heart.

And as the door swung shut behind him Matteo used the sound of it crashing closed to ignore the voice inside his head that whispered: *Not replacing. Something new.*

Was it time for something new? Not Isabella, not love—there were still too many reasons that Gabe didn't understand why that wasn't an option.

But he'd completed Giovanni's list. He'd done everything his brother had ever dreamed of.

He was done. And that revelation felt like a weight off his shoulders, as if he were flying again, rather than held down by reality.

For so many years, ever since he'd made his promise to Giovanni, he'd been living by someone else's beliefs, following someone else's dreams. And it had brought him so far, given him so much, he couldn't regret it—especially not when he knew what it would have meant to his brother.

But still…

Now he had fulfilled his promise, that meant it was time for Matteo to live by his own beliefs, follow his own dreams. Set his own challenges and meet them.

Once he figured out what they should be.

He needed new adventures. Bigger, riskier ones. He needed to take life to the edge.

That was what he'd done when Giovanni died: filled the gaping hole where his brother had been with experiences. With reminders of everything the world had to offer.

With proof that he, at least, was still alive.

He needed to do the same thing again now. That was all.

Lost in thought, he reached across the desk to grab a blank piece of printer paper and a pen and started to write.

CHAPTER TEN

A WEEK LATER, Isabella stared at the diary on the desk in front of her and sighed.

'What's with the sighing?' Gianna peered over her shoulder at the blank boxes. 'It's a quiet week. I thought you'd be pleased.'

'I am. Mostly.' Her weeks at the palace didn't tend to be busy anyway, given her aversion to public events. But sometimes things snuck into her calendar when she wasn't there to stop them, and a few had definitely been added to her future diary while she was away in Switzerland. She'd struggled through the ones in her first week back and was already thinking of ways to get out of most of the others, even though they were weeks away.

But she'd asked for a quiet week this week, and she'd got it.

Except now she had no idea what to do with the free time.

Sitting alone with her thoughts simply wasn't an option, because her thoughts all revolved around one thing. Well, two, technically, although they both linked back to the same man.

Number one: she missed Matteo, with the kind of ache she'd never felt for Nate.

Number two: her period was late. Four days late, to

be precise, since she should have had it a week after her return from Switzerland.

She didn't need it circled in red in her official engagements diary or anything to know that; she'd been counting the days ever since she left Lake Geneva. Her period was normally like clockwork—the same as her schedule. She'd have assumed Gianna had organised it like the rest of her life, except that Gianna was all about Isabella's public persona, and nobody in Augusta wanted to think about the royals having bodily functions like that, surely?

Matteo had urged her to take risks, to get out there and live life while she had the chance, in Switzerland. But she was pretty sure he didn't mean this kind of risk.

Gianna was perched on the desk beside her, looking down at Isabella with concern.

'Is it still…him?' she asked softly. 'You're thinking about him again?'

'Yes.' There was no point lying about it. While she'd tried to keep the details about her time at the villa to a minimum, Gianna had organised the whole thing. She knew why she'd been there, and she'd seen the state she was in upon leaving.

'I should never have sent you there,' Gianna said now, shaking her head sadly. 'I never thought… I know they claim to find a perfect match, but I never imagined you could fall like this in just one week.'

Isabella looked up sharply. *A fallen woman.* How did she know? 'What do you mean? Fall?'

'In love,' Gianna replied. Her eyes were pitying. 'Your Highness, you have to believe I'd never have sent you there if I really thought you were going to fall in love. Not with someone you can't be with.'

'I'm not in love.' She wasn't. *But I could be.* If she let

herself fall, let herself spend more time with Matteo... she knew in her heart he was someone she could love, for real this time.

She just wouldn't let herself, because what good would that do them?

'Isabella—'

'You said it yourself,' she said sharply, cutting off her friend. 'Who falls in love in a week? Besides, whatever M claim, how could they find my perfect match without knowing the truth of who I am? You filled in those forms for me, and I didn't even know what that video interview was for. And since Matteo was in hospital with a broken leg when his application went in, I don't even think he did it all himself either. He said his manager set it up for him to keep him out of trouble.'

Gianna looked sceptical, but she didn't push it. Well, not too far. 'But you're still thinking about him.'

And the possibility he knocked me up.

She was going to have to talk to him, and soon. He deserved to know what was going on—and she could do with someone else to freak out about it with. If she told Gianna...her assistant was a friend, but she was also a royal employee. If she knew that the Princess was pregnant out of wedlock...and without even a romantic story to tell beyond a week-long Swiss booty call...she'd be obliged to tell the King and Queen.

Which was the absolute last thing that Isabella wanted.

Of course, then she'd have to confess her own part in the whole plan, Isabella supposed, but she liked Gianna too much to let her take the fall for that, anyway. No one had pushed her into Matteo's arms, or his bed. In fact, she'd stripped off in front of him and run there herself.

God, this was so much worse than anything Aunt Josephine had done. Especially if there was a baby...

She shook her head and forced a smile for Gianna. 'Well, then, I guess I need something to take my mind off things, don't you think? There must be something fun going on here at the palace, or some sort of royal trip that could benefit from a little bit of princessy sparkle, right?'

Anything to stop her wondering what would have happened if she hadn't run out on Matteo that last night. If they'd actually talked about what happened when they went back to reality, instead of trying to pretend it wasn't happening until the last minute.

If she was surprised at Isabella's sudden—and mostly unprecedented—interest in palace events, Gianna didn't show it. Probably because she knew how much she needed the distraction.

Instead, her assistant flipped through the giant paper organiser she insisted on using, even though the palace had invested in the latest technology for such things. 'There's a tea party for some of the country's most successful charitable fundraisers in the rose garden on Thursday. A visit from Augusta's greatest living novelist—'

Isabella groaned. 'Again? Why can't he just stay home and write more books?' She liked his novels far more than his company, and he always seemed to try and sit next to her at formal dinner, especially since he'd been appointed the Royal Writer last year. 'I definitely need something to get me away from the palace if he's visiting.'

'Well, Prince Leo is taking a trip to Rome at the weekend for a charity ball, if you *really* want to get away?'

Rome. 'Really?' She hadn't told Gianna that Matteo was Italian. Or that, according to his social media accounts—which she was only stalking under an anonymous account—he lived in Rome. Was there right now, in fact.

Why call, when she could talk to him face to face?

'Want me to ask your brother if there's space for one more on the trip?' Gianna asked, looking thrilled to have found something that distracted Isabella from her mysterious lover.

If only she knew...

'Well, I have been meaning to practise my Italian,' she said nonchalantly. 'Why don't you set it up, and I'll see if I have anything suitable to wear for a ball?'

And for seeing Matteo again, she hoped.

Matteo didn't know how Gabe talked him into stuff like this.

He was a racing driver, not some sort of wannabe philanthropist actor. Sure, he did what he could for causes that mattered to him—especially the cancer charity that had helped Giovanni in his last days. Most of his riskiest adventures were sponsored to raise money for them. But that was the point, wasn't it? He liked *doing* things for charity.

Showing up at some fancy ball in a tux and having his photo taken a lot really didn't count.

Still, it *was* for charity, and Gabe was right that his face was the most recognisable on the team. So Matteo had put on his tux jacket and bow tie and his best celeb smile and prepared himself for a dull evening.

If he'd seen the guest list earlier, he'd have known it would be anything but, he realised belatedly as a tall man with coal-black hair and dark eyes entered the room followed by a whole retinue and was announced.

'His Royal Highness Leonardo, the Crown Prince of Augusta.'

Matteo's chest tightened. So this was Isabella's brother, Leo.

There was no reason to think that he'd have brought his sister with him, but Matteo couldn't stop himself craning around to see if there was another royal hiding behind the Prince.

'Looking for someone?' Gabe asked, sounding amused.

It occurred to Matteo rather too late that his manager, in setting up the whole 'perfect week in paradise' thing, had probably got to see a lot of the paperwork, before and after the trip. Including the name of Matteo's perfect match.

Damn.

'Her Highness Princess Isabella of Augusta.'

Matteo's heart stopped at the herald's words, and he ceased caring about what Gabe knew or didn't know. Instead, he turned to face the doorway full on, and tried to remember how to breathe as Isabella walked through it.

She's here. She's really here.

He'd honestly thought he might never be in the same room as her again, and now here she was.

Her ball gown, a deep midnight blue, sparkled under the lights of the ballroom, caressing her curves as he wanted to do. Her dark curls were piled on the top of her head, the creamy skin of her neck and shoulders bare except for the glint of sapphires, and her lips red and kissable.

She looked every inch the Princess, and Matteo wanted her so much he could hardly breathe.

As he watched she surveyed the room, chin held high and her gaze cool and assessing. Her manner was as many light years away from the relaxing, laughing, smiling, *touching* Isabella he'd spent the week with as her ball gown was from the light sundresses she'd worn there.

Then her gaze landed on him, and he saw the Isabella he'd fallen for in Switzerland behind all of her jewels and her title.

If she was surprised to see him, she didn't show it. But her gaze turned warmer, and he felt his body respond to her smile the way it always did.

Then her brother motioned to her, and she turned away to follow him as he toured the room, being introduced to the rich and charitable gathered in Rome for the occasion.

Matteo knew he should be circulating too, having the sort of conversations that led to donations, or someone offering him the opportunity to go and risk his neck to raise money for causes that mattered to him. But it was hard to concentrate on anything except the Princess in the room. Gabe, obviously aware of his distraction, covered for him in most of their conversations, and Matteo made a mental note to thank him later, when he wasn't so distracted.

Eventually, though, the Crown Prince had been introduced to and conversed with all the people who actually mattered in the ballroom and, as the orchestra struck up again after a break in the entertainment, and people began to flood back onto the dance floor, Leo and Isabella finally reached Matteo and Gabe.

'Your Royal Highnesses,' their guide said, 'may I introduce Mr Matteo Rossi, the current world champion racing driver, and his team manager, Mr Gabriel Esposito.'

The Crown Prince probably said something, but whatever it was Matteo didn't hear it. Not when he was taking Isabella's hand in his and lifting it to his lips, kissing it and wishing he could hold on for ever.

Never mind cliff diving, bungee jumping or jungle trekking. Seeing Isabella again made him feel more whole than any of those risky adventures ever had.

Gabe, as so many times before, was his saviour. In seconds flat he'd diverted Isabella's brother with a deep and meaningful conversation about something or other, guiding the Crown Prince's attention away from his sister and the racing driver she had supposedly just met.

'Do you dance, Mr Rossi?' Isabella asked, her voice a touch more formal than he was used to. He'd *never* been Mr Rossi to her before.

'I can try,' he said honestly. Because while his mother might have instilled good manners in her boys, dance lessons hadn't exactly been included.

Isabella flashed him a smile that made her look much more like the woman he knew and wanted. 'Just follow my lead.'

'Anywhere you want to go,' he replied.

Because if it meant being with Isabella tonight, he'd follow her into hell.

Matteo might be fast on his feet when chasing her to the bedroom, but he was not a born dancer. Not that it mattered to Isabella, since dancing together was nothing more than an excuse to get him alone—and lead him away from Leo.

Oh, and maybe an excuse to have him hold her again. She definitely wasn't overlooking the benefits of that.

He knew where to put his hands, at least, and Isabella managed to half dance, half drag him across the dance floor, towards the balcony she'd spotted on an earlier tour of the room. If she was lucky, it would be empty—but even if not, it would still be dark and more private than a crowded ballroom with all eyes on her. And besides, they'd always had good luck with balconies.

'I didn't expect to see you again,' Matteo murmured as they attempted a sort of waltz. She half expected him to add 'so soon', but he didn't, and it made his words sit all the heavier in her heart. He hadn't expected to see her at all. He'd expected that they'd both go their separate ways and that would be it.

Was that what he wanted? She'd never know if she didn't ask. And she *had* to know, before she told him about the apparent consequences of their week together.

'Disappointed?' she asked, as lightly as she could.

'Amazed. And thrilled.' His hand at her waist gripped her tighter. 'And a little hopeful.'

That made her smile—even though she wasn't sure how his mood might change when she told him why she was here.

'I was surprised to find it so easy to see you,' she admitted. 'When I found out Leo was coming to Rome, I tagged along in the hope of finding you. But I hardly expected you to show up at an event on my first night in town.'

'Fate, perhaps,' Matteo said. 'Or luck. Or maybe M had it right with that soulmates thing…'

'You think we'll keep being drawn together for ever, now we've met?' They'd reached the balcony, at last, and stopped dancing. Isabella raised an eyebrow as she waited for his answer.

In a moment, she'd open the door and lead him outside and tell him that she might be pregnant. For these last few seconds, she just wanted to enjoy being the way they'd been together in Lake Geneva.

'I think I wouldn't complain if we were.'

'Good answer.' Because there was a solid chance they were bound together for life, now, by a small cluster of cells growing inside her womb.

Moving out of his arms, she reached for the door handle to the balcony and pushed it open. She glanced around the ballroom, ascertaining that Leo was still fully occupied in conversation with Matteo's manager, and a few other guests who had joined them, and was unlikely to notice her absence for a while.

'Come on,' she said, dragging him with her into the cooler evening air of the balcony. He followed easily, shutting the door silently behind them.

They were lucky; the balcony was deserted. Isabella let out a long, relieved breath, as she moved away from the ballroom and to the stone and metal barrier at the edge of the balcony.

Matteo moved behind her, his whole body pressed up against hers as they looked out over the city below them—ancient and modern by turn, lit up by the moon and the yellow streetlights as the summer evening passed into darkness. She could see the curve of the Coliseum in the distance, the remains of Trajan's market beyond. Traffic and chatter and laughter hung in the air; the city was very much still awake, despite the hour.

It was late. She'd been travelling all day, then rushed to prepare for the ball that night, and then she'd been introduced to so many people her head was spinning with names and information, not to mention the worries she'd brought with her. She was exhausted.

But when she stood with Matteo at her back, when she felt his warmth through her ball gown, his kiss against the bare skin of her neck, above her mother's sapphire necklace…all of that faded away.

She forgot about Leo, inside, probably wondering where she was. She pushed out of her mind the reason she'd come to Rome. And instead, she relaxed against her lover, and let him carry the weight of all her thoughts for a while.

Matteo, for his part, seemed content to stand in silence with her, just enjoying their closeness. Every few moments he'd press a kiss to her hair, her throat, even the swell of her breast over her ball gown. But that was enough.

Until, apparently, it wasn't.

'Isabella,' he murmured against her ear. 'Why did you come to Rome?'

Because I might be pregnant.

The truth, but not all of it. There was another truth she wanted him to know, too. So she gave him that, instead.

'Because I missed you.'

Matteo spun her round, pulling her tight against his chest as he kissed her soundly.

'You missed me too?' She laughed as he finally broke the kiss.

'More than I like to admit.' The truth of it was there in his eyes as she met his gaze.

She needed to tell him. And she would.

Just not yet.

Was it so wrong to want to enjoy this reunion just a little longer? To recapture everything she'd loved about being with him in Switzerland, before their situation got a lot more complicated?

'I dreamed about you,' she murmured, and watched his green eyes darken.

'Yeah? What did you dream?' His voice was gravelly and low, and it made her ache for him to touch her more.

'I dreamt of your hands on me.' At her words, Matteo slid his hands up from her waist, up to her breasts, rubbing his thumbs across her nipples through the thick fabric of her ball gown.

It wasn't enough; the fabric was too thick, she couldn't get the touch she needed. She whimpered her need to him, and it seemed Matteo understood. Without warning, he tugged it down just a couple of centimetres. Just enough to release her aching nipples. This time, when he brushed his thumbs across them, she moaned.

God, she hoped the music inside the ballroom was loud enough that no one heard her and came out to investigate.

'What else did you dream of?' Matteo's voice was rough with need, and Isabella thought longingly of the balcony at the villa in Lake Geneva, and how it conveniently led right to their bedrooms.

'Your mouth.' The words came out as a gasp, and Matteo flashed her a wicked smile before dipping his head lower.

His lips wrapped around first one nipple, then the other, giving each enough attention to make her squirm in his embrace.

'Anything else?' he asked, against her skin.

Time for some payback. Her hand snuck down to the front of his tuxedo trousers and pressed against the hardness she found there. 'I definitely dreamt about this, too. Inside me.'

Now it was Matteo's turn to let out a groan. 'Trust me, if I thought I could get away with making love to a princess here on a balcony, with the whole of Rome watching, I would.'

'Too much risk even for you, huh?' Isabella's smile faltered as she remembered what other risks they'd taken.

'Maybe I'm just worried I couldn't make it good enough for you, up here,' Matteo countered.

'I doubt that. You managed fine on the balcony in Lake Geneva.'

'True.' Matteo's smile turned wicked. 'Want to find out if I still have the magic touch?'

God, she did. So much.

But her real reasons for being in Rome were too heavy

in her mind—not to mention the risk of Leo coming out
here to find her. That would be the end of her royal reputation for good.

She stepped away, tugging her dress back into position, as Matteo watched her, his eyes suddenly wary.
And she knew she wouldn't be able to hide the truth
from him any longer.

'Isabella, I'm going to ask you again. Why did you
come to Rome?'

CHAPTER ELEVEN

MATTEO WASN'T ONE hundred per cent sure what the feeling thrumming through his body was, but he suspected it might be dread. Isabella bit down on her lower lip as she looked up at him, her warm brown eyes wide and guileless.

'I think I might be pregnant.'

All the dread that was bubbling through him gathered in his stomach, sinking it like a stone.

Pregnant. She might be pregnant. With his baby.

That last night. The broken condom. The risk that was so much greater than all the others he'd taken before.

Seeing Isabella again here in Rome…for a moment, he'd let himself get carried away, as he'd been able to do in Switzerland when it was just the two of them. For all of his protestations, he probably *would* have made love to her right there on the balcony if she'd let him.

She was a risk on a different level from any skydive or impossible climb. The Crown Prince could probably get him arrested, and if someone down below had spotted them and the Rome *polizia* were called, he'd *definitely* have been spending the night in the cells.

And yet she was a risk he couldn't resist. Not for the adrenaline, like all the others. Just for her.

He'd made a lifestyle of outrunning risk, of beating all the odds, every time.

But this time, it looked as if it had caught up with him.

'We need to get you back in there before you're missed.' He brushed down the back of her ball gown and hoped that no one would notice any specks of balcony dirt in amongst the embroidery and the sparkly bits. Her lipstick was mostly gone, but hopefully she could replace that. And he'd managed not to muss up her hair too much.

'Matteo, we need to talk about this.'

'I know! I know. And I want to. Just…' The door to the balcony opened for a brief moment, a laughing couple audible in the gap, until they obviously realised the space was occupied and closed the door again to seek another spot for privacy. 'Not here,' Matteo finished, redundantly.

'Okay.' She didn't look happy about it, but at least she seemed to understand.

He hoped so. It wasn't that he didn't want to discuss the situation. He just needed to get his head around it a bit first.

Having a baby *definitely* wasn't on his list of adventures. But it seemed that someone else was writing his bucket list, once again.

'I wish we had more time,' he said. 'How long are you in Rome for?'

'Another few days. Come and find me at my hotel tomorrow?' she suggested. 'You can show me the sights of Rome. And we can talk.'

She wanted to escape her security *and* her brother in a strange city, with him? He'd taught her the fun of taking risks well, it seemed.

'I will,' he promised. He knew he wouldn't be able to stay away, not as long as he knew Isabella was so close. 'But we need to get back in there now.'

The thought of leaving her, of having to deal with all this, was making him shake. He stumbled, his hand slipping on the door handle until it opened, and the sounds of the ballroom surrounded them.

'We'll…we'll talk tomorrow, yeah?' he managed, as he staggered back into the room. 'Wait here, then follow me in a few minutes. Okay?'

Isabella nodded, but he could see the fear in her eyes, even in the dim lights.

Matteo shut the door behind him and walked away. He needed to get away from the balcony before Isabella came out. He needed to be someone unsuspicious. To look as if he were having a perfectly ordinary evening—and his entire world hadn't been turned upside down.

He scanned the ballroom until he found Gabe—a solid, fixed point in his suddenly reeling world.

Gabe was a good manager and a better friend. While Matteo had no doubt Gabe knew where they were and what they were doing, he'd managed to keep Isabella's brother away from the balcony, holding him in conversation with a variety of people Matteo recognised by sight.

That was good. Taking off in the other direction, he headed for the bar, and a drink—making sure to keep the door to the balcony in his line of sight as much as he could. Leaning back against the bar, he watched Isabella reappear, slightly mussed, but still the most beautiful woman he'd ever seen. He saw the moment her brother spotted her and excused himself from Gabe. He saw Gabe clock Matteo on the other side of the room before he let him go.

And he heard the conversation between the royal siblings as they passed by him, heading towards the rest of their entourage.

'I just needed some air, Leo, that was all,' Isabella

said. But her eyes met his for a moment, and he couldn't stop his smile. Even with everything, just looking at his Princess made his day better.

Luckily, the Crown Prince was oblivious to his presence. But not his existence.

'I was starting to worry you'd run off somewhere with that racing driver,' Leo joked. 'Honestly, Bella, we really do need to stick together at these things. Who knows? I might want to introduce you to someone you might find…suitable.'

The emphasis on 'suitable' was almost innuendo, and Matteo's grip on his glass tightened at the sound of it.

Of course, *he* wasn't suitable for a princess. He'd known that from the start.

But that didn't change the fact that she might just be carrying his baby. And that as terrifying as that was…it didn't feel like the end of the world.

Matteo threw back the whisky in his glass and wondered how long he had to wait before he could get out of there.

And how long before he could steal Isabella away again, to start figuring out what the hell they did next.

Oh, he really hadn't ever prepared for *this* sort of risk. But as long as they figured it out together…maybe it would be okay.

Isabella didn't sleep that night.

She wished she'd managed to slip Matteo her mobile number, or something, so at least they could have kept in touch over the long hours before they saw each other again. But even if she had…they needed to have this conversation in person.

She just hated waiting for it.

Finally, the morning sun slipped through the curtains

of her hotel suite, and she allowed herself to get up and dressed. She chose a sundress more like the ones she'd worn in Switzerland, rather than one of the more formal outfits Gianna had packed for her; she didn't want to be Princess Isabella today. Not with Matteo.

Perhaps he had been unable to sleep, too, because when she snuck downstairs for the first breakfast serving, uncomfortably aware of her security team following her as she went, he was already seated at a table in the corner.

The hotel staff tried to usher her towards a private seating area, offering to bring her whatever breakfast foods she desired, but Isabella sent them away with a smile. She wanted to choose her own food, from the buffet, just as all the other guests would be doing; otherwise, she might as well have had breakfast alone in her room. Which, now she thought about it, was probably what the hotel staff—not to mention her security team and her brother—would have preferred.

Before Lake Geneva, that was exactly what she would have done. But things were different now.

Isabella motioned the bodyguard flanking her towards an unoccupied table in the corner, indicating that she'd follow shortly when she'd chosen her food. The buffet was in clear line of sight from the table, so he didn't object.

Helping herself to a plate, Isabella lingered by the watery scrambled eggs, and waited to see if Matteo would take the hint.

'You know, I could take you to about seven different cafés in walking distance of this hotel that would do you a better breakfast than this.' His voice, low and familiar by her ear, sent a warmth coursing through her that had nothing to do with summer.

'Then maybe you should,' she murmured back.

'Any suggestions on how I might get out of here alone, though?' She didn't risk a glance over her shoulder at her bodyguard, probably watching their every move.

Matteo didn't even pause to think; she suspected he'd been planning this all morning. 'The corner by the coffee station is hidden from sight, but there's another door out that way. Go get some coffee, and I'll distract your security guy. When you can see he's occupied, slip out the side door of the hotel and meet me there. I'll be as quick as I can; just stay out of sight.'

She nodded, to show that she'd heard him, then picked up her plate and headed for the coffee station, while Matteo walked away in the other direction. Giving her bodyguard a smile, she lifted a coffee cup from the stack to show her intention.

Her heart was racing at the idea of actually following through with the plan. But, she reminded herself, she wasn't just taking this risk for herself. It was for the baby that might be growing inside her right now.

That was most definitely worth taking risks for.

'Hey, aren't you Matteo Rossi?' she heard her bodyguard say as she ducked into the coffee area.

Smiling to herself, she listened to Matteo agreeing to sign an autograph, and getting into a deep discussion about his teammates' chances in the next Grand Prix, then slipped out of the promised door and headed for freedom.

She tucked herself behind a pillar just outside the hotel and waited. Matteo joined her not long after, grabbing her arm and taking off at a steady clip around the back of the hotel. 'Come on.'

Isabella wasn't even properly surprised when she found herself on the back of a motorcycle, a few moments later, a black helmet crammed over her head and her arms wrapped tight around Matteo's waist as he took off through the streets of Rome.

A wonderful sense of freedom, one she hadn't felt since she'd left Lake Geneva, rushed over her with the wind. This, this was what she'd been missing. Well, this and everything Matteo had given her on the balcony the night before…and everything else she wanted from him. Was it the motorcycle or him making her throb between her thighs?

Probably both, she decided as he swung around another corner and finally pulled to a halt.

'Where are we?' she asked, pulling off her helmet, and hoping her hair wasn't completely wrecked. She ran her fingers through her tangled curls and hoped for the best.

'Just around the corner from the Forum, and the Coliseum.' Matteo shrugged. 'I figured we can walk and talk, you can see a little history, and then we'll get pizza before I take you back. Sound okay?'

Isabella nodded. Leaving the bike parked in a side street, helmets attached, they headed out into the historical centre of Rome. Matteo held out a hand to her and she took it, conscious as they joined the streams of tourists wandering the ancient, excavated streets of the Forum that they could be any other couple, enjoying a summer's day in Rome.

The only thing that ruined the illusion was the tension in Matteo's shoulders, and the way she couldn't help but check over her shoulder for any sign of the palace security team catching up with them.

'So,' Matteo said, after a while of just wandering amongst the ruins. 'I guess we need to talk.'

He'd chosen a good place for it, she realised belatedly. Here in the open air, with so much conversation and chatter, and people moving past them all the time, who was there to listen in on such an intensely private conversation? And who would realise the consequences of it, even if they *did* listen?

In a restaurant, they might have been photographed together, or recognised by a waitress who later sold her story. Matteo was far more famous here than she was—her bodyguard had proved that—but with his cap pulled low over his face, hopefully no one would recognise him.

She took a deep breath. 'Yes, we do.'

'Are you sure?' he asked, and she looked at him with confusion until he shook his head and clarified. 'Not about talking. I mean, about…have you taken a test?'

'Not yet,' she admitted. 'It's not the easiest thing to do with the whole palace watching you.'

'Right. Do you…do you want to? I could find a pharmacy…'

Isabella sighed. 'I'll need to, soon. But for now… I'm over a week late, Matteo. I think we have to assume it's likely, given our last night together in Switzerland.'

That damn broken condom. Although, without it, would she even be here, in Rome, exploring with Matteo like a tourist? She doubted it. More likely, she'd be still locked up in the palace, itching to escape but not knowing where or how.

At least this had focused her. Shown her how much the freedom she'd found with Matteo had given her.

She'd already known how much she'd missed him.

'Yeah. So…assuming you are…'

'Pregnant,' she said, since it seemed that he couldn't.

'What do you want to do next?'

And wasn't that the million-euro question?

'I… If there's a baby, I want to keep it.' That part was easy. However hard it might be, however scandalised Augustan society, however furious her family. This was her baby, and no one could take that away from her. 'Is that a problem?'

Matteo looked horrified. 'I wasn't suggesting—I didn't mean—Isabella, *of course* I support you if you want to keep the baby. I guess all I meant was… I'll be guided by you on this. It's your body, your choice.'

Your reputation, he didn't add, but Isabella could hear it in the air between them, all the same.

She wouldn't have risked it for anything else, they both knew that. But a baby…that changed things.

'What about you?' she asked, to drive the thought away. 'Would you want to be involved? Or even acknowledged? I mean, nobody has to know, if you don't want to be part of this.'

Grabbing her hands, Matteo yanked her out of the path, against a crumbling ruin of a wall, and met her gaze with his own, intense green one.

'Bella. If you are pregnant with my child, of course I will be a part of that. I'll marry you in a heartbeat if you'll let me—or if the King and Queen will, I suppose. Having a family with you will be my next big adventure, I guess.' He flashed her a quick smile at that, but it did nothing to diminish the seriousness of what he was offering.

If she was pregnant, he would marry her. Because for all that he was a reckless, daredevil playboy, he was also a good man. He'd do the right thing.

Even if he didn't want to.

And that was the problem. There'd been no mention of love, in any of his grand declaration. If she hadn't come to Rome and told him about the possibility of the baby, would he have ever come to find her? She wasn't exactly difficult to locate—The Palace, Augusta would probably do it on a map search, or even a letter.

Matteo had given her a freedom she'd never experienced in her whole, pampered princess life. She wasn't going to take his away now, just to save a few shreds of her royal reputation.

So instead of the shock of an Italian racing-car driver stealing away their Princess, the Augustan crown and public might have to deal with having an unmarried single mother in the royal succession—if she was even allowed to keep her title, which was not a sure thing at all. Her stomach was cramping just thinking about her brother's reaction.

She knew she could lose everything, the same way Aunt Josephine had, and she might not even have true love to show for it.

'Let's find a pharmacy. Buy a test. Then we can plan. After pizza.'

Matteo *really* hoped nobody had recognised him buying a pregnancy test. But who else could he ask to do it? If he was recognised, at least no one would connect it to Isabella yet. If *she* was recognised, well… That was a whole different matter.

There was nothing to link him and the Princess of Augusta. Not until they announced their engagement, anyway.

Don't think about it.

It was the right thing to do, he knew that. For Isabella, and for their child. And for him, too, really. He wanted to be a part of his son or daughter's life, the way his own father never had, and if that child was Augustan royalty then the only way he was getting close was by living up to his responsibilities and marrying their mother.

He just didn't like the way his whole body clenched at the idea of being tied down as somebody's *husband*. Would he still be allowed to race? To live his life the way he wanted? He had a sneaky suspicion that his cliff-diving days would be limited, once he was inaugurated into the Augustan royal family.

If they'd even have him.

Would he cost Isabella her title by marrying her? It wasn't as if he couldn't afford to support her in the manner she was accustomed to—his billions would go a long way to providing compensation, as would, he hoped, the freedom they'd have to live their lives together unencumbered by the royal rules, if she was thrown out of the royal family.

But being a Princess of Augusta was her birthright. Giving up her country was something she wouldn't have even considered if it weren't for him. No, if it weren't for the baby.

They managed to sneak back into Isabella's hotel room by a similar distraction technique to earlier in the day. Matteo would have less respect for the security team for falling for it a second time except this time around Isabella was the distraction. With their apologetic wayward charge back in hand, all attention was on her explanation for her disappearance, leaving Matteo free to sneak into her room with the key card she'd given him.

She joined him a few minutes later, rolling her eyes as she shut the door to keep her latest bodyguard firmly outside the room.

'Okay?' Matteo asked softly as he emerged from his hiding place by the wardrobe.

'Fine. They just all think I'm still sixteen or something. I'm under orders to stay here for the rest of the evening.' She stalked towards him, a predatory grin on her face. 'Which shouldn't be a problem, since you're here with me.'

The pregnancy test burning a hole in his pocket was

totally forgotten when she smiled at him like that. But as she pushed his light summer jacket from his shoulders, it fell out onto the floor, a stark reminder to them both of why they were there.

'Do you want to take that now?' Matteo stepped away, giving her the space to decide.

He could see the warring thoughts fluttering across her face. She bent to pick up the box, pulled out the instruction leaflet, and scanned the text.

'It says it's best to do it first thing in the morning. I'll take it then. I mean, at this point, another few hours aren't going to make any difference. And I want—'

She broke off, and Matteo waited.

'I want to enjoy this last night. Before everything changes.'

He could hear the hesitancy in her voice. She wasn't any surer about this situation than he was, and who could blame her?

But the thing that had blossomed between them during their week on Lake Geneva was still as present and sure as it ever had been—hadn't he felt that last night, on the balcony?

Matteo knew what others might think and say. They'd believe that his actions the night before—attempting to seduce an honest-to-God princess in a semi-public setting—were all about the risk, the same as all of his other extra-curricular activities. But they'd be wrong. It hadn't been the risk that had him hard and desperate in the dark.

It was Isabella. Only ever Isabella.

And she was right; once she took that test and they knew for sure, everything would change. One of them would lose their dreams, their future. Either his racing career and adventurous lifestyle, or her title and her country.

But not yet. They had one last night together.

'You'll have to be very quiet,' he said, thinking of the security team waiting outside her hotel suite door. 'Do you think you can manage that?'

'I did last night, didn't I?' she asked, one eyebrow raised.

He took a step closer, and she echoed it, leaving the pregnancy test on the table behind her. 'Last night, I couldn't do half the things I wanted to do to you. Definitely not enough to make you scream.' And he'd dreamt all night of how different that might have been. If he'd been able to lift that heavy ballgown and kneel under the skirt and take his mouth to her…

'Well, maybe I'll need to fill my mouth with something to keep me quiet.' She kept her gaze trained on his as she dropped to her knees. 'Besides, I think it might actually be *you* who needs to try not to make any noise.'

There was no blood left in his brain, or anywhere except south of his belt. He didn't care about the inadequate thin curtains over the window, or the men outside the door who were trained to break him in two in a moment. All Matteo could concentrate on was Isabella's small hands unfastening his jeans, sliding them down his thighs with his boxers, until he kicked off his shoes and stepped out of them.

Then it wasn't just her hands on him. Shaking her long, dark curls away from her face, she nuzzled against the top of his thighs, pressing soft kisses against his hardness.

God. He was going to lose his mind. He was going to actually go insane with want—and if he didn't, if she did something about it, he was going to scream and get himself killed by her bodyguard.

He had to admit, it didn't sound like a bad way to go.

'You okay up there?' she murmured against his hardness, and he felt her words vibrate through him.

'More than,' he answered honestly.

'Good.' Then, with one last kiss against his thigh, she closed her mouth over the tip of him, and Matteo decided right there and then that this was *definitely* worth dying for.

Staggering back a couple of steps, he grabbed hold of the chair behind him for support, sinking into it as Isabella explored and tasted him to her heart's content. And his, for that matter. Finally, as his body started to tighten, he pulled her away before everything was over too soon for his liking.

'You don't want me to finish? Was it not okay?' She looked up at him, her mouth plump and slick and red but her eyes uncertain.

'It was perfect,' he assured her. 'I just don't want it to end so soon.'

She smiled at that, a catlike, satisfied smile. 'What would you like instead, then?'

He pulled her up into his lap, stripping her sundress over her head before letting her divest him of his shirt. 'I'd rather like to be inside you,' he whispered against her collarbone, and felt her shiver at his words.

She was wet and ready for him when he touched her, and it was only when she stood up to strip off her lingerie that his mind could work well enough to remember the essentials. 'Wait. Condoms.'

Isabella gave him a look as if to say, *Do you really think they're necessary at this point?*

He shrugged. 'No point taking unnecessary risks,' he said, which made her laugh. 'There are some in my wallet.'

She bent over to retrieve his wallet from his jeans

on the floor, and Matteo was happily enjoying the view when he heard the first noises outside. Voices. Then a bang on the door.

'Isabella!' The voice outside didn't sound patient. Or happy. 'Let me in this instant!'

CHAPTER TWELVE

ISABELLA SPUN AROUND to face Matteo, still slumped in the chair watching her, his eyes wide. 'It's Leo!'

Because of course it was.

'Your brother?' Matteo kept his voice low, and she nodded in response.

'You need to hide!'

He'd hoped his days of hiding from angry older brothers were over when he became an actual adult, but apparently not. Scooping up his clothes, wallet and—in a brief flash of inspiration—the pregnancy test, Matteo let himself be bundled into the bathroom by Isabella.

'One moment!' she called out cheerily. 'I'm just changing.'

'Isabella, I swear to God—' Whatever Leo was swearing was cut off into a mumble, probably around the time the Crown Prince realised that *anyone* could be listening. Including the press—or at least people who'd sell the video or audio to the papers.

Isabella pulled her dress back over her head and surveyed the room.

'Bella,' Matteo whispered as she pushed the bathroom door closed. 'Remember, you're an adult. He might be a prince, but you're a princess. You get to make your own decisions. No crown can take that away from you, okay?'

Biting down on her lip, she nodded, but Matteo could tell she didn't fully believe him.

He sighed, and sat down on the toilet seat to wait, glad that the door hadn't closed all the way. He was still sitting in almost complete darkness, but at least there was that sliver of light from the bedroom. *And* it meant he could hear what Isabella and her brother were saying.

'Where were you today?' Leo asked, the moment Isabella opened the door.

Matteo hadn't spent much time with him at the ball the other night, and his attention had definitely been elsewhere, but he'd seen enough photos to be able to imagine the Crown Prince's face right then. Red, flustered and angry.

'You skipped out on your security, didn't leave word where you were going, wouldn't answer your phone—'

'I'm sorry.' The apology sounded automatic to Matteo's ears. As if she was so used to saying it, it was nothing more than a reflex.

Plus he happened to know that she really *wasn't* sorry for running out with him. Not if what they'd been doing before Leo banged on the door was any sign.

'My security team…they're not in any trouble, are they? Because I really didn't give them any choice. I just… I wanted to get outside, get some air. See a little of Rome, that was all. You know how rarely I leave the palace these days.' She was trying to mollify him, to earn his sympathy, but Matteo didn't know Leo well enough to guess whether it would work.

He *did* notice, however, that his habit of asking for forgiveness, not permission, seemed to be rubbing off on his Princess.

'And you know why that is,' Leo shot back. Matteo heard him sigh, then the sound of bed springs creaking, as if he'd sat down on the edge of the bed in exhaustion. 'Bella…people were worried. *I* was worried. You don't know this city, or anybody here. Anything could have happened to you. What if some brigand had recognised you and snatched you off the street?'

'Brigand?' Isabella asked, sounding amused.

'You know what I mean,' Leo snapped back. 'The point is, you weren't *safe*. And while you're here in Rome with me, it's my responsibility to keep you safe.'

'I know. I'm sorry. It's just…what if I didn't want to be safe, all the time?'

There, hidden in that question, was the Isabella *Matteo* knew. The one he wanted, more than any other woman he'd ever met before. The one who made him laugh and chase her and think.

The one who wanted to live a life that was more than being afraid all the time, or doing what other people wanted her to, rather than what she wanted herself.

The woman he might marry, soon. Might spend his whole life with.

It was just a glimmer, though. A brief flash of the woman he'd known in Lake Geneva, who he'd seduced on a balcony the night before. One that was soon smothered by her brother's next words.

'Of course you want to be safe, Isabella. Don't be stupid.'

'Yes. Right. Of course, I do. I'm sorry, Leo. I don't know what I was thinking.'

And with that, all of Matteo's hopes about who she could be if she was just willing to take the chance disappeared.

Maybe inside, Isabella wanted to be free, wanted to live her own life at last. But her family would always stomp out the first flames of rebellion, and she would always let them. She'd build up those walls brick by brick, all by herself, to hold onto her place in the royal family.

She didn't want to be pregnant with his child; her horrified reaction the night the condom had split had made that perfectly clear. She didn't want to have to marry him—it was just the least unacceptable option to her family, and their royal expectations.

He'd marry her, if she was pregnant, because he owed her that. But he had no illusions any more that it would be what either of them wanted. Now, they enjoyed each other's company, the sex was amazing and, yes, he knew he could fall for her. Hard.

But if they married...

He'd be tied into a life he didn't want to live. And she'd be embarrassed by him forever, even if marrying him didn't cost her the title of Princess. He wasn't what anyone wanted for her—even Isabella herself.

Outside, the royal siblings were still talking.

'Look, I know we can all seem a little overprotective at times, Bella,' Leo said. 'But you know why that is. You just don't understand the world outside the palace and, honestly, I'm not sure you want to. We just want to keep you safe, okay?'

'I know that,' Isabella replied, softly. 'I'm sorry.'

The bed springs creaked again. Leo was standing up. 'Don't cry, Bella. It's okay. Just...stay where we can keep you safe. Yeah?'

'Yeah.'

There was quiet for a long moment, before Matteo heard the door to the suite open and close again. He waited.

Isabella's eyes were red when she opened the door. 'I'm sorry you had to hear that.'

Maybe it was just as well that he had. At least it told him exactly what the future held for him.

He held out the pregnancy test. 'I think maybe you'd better take this now. Don't you?'

Negative.

How could it be negative?

'Could it be a false result?' Matteo's voice was tense as he sat beside her on the bed, but she was sure she heard relief in it, all the same.

Isabella shook her head. 'I mean, it *could*, but…'

She could feel it now, those telltale signs she'd been ignoring all day. The slight cramp in her lower back. The tiredness. The stupid tears when she'd been talking to Leo.

Her period was on its way.

She wasn't pregnant.

She might not have proof for another day or so, but she knew it, inside.

'I'm pretty sure it's right,' was all she said.

Matteo let out a long, relieved breath. 'Okay. Well, that's good. Right?'

'Absolutely.' She hadn't wanted to be pregnant—not now, not with a man she'd barely known a few weeks, with whom she had nothing in common outside the bedroom. A man her family would disapprove of on principle. A man who could cost her everything.

So why did she feel like crying?

Period hormones. That's all.

No, that *wasn't* all, and she wasn't going to pretend that it was.

'You okay?' Matteo asked. Of course, *he* looked fine. He didn't have stupid hormones. And he wasn't going back to a life trapped behind palace walls, never daring to reach out for what he wanted from the world, in case it turned on him. In case it destroyed his family, or his reputation.

Really, she'd had a narrow escape. She should be celebrating.

'I'm fine.' It came out as almost a sob. 'Happy tears,' she lied.

'Right.' He didn't look convinced. 'So…what now?'

'You're free,' she said, with a shrug. 'No need to worry about me.'

'And you're just going to go back to the palace as if nothing ever happened?' His tone was even, his expression blank. But Isabella could still feel the tension between them.

'What else can I do?' She was a Princess of Augusta. The privileges that gave her came with a cost—and a lot of expectation. 'I've already pushed about as far as I can coming here, especially so soon after my Switzerland trip. And it's a miracle nobody caught onto that, either.'

She shuddered at the thought of Leo bursting into her suite asking, 'What's this about you spending a week having sex with a racing-car driver in Lake Geneva?'

'I thought…' Matteo looked away, as if he wasn't going to finish his sentence. And suddenly it was vitally important to Isabella that she know *exactly* what he thought.

Because he was the first person in her life who had got to know her as a woman, not a princess. Who hadn't cared about titles or palaces or money. Who hadn't held expectations for what she should do and who she should be. Who loved risk enough to be with her anyway, even when it looked as if they might have been caught out by it.

His opinion mattered, more than almost anyone else's. She needed to hear it.

'What did you think?'

He sighed. Then he looked up from where his hands were clasped between his legs as he sat on the edge of the bed and met her gaze head-on.

'I thought that Lake Geneva had meant something. That coming here had meant something. To you, I mean. And not about me, particularly. I thought—I hoped—that it would be your first step out from under your family's thumb. That you might finally forgive yourself for what happened with that reporter and move on with your life.'

'I came here to tell you I might be having your baby.' Isabella swallowed, his words ringing in her ears. 'If that's not flying in the face of all my family's beliefs and expectations, I don't know what is.'

'And now that you're not? What are you going to do now that you're not pregnant, Isabella?'

She didn't know. She hadn't thought this far. Hadn't thought beyond finding him again, telling him about the baby.

Letting him figure out what she should do next, the way she'd always relied on her family to.

But he had no stake in her future now. No investment in what happened to her next.

She could go back to the palace, to her old life, but she already knew how stifling that felt, now she'd experienced something more. Last time, after everything had happened with Nate, she'd been so grateful for the safety of the palace, the security of her family around her, an impenetrable barrier against the real world outside that only seemed to want to hurt her.

This time...this time it was different. She was comparing her experience with Nate and her time with Matteo as if they were the same, but they weren't. Beyond the fact that they both included her having sex with a man the palace wouldn't approve of…the details were worlds apart.

Matteo didn't want to hurt her. Matteo could be trusted, even if his attitude to risk and opinions on suitable behaviour for a princess would scandalise the whole royal family. He was on *her* side; Nate had never been.

And she knew, now, that she'd never been truly in love with Nate. She wasn't a hundred per cent sure she could say the same about Matteo.

So what *was* she going to do now? What *could* she do?

'I need to go back to Augusta with Leo,' she said, thinking aloud. 'And obviously you don't now need to come with me. We don't need to go tell my parents I'm pregnant and they have to let us get married.' She flashed him a smile at that, ignoring the pang in her heart at the idea. He didn't smile back.

'So you just go back to your old life, and I go back to mine?'

'I guess.' Except that felt so wrong, Isabella knew it wouldn't work. Not for her, anyway. But maybe that was what Matteo wanted? His old life back—racing and risks and other women. 'Is that what you want?'

His smile was sad. 'I'm trying to find out what *you* want, Princess.'

When was the last time someone had asked her what she wanted and actually listened to the answer? Even the staff serving dinner at the palace brought her whatever dish the diet plan her mother's nutritionist had set her said she should eat, rather than what she actually fancied.

But Matteo was asking, and she knew he meant it.

What did she want? She wanted everything. He'd taught her the value of taking a risk, when it was the *right* risk. And maybe there was a way she could do it that wouldn't ruin everything else, too.

She took a breath, and a risk, and answered him honestly.

'I want to see you again. I want to *keep* seeing you. I don't want to say goodbye.'

Matteo's heart lurched in his chest as she spoke the words he'd been hoping—though not expecting—to hear. But before he could answer, she went on.

'I mean, we'd need to keep it a secret. God only knows what Leo would say if he found out. But we've managed this far, right? I think as long as I stay out of trouble at the palace, or when I'm with my family, nobody is going to mind if I take the odd weekend off. We can plan ahead, arrange to meet places where no one knows either of us. I might need to speak with Gianna about my security team…'

She had it all figured out, Matteo realised. Exactly how to have her cake and eat it.

Or have him, and not disappoint her family.

And it *should* be perfect. It should be exactly what he wanted. The freedom to live his life how he wanted and still see Isabella, without getting tied into her world and the expectations that went with it.

So why did his chest ache so much?

Because I'm not enough for her.

Ever since he was a teenager, he'd tried to live enough for two, to make up for everything Giovanni had lost. He'd done more, seen more, risked more than most people on the planet.

But he still wasn't enough for Isabella.

'Matteo?' She looked up at him, a tiny line forming between her eyebrows.

'I can't.' Pushing up off the bed, he paced across to the window. 'Isabella… I can't just be some dirty secret for you, the guy you're ashamed to bring home to your family.'

Her eyes widened at that, and she reached out towards him before sitting on her hands. 'That wasn't… I didn't mean it that way.'

'I know.' He sighed. 'But…when you told me you thought you were pregnant, I was scared, sure. But excited too. Because honestly? I've never felt anything like what I feel for you for any woman before now. I thought that maybe we could make this work. Until I heard you talking to your brother.'

'Leo? You can't… I just had to say whatever he needed to hear to get him out of here, before he found you hiding in my bathroom!'

'Yeah, but you meant it, too. And if I'd doubted it at all…you just confirmed it now.' God, he hated saying this. Hated thinking this. Realising it was true.

After so many years of pushing love away, of keeping it at arm's length to avoid the inevitable losses that came with it…now he found himself here. Wanting, wishing for a princess's love—and knowing that he couldn't take the loss that came with it when she didn't love him enough in return.

He'd been looking for an excuse to upend his whole life for her—to make her upend her life for him. But if she really wasn't pregnant, that excuse was gone. And he wasn't such a terrible human as to try again and bring a baby into a relationship they didn't have the courage to seek anyway.

He had honestly believed there was no risk he wouldn't take. Turned out that loving Princess Isabella of Augusta when she didn't love him was the line he couldn't cross.

'I'm not saying we *never* tell them,' she tried, but Matteo shook his head.

'It's okay, Isabella. We never—this wasn't ever the love match M wanted it to be. We weren't matched together because we were soulmates who were going to live happily ever after. We were put together because my manager wanted to keep me out of trouble and your assistant wanted to give you a week off from being a princess.'

'It was more than that,' she said softly.

'Was it?' Because it was hard to remember that right now.

'You know it was.'

'It was great sex, I'll give you that.' His heart was breaking, but he knew he couldn't give in. Couldn't let her say anything that would persuade him to stay. To hide away and follow her rules instead of his own.

For seventeen years he'd worked every day to fulfil his late brother's ambitions. To cross off every item on the bucket list he'd written before he died. And now, here he was, thirty-three years old and no idea what he wanted from his future for himself. Nothing except a half-scribbled list of adventures still to be had.

But he knew what he didn't want. And surely that was a pretty good place to start.

'Isabella, think about it. We sneak around, we have some fun, and, sure, I'm not denying I want that too—I want more time with you. But it wouldn't be enough. Not for me.' He'd never been the marrying type. Until he met Isabella. 'Eventually, the secrecy would break us. Or we'd get found out, and you'd have to choose. Your family, your title, or me. We dodged a bullet, this time. I won't put us in front of another one.'

'So what? We just never see each other again?' There were tears in her eyes. Matteo had to look away.

'I think it's for the best.' Even if it broke his heart. 'I can't live by your royal rules, even if they'd have me. I can't hide away my love for you, either. I need to go out there and live my life—not yours, not my brother's—just mine. I'm sorry.'

He didn't kiss her goodbye. Couldn't even meet her gaze.

Instead, he walked straight out of the hotel suite, and pretended not to see the astonished look from the body-guard as he headed back to his old life once more.

CHAPTER THIRTEEN

ISABELLA SLIPPED HER sunglasses over her eyes as she stepped out of the car at the small airfield outside the city. She'd pretended to sleep during the short drive out there—believable, given the early start—but now she needed something else to hide her red-rimmed eyes from her brother.

Not that he was looking at her, of course. He had work to do: emails from the prime minister, or something. Leo was being groomed to take over the throne, possibly sooner rather than later if their father decided he'd like to step aside and retire to the country. It wasn't unprecedented in Augustan history, and King Leonardo *had* been looking tired recently.

Musing on royal successions distracted her brain from the only other topic it seemed able to hold until they were seated on the royal plane at last. But then, as they prepared for take-off, it occurred to her that once Leo became King her role would be even less clear.

Her brother had married three years ago in a royal pageant like none the country had seen before. His wife, Princess Serena, was still in Augusta with their adorable toddler son, pregnant with their next child already. The succession was secure, and Isabella was happy for it. The further she got from the throne, the less pressure on her to be perfect.

But since she *was* further from the throne…what was the point of her? As a princess, at least? Serena had happily taken over a lot of the public-facing duties; the daughter of an ex-prime minister and a famously beautiful duchess, she was used to the spotlight. She was also a huge favourite with the Augustan people, mostly for having cute babies, but also for her keen fashion sense and ability to look empathetic on demand.

Isabella just wore whatever Gianna told her to wear. And, having grown up in a palace, was generally seen as unable to empathise with the Augustan public, even more than a woman who'd also had nannies from birth and gone to the same boarding school.

The point was, there was no place for her in Leo's new palace. If her father *did* hand over the crown sooner rather than later, would she even be welcome to stay there? Or would she move to the country with her parents, a spinster princess for ever?

More likely, they'd marry her off to some duke or lord they needed support from for something. Because Augusta liked nothing more than tradition—and the tradition of using princesses as pawns was well established.

Are you just going to do what they tell you for ever? The words sounded in her head in Matteo's voice.

Suddenly, she had to know.

'Leo.'

Her brother looked up from his papers and his laptop, his reading glasses perched on the end of his nose, and irritation in his eyebrows. 'Yes?'

'When you become King, what happens to me?'

'What do you mean? You can carry on as you always have.' He looked back down at his papers.

'No, I mean… What role do I play in the country?' she pressed.

Sighing, Leo removed his glasses and rubbed his temples. 'You want to talk about this now?'

Isabella shrugged. 'We're not going anywhere. Why not now?'

'Because you haven't shown any interest in your future, or how you can support the country or the monarchy, in years. So I'll ask again, why now?'

'That's not true.' The words were automatic, but they didn't quite cover the sinking feeling in Isabella's stomach that, actually, it might be. 'I care about our country. I do the public appearances I have to. I smile for the cameras. I stay out of trouble… Just because I haven't married any of the titled idiots you keep throwing my way—'

Leo cut her off with a weary sigh. 'Bella… Do you really not get it? After everything that happened with that reporter chap—'

'None of you trust me to make my own decisions! Trust me, I get it. I have to follow The Rules, more than anyone else, because I can't be relied on to choose good people, to know who to trust. To fall in love responsibly.' As if she could ever have missed that.

Even after all the stories about Aunt Josephine, she might have had hope that Augusta was changing with the times.

If it hadn't been for everything that had happened with Nate, maybe she'd have had the courage to take Matteo home to meet her parents. To tell them that, while he might not be the Augustan lord they'd hoped she'd marry, she loved him, and she hoped she had their blessing—but she'd marry him without, if he'd have her.

If there'd been a baby, they'd have had to let her. But now…she knew they'd remind her of her past mistakes and steer her away from what she thought could make her happy.

'That's not… Bella, it's not that we don't trust you.' Leo sounded amazed that she could even think it, which, considering the number of lectures he'd given her over the years on the 'right sort', was a bit rich.

'Of course, it is—' she started, but Leo kept talking over her.

'It's that you don't trust *yourself*.'

She fell silent.

Oh. *Oh.* Leo's words resonated in her ribcage until she couldn't deny the truth of them.

All these years, she'd thought she was toeing the royal line for them. Because it was what she needed to do to have their love, their faith. To keep her position.

And Leo had torn that away with just one line.

She'd been using The Rules as an excuse, thinking she was protecting her reputation, her family—but in truth, she'd been protecting her heart.

'Do you blame me?' she asked, slumping down in her seat to consider the implications of this revelation. 'The last time I thought I was in love, I almost brought down the monarchy.'

Leo chuckled. 'I don't think it was quite *that* bad. Although at the time, I was a little worried that the prime minister was going to have a heart attack.'

'So why all the awful set-up dates with your friends and other lords?' Because she definitely hadn't imagined those.

'Because… Bella, after everything that happened, you sort of drew in on yourself. You shut yourself up in the palace, avoided as many public events as you could, and only spent time with people you'd known practically since birth—like Sofia, or Gianna. We were worried about you. So yes, we tried to get you back out there—to help you get some confidence back—by getting you to spend time with people we knew we could trust. And yes, I can't deny that we were hoping you'd find love with one of them. Because we want you to be *happy*, and you so obviously weren't.'

Isabella looked quickly out of the window, so her brother wouldn't see the tears in her eyes. 'I thought it was because you didn't trust me.'

'It was because we loved you. And we wanted you to trust yourself again. To find your way back to us.' Leo sighed. 'But apparently we only pushed you further away. Serena warned me...well, never mind that now. The important thing is, when I am King, the same as now, there will always be a place for you in my palace, if you want it.'

'Thank you, Leo,' she said softly. 'And...and I think that, maybe, I'm ready to do a little more for the family business, so to speak. If you want me?'

'If?' Leo laughed. 'Serena would *love* it if you could take some of her events and visits off her plate right now. This pregnancy is exhausting her even more than the last, and I've been worried about her trying to do so much.'

Guilt twinged in her chest. 'I'm sorry. I should have noticed—should have offered sooner.'

Reaching across the aisle between them, Leo took her hand. 'None of that. We're all at fault for not realising things sooner. Not talking about them. I know our parents...they're a different generation, and for them feelings are very private, not to be discussed. But it doesn't have to be like that for us, Bella. I'm always here if you want to talk.'

She smiled, although it felt weak on her lips.

Maybe she'd never be what Matteo wanted—she

couldn't stop being a princess, and she didn't *want* to walk away from her heritage, her country. Quite the opposite. She was finally ready to take her proper place and do her part—and it seemed that Leo would let her.

'You said "last time", before,' Leo said cautiously. 'The last time you fell in love. Does that mean…? Is there someone you think you might—?'

'No.' She cut him off quickly. 'That's not…don't worry about that.'

The lines on Leo's forehead told her that he *was* worrying. Isabella sighed.

'I met someone when I was in Switzerland I thought might…but he didn't want the royal life. Or me.' All the truth, even if Leo still believed her trip to Geneva was to visit their cousin Sofia. It was plausible that she might have met someone there, and she wasn't quite ready to confess *everything* to her brother, yet.

'Are you sure? Because, Bella, you put up walls. One day you're going to have to let someone in. And when you do, I'll support you. Whoever they are.'

But she had, hadn't she? That was the problem. She'd let Matteo all the way in. She'd been so afraid of falling in love again, and now it had happened she could see why.

Except that following The Rules meant she'd be heartbroken for ever, separated from the man she finally admitted to herself that she loved. Completely and totally.

She couldn't regret her time with him, even now he'd walked away from her because of who she was. Because loving Matteo had shown her that love was worth taking risks for.

'What about Aunt Josephine?' she asked suddenly, remembering all the stories that had swirled around the palace. 'You said "whoever they are" but that wasn't true for her, was it?'

Leo's brows met in a puzzled frown. 'Aunt Josephine… Bella, she left the palace before you were even born!'

'Was driven out, you mean. Because the King and Queen—our grandparents—didn't approve of who she fell in love with.' Everyone knew that.

'Bella, she *chose* to leave. She didn't want the life of pageantry at the palace. She wanted to run a racing stables with her husband, so they left.' He shook his head. 'I know there was a lot of gossip—I heard plenty of it myself. So I sought her out and asked her, and she told me the truth. I guess it didn't occur to you to do the same?' he asked, looking amused.

'Well…no.'

Leo sighed. 'But you're not entirely wrong. Josie knew that there'd be a lot of talk when she married her groom. I'm sure that weighed into her decision to step away from royal life. But I promise you that no one *made* her. And if you fell in love with someone…perhaps not entirely in keeping with royal expectation, we'd find a way to make it work. *I* would make it work for you, if he made you happy. Okay?'

'Okay,' she said, blinking away tears. 'Thank you, Leo.'

'So, with that in mind, are you *sure* there isn't a certain gentleman you'd like me to meet? I can have the pilot divert to Switzerland, if you want? Or return to Rome, perhaps…?' He left the suggestion hanging, and Isabella wondered how much he'd already guessed about the man she loved.

It was so tempting, to head back and find Matteo and tell him they could be together. But Leo was right about Aunt Josephine's decision, too. She'd chosen to move away from the royal life because there *would* be a scandal, and she didn't want to live it.

Whereas Isabella had only just reconfirmed to herself how much she wanted to step back *into* royal life. She loved Matteo, but she had to live her own life, too—just as he needed to live his. And she couldn't decide for him on this one. If he wanted to be part of her royal life, that would be up to him—and without the baby to bind them together, it didn't seem as if he would.

'I can't live by your royal rules, even if they'd have me.' His words echoed in her brain, and she knew there was no point turning around.

'I'm sure,' she replied to her brother.

Leo gave her a sad smile. 'I'm sorry, Bella. But one day, you'll find the right one.'

Isabella tried to smile, to look as if she believed him. But her heart was telling her that she already had.

She just hadn't been able to hold onto him.

Matteo slammed back into the team hotel, ignoring all the fans and press he passed on the way. No way he was talking to any of them—not after a race like that.

There was, unfortunately, one person he *couldn't* avoid, though.

Gabe slipped into his hotel room behind him, before Matteo could take out his rage on another door.

'So. That was quite a race.'

'It was a disaster.'

'It was definitely close,' Gabe admitted.

Throwing himself into the chair by the window, Matteo put an arm over his eyes, only to find those final moments of the race running behind his eyelids like a video. The way the barrier had seemed to rise up before him. The roar of the other car's engine, too close at his side.

The split second when he'd honestly believed that this could be it. The last risk he ever took.

He removed his arm and opened his eyes, to find Gabe perched on the edge of the bed across from him.

'What happened, Matteo?'

'It was a bad race, that's all.' Matteo shook his head. 'That idiot Rennard was too close.'

'There was no penalty given,' Gabe observed, mildly. 'There seemed to be room as he overtook.'

Except he shouldn't have been overtaking in the first place, should he? Matteo had never lost to *Rennard* of all people before now.

He'd lost his nerve, that had to be it. He'd seen that corner and, for the first time, thought about the risks.

Was this what love did to a person? If so, he needed to get over it, fast.

'Matteo…you've not been the same since you came back from Switzerland. I think everyone can see that. It's not just the race,' Gabe added quickly, when Matteo started to object. 'It's *you*. Before, you were happy, racing along through life, living it to the full. Ticking things off Giovanni's list.'

'How did you know about that?' Because Matteo was damn sure he'd never told him. He'd never told anyone except Isabella.

But Gabe just gave him a look. One of those, *When will you learn that I see everything and I know everything?* looks.

'The point is, you're not happy now,' Gabe said. 'Are you?'

'No.' It was hell to admit, but he wasn't.

How could he be unhappy? When he lived and Giovanni didn't? When he'd achieved everything his brother had ever set out to do?

He'd even started ticking things off his own bucket list—booking a trip to swim with sharks, during his next break. He had things to look forward to, a life to live. And, today's race notwithstanding, a career he loved and was great at.

'It's the Princess, isn't it? Isabella.' Because of course Gabe knew that too. He'd even kept her brother occupied while Matteo had whisked her out onto the balcony at the ball. 'You're in love with her.'

'I can't be.' Because she didn't love him back—not enough to go against her family, or her title.

She wouldn't take the risk to be with him. And he…he couldn't take the risk of trying to live someone else's life again. He'd done it for his brother, but once was enough.

'I don't think love works like that, son.' Gabe creaked to his feet—for all that he was only fifteen years older than Matteo—and pressed a hand against his shoulder. 'Trust me on this. If it's love that's the problem, there's only one way to fix it.'

'And that is?'

'Tell her. Talk to her.'

'Don't see how that fixes anything,' Matteo grumbled. All the reasons they weren't together would still be there, after all.

But Gabe gave him a knowing smile. 'You'd be surprised. I saw the way she looked at you in Rome, Matteo. So I don't think the problem here is unrequited love. Which means there's something else keeping you apart. And maybe that something else is insurmountable, I don't know. But what I *do* know is this: once you tell her? Then it's not just you against this thing. It's the two of you, together. And two people in love against the world? I'd back those odds every time.'

With one last squeeze to his shoulder, Gabe let himself out of the room, leaving Matteo thinking in his chair. After a moment, he pulled an already tattered piece of paper out of his pocket and stared at it.

His new bucket list. The one he'd started after Lake Geneva, to replace the one that Giovanni had left him with. He'd been adding to it piecemeal ever since, whenever a new adventure occurred to him.

Now, he read through it and realised something he'd never have believed if someone else had told him.

He didn't care about any of them.

If things had gone the wrong way on the track that day, in that split second when he'd believed it might, he wouldn't regret not having done any of the things on his bucket list. Hell, in that moment he wouldn't have even been able to remember what any of them were.

Because his mind had been filled with only one thought.

The thought that he'd never see Isabella again.

That would be his only regret.

Lurching to his feet, Matteo crushed the paper in his fist. He didn't need it any more. Didn't need a bucket list at all.

She was his list.

He'd been holding onto his freedom, his adventures, but ultimately, what did they matter if he didn't have her?

Maybe he'd never be enough for her, maybe she'd never love him enough to take the chances that were needed for them to be together. But he knew he had to try.

Until today, he'd always risked his body, freely, happily, loving that surge of adrenaline it gave him. The power over the universe he felt when he survived the odds. Every experience was proof that he'd outwitted the world. That he was *alive*, even if Giovanni wasn't.

But he'd only ever risked his body.

And now, he knew, it was time to risk his heart.

'Are you sure you're okay doing this?' Princess Serena lowered her very pregnant body into her chair and Isabella smiled at the obvious relief her sister-in-law immediately felt.

'Of course. I'm happy to. And at least it's only kids, right?' Some of the children Isabella would be talking to on their visit to the palace rose garden today had been barely walking when she'd embarrassed herself so horribly with Nate. Of course, their teachers would probably remember. But Leo had assured her that most of Augusta had moved on with their lives since then, and forgotten.

It was only Isabella who hadn't. Until now.

'Your Highness? When you're ready?' Gianna called her from the door, and Isabella nodded to tell her she was coming.

Her assistant seemed pleased that she was doing more, too. Isabella supposed it couldn't be much fun organising royal appointments for a princess who refused to do any beyond the odd video interview.

Of course, it was one of those video interviews that had led her here—via Lake Geneva, and Matteo.

As always, her heart twinged at the memory of him. Her period had come and gone as predicted, just two weeks later than planned. Apparently that could be due to stress, which Isabella supposed was possible. Whatever it was, with it the last piece of Matteo that she could have hoped to hold onto was gone too.

Time to start over.

A new life, new responsibilities.

She followed Gianna out along the endless hallways

to the rose garden door, taking care to keep her breathing even and her smile in place. Her hair was styled, her simple dress and cardigan polished but not overwhelming for a group of seven- and eight-year-olds. Apparently these were the children from the capital's schools who'd achieved the most over the school year and so, as a treat, they got to spend a day of their summer holidays in school uniform touring the palace—and meeting a real-life princess.

And this year, for the first time in years, that princess was Isabella.

'Ready?' Gianna asked, before she opened the door.

Isabella nodded, and stepped out into the August sunshine, smiling at the crowds of small children and teachers who clapped her appearance, even if she hadn't really done anything yet.

The speech she'd been asked to give had been written for Serena, but Isabella thought she gave it well enough all the same. Talking about doing your best, helping others and working hard—all the things the children were being commended for—reminded her a little too much of how many years she'd spent *not* doing those things. But she was changing that now, and that was something.

Once the speech was over, and cake and drinks were brought out for the children, Isabella spent her time chatting with them, and their teachers, individually—learning more about their lives, about how they viewed their country. It was only a start, but she felt closer to the people her family ruled over than she had in years.

She was so engrossed in her conversations that she only vaguely noticed when Gianna slipped away, after talking with one of the palace guards. And only realised she'd returned when she heard her clear her throat behind her and say, 'Your Highness? I'm sorry to interrupt, but there's someone here to see you.'

The teachers were already chivvying the children back towards their bus; the visit had gone on longer than planned, Isabella knew. She said her goodbyes to the group she was talking to, and turned to see who else wanted to speak with her—

And promptly lost the ability to speak.

'Wait! Aren't you Matteo Rossi? The racing-car driver?' One of the boys who'd been on the school visit had escaped his teacher's grasp and raced back across the grass, promptly followed by most of his friends.

Matteo smiled graciously and signed autographs on request. At least it gave her the chance to gather her thoughts and stop her heart from racing quite so fast at the sight of him.

Why was he here? Hadn't they said everything they needed to when they'd parted? Unless things had changed...but how could they?

She'd changed, though, hadn't she? One conversation with Leo on the plane home from Rome and she'd found a whole new path—and a better understanding of herself, her past, and maybe even her future.

Perhaps the same had happened to him.

Was it wrong of her to hope so?

Eventually, the teachers won the battle to get the children to go home, and the rose garden emptied of people. Even Gianna had found somewhere else to be, and the palace guard were back at their posts, studiously ignoring them.

And so it was just Isabella and Matteo again, as it had been at the start.

'You came,' she said. '*Here.* Why?'

'Because I couldn't go the rest of my life without seeing you again,' Matteo replied. 'In fact, I'm not sure I could go without seeing you every single day for the rest of my life, if it comes to that.'

'I'm not pregnant,' Isabella blurted. 'I mean, I know I said…but definitely. You don't have to marry me to save my honour or anything.'

'I know that.' Matteo's smile was half amused, half fond. 'What else?'

'I'm not going to stop being a princess. I mean, I only just remembered why it's important in the first place.' She couldn't let her hopes get too high, if that was still a deal-breaker.

But Matteo just asked, 'Which is?'

'Because I can do things that matter to me. Help people, raise awareness, support my country. That sort of thing.'

This time, his smile almost split his face. 'Doing things that matter to you is the *only* good reason, I've come to realise, to do anything. To risk everything.'

He stepped closer and she moved into his arms automatically, as if that was where she belonged. It felt as if she did, anyway.

'So…what now?' she asked.

'I can't be a secret,' Matteo said, his eyes serious. 'If we're together, I need to be able to tell the world. Because hiding it implies there's something wrong or bad about it, and there isn't. I love you, Isabella, and I don't ever want to hide that.'

'I don't, either,' Isabella admitted as the warmth of his words filled her. *He loves me.* 'I hadn't realised how much I'd hidden myself away, how afraid I was to trust my own instincts, to trust *anyone*. I was using my past as an excuse to put up walls. But I trust you, and I know how I feel about you.'

'What will your family think about that?' Matteo asked.

'My parents might be…not thrilled. Especially if you're planning to carry on racing?'

'I am.'

She nodded. Of course, he wouldn't give that up; it was who he was, not just for his late brother, but for himself. And she'd never want to stop him being himself—not when she was only just learning who she wanted to be herself.

'But I've come to see that actually my family do want me to be happy, more than anything else.' And some of the barriers to their relationship might have been in her own head rather than other people's. 'I can't promise it's going to be easy—I mean, a lot of the people in power here are old-school conservative. They'd be happiest if I married a second cousin or something, but…'

'But?'

It had taken a lot of courage to talk to Leo about her future. More to start putting herself back out there again. But this was the real test—and the only one she truly cared about passing.

Isabella took a deep breath. 'But I don't want to marry anyone but you. Because I love you, Matteo Rossi. And I'm willing to take any risk to keep you with me—if you're willing to submit to everything that comes with loving a princess.'

He swept her up into his arms until her toes barely touched the floor, kissing her passionately enough that she didn't need words any more to know how he felt. From behind the rose garden gate, she thought she might have heard a palace guard give a congratulatory whoop.

When she was finally back on solid ground again, she smiled up at him. 'So is that a yes, then?'

Matteo raised an eyebrow. 'Was there a question?'

'Matteo Rossi, will you marry me, and be my Prince?' She batted her eyelashes at him, and he laughed.

'Only if we can honeymoon in Lake Geneva.'

'Deal.'

'And have sex on the balcony again.'

'Definitely.'

'Then, yes, Princess Isabella of Augusta.' He pressed a light, chaste kiss to her lips. 'I'll marry you. Because life without you is one risk I'm just not willing to take.'

EPILOGUE

'I WASN'T SURE, you know,' Leo said as they stood at the front of the Cathedral of Augusta, listening to organ music and the buzz of excitement from the crowd behind them.

'About the outfits?' Matteo guessed, looking down at the traditional Augustan dress he'd been forced into for the occasion. Gabe had laughed out loud at the sight of it until he'd realised that, as Matteo's best man, he'd be required to wear it too.

'About *you*,' Leo clarified. 'I mean, after you stole my sister away at a public ball, then helped her escape her security team to roam about Rome with you...'

Matteo winced. 'She told you that?'

'No. I am just not an idiot.' Leo gave him a long, assessing look, and Matteo was very aware of Gabe not trying very hard to hide his smile beside him. 'I admit, I was not sure about you. But,' he went on, over Matteo's attempts to interrupt, 'I promised my sister that when she found the man she loved, I would support her. Whoever he was.'

'Well, thank you for that, anyway,' Matteo replied. He knew that her brother's support would have gone a way to giving Isabella the confidence she needed to take a chance on him.

'And having you here this week preparing for the wedding, I admit, has helped me change my mind.'

'It has?' Matteo asked, surprised. Especially since he and Isabella had, as much as possible, eschewed wedding prep in favour of getting to know one another all over again, away from that private villa on Lake Geneva. Which had mostly meant hiding away in her private rooms. In bed.

'You love my sister.' Leo shrugged. 'That's all I ever really wanted for her.'

'I do love her,' Matteo admitted. 'More than anything.' That part might have taken him a little while to realise, but now he had, he couldn't believe he'd ever thought otherwise.

They might be from different worlds, and have lived very different lives before they met, but they were a pair. He brought her out from behind her terrified walls, and she helped him find a way to live in the world that didn't mean risking his neck all the time, just to feel alive. To justify his existence.

Oh, he'd still have adventures, and she'd still have days where she needed to hide away. But mostly, they'd have adventures or hide together. Because together, they were so much stronger than they were apart.

And now he got to have that for the rest of his life.

'Good,' Leo said as the organ music changed. 'Because it's time to show the world that.'

Matteo turned as the huge doors to the cathedral creaked open. The pews were filled with the great and good of Augusta, as well as a couple of rows of schoolchildren, and another few of people in uniforms—nurses, soldiers, doctors, police, firefighters. Isabella had insisted on opening the wedding up to the people who really made a difference in her country—and Matteo had supported her.

His friends and teammates were in attendance too,

and Matteo sent a quick smile their way before turning his attention to the far end of the aisle. Past the camera crews, broadcasting the occasion live to the world. Past Madison Morgan, smiling with satisfaction in the final pew. To the vision in white appearing on the King's arm as the doors parted.

Isabella glided down the long aisle to sighs and gasps from the congregation. Matteo stared at her dark curls, pinned up to reveal her long, elegant neck, and the lace neckline of her gown. Below the lace, white silk clung to her curves, down past her hips, before flaring out into a train that was still entering the cathedral when she'd almost reached him at the altar.

Her dark red lips jumped into a nervous smile as she kissed her father on the cheek, then took the last couple of steps alone.

Steps towards *him*. Matteo Rossi—daredevil, racing driver, orphan, world champion. She had chosen *him*. And no race or accolade or adventure had ever made him feel so alive as knowing that Isabella would be at his side for the rest of their lives.

'You look so beautiful,' he whispered as she stood beside him. 'That dress is…'

She flashed him a wicked smile that really had no place in a cathedral. 'Just wait until you see what I'm not wearing under it.'

Beside him Leo made a choking noise, and Gabe stifled a laugh.

Matteo gave thanks for the ridiculous, but concealing, Augustan state dress, and smiled back at his soon-to-be wife. Yeah, being married to a princess was going to be a lot of fun.

* * * * *

COWBOY IN
DISGUISE

ALLISON LEIGH

This book is dedicated to my husband, Greg.
You keep me sane.

Chapter One

January

"I thought you didn't eat bread anymore."

Arabella Fortune jumped guiltily and used the corner of her napkin to cover the roll she'd dropped in her lap, where it sat next to two others just like it. She looked from the empty bread basket to meet her brother's laughing eyes.

"More bread?"

At the question, she swiftly looked from Brady to the handsome owner of the deep voice. His name badge said Jay Cross and he'd been attending to their table throughout the birthday party for her nephew. She picked up the basket, smiling into his deep green eyes.

"Yes, please." She sounded breathless and didn't really care. "If it's not too much trouble." Jay was gorgeous. And every time their fingers brushed—when he'd given her a fresh napkin after she'd dropped hers, when he'd refilled her water glass, when she handed him the bread basket for the third time—there was an undeniable zing.

And she knew he'd felt it, too. Right from the start. The way his gaze had zipped to hers…and clung…had made her certain of it.

He had long fingers. She didn't know if they were smooth or calloused, though he had a raised scar over one knuckle, long and whitish against his tanned skin, that made her think he didn't spend all of his time on a catering crew.

His smile widened and his gaze was as warm as a caress when he took the basket from her. "No trouble at all." His fingers grazed her hand and she felt butterflies take flight inside her. That brush of his fingers *had* to be deliberate. "I'll be right back." He walked away with the basket in hand.

"Why are you staring at that wader?"

Arabella heard her brother's grunt of laughter and she pulled her attention away from Jay to focus on Tyler's four-year-old face. Since Brady had been left guardian of his best friend's twins the year before, she'd become adept at telling the two boys apart. "Was I staring?" she asked innocently.

Tyler nodded earnestly. "At his butt." His young voice was piping clear. "The wader's butt."

"It's waiter. Not wader," Brady corrected almost absently. He was busy trying to keep Toby—the more rambunctious of the two children—from unbuttoning his shirt because he was too hot. It wasn't really too warm inside the hotel restaurant where the party was being held. It was January. Back home in Buffalo, they'd be under a few feet of snow, but here in Rambling Rose, the balcony doors were thrown open and the occasional breeze that flowed in was beautifully balmy. The other two occupants of their table—her brothers Kane and Joshua—obviously felt the same. As soon as they'd finished their entrées, they'd taken refuge from Toby's and Tyler's unrelenting chatter at the bar set up near the balcony and they both had their shirtsleeves rolled up.

"Not another button," Brady warned Toby before looking back at Tyler. "And don't say butt," he directed.

"At his bottom," Tyler revised obediently. But he still had a glint in his eyes. He might be the more sensitive of the two, but like Toby, his genetic makeup seemed to be half mischief.

As the only girl among five protective older brothers, handling the four-year-old variety of male was almost a breeze. She leaned closer to Tyler. "D'you want to go outside for a few minutes?"

He nodded so hard he nearly fell out of his chair.

She looked to his twin brother, placed on her other side between her and Brady in a relatively successful attempt at helping them behave during the family event. "D'you want to go outside for a few minutes, Toby?" The restaurant, Roja, was located in the brand-new Hotel Fortune and though she hadn't had a chance to see much besides her hotel room, she was sure there would be someplace where the kids could work out their wiggles.

Toby was out of his chair before she even finished speaking, and hung on to the back of Brady's while he bounced on his bare feet.

Brady looked resigned at this latest discovery. "When did you take off your shoes and socks?"

The little boy shrugged innocently.

Arabella hid a laugh and slipped off her seat, prepared to dive under the table to retrieve the items. But she'd forgotten all about the rolls she'd snuck away in her napkin and they bounced onto the carpet like a cascade of ping-pong balls.

Brady gave her a look that, lately, had been reserved for his young charges. "Subtle, Airhead."

She crossed her eyes at him and ducked under the floor-length tablecloth, dashing the rolls out of sight along with her, and fished out Toby's shoes and socks then backed out again on hands and knees.

A pair of shining black cowboy boots met her eyes.

She looked up the long legs encased in black pants and felt her face heat at the laughter in Jay's eyes as he set the fresh bread basket on the table. "Can I help you up?" He extended his long-fingered hand down toward her.

The scarred knuckle hovered near her nose and those fluttering wings inside her took flight all over again.

She placed her palm in his.

Oh, hello. Forget *zing*. Palm-to-palm meant full-on heart palpitations.

She didn't even know how she got to her feet without catching her high heels in her maxi-length dress. Maybe she just floated upward, borne on the delight of his hand clasping hers. Regardless, she found herself standing a little closer than was probably appropriate for the moment—her nephew Larkin's first birthday party. But she just couldn't make herself put a few more inches between them.

She looked up, then up some more, until her eyes met Jay's.

She'd already noticed how green they were. But standing so closely now, she could see the circle of yellow around his pupils. The spokes of darker color that radiated out to the deep green edges of his irises.

She realized he was still holding her hand. Was, in fact, grazing his thumb ever so lightly over the back of her hand.

She also realized that both Tyler and Toby were bouncing around her, impatient for the promise of an escape from the party. And that Brady was giving Jay a narrow-eyed stare. As was Brian who'd joined their brothers Kane and Joshua at the bar. Fortunately, Adam—the eldest of her siblings—was busy with Laurel and their little boy across the room or she had no doubt his suspicious glare would be trained her way, too. Instead, he and Laurel were talking animatedly with their folks.

Catherine Fortune was smiling and nodding. Gary Fortune, however, had the same sour look on his face that he wore whenever he was faced with any of the extended members of the Fortune family. One might think discovering you had half-brothers out in the world that you'd never known about would be exciting. Not for Gary, though. Arabella knew for a fact that if not for Larkin—whose very survival had been in question not even six months earlier—her dad would sooner choke than have anything to do with "those" Fortunes.

The ones who had money.

More than they had, anyway.

The ones who had success.

Also more than Gary figured they had.

But Larkin *was* his first grandchild. And the baby was now thriving. He'd made it to his first birthday. His parents—her brother Adam and Laurel—were together. Finally. Those blessings had provided enough impetus for her dad to put aside his usual animosity, at least long enough to come to Texas for the party.

Brady nudged her from behind. "You going to let the guy get back to his job anytime this century?"

She looked into those green, green eyes again and reluctantly tugged her hand free of Jay's. "I was just going to try to find a place outside for these two to get some fresh air before the cake is served."

"I want cake," Toby and Tyler both said, nearly in unison. "Cake, cake, cake!"

"Run off some energy, you know, before we give them a sugar rush," she added above their chanting.

Jay's smile widened. "There's a perfect place downstairs. I can show you a shortcut."

Fluttering galore. "That's so sweet of you." She ignored the muffled sound of disgust that came from Brady and swept Toby up in her arms. He could put on his shoes and socks outside.

"Ten minutes," she told Brady, warning him with her glare not to embarrass her. He still rolled his eyes at her the same way he'd been doing for all of her life.

She ignored him and turned with the boys to follow Jay's extremely perfect backside out of the room.

As soon as they'd passed through the door he held open for them, he let it swing closed and the chatter and music from inside went hushed.

She felt a quick dart. "Are you sure this is okay? I didn't intend to take you away from your work." Not that she wasn't going to enjoy it while she could.

His dark brown hair was short. Thick. Light caught in the glossy strands as his head dipped slightly toward hers. "Job of the day is to take care of the Fortunes," he said conspiratorially. He really did have the sexiest deep voice. "You're a Fortune, so…" He touched her elbow lightly, directing her into a waiting elevator.

She couldn't help her shiver any more than she could help the laugh that escaped. "I'm not one of those Fortunes, though, so I'm not sure this counts."

The elevator car was narrow, long and tall and had padded walls. He punched the ground floor button. "I didn't know there were a *these* and a *those.*"

Her smile widened. If he'd been waiting on the table where her parents sat, he might have thought differently.

The elevator lurched softly as it stopped and the doors opened again. Jay led them through a back corridor made even narrower by tall racks sitting on one side, then pushed through another door into the fitness center. They crossed the spacious room and stepped through another door and outside onto a grassy area.

The music and laughter from the party upstairs carried easily down to them.

Toby was squirming so much she set him down on the grass. "Put these on before you move an inch," she ordered, handing him the shoes and socks.

Tongue sticking out between his teeth, he quickly pulled on the socks. The heels weren't in the right spots, but he didn't seem bothered by it as he worked on the shoes. She knew better than to offer help. He had an independent streak a mile wide. Meanwhile, Tyler crouched down and began running a car she hadn't even known he'd had along the cobbled pavers next to them.

She looked up at Jay. "Thanks for this." She gestured at the boys. "My brother's their guardian."

He looked surprised. "Sorry, I thought they were yours."

She shook her head. "Nope. No kids. Not married." She felt her face flush.

His smile widened.

Butterfly wings fluttered inside her chest. "So, uh, how long have you worked at Hotel Fortune?"

"Almost a month now. They're good folks here. *Those* Fortunes. Hey, pard, want a little help there?" He crouched alongside Toby who was still struggling with his shoelaces.

Toby duly considered the matter, then to her amazement, he shot out his small foot.

"Always had trouble with laces, myself," Jay told the boy with a grin. "So my granny kept buying me cowboy boots. Just like these." With a wink, he wiggled the toe of his boot and Toby giggled. "My mama, though, she said I couldn't play baseball wearing boots so she taught me like this." He stretched out Toby's laces in a slightly exaggerated way. "Cross 'em over in an X," he sang softly, "pull 'em down and now what's next?"

Tyler came over to see. "Bunny ears."

"Right," Jay agreed. "Only my mama called them donkey ears. Cross 'em over in an X," he repeated, in the same deep singsong drawl, "pull 'em down and now what's next? Donkey ears—" he nodded encouragingly when both boys shouted the answer "—get all crossed up. Make 'em do a somersault. Now that's done, what else is left? Pull 'em tight and kiss an elf."

The boys wrinkled their noses and hooted. "Kiss an *elf*!" Toby stuck out his other foot and wiggled it back and forth. "Do it again!"

"All right," Jay agreed, catching the toe of Toby's shoe. "But you do the laces this time."

Unspeakably charmed, Arabella watched them as Toby grabbed his shoelaces.

Jay started singing again. "Cross 'em over in an X…" He trailed off, as the twins took over the words, easily remembering the simple, catchy tune while Toby's fingers tried to replicate the motions. Jay straightened then and his eyes seemed to linger on her face.

She raised her eyebrows at him. "Kiss an elf?"

"Mom was—is—a piano teacher." His smile was so easy. So sexy with that slash of a dimple that appeared beside his mobile lips. "She never claimed to be a lyricist."

Shoes successfully tied, Toby hopped to his feet and even though Arabella would have loved to linger a little longer with Jay, she knew she shouldn't keep him. "Thanks for showing us the shortcut down here." Already the two imps were chasing each other around the grass, burning off some of their never-ending energy.

"My pleasure." He gestured at the hotel. "Afraid you'll have to use the main elevator to get back upstairs. The door we came out doesn't open from the outside."

"What time do you get off work?" The words blurted out of her and she flushed. Not just because of the impetuous question, but because of the slow look he sent her way.

"Jay." Another one of the servers from the party stuck her head out of the door, obviously looking for him. "Need you upstairs, dude." She stood there holding the door open, pointedly waiting.

Jay offered Arabella a slightly pained shrug. "Sorry."

"No." Arabella waved her hand. "I'm sorry for keeping you." She moistened her lips. "We can, uh, we can talk later." She was practically stuttering.

She really wasn't good at this. Inside her head, she pictured herself all smooth and maybe even a little sophisticated and sexy. Reality, though, fell far short.

Fortunately—miraculously—Jay didn't seem any more bothered by her awkwardness than Toby was by his backward socks. "That sounds good," he said and she was pretty sure it wasn't her imagination that his deep voice seemed to go even deeper.

"See you later, pardners," he told the boys as he went back inside. "Make sure you run enough to make room for birthday cake."

Arabella let the boys run around a little longer than

the ten minutes she'd promised Brady. But since she could see him upstairs in the restaurant through the opened balcony doors, she figured he wasn't too anxious.

Which was fortunate because the butterflies fluttering madly inside her veins needed to burn off some energy as badly as the boys did.

Lights were coming on around the property when she herded the twins back inside through the main entrance and upstairs.

Fortunately, they were just in time to see Larkin smashing his way through his truck-shaped birthday cake, earning *oohs* from the twins who raced to the table and onto Catherine's and Gary's laps—proof that they were perfectly normal little boys despite the tragedy of their parents' deaths last year.

Arabella spotted Jay and he jerked slightly when she touched his sleeve, but his smile was warm as ever. "Hello again."

Aware of his responsibilities there, she snatched up an unused coffee cup from the abandoned guest table next to them. "Fill me up?"

One of his dark eyebrows peaked. "With coffee?"

"Are you offering anything else?"

His eyes didn't let go of hers as he tilted his coffee carafe over her cup. "That depends."

"On what?"

He shook his head slightly as if he were as bemused as she. "Arabella."

She moistened her lips. "Yes?"

"I've never met an Arabella before."

Her heart had climbed into her throat and she felt almost dizzy. "Is that a good thing?"

His dimple flirted into view. Just for a moment before disappearing again. He set the carafe aside. "I've really liked meeting you, Arabella. A lot." He took her free hand in his. His thumb stroked over her wrist. She knew he had to be able to feel the insane thrumming of her pulse. "And I get off at ten."

Choruses sang inside her head. "Okay," she managed almost soundlessly.

"But I think you should know that—"

A huge screech rent the air just then, and they both jerked. A horrible rumbling juddered up from the floor as the balcony and everything on it fell away.

In the horrified void that followed, a balloon of dust rose silently in its place.

Then a woman screamed.

Followed by another.

And suddenly people ran.

Kids cried.

Jay shoved Arabella to one side just in time to avoid a chair flying toward her and she stared numbly at the cause as Brady vaulted across the room to scoop up Toby and Tyler.

She lost sight of Jay then in the melee while Callum— one of *those* Fortunes who'd built the hotel in the first place—ushered guests off the second floor.

Arabella gasped when her dad grabbed her arm in an iron grip.

"I *knew* it was a bad idea coming here." He had her

mother's hand in his other and Catherine stumbled over a spilled tray of dishes trying to keep up with him.

"Daddy!" Arabella pulled on his hand, slowing him long enough to notice her mom. She was glad at least to see the true dismay in his face when he helped her mom to her feet. But that didn't stop him from shackling Arabella's wrist again as if she were a wayward toddler and joining the exiting guests.

Outside, the sound of sirens ought to have been reassuring—help was on its way—yet it only seemed to add to the horror.

"Was anyone hurt?"

"Where's Wiley?"

"Was it a bomb?"

"Dear God, Grace was—"

"The mayor's here. She can—"

The voices swirled and Arabella saw a mountain of rubble where only minutes earlier, Toby and Tyler had been running around the bushes below the balcony.

Nausea assaulted her and she looked away, numbly letting her father pull her and her mother even farther away from the scene. He hustled them into the car he'd rented at the airport in Houston. He was muttering to himself the whole while, but Arabella barely heard.

The evening wasn't cold, but her teeth chattered hard as she looked out the back car window as her dad drove away from the hotel. Emergency lights flashed as one vehicle after another turned into the parking lot, tires squealing. She knew her brothers were safe. They'd all been inside Roja and well away from the balcony when she'd been talking with Jay.

I think you should know that...

"Gary, surely the entire hotel isn't collapsing! Shouldn't we—"

"No," her dad said flatly, cutting off whatever her mother had been going to suggest. "We're going straight back to New York where we belong."

Jarred from her stupor, Arabella envisioned her over-night bag still sitting on the foot of her bed. Because the party was being held right there in the hotel, she'd seen no reason to take her purse to the party. "Dad, our luggage—"

"Can be sent to us. It's the least *those* Fortunes owe us."

"Maybe, but I'm still not going to be able to get on a plane without ID! And that's still in my hotel room." In his present mood, she knew he wouldn't welcome any comments from her, but if they drove all the way to Houston only to have to turn around again, he'd be even more furious.

"Don't you know better than to go anywhere with-out your ID?" He obviously didn't expect an answer because he was swearing under his breath as he turned around and started back to the hotel.

She hadn't *gone* anywhere until he'd dragged her out of the hotel. But she was pretty sure pointing that out wouldn't earn her any points.

"How many times have I told Adam that moving to Rambling Rose would be nothing but bad news? Kane's no better. That family just invites trouble. I told you about that wedding," he said to Catherine, repeating words that Arabella had heard again and again over the past few years. "Deranged women. Kidnapping. Car chases. Now this? Those Fortunes are cursed!"

Her mother's voice was meant to be soothing. "That was years ago. What happened at your brother's wedding in Paseo—"

"Gerald Robinson is not *my* brother," Gary snapped. "How many times have I told you that?"

Julius Fortune's copious spreading of his gene pool said otherwise. Arabella kept that thought to herself, too. She'd never met Julius, who had fathered not only one legitimate son—Gerald—but at least four illegitimate ones, including her father. Everything she knew about the wealthy philanderer who'd died before she was even born was what she'd gained via the internet and snippets of gossip from her brothers.

When they arrived back at the hotel, the number of fire engines and police cars had doubled.

"Oh, dear," Catherine fretted as they slowed for a stretcher being rolled toward the opened rear doors of an ambulance. She fumbled with her purse—*she* hadn't left hers in their room—and pulled out her cell phone. "Oh dear, oh dear, oh dear," she kept moaning under her breath as she dialed.

Arabella could see her mother's hands trembling and felt another wave of nausea. "Send text messages, Mom," she advised, knowing that her brothers were likely to respond more quickly to a text than a phone call. For there was no question that Catherine Fortune was checking on her boys.

After waiting for the stretcher to be loaded, her dad pulled as close to the hotel entrance as the congestion of vehicles allowed. The second the wheels stopped rolling, Arabella unsnapped her safety belt. "I have my room key." She pulled it from her bodice where she'd tucked it and held it up.

Her father plucked it right out of her fingertips. "Stay here," he ordered, and got out of the vehicle.

"I'm twenty-five years old," she grumbled but he'd already slammed his door shut. "I'm capable of retrieving my own damn luggage."

"Don't swear," Catherine said, holding her phone to her ear. "It's unbecoming of a young lady. Oh, *why* won't Adam answer his phone? Maybe Kane."

"I told you, Mom," Arabella said with a sigh. *"Text."*

Her mother clucked her tongue and redialed. "I don't like texting. You know that."

And her brothers didn't like getting dragged into lengthy conversations with their mother that inevitably went nowhere.

It wasn't that they didn't love her. But Arabella also knew her brothers were frustrated with the chip their father had on his shoulder against the rest of the world— and of late, *those* Fortunes—and their mother's support of her husband no matter how unreasonable his attitudes were.

Was it any wonder that Arabella had spent most of her childhood with her nose buried in the books she loved? It was so much more pleasant losing herself in the excitement of a mystery or the throes of a love story than dwell on her overprotective big brothers, her old-fashioned mother and her perennially disgruntled father.

She pushed open her car door and got out.

"Arabella, where are you going?"

"Just to see what's happening." She childishly crossed her fingers where her mother couldn't see and started weaving around cars to get closer to the side of the hotel where the action was most concentrated.

Arabella spotted Jay at once.

He stood on the far side of the debris. Yellow police tape already cordoned off the area. He was looking in her direction and she lifted her hand, hoping he would notice, but she got jostled aside by the arrival of a television crew headed by a helmet-haired woman who was clearly ready to bat her pathway clear with her big microphone.

"Focus on that pile of debris and crushed landscaping," she was ordering her cameraman. "And cut back to me in five, four, three—"

Arabella looked toward Jay again.

But he was gone.

Disappointment sagged inside her.

I think you should know that...

What had he intended to say?

...I do believe in love at first sight. With you, Arabella.

Her arm was grabbed again, this time from behind.

"I told you to stay in the car," Gary said tightly. "You want to get hurt out here?"

"The person who got hurt was on that stretcher we saw." She craned her neck, trying to find Jay again.

"Police," Gary muttered, obviously not listening. He was practically frog-marching her back to the car. "Everywhere."

"Doing their job, it looks like to me."

"Yeah and those Fortunes give them plenty to do." Her dad pushed her into the back seat and tossed her overnighter in after her. "Just watch. They'll buy their way out of this latest trouble. That's what people like them do." He slammed her door shut and got behind the wheel while Arabella was trying to untangle her high heel from where it had punctured her hem. "Who would have thought that *Arabella* would be the one to show the most common sense? She's perfectly happy in New York. Not trying to act like some hifalutin Fortune."

"Gary," her mother started again. "If you just gave them a chance, maybe—"

"I don't want to hear it, Catherine."

Neither did Arabella. She closed her eyes, envisioning Jay's brilliant green ones. Remembering the touch of his hand on hers.

I think you should know that...

Chapter Two

Five months later

"Come on, Cross. Why don't you make things easy here and just confess?"

Jay shoved his fingers through his hair and stared blearily at the cop on the other side of the hardwood table.

Supposedly, he was just there at the Rambling Rose Police Station to have a "conversation."

Except he'd been sitting in this room with the detective for two hours. And even before that, he'd been sitting in the room alone for twice that long.

"Confess what?" he asked for about the millionth time.

"What were you doing that afternoon back in January when the balcony collapsed at Hotel Fortune?"

He rubbed the pain centered between his eyebrows. "My job," he said. Again. For about the millionth time.

"Which is what?"

He dropped his hand onto the table a little harder than he probably should have. The sound of it echoed loudly in the stark room.

He stretched out his fingers, mentally counting to ten, then relaxed them again and looked at the investigator, Detective John Teas. "Whatever the GM decides I should be doing."

"GM?"

"General manager."

"That's Grace Williams."

"She's the general manager now, but she wasn't in January."

"No. She was standing on the balcony when it collapsed. And every single witness that we've interviewed about that day can't recall where you were prior to that collapse. Why is that?"

Jay sighed again. If he told the detective the whole truth and nothing but the truth, would it make things better for him?

Or worse?

"I have no idea," he replied evenly. "On that particular day in January, I was one of the servers at the birthday party being held at Roja. I spent the day running back and forth from the kitchen to the banquet room."

"Doing?"

The vision of a petite blue-eyed redhead swam easily in his head. "Delivering a lot of bread baskets," he deadpanned.

The detective didn't look amused.

Jay sighed. "I served food. Cleared away plates. Poured coffee. You know. Waited tables at a birthday party." Avoided getting caught on camera when that news crew arrived after the balcony collapse.

He pushed away the thought.

"The day before I was helping out in maintenance. The day after, I was off." As was most everyone else, which the detective knew perfectly well since Jay was pretty certain the man had already questioned everyone who worked at Hotel Fortune, from the owners on down to the lowliest of low—which included Jay Cross.

Just simple Jay Cross.

"One of your coworkers stated that you were seen outside the hotel prior to the balcony collapse."

"Yes. I'd escorted one of the guests and her nephews—" he figured the description was close enough since Brady Fortune, the boys' guardian, had been hired as the hotel concierge and gossip had it that he was in the process of adopting them "—outside so the two little boys could get some fresh air."

"It was early January."

"And the weather was beautiful," Jay returned, exasperated. He shifted on the hard chair and spread his hands, palms upward. "Come on, Detective. Do you have kids? These two boys had energy to spare and had been behaving through an entire dinner. I showed them a back way down to the first floor and outside so they could run around a little."

"Near the balcony."

"The entire back side of the hotel is near the balcony," he pointed out. "What possible reason would I have to be involved in that collapse?"

"That's the question, isn't it, Mr. Cross?" Detective Teas leaned back on two chair legs, seemingly oblivious to the danger that his generous girth presented to them. He tapped a pencil eraser against the tabletop. "You're aware of the food tampering incident during the Give Back barbecue at the hotel just last month."

If the guy expected Jay to blink, he would be disappointed. "I worked the barbecue. Like usual." Except there'd been a news crew on the premises that day, too. Not to cover a disaster—though they'd gotten that in the end—but to promote the community event. Jay had spent more time finding excuses to be out of sight in the kitchen than out in the open where the reporter and cameras were.

He hadn't thought it was all that likely he'd be recognized. Not the way he looked now. But he hadn't wanted to take any chances, either. He was already living proof that life could change on a dime. And if it could happen once, it could happen again.

"Running food back and forth from the kitchen to the buffet line," the detective said with a goading little smile. "Any period of time when you were alone?"

Detective Teas undoubtedly already knew the answer to that, too. "Yes, but not for very long."

"Do you know how many people had adverse reactions to the food?"

Jay sighed faintly. "It wasn't the food. It was the pepper powder someone—not me—sprinkled on it." He also knew that everyone had recovered. That, in fact, the one individual caught on camera having an allergic reaction to the pepper had set off more of a panic among the crowd than anything, and Nicole Fortune, who was the chef of Roja, had worked very hard to prove there'd been no mismanagement.

The damage was done, though.

Like all things caught in the media, sensationalism was more popular than truth. And this—the latest of the mishaps to hit Hotel Fortune—had everyone in town, including those who actually worked there, wondering if the new hotel could even survive.

For Jay, losing the job would be an inconvenience. Rambling Rose didn't exactly offer the plentiful job opportunities that Los Angeles did, but he'd find something. He was nothing if not adaptable.

If the people looking for him, however, found out where he was, it'd cause a lot more than mere inconvenience.

"What brought you here to Rambling Rose?"

Teas couldn't really be reading Jay's mind, but he showed an annoyingly uncanny sense of timing.

"My grandmother." Jay's words were true. They just weren't exactly *the* truth. But since that had nothing to do with this situation, Jay still intended on keeping silent on the matter.

In fact, the only time he'd come close to telling someone the truth had been in January. When he'd been staring down into the otherworldly blue eyes of Arabella Fortune. Strangely enough, he'd wanted her to know all about him. Everything.

The good. And the bad.

"Your grandmother. Speaking of." The detective's voice was like a boulder dropping in the center of the image in Jay's mind, sending it rippling away. The man made a point of looking at the yellow notepad he kept to one side of him as if he didn't want Jay seeing what had been written on it. "You're living with her. Sweet deal. Sponging off an elderly woman."

Jay snorted. "Have you lived in Rambling Rose a long time?"

The pencil eraser missed a beat. "Long enough."

"Then you've probably met her. And if you've met her, you ought to know *nobody* sponges off Louella O'Brien." Jay forced a smile. "Elderly or not, she sells her homemade jam every weekend out at Mariana's Market. Rain or shine." Much to his mother's chagrin. Sandra Cross wanted Louella to move to Houston. To give up the ranch—it hadn't been a working ranch since Jay's grandfather died twenty years ago—and move closer to her and Jay's dad. To give up her gardens and her jam business and behave the way she figured a nearly ninety-year-old woman ought to behave.

Not surprisingly, Louella was having none of it. With Jay living out at the ranch, his mother had given the subject a rest. At least with Louella. Unfortunately for him, instead of calling her mother every day to nag her about moving, Jay's mother now called *him*.

"Are you talking about Lou's Luscious Jams?" The detective looked surprised. "My wife buys it every chance she gets. She says if she doesn't get out to the flea market early enough, everything's sold out in the first hour and she ends up having to settle for some other seller out there."

"Luscious Jams are my grandmother's." In fact, he could stand some of it right now, along with his grandmother's homemade bread. He was starving. He spread his palms once again. "You said this was voluntary. I've answered all of your questions a dozen times over. So unless you're going to tell me I can't, I'll be leaving now." He put words to action and stood.

The detective didn't try to stop him, which was a relief. Jay didn't particularly relish the idea of having to call a lawyer. One, it would upset his grandmother. Two, it would necessitate being more forthcoming with the lawyer than he had been with this well-intentioned but misguided cop. And even though a lawyer would have a duty for confidentiality, these days, Jay wasn't taking any chances.

He'd closed the door on the man he'd been and he didn't want it opening up again.

Teas didn't rise, though he did let his chair go back down onto all fours. "Yeah, you can go, Mr. Cross," he said in a smooth way that had probably put the fear of God in any number of suspects. He bounced his pencil eraser a few more times. "Just don't leave town."

After a decade spent in the City of Angels, Jay had acquired his own smooth smile. "I have no intention of going anywhere." He scooped up his cowboy hat from the corner of the table and jammed it on his head. He flicked the brim, mockingly, he had to admit, and walked out of the stifling room.

The police department took up only a portion of

the building that also housed the municipal courts and
the motor vehicle department. Given Rambling Rose's
affordability and proximity to larger cities like Jay's
hometown of Houston, Rambling Rose had become
quite the boutique city since Jay had been a kid. But
he could still remember visiting the building with his
grandpa whenever he was staying with Louella and Herbert O'Brien because Herb's penchant for collecting
parking tickets had been legend.

Jay followed the tiled corridor until he reached the
public lobby that all of the departments held in common and checked his motion to pull his sunglasses out
of his pocket.

He didn't wear sunglasses anymore. Ergo the cowboy hat.

At first, it had seemed like a stupid thing. More sym-
bolic than anything.

He'd gotten rid of everything that smacked of his old
life after his old life had gotten rid of him.

Girlfriend.

Manager.

Career.

His trademark shades had gone in the trash the same
day he'd shaved his beard and cut his hair short.

Now, he was glad he'd changed his appearance. His
return to good ol' boy Jay Cross was complete.

Nobody in Rambling Rose had a reason to connect
him with his old life. And if that left him with a few
missing spots in his history as far as Detective Teas was
concerned, Jay wasn't going to worry about it.

He wasn't responsible for the problems that had befallen Hotel Fortune, which meant there was no way that Teas could prove otherwise. Pure and simple.

The-late afternoon sun was shafting through the glass entry doors. Another thing that hadn't changed since Jay was a kid. You'd have thought they'd have at least tinted the glass by now. But no. The sun still streamed in, turning the lobby into a sauna that no amount of air-conditioning could combat.

He tugged the brim of his cowboy hat down farther against the glare and pushed through the door, quickly sidestepping the person who was hurrying to get inside.

"Sorry," a breathless voice said from behind a tall vase of flowers. "You're the second person I've bumped into."

Jay chuckled and held the door wider. "Not surprised. Those things are taller than you." He glanced around the enormous bouquet and felt the impact straight to his solar plexus.

Her hair was mostly hidden by the ball cap she wore, but the long ponytail hanging out the back was distinctively red. And though her eyes were hidden behind a pair of reflective aviator-style sunglasses, he knew they'd be distinctively blue.

Her smile widened. "Jay!" Juggling her gigantic burden, she whipped off her sunglasses.

And sure enough, Arabella Fortune's aquamarine eyes were exactly how he remembered.

It was his own damned luck that Teas was heading directly for them.

Suddenly, he felt cornered. Hemmed in by a beautiful young woman on one side and a determined cop on the other. His frustration coalesced. "What are *you* doing here?"

Her wide smile faltered, making him feel like a total ass.

"Delivering flowers," she said, stating the obvious. "What are *you* doing here?"

Even though he'd gotten good at pretending the last decade of his life had never occurred, he ought to have been quicker with a response.

Instead, he saw Teas now just a few feet away.

He saw the POLICE sign with the big arrow right behind him.

And he could imagine the horror in Arabella's eyes when she found out he was Rambling Rose's latest "person of interest."

"Leaving," he said abruptly, and backed the rest of the way out the door.

Arabella stared after Jay. Sudden tears burned deep behind her eyes.

I think you should know that...

...I'm just not that into you.

"Can I help you?"

Swamped in disappointment, Arabella let the glass door swing closed. She blinked hard before looking up at the tall man who'd spoken. He wasn't wearing a uniform but he had a police badge clipped to his belt. "I'm sorry?"

"I recognize Petunia's Posies when I see them." The officer had a kind look in his eyes and he gestured slightly at the enormous bouquet. "Usually it's the Bellamy boy who delivers them."

If she needed proof that Rambling Rose was a small town compared to what she was used to, this was it. He probably knew Jay Cross as well. Certainly better than she did.

Or ever would.

The cop was still waiting.

"I'm filling in for Todd." She knew the kid only by name. "Temporarily. I understand he's on vacation for a few weeks."

"Oh, right." He nodded. "Big Disneyland trip. I remember now. Usually Petunia gets her dad to pinch-hit when Todd is gone."

She wasn't sure what sort of response he expected to that, so she just shrugged. "All I know is she needed someone for two weeks to fill in. I'm Arabella. New in town. And—" she glanced at the delivery slip that she still had tucked between two fingers "—looking for Mrs. Jones in Central Records."

Happy anniversary, my beloved. Arabella herself had written the customer's message on the card included with the flowers.

"Third floor. Back of the building," he said immediately. "Fastest way is the stairs. Elevator takes forever."

"Thank you, Officer—"

"Detective, actually. Detective Teas." He walked away from her in a much nicer way than Jay had.

I think you should know that...

...you should never take flirting seriously.

She huffed out a breath and headed for the wide

staircase situated in the center of the lobby. The detective hadn't exaggerated about the elevator. There was a small line of people standing outside of it waiting for the bronze arrow to move on the old-fashioned dial above the door.

She could handle two flights of stairs to the third floor a lot easier than face the fact that she'd actually moved away from New York to find out exactly how Jay Cross had intended to finish that sentence.

It had been five months since that day.

Five months of weaving romantic fantasies about the words he *hadn't* said.

She found Central Records and delivered the flowers to Mrs. Jones, who turned out to be a young woman who looked no older than Arabella. She had an enormous diamond ring on her finger and gushed over the flowers.

"How long have you been married?" Arabella was afraid her smile was wistful but the young Mrs. Jones didn't seem to notice.

"One month today!"

As Arabella went back down the stairs again, she couldn't help but wonder what sort of display the girl would be getting when she and her husband reached one year.

Arabella couldn't even get a date.

And whose fault is that? Spending the last five months daydreaming about a man you met only once?

Thank heavens Arabella was smart enough not to have shared that particular fact with anyone. Her family already accused her of always having her head in the clouds. And her girlfriends were all too busy with

their own love lives—ones that were much more fruit-
ful than Arabella's.

She'd lost count of how many bridal showers she'd
been invited to lately. And being asked to be a bridesmaid for the fourth time in as many months had been
just one time too many.

She'd been toying with the idea of returning to Rambling Rose almost as soon as her dad had dragged them
away in January from Larkin's birthday party. But when
Arabella had gotten a wedding invitation from her nem-
esis, Tammy Jo Pendleton, something inside her had
snapped. For one thing, it was a destination wedding.
In Bali.

If the invitation had been heartfelt and genuine, Arabella would've felt regretful having to decline. There
was no way she could afford to travel to Bali on her administrative assistant wages, which was something that
Tammy Jo knew perfectly well. But the invitation had
not been genuine. Tammy Jo had sent it for one simple
reason—to drive home the fact that *she* was getting
married to Hamilton Dawes.

Arabella might have dated Ham once upon a time but
it was Tammy Jo who'd actually landed him. And now
Tammy Jo was the one having the fairy-tale wedding
with the most eligible bachelor in their town.

Arabella reached her car and climbed behind the
wheel. She rolled down the windows to let the heat escape. Even though it had only taken a few minutes to
make her last delivery of the day, the car interior had
become stifling hot. Her car was old. It wasn't equipped
with air-conditioning. She probably should have sold it

before she'd left New York and figured out a way to get around in Rambling Rose until she could afford to buy another vehicle. But she'd been determined to prove she wouldn't be a burden on her brothers in Texas.

Because, despite what her brothers and parents thought, just because she had a head full of dreams didn't mean she had no common sense or pride.

And just what kind of common sense did it show to fantasize about Jay Cross all these months?

She twisted the rearview mirror slightly until she saw her own reflection. "Shut up," she muttered.

For once, the mocking voice inside her head obediently went silent and she readjusted the mirror and turned the key.

The engine tried to turn over, but didn't.

The car had some power because the radio came on playing the same song that had been on the radio incessantly for months now. On the long drive from New York, every time she caught a radio signal as she drove from town to town, it had been an obvious staple.

"'Givin' it all up,'" she muttered along with the singer's deep voice before she snapped off the radio. She didn't even listen to country music but the song had still become an earworm, sticking inside her head for hours at a time. "Right now I'd like to give it all up and be back home in New York."

But saying the words was enough for her to know that wasn't strictly true. She was twenty-five years old and it was time that she began doing something with her life. Even if that meant moving to Texas like half her brothers had done.

"All right, car. Don't let me down now." Eyes closed as if that might influence the outcome, she turned the key again.

Silence reigned.

She pulled out the key with a sigh and leaned back in the seat. She tossed aside her ball cap and swiped her sleeve over her sweaty forehead.

She loathed having to call Brady. Not that her brother wouldn't help. Any one of them would. But Adam and Kane both were busy with their own lives. Which was why Arabella had first broached the subject of moving to Rambling Rose with *Brady*. He'd already gone to work for the Hotel Fortune as concierge at that point and she'd had the idea that if she helped take care of the twins for him, not only would she be helping him, but also she could get by without having to pay him rent until she got herself established. She was *pretty* sure he wouldn't have tried to charge her rent anyway, but he also would have totally lorded it over her that he was taking care of her.

Only in the time since then, Brady had fallen for the twins' nanny, Harper Radcliffe.

Which meant that now, instead of moving in with her brother and his rambunctious twins, she was imposing on the engaged couple and their rambunctious twins. They even had a dog now. All that remained was the official *I do*'s.

They never said there wasn't really room for Arabella, but that didn't mean there was.

Harper was lovely and brilliant with the boys and they adored her. Once she and Brady married, Tyler and

Toby would have a new mother to care for them. They certainly didn't need Arabella's help now.

Pity party, much?

This time Arabella didn't try to shut up the voice.

She tightened her ponytail, pulled on her ball cap again and tried the key one more time with no more success than before.

Not even the radio turned on.

Nor could she roll up the power windows.

She glanced around the interior of the car. Was there anything she was afraid of being stolen, anyway?

Plus, in a town like Rambling Rose, was there even any danger of leaving a car open like this? She *was* parked right outside the police station, after all.

She grabbed the book bag that was both a holdall and purse and even though she knew it was pointless, she pushed down the door lock after she got out of the car.

She hefted the long strap crosswise over her shoulder and looked up and down the street.

She'd been in town for only a week, but thanks to Petunia's brisk floral business, Arabella already had a good lay of the land and she set off for Provisions. Adam managed the restaurant, but he and Laurel had gone to Houston with Larkin for one of his doctor's appointments. She knew they wouldn't be back yet.

Which meant Arabella could at least satisfy the hollowness in her stomach in privacy while she dealt with her car.

I think you should know that...

...I can be a rude jerk.

She picked up her pace and was breathless when she reached the cool interior of Provisions.

There were people waiting for a table but she by-passed them for one of the few empty seats at the bar. She ordered an iced tea when the bartender came over, then pulled her cell phone out of the book bag before plopping it on the floor.

She called the flower shop first to let Petunia know that she'd finished her deliveries for the day. She did not, however, tell her boss about the dead car battery. One of the only requirements for the job was posses-sion of an operable vehicle.

Just as Arabella finished her call, the bartender slid a tall glass in front of her. "Get you a menu?"

"That would be great, thanks." She wrapped one hand around the blessedly cold beverage and took the offered menu with the other. "Say—" she quickly read the bartender's name badge "—Evan. Any auto places in town you recommend where I can get a car battery?"

Evan reeled off three places. "But," he added as he glanced at his wristwatch, "I think they all closed at five."

Great. She smiled weakly. "Thanks."

He smiled back far more cheerfully and headed off again.

She chugged half the contents of her glass while she verified that the auto supply stores were closed. Only one was still open, but it was all the way across town. She didn't have a hope of finding a ride there in time.

She heaved out a breath.

"That sounded heartfelt."

She jerked slightly, and then looked behind her to see her cousin Ashley who, along with her sisters Megan and Nicole, had opened the restaurant the year before. Arabella flashed the screen of her phone at her, displaying her search results and made a rueful face. "Car problems."

Ashley's brows knit. "Oh, no. Anything I can do?"

Though Arabella hadn't even met Ashley and her sisters until that January, she'd gotten to know all of them better in the time since—mostly via text messages. But that didn't mean she felt comfortable taking advantage of that fact. Ashley was obviously working. "No worries. It's just the battery." She wouldn't allow herself to think otherwise. "I've got it covered."

"Well, at least order some dinner. On the house."

"You don't have—"

"Please." Ashley waved her hand. "You're family. It might as well be policy."

Arabella couldn't help but laugh. "I know from Adam that half the people who come in here are Fortunes. You'll lose far too much of your profits with a policy like that."

Ashley just grinned as she gave a sideways nod to the hostess who was trying to catch her attention. She squeezed Arabella's shoulder. "I'll check on you later."

Arabella wasn't sure if it was a promise or a warning. Either way, she didn't really see how Ashley would have the time. The restaurant was already busy and Arabella knew it would only become more so as the evening progressed. Adam had said many times how impressed he'd been by their young cousins' success not only with this restaurant but with Roja in the Hotel Fortune as well.

Unsaid, at least in Arabella's mind, was how little *she* had accomplished so far.

And she was a year *older* than the triplets were.

Evan appeared again with a pitcher. He refilled her glass. "Can I put an order in for you?"

She hadn't even glanced at the menu yet. "Hamburger and fries."

"Cheese? Bacon? Avocado?"

"Yes, yes and dear God no. Pack it to go, though, would you please?"

"You bet." He slid the menu away from her and headed away again. While she waited for the food, she sent her daily reassurance to her mom—which necessitated several follow-up texts that yes, she was taking her daily vitamins, yes, she was getting enough sleep despite what Brady must have said, and no, just because she was delivering flowers these days didn't mean she'd stopped looking for a "proper" job.

Proper in her mother's vernacular meant nine-to-five with insurance benefits and a retirement plan.

By the time Catherine Fortune's questions were finally spent, Arabella had received her order of food. She gave Evan enough cash for his tip before she left.

The sun was no longer blazing, but it was still a long way from setting. On the way back to her car, she passed a bus stop and sat on the pretty wooden bench in the shade where she ate her fries and hamburger, and dialed Brady's number—twice.

She hung up both times before it could ring, though,

and finally tossed her phone inside her book bag. Calling any one of her brothers would be her last resort.

According to the bus schedule posted on a sign next to the bench, the next bus wasn't due for another hour. She could eat at her leisure, enjoy the shady spot and pretend that she hadn't foolishly given it all up in New York.

The hamburger was enormous.

She still managed to polish it off. Then she slowly dredged french fry after french fry through her mustard and contemplated whether she could stand the humiliation of returning to Buffalo so soon after coming to Rambling Rose.

On the plus side, her dad would get over his apoplectic anger that she'd defected to the "other side," which was how he viewed the rest of the Fortunes of the world.

"Need a lift?"

She looked beyond her mustard and fries to the street.

A bus hadn't stopped in front of her bench, but a dusty blue pickup truck had.

The french fry stuck in her throat as she looked through the opened window to see Jay Cross sitting behind the steering wheel.

She coughed slightly and sucked iced tea through her straw, forcing the fry down. "Not from you," she croaked.

His lips compressed and she thought he'd drive off.

But instead, he leaned over and pushed open the passenger-side door a few inches.

It was embarrassing the way her heart skittered around so easily.

She stiffened her spine and said nothing. Just raised her eyebrow. She'd perfected the motion when she'd been a teenager—a baby sister's defense against so many protective older brothers—though she figured the effort right now was pretty well lost under the brim of her baseball cap.

"Come on, Arabella." Jay pushed the door open a little wider. Wide enough now that she could see the way his shoulder stretched the fabric of his gray T-shirt. Not so stretched out that it was in danger of splitting, but definitely stretched enough to be…interesting. "At least let me apologize."

"For what?" She was rather pleased with the bored tone.

"For not saying…more…earlier at the, uh…" He looked pained. "You know. At the municipal building."

She gathered up the long strap of her book bag and tossed the rest of her french fries in the cement trash bin next to the bench before she stood.

Maybe it was childish, but she enjoyed the look of relief on his handsome face when she smiled.

Enjoyed even more the glimpse of his frustration when she turned aside and walked away.

Chapter Three

Jay swore as Arabella marched off along the sidewalk. The tail of her red ponytail bounced against her spine and a giant olive-green bag banged against her jean-clad hip with every step she took.

She looked a lot different than she had all those months ago at Hotel Fortune. But whether she was in a clinging green halter dress or jeans and T-shirt, there was still no mistaking her beauty.

He nearly strangled himself with his safety belt when he reached over to pull the passenger door closed again. He was able to troll along behind her only because there were no other vehicles parked alongside the curb, and he saw the way she angled half a look over her shoulder at him before her ponytail bounced with even more pronounced vigor.

He followed alongside her that way for two blocks before she about-faced and propped her fists on her narrow hips, giving him a glare.

He had the random thought that having her glare at him with those incredible eyes for the rest of his life would be better than having a dozen others looking at him with adoration.

Then he thought that there was probably a song in there somewhere.

He shook off both thoughts and rolled to a stop at the curb.

"I don't know why you're bothering to follow me," she said testily.

"Because I want to—" What? Apologize? Explain? "You surprised me," he said and cringed at his own lameness.

Her eyebrows disappeared from view beneath the ball cap. It was blue. Not quite as blue as her eyes. And it didn't sport the name of a sports team. Instead, it just sported an emblem of an open book.

"I didn't expect to see you," he tried again. "There."

"Where?" She lifted her arms at her sides. "In Rambling Rose?"

When the universe tosses you a nugget, you run with it. At least that's what his manager claimed.

Former manager. If Michael Devane hadn't already cut him loose, Jay would have done it himself.

"Right," he said to Arabella. "In Rambling Rose. I know I came off—"

"—rude?"

"Yeah." He cleared his throat. "I'm sorry. I never

intended to be rude. I just—" Couldn't explain. He switched course. "Are you visiting?"

She shrugged noncommittally and folded her arms across her chest. Obviously not going to make things easy for him. But then again, she hadn't started walking away from him again, either.

"I hope your visit is longer this time," he said honestly.

She looked away, presenting him with her very lovely profile. Her lips twisted slightly, revealing a dimple that he knew was glorious when it accompanied an actual smile.

"And less upsetting than last time," he added.

That earned him such a fast look that her ponytail flew forward over her shoulder. "Upsetting?"

"After the balcony collapsed." Even as he mentioned it, he wondered what sort of masochistic streak he'd developed. He didn't want to talk about the balcony collapse. Especially after his encounter with Detective Teas. "You disappeared so quickly afterward."

Her shoulders looked a little less stiff and she mumbled something.

He leaned across the cab of his truck again toward the opened window. "Sorry?"

She released her arm-clench and took a step toward the curb. Probably an unintentional one, because as soon as she seemed to realize it, she went stiff and still all over again. "I said," she uttered louder, more clearly, "my father was anxious to get home."

He was pretty certain that had *not* been what she'd muttered, but he wasn't going to call her on it. "Once things calmed down, I discovered y'all had left the hotel." He didn't add that he'd also heard through the hotel grapevine that their luggage had been shipped back to them. As if they hadn't been able to leave Rambling Rose fast enough.

Not that he believed *anyone* had been responsible for the balcony accident, but if Teas felt the need to be suspicious of someone, why couldn't he be suspicious of someone making such a quick getaway like that? The entire team working the front desk had talked for a week about how obnoxious Arabella's father had been.

She took another half step. "You checked?"

"Of course."

Her eyes narrowed as she looked at him. Then her head shook slightly and the tail of her ponytail drifted off her shoulder again. "Why?"

"Because I really liked meeting you. Now can I at least take you wherever you were waiting for the bus to take you?"

She moistened her lips. "I wasn't actually waiting for the bus. I was—" She broke off, taking another step nearer. So near that she could close the fingers of one hand over the truck door. "I was deciding whether or not I wanted to stay in town. For a while."

"I hope you do."

"Why?"

"I told you. I really liked meeting you."

She angled her head slightly. "But…?"

"But…" He mimicked the way she drew out the word questioningly. "What?"

She pressed her lips together. They looked soft and pink and perfectly, entirely natural.

Entirely enticing.

As if coming to a sudden decision, she pulled open the door and worked the strap of her bag free. She dumped it with a thud on the floor and climbed up into the passenger seat. "You can drop me off at my car. It's still at the police station. Or as you call it—" her dimple appeared, again in an unsmiling sort of way "—the *municipal* building."

Whatever it was called, Jay wanted to go back there about as much as he wanted a hole drilled in his head.

But since that wasn't something he wanted to admit, he waited for a passing car and then pulled out onto the street.

He glanced at her. "It's a long drive here from New York if you're not planning to hang around awhile."

He received the side-eye on that one. "Or maybe I just don't like flying," she countered.

"Do you?"

Her lashes swept down as she fastened her seat belt. "I haven't done all that much of it, if I'm being honest."

"I like flying."

"Suppose *you* have done a lot of it."

He tightened his grip on the steering wheel and shot her a quick look. "Why's that?"

She shrugged, seeming oblivious to his sudden suspicion. "Everyone's done more flying than me."

The tension leaked out of his shoulders. "Well, I have done enough flying to get my license."

She looked at him with even more surprise than he felt making the admission. "You're a pilot?"

"I have my private."

"Which means what? You fly private jets?"

He laughed. "No. It means I can fly a single engine in clear conditions. I don't have an instrument rating." He'd intended to get it but life and circumstances had gotten in the way.

"You're talking the tiny little planes, then?" She shuddered. "They look terrifying."

"They're exhilarating," he corrected.

"I'll have to take your word for it," she said dryly, then pointed. "That's my car there. End of the block."

When he'd left the police station earlier, the street had been lined with parked cars. Now there was only hers.

He pulled up behind the small tan vehicle. "I can prove it to you."

She'd released her seat belt and was gathering up the long strap of her bag. "Prove what?"

"That it isn't terrifying at all. I'll take you up sometime." He didn't stop to think about the complications of that particular offer. Yeah, renting the plane would be pricey for a guy on Jay Cross's salary, but he could explain it away.

She gave a laugh that was full of disbelief. "My brothers are always telling me my head is in the clouds, but I think I'll keep my feet firmly on the ground." She hopped down out of the truck. "Thanks for the ride." She closed the truck door and quickly hurried around to the driver's side of her car.

He watched her toss her bag through the opened window. Then she opened the door and got behind the wheel.

And just sat there.

He waited, his curiosity mounting even more when she got out a few seconds later and walked back to the truck. She stopped next to his door. "You don't have to wait for me."

"Blame it on my upbringing. A guy just doesn't drive away until the girl is safe inside."

"I *was* safe inside and you didn't drive away."

"Safe inside a car that wasn't locked to begin with doesn't exactly count."

She showed him the cell phone in her hand. "I have a few calls to make. So, you know, feel free to go." She jerked her chin toward the building next to them. "I'm sure you've got better things to do than sit parked in front of the police station while I make them."

He'd been glad as hell to be finished with Teas earlier, but the more words that came out of Arabella's lips, the less he cared about parking in front of the man's office now. "You're not living in your car, are you?"

She looked genuinely shocked. "What on earth makes you ask that?"

He shrugged. He wasn't about to tell her how often he'd had to choose between rent money and gas money. Rent was a roof over his head. Gas meant the means to get to his next gig. "No reason. Make your calls. It's a nice evening. I'll wait."

"There's no reason—"

"I'm not leaving until you leave, too, Arabella."

She huffed out a breath. "You know, I think you're as bad as my brothers."

"I don't look at you and think *sister*," he said dryly. "Trust me on that one."

Her gaze grazed against his then danced away. "My battery is dead," she admitted abruptly. She waved her phone again. "But I'm going to call someone and take care of it."

The level of his relief was almost laughable. "Someone's already here." He gestured. "Go wait on the sidewalk. I'll pull around in front of you and give you a jump."

She looked like she wanted to argue, but went over to the sidewalk and he moved the truck around until the vehicles were nose to nose. He turned off his engine and pulled out the jumper cables that were stored in a coil behind his seat. Five minutes later, her car was running and he returned the cables to their spot while she got behind the wheel of her car.

He dusted off his hands and looked through her window. "How far do you have to go?"

"I'm staying with Brady. Not even a couple miles from here."

"But you didn't call him for help with the battery?"

She looked resigned. "Do you have older brothers?"

He shook his head.

"Then you don't know what it feels like to grow up with big brothers constantly thinking you can't take care of yourself."

Lack of personal experience didn't mean he was incapable of understanding her feelings. "Can I see your phone?"

She narrowed her eyes at him, but passed the phone to him through the opened window.

He entered his number and handed the phone back. "If it doesn't start in the morning, you can call me." He knew what sort of hours Brady Fortune worked at the hotel. "We can get a new battery installed if it needs one and your brother never even needs to know."

"You'd do that?" She pressed her chin against her arm that was hung over the door and peered up at him. "Why?"

"Told you." He brushed his thumb lightly over her arm. Just a quick graze. One that satisfied his need for contact and one that gave him the added perk of seeing her eyes dilate for just a moment. "I hope you'll stick around awhile."

Her car engine was humming smoothly when he walked back to his truck and got inside.

She was watching him through the windshield, looking a little bemused, a little wary, and a whole lot of beautiful.

Then she smiled, shook her head a little, and put her car in gear.

He watched her drive away until she was out of sight.

Only then, wearing a smile of his own, did he pull out onto the road and finally head home.

And if there was a part of him that hoped her battery would be dead in the morning, he wasn't going to apologize for it.

* * *

"Auntie Bella." A small solid body bounced onto the foot of her bed. "You're late for breakfast!"

Arabella peeled open her eyes and tried to avoid the slathering tongue of the small dog who'd followed Toby onto the bed. "Murphy, stop." She squinted at her nephew. "Says who?"

"I do." Brady spoke from the doorway. His hair was wet from the shower and he still had a towel around his neck above his robe. "You've been here a week. You know the drill. Routine is what keeps the masses sane here."

"Routine for the *boys*," Harper said, also from the hallway. She, too, had wet hair and a towel around her neck. "Morning, Arabella!" She peered around Brady. "Toby, come on. Leave your auntie alone. Murphy, get off the bed." She snapped her fingers and the dog hopped down. He'd been a rescue and with a few exceptions was generally well behaved.

Arabella closed the notebook she'd fallen asleep writing in the night before and moved it to the nightstand before swinging her legs off the narrow mattress. "Yeah. Leave your auntie alone." She reached over to tickle her nephew's skinny ribs. He rolled with laughter, and unlike Murphy, made no attempt at all to get off the bed *or* to leave her alone.

She didn't mind.

She scooped him up by the waist as she got out of bed and carried him like a sack of potatoes toward the door, being sure to lightly knock his swinging feet against a few objects along the way.

He laughed even harder and for some reason found it particularly hilarious to try to muffle that laughter.

Arabella stopped in front of her brother and his fiancée. She looked from their twin wet heads and towels. "Conserving water again? Very…ecologically minded of you."

Harper snickered and padded along the hallway, disappearing behind the master bedroom door.

"Have to do something to offset the hour-long soaks you take," Brady countered. He slanted his head, studying the boy slung sideways over the hip of her striped pajamas. "Might want to see a doctor about that human appendage you've developed out of your side."

"Might have to," she agreed, managing to work her fingertip against Toby's ticklish ribs. "And once I find a real job, you won't have to complain about my so-called hogging of the shower." She bumped into her brother as she lopsidedly left the bedroom with the awkward, wriggling appendage.

"What's that supposed to mean?" Brady followed on her heels.

"It means I can't very well crash here forever." She reached the staircase and set Toby down. "Bet you can't finish your oatmeal before I finish brushing my teeth," she whispered in his ear.

Predictably, he was down the stairs like a shot.

She straightened again and arched slightly, working out the ache of carrying him that way. Both boys had grown noticeably in the last five months.

"And where do you think you're going to crash?" Brady followed her again, this time back to the bathroom, where he stood in the doorway as if she were still five instead of twenty-five.

She widened her eyes dramatically. "Somewhere wild and crazy like my *own* place?"

He looked askance. "You can't live on your own."

She propped her fists on her hips. "And why not?"

"Because you've *never* lived on your own."

"Then it's about time, don't you think?"

"No, I don't think!"

She made a face at him and shut the bathroom door in his face. And made a point of noisily locking it.

"Bella!" He banged once on the door.

She rolled her eyes at her reflection in the mirror over the sink and turned on the faucets until the water rushed loudly in the pipes.

Eventually she heard the creak of his footsteps moving away and her shoulders slumped with relief.

For all of Brady's insistence that he was nothing like their father, sometimes he showed a dismaying similarity to him.

Despite her brother's claims that she was a bathroom hog, she sped through her morning routine like usual. Because she *was* aware of the fact that she was taking up the bathroom in an already busy household. Plus, she'd learned her first morning there that the hot water ran out halfway through shampooing her hair if she dallied too long.

Also, there was that bet with Toby.

Her hair was streaming wet down the back of her T-shirt when she got downstairs a short while later.

Sitting at the kitchen table, Toby was still scooping

up oatmeal. Tyler was drawing on a paper with a crayon, his cereal already finished. Arabella filled a mug with coffee and sat down across from them before reaching for a slice of toast from the stack sitting on a plate in the center of the table.

Without being asked, Harper passed her a small jar of jam and Arabella smeared some on her toast. She took a bite of the deliciousness and chased it with hot coffee.

She looked from Harper to the boys and back again. "So what's on your schedule today?"

"We are going out to spend the day with Laurel and Larkin at the ranch. She's offered to start teaching the boys how to ride horses." Harper sipped her own coffee. "You can come, too, if you're free."

Arabella thought about her car battery and actually found herself hoping that it'd be dead. Just so she'd have an excuse to use Jay's number that was stored in her cell phone. She'd only been out once to Laurel and Adam's place located in the guesthouse at Callum's Fame & Fortune Ranch. "Sounds like fun, but Petunia's expecting me."

"Even on a Saturday?" Brady asked, entering the room. His robe and towel had been replaced by jeans and a necktie that hung loose over his dress shirt.

"Yes, even on a Saturday," Arabella said a little waspishly. The flower shop was open until noon. "*You're* the concierge at Hotel Fortune. *You're* working on a Saturday."

"Sadly," Harper said lightly. She rose and took the ends of Brady's tie and deftly crossed one end over the other. "He's going to miss out on all the fun."

Arabella had a vision of Jay helping Toby tie his shoes the day they'd met.

She felt suddenly flushed and looked down at her toast, willing the heat to fade.

"I'll leave the saddle-sore fun to you," Brady said. "When you need a massage as a result, that'll be fun for me."

Arabella felt an urgent need to wash out her ears. She was glad her brother was ridiculously happy with Harper, but still…

"Maybe neither of you can make it out there for the riding lesson," Harper said, "but we'll be having a cook-out later this afternoon. You can come for that, at least. About three o'clock. Brady, you'll be off for the day by then. I'll expect you both."

"Yes, ma'am," Brady drawled. "Any more orders?"

"None for the moment," Harper said with a laugh.

Arabella tuned out their flirting as she slathered more jam on her toast and looked over to focus on Tyler's drawing. There was a sun on one corner of the page and a brown blob with a long tail in the other corner. Murphy, obviously. And in between, four people. "Impressive. Is that you and Toby?" She pointed at the two smaller figures with shocks of dark hair standing next to the two taller figures.

"No, that's the new babies," he said, without missing a stroke of his crayon. "That's me. That's Toby." He added slashes of bright red across Toby's chest, obviously mimicking the red-and-white stripes of the shirt his twin was presently wearing.

Arabella cast her brother and future sister-in-law a sideways look. "New babies, huh?"

Harper's cheeks went red. "Don't look at me!"

Arabella raised her eyebrows and decided studying her coffee was safer than interpreting the look passing between Brady and Harper. Soon enough, though, her brother was off to the hotel and after reminding Arabella to turn on the radio before she left, too, Harper and the twins were off to their day of riding lessons.

Music soothed not only the savage beast, but it soothed Murphy, too. Even though Brady had put in a doggie door so the animal could go in and out of the house at will, without the radio playing Murphy got up to all sorts of mischief when he was left alone.

Since Arabella had already sacrificed one pair of shoes to the dog when she'd forgotten to leave the music on, it wasn't a mistake she intended to repeat and she turned on the radio as soon as the door closed behind Harper and the boys.

Fortunately, at least the dog wasn't picky about what type of music and with Adele singing in the background, Arabella rinsed the dishes that were left in the sink. Then she loaded the dishwasher and wiped up the table while the DJ warned her listeners that it was going to be a record-breaker of a hot day.

She refilled the dog's water bowl and with her heart feeling jittery inside her chest, she went out to her car.

The engine started just fine.

And the little jitters jittered no more.

She had no reason to call Jay at all.

Feeling decidedly disgruntled, she drove to the flower shop.

Petunia was on the phone when Arabella walked inside. She was obviously taking an order and Arabella walked around her at the counter to go in back where two large worktables were covered with the makings of several bouquets.

She checked the delivery schedule; her first one of the day wasn't for another few hours. Petunia was still busy on the phone, so Arabella began sweeping up the bits of stems and leaves that surrounded the work area. She'd moved on to polishing the glass of the refrigerated cases when Petunia finally entered the workroom.

"Ever wrapped a hand-tied bridal bouquet?"

Arabella glanced over her shoulder. Petunia was holding up one of the lush bouquets, an inquiring look on her face.

Arabella shook her head. "Have only carried more than my fair share of bridesmaid bouquets."

"Close enough." Petunia gestured with the flowers in her hand. "Gerrie called in sick this morning."

Arabella gave a final swipe over the glass. "What do you need me to do?"

Petunia pulled a box of ribbons from beneath the worktable and set it near Arabella. "Need to have all of these bouquets wrapped. Bride wants the ivory ribbon." She withdrew the tail of one of the spools of ribbon inside the box. With enviable ease, she spun the bouquet, deftly encasing the fat bundle of stems in lovely ribbon that she fastened with a pearl-topped pin at the top. "Easy peasy." She handed the finished bouquet to Arabella. "Have twelve of them to do."

"Twelve! For one wedding?" Not even Tammy Jo was having twelve bridesmaids for her fairy-tale wedding.

Petunia shrugged. "Even here in Rambling Rose, some brides are prone to overdoing it." Her lips twitched. "What should I tell them? No, I don't want the business?" She gestured at the ribbons. "Let's see how you do. It's not rocket science."

"Which is also fortunate," Arabella murmured as she gingerly plucked the end of the ribbon and tried to emulate Petunia's work, albeit much more slowly. When she reached the top of the stems, Petunia cut the ribbon and showed her once more how to fold it back on itself so none of the raw edge showed, and pin it in place.

Then Petunia peered through her glasses at Arabella's work and nodded in satisfaction. "I'll have you making corsages and boutonnieres in no time."

She obviously recognized Arabella's horror, because she laughed. "I'm kidding, girl. I know you're looking for a permanent job. But today I am very glad to have you. My father usually fills in for Todd and even though the man is a regular MacGyver, he'd be all thumbs when it comes to this sort of thing." She moved down the table to continue working on the rest of the order. "Heard there's an opening for a cashier over at the grocery on Main."

"No offense to all of the grocery cashiers of the world, but if I'm going to stand on my feet all day, I'd rather be surrounded by the beautiful flowers here than scanning canned beans and heads of lettuce."

Petunia chuckled. "Pay's probably better at the grocery." She plucked a spray of greenery from the stems lying on the table in front of her and after a brief study, snipped off a trio of leaves. "Don't know why you haven't applied over at Hotel Fortune. Goodness knows you've got the connections there."

Arabella chewed the inside of her lip, not wanting to admit that working at the hotel—where Jay worked— had of course figured prominently in her dream world.

Reality, though, was that she had no experience in hospitality whatsoever.

"You know that one of the goals of the hotel was to fill as many positions with locals as possible." She studied her bouquet, trying to decide if the ribbon looked straight or not.

"You're a local now, too."

She unwound the ribbon and started again. "I appreciate the sentiment, but we both know that's not really true."

"Haven't you moved permanently to Rambling Rose?"

"Well, yes, but—"

"Makes you qualify in my mind, girl." Petunia's hands were fairly flying as she plucked a flower here, a bit of leaf there, and fastened them all together into something small and lovely. "Besides which, my nephew Jason works over there and he says they've been having trouble filling all the positions."

Arabella chewed her lip again, stifling the automatic urge to confirm that point. But the things that Brady spoke about over the dinner table at home probably weren't things that he wanted her broadcasting. So she stayed silent and reached for the scissors.

"No wonder, really," Petunia mused.

Arabella couldn't help herself. "Why is that?"

Petunia placed her finished corsage onto a bed of crimped tissue slices filling the bottom of a clear plastic container. "Well, the place seems cursed, doesn't it?"

Arabella's shoulders stiffened. "No."

Her boss must have recognized Arabella's offense because she looked up from her work again. "I'm not saying it *is*," she said quickly. "Or even that I agree. But there's no denying the accidents that have occurred there. That balcony collapsing?" Tsking softly, she snapped the plastic lid in place and set the corsage in a shallow box alongside several others, then immediately began selecting another flower. "My husband insisted Jason find a job somewhere else. At the time, I thought he was overreacting, but he can't very well control what Jason does."

A lot of people had overreacted to the balcony collapse, Arabella thought, her own father included. But it had been a fluke. A terrible accident that mercifully hadn't caused any more injuries than a broken leg for the woman who now managed the hotel.

"Jason listens way more to my father, anyway," Petunia went on, though Arabella was barely listening. "The two of them are thick as thieves. And my dad's been all for Jason working at the hotel." She glanced at Arabella over the rims of her glasses. "You're doing a good job. Going to have to give you a raise."

She was clearly joking and Arabella smiled obediently as she reached for the next bouquet. "All of this stuff is for the 10:00 a.m. delivery?" There were so many left to do and the clock was ticking along.

"It is. Don't look so worried," Petunia assured. "Everything will be ready in time. What kind of career *do* you want to have?"

Arabella let out a laugh that was a little short on humor. "I don't think in terms of a career," she admitted not quite truthfully.

"College?"

"Some." She focused hard on starting the ribbon off at the right spot, even though the task didn't take all that much focus. "It wasn't really for me." More to the point, her average grades hadn't been good enough to garner scholarships and there'd never been any hope of her parents footing the expense for college. She'd quickly learned that spending her paycheck on classes that she wasn't really interested in anyway was a lot less palatable than spending her paycheck on things that *did* interest her.

"Me, either. My father was less than pleased at the time. He's a military vet. He figured either you went to college or you went into the service. No middle ground. Oh, my Lord, the battles that went on between my mom and him. I think that was the last straw in their marriage." Petunia selected another small bit of leaves that would have looked like trimmings to be swept up had it been on the floor instead of the work surface and added it to the corsage taking shape between her fingers. "But I was straight out of high school and wasn't going to listen to anyone, least of all my dad. It wasn't until I was quite a bit older and realized I needed to learn how to run this business I loved that I went back for classes that seemed a lot more relevant."

The bell over the front door jangled then and Petunia went out to deal with the customer.

After giving up on her community college experience, Arabella had taken classes that seemed a lot more relevant to her, too. The only problem was that nobody else appreciated that relevance at all.

And she had no successful business, like Petunia's Posies, to show for herself.

As far as her folks were concerned, creative writing classes were pointless unless you planned to make a living teaching it. Thinking that she might be able to make a career out of it otherwise was just a pipe dream.

And so she continued spending her days in one deadly dull office after another, simply because she could type fast and follow instructions reasonably well, and spent her nights falling asleep over the unfinished stories in her notebooks.

She'd finished three more bouquets by the time Petunia finished with the customer, and by the time Arabella needed to load up her vehicle for the day's deliveries, Petunia's confidence that the wedding flowers would be ready was rewarded.

With the clipboard of delivery addresses sitting beside Arabella on her front seat, she set off.

The church was locked up tight when she arrived and she had to hunt around to find someone possessing keys to open up so she could place all the flowers in the sanctuary per her instructions. After that, she was off to the other side of town to deliver a dozen roses to a woman who took one look at the card included and dropped the long-stemmed beauties to the doorstep, where she ground her heel on them until they were pulp.

Then, taking in Arabella's horrified fascination, smiled and tipped her a twenty.

Arabella returned to her car and the potted plant that was her final delivery for the day. She didn't recognize the street at all, so she plugged the address into her phone's GPS and set off.

Twenty minutes later, she'd left the outskirts of Rambling Rose behind and was beginning to wonder why the GPS-lady was sending her down a dirt road. There was nothing on either side of the road. No cows grazed in the green fields. In fact, whatever was growing in the fields looked more like weeds to her than actual crops.

She was almost ready to stop and call the number on the order slip for better directions when a white two-story farmhouse surrounded by rosebushes came into view. Unlike the unkempt fields, the rosebushes were entirely orderly and filled with roses just as red as the ones that had ended up beneath the woman's heel.

The message on this card said "For my favorite granny" and the potted plant accompanying it would surely have a happier fate.

Arabella parked in front of the house, carried the plant up to the front door and used the eagle-shaped door knocker since there didn't seem to be a doorbell. She soon heard footsteps and was already smiling when the door pulled open.

But instead of a delighted granny named Louella standing on the other side of the door, it was Jay Cross.

And Arabella was pretty sure *she* was the one who looked delighted.

Chapter Four

"I wondered when you were going to get here."

"You did?" Arabella felt breathless looking up into Jay's smiling green gaze. "Why?"

"I was hoping the plant would be here before my grandmother got done at Mariana's Market."

Arabella rather stupidly remembered the fern in her arms. "*You* ordered this?"

He leaned his shoulder against the doorjamb. His dimple deepened. "I did."

"Special occasion?"

"Definitely."

He didn't elaborate and she handed him the plant. "Well, I hope she enjoys it. Tell her that Petunia says it wants filtered light and moist soil so…" She trailed off as his smile widened. "What?"

"Appreciate the instructions, but my grandmother can grow anything. You should see her garden out back." He straightened. "In fact, come on in. I'll show you."

Certain her smile was engulfing her entire being, she stepped past him into the cooler shadows of the foyer. He reached out, his arm brushing her shoulder, and her breath caught in her chest.

Then the door closed with a soft click and she realized he'd been only reaching around her to shut it.

Feeling as mature as a giggly girl, she stepped aside and glanced around.

The short foyer fed to a staircase on the left and an airy kitchen and living area on the right. Straight ahead, she could see through to tall, narrow windows at the back of the house. They overlooked another porch similar to the one at the front of the house. Beyond the porch were row upon row of fat, green bushes.

Obviously the garden Jay mentioned.

But the plants weren't relegated only to the outdoors.

As she followed Jay deeper into the house, she saw houseplants thriving in nearly every corner and crevice.

He set the plant she'd delivered on the wooden dining table as they passed it. At the shop, she'd thought the fern was one of the larger ones they had, but here, amongst all these others that his grandmother was already growing, it seemed positively tiny.

"You weren't kidding," Arabella commented. "Your grandmother must really love plants." Whatever the special occasion was, the plant that Jay had ordered barely stood out in comparison.

"That she does." He pushed open a door and the old-fashioned metal blinds hanging over the window on the upper half swayed. "She adamantly refuses to leave her garden, much to my mom's dismay."

He, on the other hand, didn't sound dismayed at all. "Why is that?"

"Mom figures my grandmother is too old to live here by herself, even though she's lived in this house since she married my grandfather when she was eighteen years old." He stopped on the covered porch and spread his arms. "She's spent seventy years here and she keeps up with all of this, but Mom still worries." He dropped his arms. "Come on."

His hand closed around hers as if it were perfectly natural and she nearly tripped over her own feet as they went down the porch steps. "I'm guessing *you* don't worry?"

He laughed softly. "Louella O'Brien defies worry." He tugged her around the end of one row and stopped next to a raised bed positively bursting with ripening strawberries. He plucked a bright red one and held it in front of her lips. "Taste."

She blinked, still too surprised by his presence there, much less his hand still clasping hers, to do anything at all.

His brows drew together and he pulled the strawberry away again. "Wait. You're not allergic, are you?"

"No," she said faintly.

"That's good. Nobody's berries taste better than my grandmother's." He held the fat berry closer to her lips. So close she could smell the sweet aroma. "Taste."

Feeling caught in his gaze, she obediently opened her mouth and bit into the fruit. Sweet juice exploded in her mouth and she chewed more quickly, laughing a little as she wiped her lips. It really was the sweetest strawberry she'd ever tasted. She swallowed. "Is her secret growing the plants in sugar?"

"You'd think." He grinned and popped the other half of the large strawberry into his mouth.

Arabella's stomach hollowed. Feeling hotter than the sunny day warranted, she pulled her hand free and walked alongside the raised bed, pretending to study the plants. What she saw were a lot of great fat leaves and a massive amount of strawberries. Surely more than one person—even one family—could consume. "What does she do with it all?"

"Makes jam." He'd plucked several more berries and handed her one as they moved down the row. "She sells jars of it at Mariana's Market. Lou's Luscious Jams."

"That's the jam that Harper buys. I had it on my toast this morning!"

"Then you know why it's so popular." He popped another strawberry in his mouth and grabbed her hand again as they continued walking along the rows. "Only one who comes even remotely close competition-wise is Mabel's Marmalades." They passed a three-sided potting shed that was as big as the bedroom Arabella occupied at her brother's house. On the other side of the shed were rows and rows of trees. The shade they cast was welcoming.

"Peach trees?"

"With fruit almost as good as the strawberries." He

lifted their joined hands and pointed his finger beyond the trees. "That's my place."

He was pointing at a small stone barn situated on the bank of a narrow stream. Beyond that was a green pasture surrounded by a white-rail fence where several horses grazed near a three-sided shelter.

It was all so picturesque that every little romantic cell in her body quivered in delight. "You live in a converted barn? Can I see inside?" She heard her own eagerness and was vaguely embarrassed by it.

But there was nothing in his expression that suggested she ought to be embarrassed. "If you won't judge me for my housecleaning."

She crossed her heart with her finger. "Promise."

His hand tightened on hers again and he headed toward the barn. But they hadn't emerged from beneath the shade of the peach orchard when the coughing rumble of an engine cut through the quiet.

"Sounds like my grandmother is back." He about-faced and started back through the trees.

Arabella couldn't really complain. Not when he was still holding her hand the way he was.

They rounded the potting shed again and passed the strawberry beds and were halfway up the rows of big green bushes when a thin woman with dark gray-and-silver hair appeared on the back porch. She looked a lot younger than Jay had indicated and in her hands was the plant that Arabella had delivered.

"Favorite granny?" Louella O'Brien had a sturdy drawl and an equally sturdy tone. "Your *only* granny, you mean." She balanced the plant on the porch rail and waited until they reached the steps. "If this is another attempt at bribing me to call your mama—"

"It's just a plant," Jay assured lightly. "So don't get your hairnet in a knot." He let go of Arabella's hand and dashed up the steps, leaning down to drop a kiss on the woman's tanned, lined cheek. "The plant was just an excuse, anyway."

"I thought it was a special occasion." The words escaped Arabella without thought and she saw the raised-brow look that Jay's grandmother sent him.

"It is." He beckoned Arabella closer. "Gran, this is Arabella Fortune. She delivered the newest addition to your indoor jungle. Arabella, my grandmother, Louella O'Brien."

Arabella hurried forward, extending her hand. "I'm pleased to meet you, Mrs. O'Brien."

Jay's grandmother's hand grasped hers in return. Not only were her fingers longer than Arabella's, they were more darkly tanned and much more calloused. "Another one of those Fortunes, hmm?"

Arabella's gaze collided with the amusement in Jay's. "I don't know about that," she demurred. "But…related. I just moved here from New York."

His eyes glinted. "You've decided to stay, then?"

She felt like steam might be radiating from her skin, but she kept her eyes from shying away. "The odds are beginning to look up."

His grandmother cleared her throat noisily.

Arabella flushed and belatedly released the woman's hand. She pushed her fingers into her back pockets and glanced over her shoulder. "Jay was showing me your garden, Mrs. O'Brien. It's amazing."

"Yes, it is," Louella agreed matter-of-factly. "Do you garden?"

Arabella shook her head. "I couldn't even keep the succulent a friend gave me last year alive."

"No matter what people think, succulents can be touchy. Come out here tomorrow. I'm making cuttings and a new batch of jam."

"Arabella has a job, Gran. At Petunia's—"

"Posies," Louella finished. "I can read well enough." She flicked the embossed card that was tucked among the potted plant's glossy leaves. "And I happen to be well aware that Petunia's shop isn't open on Sundays." She gave Arabella a look. "Churchgoer?"

Only if one counted Christmases and Easters. "Umm—"

"Ten sharp," Louella said, as if that settled it. "Jay? A word?"

Something in his gaze flickered, but he nodded. "Be right back," he told Arabella before following his grandmother inside the house.

They closed the door after them, which only increased Arabella's sudden sense of awkwardness. She stepped off the porch again, reaching out to steady the plant that was propped on the flat rail when it wobbled.

"An excuse or a special occasion," she murmured, placing it more squarely on the rail. "What are you really?"

The plant provided no answer and she turned away, moving back over to the first row of bushes. She glanced over her shoulder, but the door to the house was still closed.

Maybe Jay's grandmother was warning him not to get involved with one of those Fortunes.

The sun was getting higher in the sky and hotter and the faint buzz of insects seemed like summer music. Maybe when she found a real job and started looking for a place of her own, she should look for one that had space for a tiny garden. Growing something outdoors might be easier than keeping a container succulent happy on a windowsill in her bedroom.

She glanced back at the house. Door still closed.

She told herself there wasn't any reason to be concerned. If Jay's grandmother were warning him not to get involved with one of those Fortunes, then why would she have invited Arabella to come back the next day for cuttings?

From between the slats of the window blinds, Jay watched Arabella disappear into the shade of the potting shed. "She's just a friend, Gran," he insisted for the third time and his grandmother made a third, disbelieving snort in response.

"I've been able to read your mind since you were knee-high to a grasshopper." Louella set two glasses on the round serving tray she'd pulled from a cabinet. "I can read it now, too." She opened the refrigerator and pulled out a glass jug of homemade lemonade. "You're interested in that girl."

He spread his hands, exasperated. "So what if I am?"

"Goin' to tell her the truth, then?" She added the jug to the tray and turned back to the fridge.

Jay felt a faint pain start up inside his head. He'd been on the verge of telling Arabella the truth in January when they'd first met. But a lot of time had passed since then. Time for him to get even more settled into the routine of Jay Cross. Time for him to get further away from the man he'd been. But the further away he remained, the more interest kept growing to flush him out. "Eventually."

His grandmother gave him a look as she pulled a tray of ice from the freezer.

"Probably," he amended.

She said nothing. Just filled the two glasses with the ice, her lips compressed.

"Maybe," he tried again.

"I *knew* you were waffling!" She peeled the plastic lid off an old metal coffee can and removed several cookies from inside. She spread them on a flowered plate and added it to the serving tray along with a few of her fabric napkins that she kept in a drawer.

"And you don't approve."

She slid her finger between two slats in the window blind the same way he had and peered through the narrow slit. "She's a pretty girl."

Arabella was a lot more than pretty, but he wasn't going to argue the point.

"Not like that other one." The slats snapped together again.

He didn't have to ask who she meant. Louella had never pretended to like his ex-girlfriend. And Tina had never pretended to like Louella. The only thing Tina liked about Jay's background was that he came from Texas.

In her opinion it gave him a sort of credibility.

Not that he'd recognized that at the beginning. In the beginning, he'd been totally taken in by her.

"You ought to be happy about that," Jay said aloud. "Arabella being different than Tina."

"I am."

"Then what's the problem?"

His grandmother picked up the laden tray and pushed it into his hands. "You're a smart boy," she said irritably. "So be smart. Start as you mean to go on."

"She's not even certain she's going to stay in Rambling Rose." The words were as much for himself as they were for his grandmother. A reminder that jumping in with both feet was fine when you were eight and standing on the precipice of a cool swimming hole on a hot day.

But his life was a lot more complicated now than it had once been. More complicated even than it had been in January. Staying two steps ahead of the man he'd been was getting harder by the day.

"Are *you* staying in Rambling Rose?" she asked pointedly.

He sighed noisily. She knew he didn't have an answer. "You know I'm working tomorrow," he told her. "But you invited her to be free labor for you."

"She'll learn a little about gardening and a little about jam-making. It's a fair trade. Don't worry. I won't tell her who you really are, *Jett*."

"I'm *really* Jay Cross," he said flatly.

She gave him a steady look. "We'll see 'bout that, won't we?" She pulled open the door. "It's hot out there. Go have lemonade and cookies with your girl."

"Don't think I miss the significance, Granny."

Her eyebrows rose. "Can't imagine what you mean."

He made a face and passed her through the doorway.

He found Arabella in the potting shed. She was sitting on a stool at the scarred metal workbench, paging through one of his grandmother's binders that were stored on one of the many shelves above the bench.

"Did you know she keeps notes on what she plants?" She glanced at him. "The dates and what the weather's like and all sorts of little details?"

"As a matter of fact, I did know." He set the tray next to the binder. "She has binders going back for decades. Before I was born, even. How else do you think she developed her sugar-soil recipe?" He filled both glasses with lemonade and handed her one. "Better drink it all. She squeezes the lemons by hand, too."

Arabella's eyes danced. "Did she mill her own flour for those cookies, too?"

He grinned. "Anything's possible." He lightly tapped his glass against hers. "Cheers."

She took a quick sip of lemonade, made a soft, appreciative "mmm" sound that slid down the base of his spine and took a longer drink. "Delicious."

He had to force himself to look away from the way her lower lip glistened. "Best lemonade in the county." He chugged down half his own glass, feeling parched in a way that lemonade would never quench. "She has a box of blue ribbons from the county fair that goes back about as far as the binders do."

Arabella picked up one of the golden cookies. "Chocolate chip?" She didn't wait for his nod before she broke off a little piece and popped it in her mouth. She made that same throaty "mmm" sound. "How many blue ribbons did she win for her cookies?"

"No idea," Jay admitted. "But she did win my grandfather with them."

Arabella looked even more delighted. "Really?"

If her eyes hadn't held such vivid interest, he would have wished that he'd kept his mouth shut. "They met when she was just seventeen. Her father wouldn't let her go out with him because he was eight years older. But her mother, who was a piano teacher, said he could come to their house on Sunday afternoons for piano lessons. After which, my grandmother would serve him her homemade lemonade and chocolate chip cookies. He always claimed that it was the lemonade and cookies that kept him coming back. They eloped a week after she turned eighteen."

Arabella propped her chin on her hand. "That's the sweetest story. Is she your mom's mom or your dad's?"

"Mom's. She was their only child. Lonely only, as my mother says."

"Are you a lonely only, too?"

A crumble of cookie caught in his throat. He coughed slightly and nodded.

"Do your parents live here in Rambling Rose also?"

"Houston. That's where I grew up. My dad's a math teacher. Mom's a piano teacher."

"I remember you mentioned that the day we met. Like your great-grandmother."

He nodded. "But I spent a lot of summers here with my grandparents." Until he'd turned fifteen and decided he was too old for such nonsense. It had taken him another ten years before he'd begun to appreciate the error of his ways. Fortunately, his grandmother hadn't held that against him too much when he'd needed a bolt-hole.

"And now you live here with her."

"No, I *live* in the barn," he corrected dryly. "Which she tolerates only because I feed the horses she refuses to give up and my presence here keeps my mother relatively quiet on the subject of moving Gran to Houston. In case it's not apparent by her choice to live way the hell out here, my grandmother likes her privacy." Something that also suited him very well these days.

Arabella shook her head. "I'll bet she loves having you here. You, who surprises her with potted plants."

"One plant." He rotated his glass in the pool of condensation that had formed around the base. "And it was just so you'd have to deliver it," he admitted.

Her eyebrows pulled together. The corners of her lips curved again. "You're joking."

"You didn't call me this morning to tell me your battery was dead. What else was I supposed to do?"

She looked down at the tray between them. Her lashes were dark and long and looked entirely natural. "So the plant really was an excuse?"

"For a special occasion."

She wrinkled her nose and looked at him. "Special occasion being…?"

He was barely aware that he'd leaned down on his arms on the workbench, putting him at her level. "Getting to see you again."

Her eyes softened. "Jay."

"Arabella." He couldn't help himself. He touched the ponytail hanging over her shoulder. The red strands might look fiery, but they slid through his fingers cool and silky.

"I think you'd better kiss me," she murmured and her cheeks turned rosy.

"Yeah?" His voice dropped also.

"If you don't, then I'll know this is just a dream."

"And if I do?"

She moistened her lips. "Then I'll know this is just a dream."

He smiled slightly. He brushed the silky end of her ponytail against her cheek and leaned closer. "Dream, Bella," he whispered, and slowly pressed his lips to hers.

He felt her quick inhale and his own quick rush. Tasted the brightness of lemonade, the sweetness of strawberry.

He slid his fingers from her ponytail to the back of her neck and urged her closer.

Her fingers splayed against his chest. She murmured something against his lips. He barely heard. His head was full of sound. Full of pulse beats and bells.

She murmured again. This time not against his lips.

He frowned, feeling entirely thwarted. "What?"

She pulled back yet another inch. Her fingertips pushed instead of urged closer. "Do you want to answer that?"

It made sense then. His cell phone was ringing.

He exhaled his annoyance and pulled the offending device from his back pocket. The number showing on the screen wasn't familiar, but the area code was. He declined the call, the ringing went quiet and he shoved the phone into his pocket again.

"Nobody important?"

He shook his head, but some piece of conscience in him prickled.

Start as you mean to go on.

When had he stopped believing in that?

"Bella. Arabella—"

"I like when you call me Bella." Her hand had found a place against his chest again, her fingertips grazing his neck.

The urge to pull her out of the potting shed and beyond the peach orchard to his barn was painful.

He closed his hand around hers, moving it away from his chest. "Then you'll always be Bella to me." He kissed her fingertips. "But I—" He broke off with a curse when his phone rang insistently again. He didn't need to look at the screen to know it would be the same caller. Just as he hadn't needed to recognize the number to know it would be the same caller.

Despite their long alliance, Michael Devane had cut Jay loose the year before without a speck of regret.

Then everything changed and Jay had been dodging Michael ever since. When there was money on the line, the other man was like a bulldog.

He pulled out his phone again, turned it off and left it facedown on the bench.

But even though he wanted to start up right where he'd left off—namely the pouty curve of Arabella's lower lip—that damn piece of conscience prickled harder than ever. So instead, he raked his fingers through his ruthlessly short hair and refilled his glass of lemonade. "Damn, it's getting hot out, isn't it?"

She looked vaguely confused. "The heat isn't so bad, but the humidity is worse than I'm used to." She freed her ponytail, only to bundle her hair up into a knot on the top of her head and secure the tie around it again. "I actually ought to be going. I have a thing I have to go to this afternoon." She closed the binder and stretched up to replace it on the shelf. Her shirt rode up above the waistband of her jeans, briefly revealing a narrow strip of creamy skin.

He looked away and chugged another quarter glass of lemonade. "A thing?"

"Barbecue. My brother's fiancée is expecting me." She went back down on her heels and tugged the bottom of her shirt. "You know, if you don't want me to come tomorrow, you can just tell me."

His mind had been occupied with fantasies of exploring that soft-looking skin. To see whether the sprinkle of light freckles across her nose were repeated anywhere else. "Why wouldn't I want you to come?"

"I don't know." She tugged at her shirt again, but this time he knew it wasn't an unconscious act but an indicator of uncertainty. "Just thought I should make sure. She's *your* grandmother. Maybe she doesn't really expect me to take her up—"

"You haven't spent enough time with her yet," Jay

said wryly. "She doesn't say things she doesn't mean." Which was why he trusted that she wouldn't tell all to Arabella just because she figured Jay ought to. "You didn't decline her invitation. She's going to expect you tomorrow. And she's going to put you to work, so you might as well come prepared."

"And you? Is she putting you to work, too?"

"She would if I didn't have to be on duty at the hotel. Can't tell you how many hours of weeding she's gotten out of me since I moved into the barn."

She looked crestfallen. "You have to work at the hotel tomorrow?"

Her disappointment was ego-boosting to say the least. "Afraid so." He tucked his finger beneath her chin. "Which means I'll have to think of some way to make it up to you."

"Really?" It was practically a squeak and she blushed. "Really?" she repeated in a much lower register and with a lot more aplomb.

Everything about her charmed him. "Really." He wrapped the remaining cookies in one of the napkins and handed them to her. "Gran'll figure I screwed up if all of the cookies aren't gone."

Their fingers brushed as she took the napkin from him. "Can't have that."

He walked her back to her car, going around the house rather than through it. But his attempt at avoiding his grandmother was futile, since she was outside at the front of the house anyway, tending her rosebushes.

She peered from beneath the brim of her ancient straw hat. "Leaving already?"

"Arabella has a family thing to get to," Jay answered, knowing that was one thing that would quell his grandmother's well-intentioned nosiness.

"I do," Arabella confirmed. "Thank you for the cookies and lemonade, Mrs. O'Brien. They were delicious."

"Pleased to hear it," his grandmother said. "Nothing more satisfying when everyone's feeling warm."

Arabella obviously took the words at face value, but Jay was glad his grandmother's straw brim shaded her undoubtedly crafty expression.

He opened Arabella's car door for her and closed it again once she was behind the wheel. When she turned the key, the engine started immediately.

She smiled wryly. "Guess the battery thing must have been a fluke."

"Fluke. Divine intervention. Either way, I'm grateful."

Her smile widened as she put the car in gear. "You don't happen to be Irish, do you?"

"Are you kidding?" He took a step back when her tires began to slowly crunch over the drive. "Gran's name is O'Brien."

"That doesn't necessarily mean you're Irish. But if you are, it at least explains the gift you have for blarney!" Then she was driving away, leaving behind the sound of her laughter.

He stood there, long after her car was out of sight and the dust she'd kicked up was finally settled.

"Didn't tell her, did you." It wasn't a question.

He exhaled sharply and turned to face his grandmother. "Do you ever get tired of being right all the time?"

"It's a burden I've learned to bear," she deadpanned.

Then she wielded her snips with deliberation and a dying rose fell to the ground.

Chapter Five

"*...And that's 'Giving It All Up' by the newest sensation—*"

The radio went silent as Arabella turned off her engine. She stared through her windshield at the front facade of Hotel Fortune and wondered for about the hundredth time if she was really doing this.

Applying for a job at Hotel Fortune.

Any job.

Three days ago, Todd Bellamy had returned from his family vacation and three days ago, her job at Petunia's Posies had ended.

She also hadn't heard one word from Jay Cross. Not even after she'd spent several hours working in his grandmother's garden more than a week ago.

Which, considering the way he'd kissed her in the

potting shed, left her once again mired in a swamp of uncertainty. Was he interested in her or wasn't he?

You're the one who asked him to kiss you.

She swatted away the thought like an annoying fly. But like any respectable annoying fly, it just kept returning to the picnic.

She couldn't even be certain whether or not her decision to actually seek a job at Hotel Fortune was because of Jay or in spite of him.

She got out of the car, slamming her car door harder than necessary, and straightened her shoulders as she marched through the entrance of the hotel.

She hadn't been there since January. The only noticeable change to the Spanish Mission–style lobby since then were the flowers in the massive arrangement on the table positioned beneath a skylight centered in the soaring ceiling.

She stopped at the reception desk. "I have an appointment in human resources?"

The attendant was a young man who didn't even look old enough to shave. "Third floor. Just follow the signs."

"Thanks." She headed for the elevators. There were very few people about. Only one middle-aged couple sat in the massive leather chairs in one corner of the lobby near the door. They had small suitcases sitting on the terra-cotta tiled floor next to them. Probably waiting for transportation. Another couple exited the elevator when the doors opened and Arabella stepped into the empty car and punched the third-floor button.

As the doors closed, she couldn't help remembering

the small elevator that Jay had shown her the day of Larkin's party when she'd taken the twins outside to play.

"Stop thinking about Jay Cross," she said under her breath. The soft bell chimed at the second floor and the doors slid open to reveal an empty corridor.

Arabella poked her head out of the car and seeing nobody standing by, ducked back inside and poked the close button a few times to hasten it along. She wouldn't be cutting the time so closely for her appointment with the human resources department if she hadn't had to change her outfit at the last minute thanks to Murphy's muddy paws.

But the doors stubbornly refused to close at all. Not even pressing the third-floor button again garnered any results.

Huffing in frustration, she left the elevator and pressed the call button for its mate, but that button didn't even light up and after another minute waiting for it to respond, she huffed again and headed down the corridor looking for signs for the stairwell.

As she went, she passed the entrance for Roja's banquet room. The door was open and she glanced inside as she hurried past. Round tables—currently naked of tablecloths—were situated around the room. Then she remembered the stairwell they'd used in January and quickly found it around another corner. The heavy door clanged shut behind her and her heels rang out as she raced up the cement steps. She reached the landing where a door was marked with a black numeral 3.

She'd been on dozens of interviews in her life. She shouldn't be so nervous now, yet she was. She drew in a deep breath and smoothed her hand down the side of her skirt before grasping the door handle and pushing it down.

The handle moved.

The door did not.

"No way." She twisted the lever up. Twisted it down. But it remained locked. Cursing under her breath, she hurried back down the stairs, the whole way to the first floor, and burst breathlessly out of the door, inordinately relieved that it hadn't been locked as well.

The stairwell hadn't been particularly confining. Just a basic square tower filled with concrete steps and a bunch of doors that didn't open, but she still felt shaky from nerves.

She smoothed her ponytail and hurried back to the lobby, passing a trio of people now waiting for the elevators along the way.

"One of them was stuck on the second floor," she told them as she walked by, heading once more back to the reception desk.

The same young guy was there.

"That was fast," he said as she stopped in front of him.

"Only because I couldn't get up to the third floor." She inhaled yet another deep, calming breath. "The stairwell doors are all locked on the inside."

"It's a security thing," he said. "Unless you're a guest with your room key, you can't enter other floors except the main floor. Of course the fire department can override the locks in an emergency. The elevators—"

"—decided to hang out permanently on the second

floor," she interrupted, wanting to cut to the chase. "One of them, anyway." Who knew about the other elevator.

"Oh, yeah." He nodded as if just now remembering. "That's been a problem lately."

Arabella wanted to ask him why something hadn't been *done* about that problem lately. "What about the service elevator?"

"Sorry but that's for staff only."

"Which I won't have a chance to even *be* if I can't get up to the human resource department. Can't you just give me a room key or something so I can get through the stairwell door?"

He frowned as if the idea of it caused him physical pain.

Arabella leaned closer and lowered her voice conspiratorially. "Isn't it a bit of a hazard having only one way to get from one floor to another?"

"Is there a problem, Jason?"

Jason got a definite deer-in-the-headlights look when a brunette with a serious expression on her face stopped next to the reception desk. "No problems, Ms. Williams."

"You're Grace," Arabella said, realizing it even before she saw the discreet name badge on the other woman's lapel. Grace Williams. General Manager.

The woman's expression was friendly but Arabella thought she detected a sense of reserve in her eyes.

"I do have the distinct pleasure of being GM," Grace said, holding out her hand. "And you—"

"Arabella Fortune." She pumped the manager's hand. "I'm Br—"

"Brady's sister!" Warmth entered Grace's eyes. "I'm so pleased to meet you. Your brother has told me all about you."

Arabella couldn't help making a face. "When it comes to big brothers, that isn't always a good thing."

Grace laughed lightly. "He sings your praises," she assured. "Are you here to see him?"

"Actually, no," Arabella admitted. Brady didn't even know what she was up to that afternoon. She cast a look toward the elevators. Two members of the waiting trio had given up and disappeared, leaving only the third standing there still staring at the unmoving illuminations above the doors. "I have an appointment with Sybil in human resources. Starts—" she glanced at her nonexistent wristwatch "—about ten minutes ago."

"You're applying?" Far from being concerned over Arabella's tardiness, Grace just looked delighted. "Your brother didn't say a word about that."

"He doesn't really know," Arabella admitted. Even though he'd teased her unmercifully about going to work at the hotel when she'd first broached the subject of moving to Rambling Rose. "I didn't want anyone thinking that I was hoping for special favors or something."

"Trust me," Grace assured. "I understand that completely."

Arabella remembered then that Grace was involved with Wiley Fortune, who was one of *those* Fortunes. Considering he was one of Arabella's cousins, she ought to have more than a vague recollection of meeting him at Larkin's party.

But the truth was that she'd been far more interested in the server named Jay than she had been with anyone else.

"Which position are you applying for?"

Arabella spread her hands. "I'm not picky. I just want a paycheck so I don't have to keep sponging off my brother."

"Well, then." Grace extended one arm in the direction of the elevators. "I have a meeting on four. I'll go up with you."

"Um—"

Grace's eyebrows rose slightly. "Yes, Jason?"

"One of the elevators is stuck on the second floor," Arabella provided because the poor guy looked like he was about ready to choke on his bobbing Adam's apple. "And the other one seems stuck somewhere also."

Arabella heard the faint sigh that Grace exhaled. But her expression was calm and still smiling as she looked at Arabella. "Excuse me for just a second while I take care of that."

Arabella wasn't going to argue. Certainly not with the woman who was not only Brady's boss, but boss of the whole place. She waited until Grace had disappeared through a doorway behind the reception desk and looked toward Jason again. "Make up your mind about that key yet?"

Jason cast a quick look over his shoulder toward the doorway. "I think she meant for you to wait for her."

Arabella actually had that same impression. But she

hadn't been able to resist asking him the question. "How long have you worked here, Jason?" She felt sure he was the nephew Petunia had mentioned.

He stood rather stiffly behind the reception desk and after her question he straightened his blue tie. "Since they first opened," he said proudly. "Two weeks ago I got promoted here to the desk."

Grace reappeared. "Maintenance is taking care of the elevators and I buzzed Sybil to let her know why you were delayed. Jason, until the elevators are fixed, be sure to direct anyone needing them to the service bay. One of the girls from housekeeping can escort them to their floor."

He nodded. "Yes'm. Um. Ma'am."

Grace's smile gentled. "And one more thing, Jason. *Relax.* You're doing fine." Then she turned to Arabella again. "Shall we?" She led the way out of the lobby.

There was no sign of the broken leg she'd sustained when the balcony had collapsed and following her, Arabella couldn't help but admire the confidence in Grace's bearing.

Maybe someday she'd exude some of that herself.

They used the same service elevator that Jay had used back in January and in minutes, Arabella found herself sitting in front of Sybil's desk.

"Take good care of her." Grace's voice was light as she departed for her meeting. "If she's anything like her brother, we don't want her getting away."

Left alone with Sybil, Arabella smiled a little awkwardly. "I'm nothing like my brother," she warned.

"You're a Fortune," Sybil said, sliding a blank job

application and a pen across the desk toward Arabella. "That's the only qualification you'll need."

Arabella picked up the pen and hesitated. "There's nothing magical about my last name."

"Says the person who possesses it." Sybil's voice wasn't unkind. But it *was* matter-of-fact.

"I don't expect to be given preference over another applicant just because I'm related to—"

Sybil cut her off with a wave of her hand. "You won't be. Right now, we have more open positions than we do applicants. Just fill out the top section. Name, address, social security number. That stuff. Then sign the bottom. We're running background checks on new hires, so assuming all that checks out, we've got positions available in everything from maintenance to housekeeping to front office to accounting. What sort of experience do you have?"

Arabella quickly filled in the boxes on the application and added her signature at the bottom. "Most recently, I was an administrative assistant at a plastics manufacturer before I moved to Rambling Rose." It was true, but Arabella had always considered the title a glorified one considering the scope of her clerical duties. She slid the application back across to Sybil. "I've also worked back office at a dental practice, had the ubiquitous phone bank job when I was still in school. Retail work—um, a department store as well as a small independent book—" She broke off when Sybil waved her hand again.

"When can you start?"

"Immediately."

Sybil made a note on the application and slid it into one of her desk drawers. She rose and rounded her desk. "The trainee program was designed with Rambling Rose locals in mind but we'll start you there for now. Come with me and we'll get you set up with a name badge and such. I'll get a copy of your ID while we're at it. And then I'll give you the tour."

Getting a job couldn't possibly be this easy. Feeling bemused, Arabella followed the older woman out of her small office. "What about the background check?"

Sybil cast her a sideways look. "You're going to pass it, aren't you?"

"Well, yes." Unless occasionally skipping to the last page of a book counted, there was nothing remotely scandalous in Arabella's background. Still, it hardly seemed prudent to just trust a person's word on that score, even if one's surname *was* Fortune.

"Then there's no reason why you can't start tomorrow—provisionally, of course."

They stopped in the security office and Sybil made introductions, then went off to get her copies of Arabella's proof of ID, while she had her photograph taken and a name badge made up right there on the spot.

"The badge is an access key. Encoded with your security rights. So don't lose it and don't let anyone else use it," she was instructed when she received the badge.

Then Sybil returned, and feeling like she was pretending to be something she wasn't, Arabella fastened the badge on her blouse and hurriedly caught up with Sybil's ground-eating stride as she started off on the tour.

She introduced Arabella to every department head

and supervisor until Arabella's head felt like it was spinning. The only person they didn't see was Brady, and that was undoubtedly because Sybil knew he was Arabella's brother.

The dizzying tour ended once more in Sybil's third-floor office. She poured herself a cup of coffee from a communal pot and sat on the edge of her desk again. "Any questions?"

Tons. Arabella smiled with more confidence than she felt. "Only two. What time do I start tomorrow and who should I be reporting to when I get here?"

Sybil looked pleased. "Eight sharp and check in at the front desk. I'll leave further instructions for you there."

"Thank you." Arabella shook the woman's hand. "I appreciate the opportunity."

"Hope you'll still feel that way after tomorrow," Sybil said humorously. She moved around her desk to sit once more and taking her cue, Arabella departed.

Arabella didn't need to use her new badge to call the service elevator because an older woman with bright blond hair in a big bun on her head was already entering.

She held the door and smiled as Arabella joined her. "New here?"

Arabella nodded, fingering the sparkling new badge. "As of an hour ago, actually."

"Well, congratulations!" The woman punched the button for the second floor and after a questioning look at Arabella, hit the first floor button, too. "I'm Mariana. I help run Roja here."

"Mariana! You run the flea market, too, don't you?" Arabella pumped the woman's hand with genuine pleasure when the other woman nodded. "That's where Jay's grandmother sells her jams."

Mariana looked delighted. "You know Jay Cross? I remember when he was just a skinny little rug rat. He's sure grown into a handsome man."

Arabella flushed. "We've met," she allowed. "Brady talks a lot about you. He says the boys love going out there because of all the food trucks. Yours is the original one, right?"

Mariana laughed even more merrily as she nodded. "Food trucks have come a long way these days from our humble roach-coach beginnings." She touched the badge on her own buxom breast. "Some might say the same thing about me." The elevator lurched slightly and the door opened. "Come by Roja soon and tell me how you're settling in." She left the elevator, stepping around the tall ladder just outside of the car. "Hey there, Jetpack," she said on her way. "Were your ears burning?"

When Jay maneuvered the ladder into the elevator, she wanted to disappear through the padded walls. She'd known the chances of running into him around the hotel were good. But she hadn't really thought it would happen like this.

He looked equally surprised to see her. "Bella. You're—"

"On staff here." She flicked her name badge and tried not to get drawn in by his emerald eyes as the elevator doors closed yet again.

"I see that." He shifted the ladder until it was leaning against the padded wall. "What department?"

She shrugged. "No idea. I'm starting off in the trainee program tomorrow."

"Same as me, then." He smiled. "Be prepared to try your hand at everything from cleaning toilets to delivering room service."

"And hefting ladders, evidently."

"I was helping maintenance with the elevators." He hooked his arm over one of the rungs and his fingers hung loosely on her side of the ladder. If she moved even half a foot, they'd brush against her.

She pressed her back harder against the padding as if to warn herself not to move toward those callused fingertips. "You've been here for how long now? Six months?"

"Little past that."

"Is it common to stay in the trainee program that long?"

"Is that your way of suggesting I'm doomed to be a perpetual trainee?" His teeth flashed. "When I joined the program, they said it was designed to last about a year. After which, theoretically, the person should be ready to move into one of the junior management positions."

"What sort of management—" She broke off when the elevator doors slid open.

She hadn't even been aware that the car had stopped moving.

Still holding the ladder propped against his shoulder,

Jay shifted sideways until his back was pressed against the edge of the door. "After you."

She detached herself from the padded wall and quickly stepped out of the elevator. It meant passing him even more closely and she only realized she'd been holding her breath when it escaped after she'd put half the width of the corridor between them. Whether or not he'd ignored her for more than a week, walking away without saying some sort of goodbye felt rude.

"Well." She pressed her palms together. "Guess I'll see you around." She turned to leave only to bump hard against the corner of one of the empty rolling racks stored against the wall. Feeling like an idiot, she steadied the cart as she moved around it.

"Bella, wait."

It was painful the way her nerve endings tingled so swiftly where he was concerned. She took another sidestep, waving her arm. "I can see you're busy and I need to get going."

"Bella—"

Her neck prickled. "Arabella, actually. Only my family calls me that."

His gaze flickered. "I should have called you this week."

Something inside her head sort of popped. "Then why didn't you?" The words flew out. Cheeks on fire, she backed up again and banged into yet another rack. "Never mind. Don't answer that."

"It's not you, it's—"

Good grief, she was going to cry at this rate. "Yeah, I know. Sorry if I don't want to hear another *it's not you, it's me* story. No sweat, you know. You don't have to explain a thing. We don't even really know each other."

I think you should know that...

She clamped down hard on that thought, cutting it off at the head.

"Tell your grandmother thanks again from me. The jam she sent me home with is already gone thanks to my brother and his family." Afraid of what she might do or say if she let him get a word in edgewise, she quickly turned and mercifully avoided running into another one of the racks as she hurried away.

It was only divine mercy that kept her feet moving in the proper direction, because she honestly wasn't sure how she ended up back in the lobby. The couple with the luggage was gone now and a curvy girl in a black T-shirt and trousers was dusting the leather chairs they'd occupied.

Arabella managed a smile as she sailed past her and out the door. She felt a little compunction for not looking in on Brady, but told herself he would have been busy, anyway.

Clouds had formed overhead while she'd been inside the hotel, and the air felt heavy and humid. Her car provided no relief, either, and she was grateful to get back to Brady's place.

The house was empty—a momentary condition, she felt sure—and with Murphy trailing after her every step, she changed out of her skirt and blouse and into cutoffs and a spaghetti tank and went down to the kitchen.

"And that's another deep cut called 'Lonely Only' from Carr's first album that was released nearly ten—"

Arabella snapped off the droning voice on the radio and opened her arms. Murphy nimbly jumped up into them. She rubbed his ears. "Did you behave?"

He licked her neck, which wasn't much of an answer, but was pretty delightful, anyway. She gave him a treat and he jumped out of her arms and darted through the dog door.

Harper and Brady had taken to leaving notes on the refrigerator for each other in an attempt to keep up with the increasing busyness of their lives. Brady's schedule. Harper's menu plans for the coming few days. Another note in Harper's neat handwriting that said simply *Love you.*

The sweet, ordinary things of an ordinary life. Arabella sighed as she traced Harper's little note.

How nice it would be to have someone with whom to share that sort of ordinariness.

Predictably, Jay filled her thoughts and she determinedly shrugged him off along with the clouds inside her mind as she pulled open the refrigerator door.

The least she could do was get dinner started and according to Harper's note, the menu du jour was hamburgers on the grill and salad.

She had the salad and burger patties waiting in the fridge and was poking at the fiery coals in the grill in the backyard when she heard the rumble tumble of the twins inside the house behind her. Several minutes passed, though, before Harper came outside, Murphy on her heels. She was wearing a T-shirt and shorts.

"Look at you," Harper greeted her delightedly. "When the boys' checkups at the clinic went later than

I expected, I figured I'd be resorting to PB&J for their supper if I wanted to get them to bed at a reasonable hour."

"Just waiting for the coals to get hot." Arabella hung the poker on the side of the kettle-shaped grill and fit the domed lid in place. She eyed the kiddie pool that Harper was manhandling through the doorway. "Need help?"

"I've got it." Proof was in the pudding. The hard plastic pool popped out of Harper's hands and rolled on its side off the edge of the patio, flopped down onto the grass. Murphy went nuts, immediately hopping inside it to sniff every blue plastic crevice. "Picked it up at the store on the way home. This humidity is killing, isn't it?" Harper didn't wait for an answer as she grabbed the end of the coiled garden hose. "Murphy, come."

The dog flopped on his belly and woofed.

Harper shook her head, resigned. "Get wet, then." She dropped the end of the hose into the pool and turned on the water.

Predictably, Murphy yelped. He disliked water as much as he disliked being left alone in a silent house. "Coward," Harper accused when the dog bolted inside, leaving the dog door swinging wildly.

With the pool filling, she flopped down onto the deck chair beside Arabella. "So, how's the job hunt?"

"I start at the hotel tomorrow."

Harper's eyebrows rose. "I knew you were putting applications in everywhere, but Brady didn't tell me you were applying there, too."

"He didn't know. They put me in the trainee program."

"Well, that's great!" Harper beamed.

"What's great?" Brady stepped out onto the patio. He was loosening the tie that Arabella still found hard to believe he wore to work every day.

She'd never thought her brother was particularly a suit-and-tie sort of guy. But as the hotel concierge, he was living up to the task as well as the look.

Harper tilted her face for his kiss. "Arabella's gotten into the trainee program at Hotel Fortune. She starts tomorrow!"

Brady gave her a sideways look. "Wondered how long it'd take you to get around applying there."

She lifted her chin. "Why's that?"

"'Cause that's where your crush works."

She stared him down, refusing to react. When it came to her brothers, she had that down to a fine art.

When it came to Jay Cross?

Pure and utter failure.

"I have no idea what you're talking about," she said with just the right amount of boredom. She got up and turned off the hose because the pool was almost over-flowing. Then she lifted the lid on the grill to check the coals and the twins and the dog raced out to join them.

Clad in only their swim trunks, the boys sent water splashing over Arabella when they jumped pell-mell into the pool.

"Guys!" Harper chided as she reached down to calm the dog who'd scrambled under her chair. "Don't splash Auntie Bella."

Arabella just laughed, though, because the cold water dripping down her front did feel refreshing.

"I need to grab towels," Harper said, heading to the door. "Brady, can you help?"

As a ploy to get her fiancé alone for a moment it was pretty transparent and Arabella didn't bother hiding her amusement.

"Bring the burgers, too," Arabella called after them because the charcoal in the bottom of the kettle had turned a perfect ashy shade around the edges. She put the lid back in place to keep in the heat and with one leap, jumped squarely into the center of the pool, splashing the boys much more thoroughly than they'd splashed her.

They rolled with giggles and before long, the pool was nearly empty thanks to the waves of water they splashed back and forth at Arabella. She was soaked to the skin when she dragged the hose back over to fill up the small play pool again. "I ought to pour bubble bath in there with you. Would save time later tonight!"

"That it would," Harper agreed, finally returning with a stack of folded bath towels in her arms. Brady followed. He carried the tray of burger patties and concentrated on the task of removing the plastic wrap covering the tray with unusual ferocity.

Harper handed Arabella one of the towels and set the rest a safe distance away. Arabella easily recognized the linens from her mom's supply. They were the "good" towels patterned with a hideous pink crest on one side from her mom's royal-watching phase several years ago.

Evidently, their mom had sent Brady off to Texas with more provisions than she'd provided Arabella. She seriously doubted Brady would have chosen to steal the towels.

"Earth to Arabella."

She looked up. "What?"

Harper was grinning. "Delivery for you inside."

Arabella frowned. She wasn't expecting anything. But she quickly mopped her wet legs and feet before going through the kitchen to the front room of the house.

Jay was sitting on the couch.

No wonder Harper had been grinning.

Arabella bunched the towel against her midriff but it didn't do diddly to squash the swirling squiggle inside her. "What are you doing here?" It was much more a demand than a welcome.

"Delivery." He reached into a paper bag at his feet and pulled out three jars of his grandmother's jam. He set them on the coffee table.

"That wasn't necessary."

"Maybe not." He pushed to his feet and her swirling squiggle squiggled faster. "But an explanation is." He stepped around the coffee table and only through sheer willpower was she able to keep her feet rooted where they stood when he reached out to lift a hank of wet, tangled hair from her shoulder.

Then she just shivered and was glad that she had the towel to clutch in front of her.

"It's been a complicated week."

She would *not* let herself be curious about the reasons why. Particularly when she wasn't convinced his words were anything more than an excuse. Though why he'd feel a need to make an excuse at all was beyond her comprehension.

His hand moved and she couldn't help her faint jerk, but he'd merely released her hair and was pushing his fingertips into his pockets.

Not reaching for her at all.

She finally took a step, turning away slightly. She tucked one end of the towel beneath her rear and perched gingerly on the arm of the sofa. She pressed the other end of the towel against her wet hair.

He paced to the end of the couch, stepping around the colorful tower of building blocks that the boys had built the night before. It was a miracle that Murphy hadn't knocked it down by now.

"My whole life is…was…complicated," he said in the void of her continued silence.

I think you should know that…

…my life is complicated.

Well, that at least fit. She lowered her hand to her lap. "What's so complicated about it?" Did he have a wife in the wings somewhere? A passel of children he'd run out on? "You work at a hotel in a town where nothing seems complicated."

His frowning gaze roved over her and she shivered again. She was too light on the curve-quality to go winning any wet T-shirt contests but she was nevertheless excruciatingly aware of how thin and wet her tank top was. And just how much it showed.

It was probably her imagination that his eyes seemed to catch for a moment on her chest, but her nipples tightened even more, anyway. "I'm getting the upholstery wet." She hopped off the couch. "I need to get another towel. You can find your way out." She bolted for the stairs, miraculously not falling over her feet in the process.

Once upstairs, she didn't retrieve another towel, though. She left her wet clothes in a heap on top of her empty laundry basket, dried off enough with the now-damp towel to pull a loose-fitting T-shirt dress over her head, and went back to the stairs.

She could see the living room was empty by the time she was halfway down the staircase. Well, good. He'd left.

She didn't want to hear more excuses anyway, right?

Twisting her hair into a wet rope over her shoulder— no, her shoulders were *not* slumping—she padded barefoot through the kitchen and back out to the patio.

"See, Jay?" Harper's voice greeted her. "I told you she wouldn't be long." She was setting out paper plates on the picnic table and she smiled at Arabella. "Jay's agreed to join us for dinner. Isn't that nice? We're ending up with a proper summer cookout here."

Chapter Six

*N*ice.

Arabella's teeth clenched but she summoned a smile. "Aren't we the lucky ones?" She started to turn right back around to escape. "I'll get the salad."

"Already have it," Harper told her.

Sure enough, the salad bowl was sitting in front of Jay.

"I'll get the drinks then," she said, annoyed that she sounded a little desperate. "Can't have a summer cook-out without libations. Milk for the boys, I know. Beer for everyone else?"

But Harper shook her head. "I'll just have milk, too." Her voice was casual. Too casual.

Arabella eyed her soon-to-be sister-in-law's down-bent head for a moment, then looked at her brother. Brady was focused on the burgers. Too focused.

The suspicion she'd been harboring since the twins had drawn that picture over a week ago warred with her consternation over Jay and won. So victoriously won, in fact, that in her effort to contain a broad smile, her gaze collided with Jay's. He, too, seemed to be struggling not to smile, though surely he couldn't understand *her* reason.

Warmth engulfed her and only being jostled by two wet, slippery little boys as they chased their ball under the table near Arabella's feet was enough to break the trance. Bad enough that Murphy was already under the table, too.

"Come on, guys. Get out from under there and finish drying off." She grabbed two towels and lightly flipped the ends under the table.

Tyler popped out and giggled madly when she dropped the towel over his head. "Can we have the radio?"

Toby popped out, too, and caught his towel midair. "Yeah, I wanna floss!"

Jay laughed. "Where'd you learn to do that dance?"

"Harper taught us."

At the sound of her name, Harper finally looked up. "Sorry, what was that?"

Arabella bit back another smile. She was convinced that Harper was pregnant. "The boys say you taught them how to do the floss. Which means we definitely need some music out here."

"Get that new Bluetooth speaker that Brady brought home the other day," Harper called after her as she went inside the house. "It's on the washing machine."

When Arabella went back outside a few minutes later with the beverages and the speaker, she was equally convinced that her brother knew about the pregnancy and was reeling. There was no other way to explain his uncommon silence, the tinge of pallor on his face and the totally abject adoration in his eyes when he looked at Harper.

She opened her streaming service on her phone, connected to the speaker and music from her favorite radio station back home in New York filled the patio as though she'd just hooked up a huge sound system. "Don't you love technology?" She had to raise her voice above the robust volume.

Jay's smile seemed to twist slightly. "Sometimes."

Brady finally looked away from Harper. "Geez, Bella. Neighbors?"

She made a face but turned down the volume. "This is *so* much better than Murphy's radio."

"The dog has a radio?"

Arabella didn't look at Jay. "Don't they all?"

"Only thing that keeps Murphy out of mischief when we're all gone is to leave the radio playing," Harper explained. "Don't ask how many pairs of shoes we sacrificed before we figured out the solution, though." She patted her lap and the dog hopped up. "Yes, you're still a good boy," she crooned, then broke into giggles because the boys were jumping around doing their surprisingly coordinated version of the floss, swinging their hips one way while their arms went the other.

"Auntie Bella," Toby called. "Come and dance."

She shook her head. "No, thanks. I'm not that co-ordinated!"

"I doubt that," Jay said.

"Go on," Harper encouraged. "You can do it."

"You're the one who taught them," Arabella reminded.

"Come on." Jay stood and held out his hand. "It's not that difficult."

Arabella eyed his hand, not wanting to be as tempted as she was.

Fortunately, Brady announced just then that the burgers were ready, which solved that. The ravenous boys sat up at the table, and with the exception of Jay sitting next to Arabella and the conversational gaps that kept happening whenever Brady and Harper looked at each other, it was just another normal night in the Radcliffe/Fortune household.

Arabella supposed it wasn't surprising that they weren't announcing anything—verbally, that was. Not with an outsider present in the form of Jay. On the other hand, she wanted to whoop and jump around the same way her nephews had been doing and hug her brother silly because nobody deserved that panicked look of awe and devotion more than he did.

After hamburgers, though, Harper and Brady disappeared inside for a few minutes, leaving Arabella and Jay alone with the boys, who'd gone back to racing around the yard with their boundless energy. The only difference now was that they'd progressed from dancing to brandishing twigs as if they were light sabers.

She rolled her empty beer bottle between her palms

in time to the beat coming from the speaker and eyed Jay from the corner of her eye. "So. Complicated week."

"Right." He sat forward and clasped his own empty bottle, his hands close to hers. "That."

He didn't say anything else, though, and she looked at him fully. Waiting. With a pained expression, he sat back again.

Frustration wore at her edges, helped along by the earworm song she detested that came on the radio just then. Again. Even from her beloved Buffalo station. "I hate that song," she muttered.

His beer bottle clattered onto its side and he righted it. "It *is* pretty annoying."

"Right? I mean the singer's got a nice enough voice but that song is played *way* too often." She fiddled with her phone and found another station, then took the empty bottles into the kitchen to toss in the recycling bin. Her brother and Harper were still MIA, so she grabbed a bag of marshmallows and went back outside. "Boys! Bring your light sabers over here."

Even though the sun was starting to set, they plainly saw the bag that she held and made a beeline from across the yard.

She checked the ends of their sticks for signs of obvious mud and, finding none, impaled a marshmallow on each one. "Hold it over the grill," she told them. "There's still enough heat from the coals to toast them. But stand right here." She positioned them as far from the kettle as possible. "Murphy, get back." She snapped her fingers and pointed behind her.

The dog interpreted that as "climb into my seat."

She let it pass and focused on her nephews. "All right, guys, no closer than right here or you might get burned. Remember when Toby burned his finger on the stove?"

They wore twin frowns of concentration mingled with wariness and she returned to her seat. The dog looked up at her, one maple-colored ear cocked forward hopefully.

Resigned, she scooped him up and sat down with him on her lap, holding the marshmallow bag out of his range.

"Cute dog."

"If you like a crooked-eared mongrel," she allowed, nuzzling the dog's head. "I guess he's okay." If she were brave, she'd tell Jay to either start talking or just leave. Instead, she shook the marshmallow bag. "Want one? I can get another stick for you. Or a proper long-handled fork if you're squeamish."

"I'm not squeamish, but I'll pass."

"Suit yourself." She plucked a marshmallow from the bag and shoved it in her mouth. She didn't need to toast a marshmallow to love a marshmallow. She leaned forward to toss the bag on the table and adjusted the volume on the speaker again.

"What kind of music *do* you like?" Jay gestured at the speaker. "It's obviously not Jett Carr."

Harper walked out onto the patio. "Isn't he that singer everyone is looking for?"

Brady was on her heels and he spotted the bag of marshmallows and aimed for it as quickly as Toby and Tyler had done. "Publicity stunt." He grabbed a handful and dragged his chair over to the boys. They were still waiting for their marshmallows to turn at least the faintest tinge of gold and they immediately climbed onto his knees. "Gotta be a publicity stunt."

Harper stood behind him, her hands on his shoulders. "Don't be so cynical." She kissed the top of his head. "When those marshmallows finish toasting, it's off to bed with you boys."

"What's cynical?" Brady jabbed the coals with the poker, spurring them along. "The guy puts out a music video that supposedly goes viral just when he seems to disappear off the planet? Too coincidental if you ask me. He's probably sipping margaritas sitting on some beach in the Bahamas, raking in the money."

Jay snorted. "There're more singers scraping by than sitting around raking in money."

"Says the hotel trainee," Arabella drawled. "What *did* you do before you started there? Aside from getting your private pilot's license, I mean."

He reached for the marshmallow bag, evidently unable to resist the lure, after all. "I wasn't flying drugs back and forth across the border if that's what you're wondering."

"He used to work at an insurance company in California," Brady said, then spread his hands when they all looked at him. "I checked his personnel file," he said defensively.

Jay was frowning. "What for?"

"I know exactly what for!" Arabella jabbed her finger in the air at Brady. Because he was an overprotective big brother who wanted to know more about "her crush," as he called it. "You had *no* business doing that."

"I had every business," Brady countered unapologetically. His gaze skated over Jay. "You were hired early on at the hotel. Before the balcony collapse. After that, they started doing deeper background checks on the employees."

"But the balcony was an accident!" Arabella wanted to throttle Brady.

Her brother's expression didn't change. "Tell the insurance company covering the hotel that." He looked at Jay again. "Security's reviewed the files for all of the original employees at this point, so don't take it personally."

"You're not security," Arabella said through her teeth. "You're the *concierge.*"

Jay waved his hand. His frown was gone. "He's right. No reason to take it personally. At Hotel Fortune, everyone pitches in where they're needed."

Arabella shook her head. "Stop making excuses for my brother, Jay. As usual, he's sticking his nose in where it doesn't belong."

"My marshmallow's on fire," Tyler suddenly wailed.

"It's fine," Harper assured calmly and showed him how to blow it out.

"But now it's black!"

"That's the best way," Jay told him. "Crispy and burnt a little on the outside and—"

"—gooey on the inside," Arabella finished. "That's my favorite way to eat toasted marshmallows." She addressed her nephew but from the corner of her eye, she saw Jay's dimple flash.

Somewhat mollified, Tyler subsided, leaning back against Brady's chest while he waited for the gooey marshmallow to cool enough to eat. Toby, on the other hand, had already eaten his marshmallow before it got to such an inflamed state and he was climbing onto Harper's lap now that she'd pulled up a chair along-side Brady's.

The afternoon of water play, sunshine and food had worked its magic and the twins were clearly getting sleepy. Even Murphy had abandoned her lap to curl around Brady's feet.

Arabella studied the picture they all made together. A family already. And now, she felt sure, with new ba-bies on the way as well.

She exhaled, feeling her annoyance with Brady drib-ble away. Most of it, at least.

"It's getting late." Jay pushed away from the table and stood. "And I should leave you folks to your eve-ning."

"You don't have to run off," Harper protested.

"I've got horses to feed and I usually check in on my grandmother every evening about now," he said, even though Arabella felt sure he did no such thing. If anyone did any "checking in" where Louella was concerned, it was probably Louella herself checking on Jay. "Thank you for the dinner, though." His gaze rested on Arabella. "I can't remember when I've enjoyed myself more."

Feeling a little like a slightly scorched marshmallow, Arabella followed him through the house to the front door. "Thank your grandmother again for the jam." The jars were still sitting on the coffee table in the living room. "I'm going to have to hide one away in my bedroom to keep it safe."

"You know where there's more." He stepped out onto the porch.

She suddenly didn't want him to go. "Insurance office. Really?"

He smiled slightly. "Really."

She wrinkled her nose. "That's as bad as a plastics manufacturer. That was my last job in New York."

"Surprised you were able to tear yourself away," he said dryly. "And insurance is boring only until you find yourself in need of it."

"Sounds like a slogan but I'll concede that point."

His smile widened. He suddenly lowered his head slightly toward hers. "Is your brother's fiancée pregnant?"

She gaped, and hearing a noise behind them in the kitchen, joined him on the porch so she could pull the door closed behind her. "You got that, too?" She pressed her hands over her mouth until she got control over her chortling. Then she grabbed his shirtfront urgently. "You can't say anything, though."

He covered her hands with his. "I promise."

Just that easily, her knees went weak. Thanks to her own riotous imagination, the last week and a half had been an emotional roller coaster where he was concerned.

Which meant she needed to stop overreacting at

his slightest touch and start acting like the adult she claimed to be.

She only needed to figure out how to think straight for more than ten seconds at a time whenever he touched her.

Simple enough, right?

"What's going on inside that beautiful head of yours?"

She froze. "What do you mean?"

His eyes roved over her face. His thumb brushed against the back of her hand. "I can practically see the wheels turning."

She made a face and shook her head. Her fingers finally listened to the frantic signals from her brain to release his shirt and she pulled her hands from beneath his. "The sunset," she lied. "Reminds me that I should get in there." She tilted her head toward the door behind her. "Make sure I'm set for tomorrow. Big day and all." She rubbed her hands together with false excitement. "Trainee program and such."

"You might like it."

"I'll like it fine as long as it pays my way out of the twin bed I sleep in upstairs here."

"Twin bed?"

She realized too late that was a topic better left alone. "It's a small bedroom." She fumbled behind her back for the door handle. "Maybe I'll see you around the hotel."

"Pretty sure you will."

"Well." She got the door open. "G'night."

"Arabella."

Her nerves went tight again. "Hmm?"

"It was a complicated week because of old business from California."

Her mouth dried. Business? Or relationship? "Insurance business?"

His lips compressed. "Not exactly."

Her stomach sank. Relationship then. Despite her little mental lecture about overreacting and overactive imaginations, she was as certain of that as she was about Harper being pregnant. "Are you married?"

His eyebrows yanked together. "*That's* what you're worried about?"

She didn't like feeling foolish any more than the next person did and she lifted her chin. "That's not an answer."

"No, I am *not* married," he said emphatically.

She felt a little like Tyler, then. Somewhat mollified. Somewhat reassured. But not entirely convinced. "People have lied about that before."

"You were involved with someone who was married?"

"Well, not once I learned the truth!" She cleared her throat and lowered her voice again. "It was just one date. We didn't—" Her words freeze-dried on her tongue when he curled his palms over her shoulders.

"Arabella." He exhaled and she felt the press of his fingertips through her knit dress. "One of these days, I hope you'll want to be Bella to me again."

Her knees went weak all over again.

"I am *not* married," he said softly. "Never have been married." His fingers squeezed her shoulders slightly. "The stuff from California is just…old…stuff.

An inconvenience. And it doesn't have anything to do with us."

Forget freeze-dried. Her mouth was suddenly watering and she swallowed hard. "Us? Is there an *us*?"

His fingers slipped her hair behind her ear before trailing along her jaw. "I think there could be." His thumb reached her chin. Rested right below her lower lip. "Don't you?"

The entirety of five months of fantasizing couldn't match that single moment standing on her brother's porch while the sunset beamed red and gold and orange behind Jay. "Yes," she breathed.

"Then let's just go one day at a time and see where it takes us. Hmm?"

She nodded jerkily. Every fiber of her soul wanted him to kiss her. But she'd asked for his kiss the last time and then he'd gone a whole week and then some before speaking to her. And then only because they'd run into each other at the hotel.

She didn't have the guts to ask again.

Not even when he ran his thumb slowly over her lip.

Her knees were already mush. The rest of her bones followed suit.

As if he knew it, he smiled slightly. "G'night, Arabella."

Then he turned and walked away.

Thankfully, the front door was hard and substantial. It held her up when she leaned weakly against it while she watched him climb into his truck parked at the curb. A moment later, his taillights were disappearing down the street.

"Call me Bella," she whispered soundlessly.

Then the door opened behind her and she fell back, knocking straight into Brady.

"What the hell're you doing?" He set her back onto her feet.

"Thinking that I can't wait to have a place of my own!"

"Not that again. You can't afford a place of your own."

"Not yet, but I will. And I'd think you'd be glad about that." She poked him in the chest. "Seeing how you're going to need the room I'm using."

"What for?"

She went around him toward the staircase. "Who for, would be more the point, wouldn't it?"

"Bella—"

"Don't worry." She started up the stairs. "I won't say a word more about it until the two of you are ready to announce it. But—" She shot him a look. "I just have to say one thing first."

"Just *one*?"

She let the sarcasm pass and smiled broadly. "You're already a heck of a dad, Brady. I can't wait to see you with a baby, too."

He frowned suddenly and seemed to find the newel post at the base of the staircase inordinately interesting. "What if I screw it up?"

She went back down a couple steps until she was at his eye-level. "Then you'll adjust and do it better. But you won't screw it up."

"How do you know?"

"Because I see Tyler and Toby." She gave him a quick, hard hug. "Gord and his wife knew what they were doing when they named you in their will as the boys' guardian."

"I can't imagine life without them now," Brady admitted huskily. "I wouldn't have moved to Rambling Rose if not for them. Would never have met Harper." He sniffed and gave an awkward laugh that just reminded her why he had always been her favorite brother. "Rambling Rose seems pretty lucky for those of the Fortune persuasion."

Arabella smiled and gave him another hug. "That's what I'm counting on, big brother."

Then, before he could make too big a deal out of that, she turned and hurried up the stairs.

"All right, then." Sybil smiled at Arabella the next morning. Instead of leaving instructions at the front desk for her, she'd met Arabella there in person and escorted her to housekeeping. "I'll leave you in Hallie's capable hands to get you started. She's an excellent floor supervisor so you couldn't have a better trainer. We'll check in again—officially—next week." Nursing her coffee cup, she walked out of the office.

Hallie, who'd turned out to be the same girl that Arabella had seen cleaning in the lobby the day before, cast a measuring look over Arabella before hunting through a shelving unit stacked high with folded shirts wrapped in plastic. She pulled one out and handed it to Arabella. "You can try it on in the night supervisor's office." She waved at a darkened doorway. "It's empty. Jordan quit a week ago and they haven't replaced her yet."

"Am I going to be fired if I admit I don't know what the night supervisor even does?"

Hallie laughed. "Night supervisor's responsible for all the public area cleaning that's done while everyone else is supposed to be sleeping and makes sure that all guest requests are answered after regular hours."

While she'd explained, Arabella had unzipped the plastic pouch and pulled out the T-shirt. It was black with the stylized Hotel Fortune logo embroidered in turquoise on the cap sleeve. "What about pants?" she asked as she headed toward the office.

"Those black jeans you're wearing are fine. Basically anything black is allowed except leggings." Hallie covered a yawn. "I'm going to grab a coffee. You want one?"

"I've already had two. Thanks, though." She stepped into the office and found the light switch on the wall before closing the door.

Arabella whipped her own blouse off her head and pulled on the T-shirt. It was identical to the one that Hallie wore, though Hallie's clung to her generous curves and Arabella's hung loosely from her shoulders.

She left the office again and went to the lockers lining one wall adjacent to the control desk where an unsmiling woman sat in front of a computer with a phone headset on her head. Her name was Beulah, which would have probably wiped a smile off of Arabella's face, too.

She'd already been assigned one of the lockers and

she stored her blouse inside along with her book bag
and lunch box that she'd crammed inside earlier. Hallie
still hadn't returned, so she pocketed her locker key and
wandered over to the bulletin board that was covered
with as many little scraps of paper as it was with large
employment posters.

She peered closer at one of the scraps—Roommate
Wanted—and made a mental note to check the board
again in a few weeks when she had her first paycheck
in the bank.

Two other young women, both wearing the turquoise-
accented T-shirts, came in. They stopped in front of
Beulah and signed in, then waited for the woman to
give them their assignments for the morning.

Hallie returned then and she, too, stopped in front of
Beulah. A few seconds later, she had a printed sheet in
hand and came back over to Arabella. "You learn quick
to stay on the right side of Beulah," she said under her
breath as she led Arabella out of the office. "She handles the scheduling for all the room attendants. Get on
her bad side and she'll either assign you enough rooms
to kill an elephant or else so few that you'll be looking for a second and third job just to make it through
to payday."

She led the way to the service elevator and they went
down to the second floor. There, Hallie unlocked a door
near the service elevator and rolled out one of the large
carts stored inside. She showed Arabella the chart on
the sheet that Beulah had given her, which indicated the
rooms that had been occupied the night before and of
those, which ones had already been vacated. "She coor-

dinates with the front desk and will update us throughout the shift as more rooms are vacated. These ones
that are circled—" she pointed out the rooms "—are
stayovers. Multiple night stays, so it's up to us to keep
an eye out for them. If the guest takes the newspaper
we leave outside the door overnight, we know they're
awake, for instance. If we see them leave for breakfast
or for the pool, that sort of thing, we can turn the room
while they're gone."

"How long does that take?"

"It's a little faster than a total turn. But on average
thirty minutes or so for a standard guest room, which
is what all of yours are today." As Hallie talked, she
was busy counting out linens and supplies and adding
them to the cart. "But it also depends on the state of the
room. Some guests are complete and utter slobs and it
takes longer." She held up the box of disposable gloves.
"Get used to these things," she said dryly.

Arabella smiled weakly.

Once Hallie judged the cart ready, they were off.

For the next four hours, Arabella reached and stretched
and squatted and crawled around, all for the purpose of
leaving each room Fortune-Hotel perfect. Linens were
changed. Every surface—from bathroom toilets to wall
switch plates—was left polished and sanitized.

By the time they took their lunch break, Arabella felt
like she'd been training for a marathon. "I never knew
cleaning could be so hard," she moaned after collapsing onto one of the molded plastic chairs at the round
table Hallie commandeered. "I've never wanted a foot
massage as badly as I do right now." She had to content

herself with curling and uncurling her toes inside her tennis shoes. For one, they were in a cafeteria so removing them was probably in poor taste. For another, if she took off her shoes, she wasn't entirely certain she'd be capable of putting them on again. "How long have you been doing this?"

Hallie set a glossy magazine on the table, followed by a can of soda. "Six years." She popped the top of the soda and unwrapped her sandwich. "I was working at a resort in Austin before I came here."

"What made you want to come to Rambling Rose?"

"What else?" Hallie looked wry. "A guy, naturally. Of course, two months after I'd already signed an apartment lease here in Rambling Rose, the creep gives me the 'it's not you, it's me' speech and heads off to Chicago with an old girlfriend."

"That stinks."

Hallie shrugged. "What're you going to do?" She winked. "Stink happens."

Arabella groaned humorously. "Terrible."

"Blame all the toilets I've cleaned in the last six years. I just hope things start picking up around this place."

"What do you mean?"

Hallie shrugged again. "The owners put on a good front, but the vacancy rate's still pretty high, even for Rambling Rose." She chewed her sandwich and flipped open her magazine. "What about you? What brought you to town?"

I think you should know that...

...there may be an "us."

"Family," Arabella said instead. "Three of my brothers had already moved here." She wasn't hiding the fact that she bore the Fortune name, but since Sybil hadn't introduced them using their full names, it just hadn't come up yet.

Hallie's dark eyes danced. "Any of 'em available?"

Arabella chuckled. "Only the two still living in Buffalo."

"Bummer. I haven't had a decent date in three months." Hallie nodded toward Arabella's barely-touched salad. "You're gonna get even skinnier if you keep bringing rabbit food like that and then don't even eat it. We're back on in ten minutes."

Arabella was starving, but the energy that it took to lift a fork seemed immense. "How many more rooms will we have?"

"Seven. We should have gotten six done this morning, but—"

"—I'm too slow," Arabella finished. She'd never thought it was that complicated to clean mirrors but she'd ended up leaving fingerprints that necessitated re-cleaning more often than not. And she was supposed to be ready to go out on her own without Hallie's help the following day.

"Get yourself a pair of these." Hallie held up the earbuds that were presently hanging loose around her neck. "You'll work faster when there's music going. Don't ask me why, but it always works."

"It better. Or I'll be lucky if I'm not fired on my second day."

"You're in the trainee program," Hallie said dryly.

"Once you're in the trainee program, you don't get fired."

"I'm only in the trainee program because they didn't know where else to put me. Is that something you wanted to do?"

Hallie shook her head. "Being a floor supervisor is enough for me." She was responsible for inspecting all the cleaned rooms before releasing them again to the front desk for use with another guest. "I'm not interested in getting into management. Too many reports to fill out. It's more fun sticking to room cleaning."

Arabella made a face. "I don't know about that."

"I even met a couple of celebrities in Austin who stayed at the resort." Hallie flipped her magazine around to show Arabella an image of a ridiculously handsome man with dark eyes and short dark hair. "This guy? Grayson?" She air-quoted the name. "He used to be big in rodeo. Now his Grayson Gear clothes are everywhere. I have a pair of his jeans. Do wonders for my butt. Anyway, he stayed at our resort a couple of times when I first started working there. All the gossip magazines said he was a real player, but I thought he was super nice. And he tipped great."

Arabella held her tongue. Hallie didn't realize that Grayson was one of "those Fortunes" any more than she knew Arabella shared the name, too. Adam and Kane had met him several years ago at that wedding in Paseo that her father was still complaining about. She knew Grayson had two identical brothers, but that was the extent of it. She hadn't met any of them herself. "Who else famous have you met?"

"Matt McIntyre. He's on a daytime soap." Hallie's eyes lowered to half-mast. "Sexy," she drawled. "But total slob." She closed her magazine and tapped an inset photo on the cover of a man with long dark hair. "Wouldn't mind cleaning *his* hotel room. He's so hot I'm not sure I'd even care if he *were* a slob."

Where in the World is Jett? was the photo's caption.

Arabella turned the magazine to get a better look. "You think he's hot? You can't even see what he really looks like. Not with those sunglasses and that beard."

"Seriously? He's got the bad-boy look nailed down."

Arabella shrugged. "My mom always says she wonders what guys are hiding behind their beards. I guess it's stuck with me." Jay's clean-shaven face danced in her mind.

"My mom says the same thing. But seriously, have you seen his music video? There's a reason why that video put his name on the map." Hallie fanned herself when Arabella shook her head. "Whether you like facial hair or not, you are missing out. Whenever I get depressed over my lack of a love life, I pull out my phone—" she did just that, pulling her cell phone out of her pocket to wave in the air "—and watch me some hottie Jett Carr crooning about his lost love and I am all good again."

Arabella couldn't help but laugh. "I'll keep that in mind." She steeled herself against her protesting muscles and stood. They packed up their lunch boxes and reported back to duty. Hallie went to inspect some of the other rooms also under her watch while Arabella went to the floor pantry and retrieved the cart. She replenished the linens and carefully began backing it through the doorway.

"How's the first day going?"

She jumped and turned around.

Jay was leaning against the wall watching her.

She forgot all about her sore feet and muscles. "It's going great." She waved her hand, taking in his appearance. "Back on food and beverage again?"

"Shows, does it?" He grinned. "Some corporate thing going on this afternoon. Using the banquet room and a couple breakout rooms. I'm on water and coffee detail. Tough gig."

She laughed softly. "Did you ever have to do a stint in housekeeping?"

"Yep." He straightened away from the wall. "After the first day, I sent flowers to my mother and grandmother for all the years they spent cleaning up after me."

She laughed again and finished pulling the cart into the hall. "I'd better get to it. I'm already behind schedule."

He glanced around the piled-high cart, then leaned closer to her. "Hot tub in the fitness center does wonders for helping with the aches and pains." His murmur next to her ear sent shivers dancing down her spine.

She turned her head slightly toward him. His green eyes mesmerized. "Fitness center is for guests."

"It closes at nine." His smile turned wicked. "And I have a connection who can get us in." Then he kissed her lightly and straightened away from her just in time to avoid being caught by Grace Williams, who stepped out of the service elevator.

"Good afternoon, Jay. Arabella. How's the first day going?"

Arabella couldn't have wiped away the smile on her face if she'd tried. "Better than I ever dreamed."

Chapter Seven

She met Jay outside the hotel that evening promptly at half-past nine.

Prompt, because she'd waited in her car around the corner to the hotel for fifteen minutes so she wouldn't look too eager.

Even though she was, in fact, very eager.

"Ready?"

She nodded and felt even more breathless when he took her hand in his and led her around the side of the hotel to the door they'd used that day in January. Although she knew the balcony had been rebuilt since then, Arabella couldn't help looking up at it a little warily as they passed it.

Jay noticed. "It's been inspected a couple dozen times over by now." He knocked twice on the door.

"I know." Even the bushes that had been growing beneath the balcony had been replaced. "Kane and Brady have both talked about it."

The door opened and Mariana peeked out.

Arabella eyed the woman with surprise, but Mariana just gave a quick look around as Jay pulled Arabella through the door and into the fitness center.

"Thanks, Mariana." Jay kissed the older woman's cheek. "You're a peach."

"Sweet and juicy," Mariana quipped, giving a broad wink. "Just be sure to get out of here before the night crew comes in to clean at eleven." Then whistling tunelessly, she hurried out of sight.

There really was no need for Jay to hold Arabella's hand as they made their way through the well-equipped room. Dim lights lit the perimeter, illuminating the way well enough.

But Arabella didn't tug her hand free and Jay didn't let go of it either, not until they reached the opposite end of the space and he pointed at the sign on the door. Women's Lockers. "You have your suit?"

She patted her trusty book bag. "Even brought a towel of my own. Just in case."

"Hot tub is through there." Jay pointed to an archway. "Meet you there."

Her eagerness reached such a peak she was possibly in danger of passing out. She nodded and hurried into the women's locker room and reminded herself to breathe again. She quickly changed into her swimsuit and pulled her hair up into a high ponytail. Then she wrapped the towel she'd stolen from Brady's around her waist, bundled her sundress and undies into her book bag and slung the strap over her shoulder.

Heart pounding, she peered around the edge of the locker room door, and squealed out loud when Jay moved. She pressed her hand to her chest and slipped through the doorway. "For a second there, I thought we'd been caught!"

His teeth flashed. "Nothing like the fear of getting caught to keep things exciting."

She swallowed hard, not certain how to take that particular innuendo.

He'd changed out of his jeans into a pair of black-and-gray board shorts, and his white shirt hung unbuttoned over his chest. It was nearly impossible to keep her eyes from straying to the strip of flesh showing. It seemed as rude as guys who just stared at a girl's chest. Or in her case, her lack of one. "What if we *do* get caught?"

"Don't know," he admitted. "Hasn't happened yet. Pretty sure *you'd* be safe, though."

Yet.

He'd done this before. Of course he had. "Why would I be safe?"

He winked. "You've got the right name."

"But it wouldn't save me from embarrassing Brady."

"Want to sneak back out?"

Arabella didn't hesitate. Not even figuring she wasn't the first girl he'd brought there was enough to sway her. "No."

His smile widened. "Good." He closed his hand over her elbow and drew her toward the archway.

The in-ground hot tub was oval shaped and large enough to accommodate at least a dozen people. It was surrounded by several mesh lounge chairs and several potted plants that looked real. The ceiling overhead was vaulted and with the lights low the way they were, gave the impression of being open-air even though it really wasn't.

Jay let go of her and shrugged off his shirt, pitching it at one of the chairs as he passed it on his way to the control panel. A second later, the hot tub lit up from an underwater light and the surface began churning. He joined her where she was still hovering near the chair. She'd hung her bag off the back of it and glanced around, because wondering if there were security cameras felt safer than getting caught ogling his bare torso.

She didn't see any cameras but maybe they were just more discreetly placed here than they were in the rest of the hotel. "How many times *have* you done this?"

"Twice before." He'd been wearing tennis shoes with no socks and he toed them off before stepping to the edge of the churning water. "Stepped wrong a while back and sprained my ankle." He stood on one foot and rotated the other. "Whirlpool helped." He stepped down onto the first step and the water swirled around his calf.

"I sprained my wrist once and the doctors put me in a sling for more than a week," she said absently. He was slim but that only made the V from waist to broad shoulder even sharper. And slim, she realized, didn't mean undefined. He was practically a textbook study in musculature and sinew. He had a small tattoo near his shoulder blade that she couldn't quite make out.

"Didn't bother with a doc. Not the first time I've sprained something. I know the drill."

He glanced over his shoulder at her, catching her in the act of squinting at him. His eyebrow rose. "Ready to take the plunge?"

She could have fanned herself in the same way that Hallie had done during lunch.

There was nothing seductive about her utilitarian tankini. The only thing it had going for it was the jaunty blue-and-white stripes of the halter top that supposedly gave the impression of curves where there were none. Feeling as self-conscious as if she were stripping down to her undies, she pulled the towel from around her hips and dropped it on the chair. He hadn't brought one, she realized. "Is it hot?"

His lips tilted. "Very." His gaze never left her face as she gingerly dipped her toe in the water. "The water's pretty warm, too."

She hoped he'd blame her flush on the steam rising from the churning water.

His smile widened and he took another step down into the water. "Come on. I remember what a workout it is cleaning rooms. Fitness industry's missing out on a whole trend if you ask me."

She glanced over her shoulder. It was a fine time to start having reservations. "Are you sure we're not going to get caught?" No matter what he thought, having the last name Fortune didn't mean they had a pass on following the rules of the hotel.

"You *are* getting cold feet."

"No, I'm not!" She made a face because it was so

obvious to them both that she was. "No," she said more firmly.

"I've known Mariana since I was a kid. She's not going to tell a soul about this," he said calmly. "And the only cameras down here are in the hallways that head to the lobby in one direction and Roja in the other. I've done my research on that score. I know where they're all located."

"The advantage of working in every department, I guess."

"Something like that. And nobody should be here until the cleaning crew." He held out his hand. "You heard Mariana. Time's tickin', sweetheart. So what's it going to be?"

She looked at his palm extended to her. Even in the dim light she could see the ridge of calluses across his fingertips.

She swallowed hard and quickly placed her hand in his. His fingers closed around hers, steadying her as she stepped down into the water.

It was like being encased in comfort and she wasn't entirely sure if that was owed to Jay's hand clasping hers or the steaming, churning pool. Either way, she couldn't stop a heartfelt groan. Nearly all of her nervousness floated away. Magical. "Oh, yessss."

"Had a feeling you'd like it." Jay didn't let go of her hand until she stood waist deep in the water. Then he moved toward one end of the oval and sat, stretching out his arms on the travertine coping behind him. The water bubbled around his shoulders. "Jets are stronger over here." He patted the curved tile.

She walked toward him and the tub got deeper toward the center of it, but never so deep that she couldn't reach the bottom and still keep her chin above water. He'd said he'd used the hot tub because of a sprained ankle, but she still couldn't help wondering if he'd been alone or not.

It was the only fly in this heavenly ointment.

She sat down near him, keeping a circumspect arm's length between them, and pretended not to see the way his lips twitched. Unlike him, though, she slumped down as far as she could in the water until the bubbles flitted over her chin, tickling her nose as they popped and spit. "I haven't had a bath since I left Buffalo," she said. "Well, *showers* obviously," she qualified hastily.

"No tub at your brother's place?"

"Yes, but it's usually filled with the twins' bath toys. And the hot water only goes so far."

"Gran has a big old claw-foot thing in the middle of her peach orchard."

Arabella turned slightly toward him and felt the thrum of water pound against her side. She arched slightly, relishing the massage. "What does she grow in it?"

"Bubbles?" His eyes smiled. "She takes baths in it. Heats the hot water in a big old barrel on wheels with a propane burner that my grandfather rigged up when I was still a kid. Sort of like those things that people use these days to fry a turkey. Only a helluva lot bigger."

She bent her elbow on the coping and propped her head on her fingertips. "Have to admit, I have a hard time envisioning that."

His chuckle was low and deep and as much a physical pleasure as the hot, bubbling water was. "Wish I had a hard time envisioning it," he said. "Accidentally discovered her using it once when I was a teenager. Couldn't bring myself to visit her again for a few years. Love my grandmother. Did not want to see her lolling around in a bathtub in the middle of a peach orchard."

She laughed softly and sank deeper in the water again. Her ponytail dragged in the water, floating like a coiled rope between them. "Your grandmother's amazing."

"Always has been. Just took me getting old enough to appreciate it."

"Is your mom like her? I know you said she'd rather your grandmother move to Houston, but—" She broke off. He was already shaking his head.

"Mom is nothing like her mom. But that's okay." He shrugged. "I'm nothing like my dad. Doesn't mean there's a lack of love because of it."

"Preferred selling insurance over teaching math, hmm?"

"I didn't sell insurance." He lowered his arms into the water and his fingers toyed with her ponytail. "I was working on becoming an actuary."

She twisted a little more, centering the waterjet against a fresh ache. "Doesn't that entail like *all* math?"

"Math. Statistics." He suddenly rotated until his legs floated straight out toward the middle of the hot tub and his arms were stretched out, hands cupping the coping as he faced her.

"Not so different than your dad, then."

He ducked his chin in the water almost to his nose and in the dim light, his green eyes looked dark above the water. She could still see the laughter in them, though. Especially since the arm's-length distance between them had somehow been reduced by half.

He lifted his chin. "I hated it. Spent all that time studying actuarial science in school and went straight into the field, only to detest every minute of it. The second I could afford to, I got out of it."

"What'd you really want to do? Be a pilot?"

He bent his arms, pulling himself closer to the edge. Closer to her.

Still floating. But closer.

"Not necessarily."

"And now you're here. Hotel Trainee Cross."

"So are you, Hotel Trainee Fortune. At least it offers a lot of variety." His expression shifted and she couldn't help wondering if he even realized it. "Expectations are straightforward," he said flatly. "Honest day's wage for an honest day's work. Nobody trying to make you into something you're not."

"Plus an illicit hot tub session now and then."

His face lightened again just as she'd hoped, and his hands inched closer to her shoulders. "Illicit." His deep drawl gave the word an added nuance.

She sucked in a breath that was too redolent of chlorine to be particularly helpful. She turned until her spine was in front of the jet again and suddenly found Jay floating directly in front of her, his hands on either side of her shoulders.

"That's a great word." His gaze roved over her face,

seeming to rest on her mouth. He drifted closer. "Evocative," he murmured, just loud enough to be heard over the bubbles and jets.

"I...like words." She moistened her lips that, impossibly, felt dry despite the water all around them.

"They have a power," he agreed. He ducked his chin in the water again and closed the distance even more.

She felt him kiss the point of her shoulder and then the curve of her neck. Her head fell back, resting against the tile. She watched him from beneath her lashes. "Who else have you snuck in here like this?"

A quick line came and went between his dark eyebrows as if the question surprised him. "Only you."

She wanted to believe him more than she wanted her next breath. The jetted water seemed to be pushing her spine away from the wall until her legs floated upward and glanced against his. Lightly. Tantalizingly.

He let go of the wall with one hand and lowered it to the seat beside her.

Then he kissed the point of her collarbone and her head fell back a little more, only this time the tiled wall wasn't behind her. It was just swirling water that seemed to bear her torso upward toward his.

Or maybe that was his hand, now splayed flat against the small of her back beneath the tank-length top of her swimsuit. They were both floating now, anchored only by his one hand on the edge of the pool.

His legs slid against hers and she trembled when her abdomen brushed against the hard barrier of his chest. His head dipped again into the water and she felt his mouth brush her skin right at the deepest V of her halter top. He raised his head again. "Yes or no?"

She realized his hand was at the tie behind her neck. "Yes, please," she exhaled the words.

His lips curved and she felt a faint tug. Then the jaunty blue-and-white stripe started to float away from her shoulders. She was in no danger of losing the top altogether. The tie merely held up the bra portion. And regardless of her insecurities where her slight figure was concerned, when his head dipped back into the water to catch a rigid nipple between his lips, some portion of her reeling sensibilities decided they were just about right for this particular moment.

For this particular man.

Borne on his arm and the swirling water, Arabella stared blindly up at the skylike ceiling and slid her hands through his wet hair. Feeling him dip and taste, dip and kiss, dip and delight.

Her legs tangled with his and her ponytail swirled around them and she hovered there in a suspension of pleasure, oblivious to everything except him.

I think you should know that...

He jerked his head up suddenly and swore. With a splash, his hand grabbed hers and her feet hit the bottom of the pool.

"Wha—"

"Someone's out there," he said under his breath. He was practically propelling her right out of the hot tub and she stubbed her toe on the step as she gained her footing and yanked at her top.

In one fell swoop, he grabbed up his shirt and her

towel and their shoes while she snatched the strap of
her book bag, upending the lightweight chair in the process. The racket it made echoed against the travertine
and Jay didn't even stop at the control panel to kill the
hot tub jets. Their feet slapped wetly on first tile, then
soundlessly on carpet as he pulled her around a corner
and into an alcove next to a large metal ice machine.

"Who was it?"

"Sshh." He cupped her head against his chest and
edged deeper into the alcove. There wasn't a lot of space
for their bodies and it was so dark she couldn't see. Only
a slight gleam of light reflected over the stainless steel
of the ice machine.

Adrenaline rushing through her veins, she slid her
arms around him and huddled close despite the bundle of shirt and towel caught between them. His heart
beat as fast as hers. She knew because she could feel it
pulsing against her cheek. When his hand drifted upward and grazed her bare breast, desire cramped hard
inside her. Until she realized he was just pulling up the
straps of her halter to tie it behind her neck once more.

She pressed her forehead against him and suddenly
wanted to laugh. And not being able to do so exacer-
bated the need to.

When the ice machine suddenly vibrated loudly and
belched out a fresh batch of cubes somewhere in its
metal innards, a muffled snort escaped, despite her best
efforts to contain it.

She felt his chest rumble with silent laughter, too.
His head dipped and his lips brushed her ear. "Sshh."

She clung to him even more tightly, plastering her

mouth against the bulge of his biceps. His rumbling silent laughter increased and he twisted slightly, picking her up at the waist and pressing her back against the narrow wall behind her. "Sshh," he murmured again and then kissed her.

She forgot about laughing, then.

She twined her arms more tightly around his shoulders and her calf knocked into the ice machine as she mindlessly wrapped her legs around his hips.

His weight against her was heady. The rub of his tongue against hers delicious. When his head lifted too soon, she slid her fingers into his hair and pulled his head back. "Don't go," she said against his mouth.

He let out a sound, equally muffled. Half exultant. Half frustrated.

All perfect to her ears.

He dragged his mouth from hers, running it along her cheek. "It's the cleaning crew," he whispered. "Hear the vacuum?"

She hadn't. Not above her pounding pulse and the ice maker and the rush of music inside her head whenever his mouth touched her.

"Stay here." He disentangled himself from her. "There's a security camera in the hall around that corner. So stay *here*." He edged out from their hiding hole.

If there was a camera, why was he leaving?

She didn't have a chance to voice the question, because he was already gone.

She exhaled deeply and unwound her book bag strap from her forearm where it had twisted around without her notice. She slid it over her head crosswise then stuffed his shirt inside. She was cautiously feeling around the floor with her foot for the towel that she'd dropped when he returned.

He grabbed her arm. "We've got to be fast." He pulled her back around the way they'd come, then he pushed her head down while they dashed—bent nearly in half—through the weight-lifting section of the fitness center. The lights were all turned on now, clearly illuminating them if they were noticed. His route made little sense to her, but there was no time to argue. Not with the way he dragged her along after him.

On the other side of the room, one person was using the big vacuum, another was polishing surfaces and a third wielded some sort of wand that emitted a fine cloud over the workout equipment.

None of them so much as glanced their way, not even when Jay pushed open the same one-way door they'd used to enter.

They slipped through, and he held on to the edge of the door with his fingertips, gingerly letting it close with a soft *snick*.

As soon as it was closed, Arabella dropped her bag on the ground and started laughing. "I can't believe they didn't see us!"

Jay's laughter was deep and rich, too. His hand curled around the back of her neck and he pressed a fast kiss to her lips. "So much for a therapeutic soak." He grabbed her hand. "The pool's free game, though. What do you say?"

"I dropped my towel. And you don't even have one."

In answer, he grabbed the strap of her bag and pulled

her around the side of the hotel to where the pool was located. "Good grief," he said as he hefted the bag. "What're you carrying in here?"

"Notebooks."

"Full of what?" He curled his arm as if he was weightlifting. "Feels like you're carting around a couple of my grandmother's garden binders."

"Nothing so productive." She rubbed her nose, feeling suddenly self-conscious. "Just stuff I…write."

"Journals?"

Sure. That was close enough. She made a sound he took for agreement.

"Dear Diary." Beneath the swag of lights crisscrossing high atop the pool area, Jay's eyes crinkled at the corners. "Tonight, I nearly got caught by—"

She reached up and pressed her hand over his mouth. "Stop!"

She felt his smile against her palm and her stomach swooped. She should have felt chilly in her damp swimming suit. Instead, she felt warm from the inside out.

She pulled her hand away and turned to face the pool again.

Even at that hour there were a half-dozen people in the water playing a noisy game of water volleyball. A few more guests lounged on the chaises surrounding it. They all had drinks in their hands, served up from the bar situated next to a small dais where a trio of musicians played live music. On the other side of the musicians sat another table with pale blue hotel towels stacked on it.

Jay gestured. "See? Towels."

He was impossible to resist even when he was being impossible. When he was grinning at her the way he was now? It was a lost cause altogether. "Why would the hot tub be reserved only for guests but the pool isn't?"

He shrugged. "The hot tub accommodates twenty people and the pool handles a lot more? I don't know. Ask your brothers. They're more likely to know the answer to that than me."

She made a face. "If my brothers find out I'm here with you swimming, you're going to regret all of this."

His lips twitched. "Pretty sure I'm not."

I think you should know that…

…I'm the perfect guy for you.

His confidence was intoxicating. "Swimming pool it is." She stepped off the paved pathway and cut across the grass diagonally toward the nearest chaise lounge. She dropped her bag on it and kicked off her sandals and slid into the water.

In comparison to the night air, it felt warm and welcoming. Not quite at the level that the hot tub had, but it was still wonderful.

She expected Jay to follow her in, and when he didn't, she slicked her hair out of her eyes and looked back at him. "Well?"

He was no longer smiling. Instead he was staring fixedly toward the bar where a tall man was watching them.

Then the man walked toward Jay and she saw the glint of a badge on his belt.

That's when she placed him. He was the officer at the municipal building.

Not officer. Detective. Detective Teas.

"Cross," he said as he stopped in front of Jay.

"I've already answered all your questions," Jay said flatly. "I don't know what else you want from me."

"I'm not here to question you again," the detective said. "Not yet, anyway."

Arabella frowned. She was barely aware of the way Jay and the police detective had drawn the attention of the guests nearest them as she started up the steps. The night air no longer felt hot and balmy, the water no longer soft and warm.

Jay's face tightened even more. He looked hard and nearly unrecognizable. "Then what—"

The detective raised his hand. "There's been an incident. With your grandmother."

Water splashed as Arabella scrambled out of the pool. She slid her hand into Jay's.

He didn't spare her a glance, but his fingers closed tightly around hers. "What kind of incident?"

The detective looked suddenly uncomfortable. "She and Mabel Forsythe got into it over at Provisions. Afraid they were both hauled in for—" He broke off, grimacing.

Arabella hugged Jay's arm to her. "For what?"

"Public brawling," the detective finally said, looking pained. "She's gonna need you to bail her out."

Chapter Eight

"Well? Anything you have to say for yourself?" Jay peered through the bars of the cell. It was empty except for his grandmother. An identical cell next to it held Mabel Forsythe.

Both women sat on the hard benches that lined the perimeter of each cell. They had their backs to one another and their arms folded across their chests.

At his grandmother's stoic silence, he sighed and rubbed his fingers through his hair. "If Mom finds out about this—"

"She'd better not," his grandmother warned. "I keep your secrets, you better be prepared to keep mine." She suddenly looked over her shoulder at the woman sitting behind her. "And if I hear you've been spreading tales, Mabel Forsythe, I'll hunt you down and finish what we started."

Mabel looked fit to spit.

"She didn't mean that, Mrs. Forsythe," Jay soothed.

"The hell I didn't!"

He eyed her. "Threats aren't going to help the situation here, Granny. If you want me to post bail—" he'd already done it, but she didn't need to know that "—then you're going to have to explain yourself."

She harrumphed and folded her arms again, looking prepared to sit there until kingdom came.

If his grandmother wouldn't talk, then maybe Mabel would.

He moved past his grandmother's cell—just *thinking* those words made something inside his head clang painfully—and stopped in front of Mabel. "What about you, Mrs. Forsythe? Do you want to explain what went on over at Provisions tonight?" Teas had already told him that Mabel's daughter-in-law was driving in from Dallas to post bail, but she would be hours getting there yet. "I might be willing to look at paying your bail if—"

"You'd damn well better not," Louella said furiously. "You'll have your grandpa rolling over in his grave if you spend one red cent on that woman."

That woman had risen to her feet, too, wrapping her arthritic fingers around the cell bars as if she were prepared to push them apart Samson-style. "Herb would still be alive if he'd married me instead of you."

"You miserable—" Louella reached through the bars and yanked on Mabel's hair, pulling the glossy brown coif askew to reveal the sparse white hair beneath.

"Ladies!" Detective Teas strode into the holding area and his bark echoed around the cement walls. "And believe me. Right now I'm using that term generously." He glared at the women. "Keep it up and I'll keep you both here all night. Is that what you want?"

"What I *want* is for her to admit she stole my strawberry jam recipe fifty years ago!" Mabel tugged her wig into place with a sharp jerk. "Just like she stole Herbert twenty years before that."

"Herb never gave you the time of day and you know it, Mabel. And that recipe was my mother's before it was mine. I have it written down in her handwriting in my recipe card box."

"Lies."

"And *you* can't cook your way out of a pot of stone soup! That's why your Donny, God rest his poor soul, kept coming over to eat dinner with Herb and me!"

Teas sent Jay a weary look. "They've been at it like this since we brought them in." He unlocked Louella's cell and pulled open the door. "Sooner you get her out of here, the sooner we'll all have a little peace and quiet." He beckoned. "Come on now, Mrs. O'Brien."

His grandmother gave Mabel a goading smirk as she sauntered out of her cell. "I'm sure your daughter-in-law will be here soon. We all know how *fond* she is of you." She glanced up at Jay as they followed the detective out of the holding area. "Only reason Donny Jr. moved to Dallas was because Charlene refused to live in the same town as his mama." She didn't bother keeping her voice down and Mabel obviously heard, because her shrieks followed them until the heavy door to the holding area clanged shut behind them.

"Here." Teas handed Jay a sheaf of papers. "Judge has ordered your grandma and Mrs. Forsythe to keep one hundred yards away from each other until their hearing's scheduled." He focused on Louella. "Ma'am, you understand that if either one of you breaks that order, you're both gonna end up in a cell for a mite longer than a couple hours?"

"Might be worth it," Louella grumbled, "just to make her suffer."

"You'd suffer, too," Jay pointed out. He gestured toward Arabella, where she sat on a bench looking worried. "Now go over there and say hello to Arabella. She's the one who drove me here."

"I don't appreciate being spoken to as if I'm five," his grandmother said thinly.

"Then don't act as if you're five," he returned.

Her lips compressed and she turned away from him, marching across the room to Arabella.

Jay blew out a breath and looked back at the detective. Even though he'd spent the last few weeks loathing the other man, he knew that Teas could've made this situation a lot more difficult. He extended his hand. "Thank you for your help tonight."

Teas looked resigned. He shook Jay's hand. Firmly. But briefly. "First time I've ever arrested two women of their…ah…"

"Maturity?"

"Afraid maturity wasn't one of the things on display." He tucked his hands in the pockets of his jacket. "Do your best to make sure she follows the judge's order," he advised.

"I will." Jay started to turn away, but looked back at the detective. "How *did* you know where I was tonight, anyway?" He hadn't seen his grandmother since morning. She hadn't known where he'd be, any more than he'd known she was going to have dinner at Provisions with her supposed friend Mabel Forsythe.

"You're not going to like the answer." Teas glanced past him.

Arabella and Jay's grandmother were sitting together now. Jay wasn't sure if the fact that they looked deep in discussion worried him more or less than whatever Teas was going to answer. "Regardless. I still want the answer."

Teas capitulated with a small shrug. "We've had you under surveillance since the day I brought you in for questioning."

Of all the things Teas could have said, that was the last thing Jay expected.

His jaw tightened until it ached. "Surveillance," he said through his teeth when he could finally form a word that didn't involve the furious outrage bubbling inside him. "You're wasting a helluva lot of time and taxpayer dollars."

Teas pursed his lips. "Not so sure 'bout that. You're hiding something, Mr. Cross. There're just too many gaps in your timeline for my taste. And I'm the kind of detective who tends to follow up on that sort of thing."

Jay pinched the bridge of his nose. "My private business has nothing to do with Hotel Fortune's misfortunes."

The detective was unswayed. "Sounds like the name of a bad song, Mr. Cross."

Jay returned the man's stare. If the cop was looking for a reaction, he'd wait a long while.

And then he felt Arabella touch his arm. "Jay."

He finally looked away from Teas.

"It's really late," she murmured softly. "I think your grandmother's exhausted."

He exhaled sharply. Of course she was exhausted. Once Jay and Arabella had arrived at the station, it had taken a few more hours before the bail had been processed. And now, it was nearly 3:00 a.m.

He didn't exchange another word with Teas as he went to collect his grandmother from the bench. Exhausted she might be, but the only evidence of it was in her eyes. He still took her arm as they left the municipal building.

Arabella led the way, glancing over her shoulder periodically as if she were nervous.

Police stations probably had that effect on most law-abiding citizens.

She'd changed out of her swimsuit into a swingy yellow sundress before they'd driven to the station. Jay, on the other hand, was wearing the wrinkled shirt she'd pulled from her canvas purse and a pair of old cowboy boots he'd fortunately had stored in his truck.

God only knew where he'd managed to drop his tennis shoes during their escape from the fitness center.

The end result, though, was that Arabella looked like

a ray of sunshine and he looked like an advertisement for Menswear Don't.

At least the only ones following him around these days were the cops who didn't care what he looked like so long as they kept trying to link him to the balcony collapse.

"I didn't tell Detective Teas to find you," his grandmother said as they left the building through the front doors. "So don't blame me that you had to come to my rescue."

"And what were you planning to do if I *hadn't* shown up?"

"I have friends. I could have arranged the bail and you'd have never been the wiser."

Jay snorted. "Worked out well for you, didn't it, then?" And it meant he needed to thank the detective for yet one more thing, he thought blackly.

"Don't take that tone with me," Louella said.

He scrubbed his hand down his face as they stopped next to Arabella's sedan.

His grandmother looked confused. "Where's your truck?"

Jay's eyes met Arabella's over the roof of the car as she unlocked the driver's-side door. And despite everything—the frustration of not being able to kiss her as long as he'd wanted, the shock of his grandmother's arrest and the fury of knowing the cops had been following him and he hadn't even noticed—he couldn't help smiling.

"Dead battery," he said.

* * *

"Well?" Brady tossed a towel patterned with a distinctively ugly pink crest on his desk and gave Arabella a look. "Anything you have to say for yourself?"

She rubbed the pain in her temple and held back a yawn with no small amount of effort.

After getting Jay and his grandmother out to their place and driving back into Rambling Rose, it had been nearly four in the morning when she'd finally crept into her twin-size bed at Brady's house. She'd been so tired, she hadn't even spent her usual hour writing. "Like what?"

Brady had made no secret that he was annoyed with her. That had been plainly obvious when he'd summoned her to his office in the middle of her cleaning shift.

"Like the fact that this—" Brady shook the towel in her face "—was found next to the ice machine on the first floor last night by the night crew."

"It's just a towel, Brady."

"It's a towel from my own damn linen closet, Bella. And I sure didn't leave it there."

"Actually, it's a towel from *Mom's* linen closet. Do you remember when she ordered them? How appalled Dad was that she'd spent hard-earned money on a set of towels just because they had a royal crest on them?"

His expression told her plainly that he appreciated neither her irony nor the little trip down memory lane.

"Okay, fine," she huffed. "I was using the hot tub after hours last night, okay?"

"Alone?"

"Of course I was alone," she bluffed. "Every muscle in my body hurt after cleaning all day and—"

He thumped a pair of men's tennis shoes on his desk. "These were with the towel. Your feet suddenly grow about four sizes?"

Arabella pressed her lips together.

"How'd you get into the fitness center?"

"Does it matter?"

Brady grimaced. He sat back in his chair and tugged at his tie as though it was suddenly choking him. "Yes, it matters."

"Why? Look, we weren't doing anything terrible." Not entirely. "Jay just—"

Brady swore. "Jay *Cross*?"

She shoved out of her chair because sitting in front of Brady's desk the way she was felt a little too similar to being called in front of the principal. And those elementary school days were long past. "So what if it was?"

"You snuck in the house at four this morning!"

She jabbed her finger in his direction. "Stop acting like Dad."

"Stop acting like an irresponsible teenager, then!"

She gaped at him, feeling stung. "I'm a grown woman, Brady. If I choose to stay out all night with a guy it is my business. Not yours."

He rose and planted his hands flat on his desk. "It's my business when it's under my roof."

She slapped her hands on the desk, too, going practically nose to nose. "Well, we know the solution to that, don't we?"

"Ahem."

They both looked over to see Grace Williams standing in the doorway to Brady's office.

As furious as Brady was with Arabella, she was somewhat surprised to see amusement in the other woman's eyes.

"Brady, the camera crew is here to get started on filming the new commercial. Would you mind getting them set up? I'm afraid I have to deal with that other matter." Her eyebrows rose slightly as if she were speaking in code meant only for Arabella's brother.

Brady looked at Arabella. "We're not finished with this discussion," he warned.

"Damn straight we're not," she muttered under her breath after he and Grace had left the office again.

Arabella plucked Jay's tennis shoes from the desk and left, too.

She knew that he wasn't on duty that day. A happy coincidence for him since he needed to deal with getting his truck battery changed. Unlike hers, his hadn't responded to charging, which was why she'd ended up driving him to the police station the night before.

On one hand, she was grateful that Jay had seemed glad to accept her help. On the other hand, she was left with more questions about him than ever before.

What had Teas said when he'd appeared at the pool?

I'm not here to question you again. Not yet, anyway.

Question Jay about what?

Even if there'd been an opportunity to ask him what the police detective had meant, Arabella hadn't been brave enough to voice it.

She could go toe to toe with Brady all day long and

twice on Sundays if she had to. But ask Jay one simple question?

I think you should know that...

...I'm wanted by the police.

She shook her head sharply. "Ridiculous," she muttered and reached out to wave her badge over the service elevator call button.

"The first sign of genius is talking to yourself."

Startled, Arabella dropped the shoes as she whirled to see Mariana walking toward her.

"I'm sorry, hon." Mariana's brows pulled together as she bent over to pick up the shoes. "Didn't mean to scare you all to bits and pieces." She handed her the tennis shoes.

"Thanks." Arabella hugged them to the front of her black T-shirt. "And you didn't. I was just, uh, just preoccupied."

Mariana tilted her head slightly as if listening for sounds of the elevator's movement. "These days, everyone here seems preoccupied."

"Why is that?" Arabella flushed at the urgency in her tone.

"Oh." Mariana waved a dismissive hand. "Nothing seriously bad has happened here in the last few months. Instead, we just have these little annoyances that keep happening." She obviously read Arabella's obliviousness. "You know. The elevators breaking down so often. The glitches in the reservation system and the security system that's registering doors as locked when they're not and vice versa."

Arabella wondered if the security system was Grace's "other matter" that needed her attending.

"Leaves a person waiting for the other shoe to fall." Mariana's gaze drifted to the tennis shoes Arabella was clutching. "No pun intended."

The service elevator rumbled softly and a moment later the door opened. Arabella gestured for Mariana to go first.

"Thank you, dear." Mariana waited until Arabella was inside the car, too, and pushed the button for the second floor. "Now, tell me how you and the Jet-pack are doing."

"Jet-pack?"

"Jay," Mariana said, as if it were obvious. "That's what his grandpa always called Jay when he was visiting. Boy had so much energy it was like he was pumped up on jet fuel. Lord, the way he'd run around out at the market. Mischievous as hell. Always wanting to sweep up inside my food truck just so he could snitch a lemon tart when I wasn't looking." She grinned. "Used to figure he'd end up flying jets. Instead, he heads off to California when he was just a young pup and was gone for so long—" The doors opened again and she stepped out. "Goes to show you never can tell," she said just before the doors started sliding closed.

Arabella hurriedly blocked them with her shoulder. "Mariana—"

The older woman paused midstep. Beyond her, Arabella could see servers loading carts in preparation for the latest event being held in the banquet room.

Aware that she was holding up Mariana from her

duties, Arabella just shoved out the words. "Do you let Jay into the fitness center often?"

"You're the only one he's ever brought with him." Mariana answered the question that Arabella *hadn't* asked. "That's how I can tell you're someone special."

The tight little fist inside Arabella's stomach that she'd almost forgotten suddenly eased. "Really?"

Mariana's eyes softened. She dashed her fingers in a cross over her chest. "Promise." Then she winked and hurried away, her big bright bun bouncing on the top of her head.

Arabella shifted and the doors finished closing.

She didn't have time to go up to the fourth floor to store Jay's shoes in her locker there, so she just tucked them in a bag on her cart after she'd pulled it from the floor pantry. With her headphones tucked in her ears, she pulled the assignment chart she'd gotten from Beulah that morning out of her back pocket.

I think you should know that...

...you're someone really special.

Hallie shook her head for the third time in as many rooms. "Sorry." She dashed her finger along the wooden cabinet that housed the flat-screen television. "This needs a better polish."

That entire afternoon—ever since she'd left Brady's office with Jay's shoes—Hallie had been critical of Arabella's work.

"I'll polish it again," she said and pulled out a fresh cloth. "Hallie—"

The other girl's lips were pursed as she raised an eyebrow.

"Did I do something to upset you? Besides my sub-par cleaning, I mean?" She tried a wry smile but it was met with a stony stare.

"What could possibly upset me?"

She waved her dust cloth a little helplessly. "I don't know. That's why I'm asking. I thought…well, yester-day, I thought you and I might become friends."

"I don't need friends who hide the truth about them-selves from me." Hallie looked back at the clipboard she used to mark off her inspections before releasing a room back to the front desk. "You'd better pick up the pace. You're an hour behind." She walked out of the room, leaving Arabella gaping.

She hurriedly applied the cloth to the offending wood, then darted out of the room after Hallie. There were only two rooms rented on this end of the floor so far, and Arabella knew the occupants were down at the pool where the marketing people were still working on filming. "It's done," she yelled, "and what truth am I supposed to have hidden?"

Hallie turned on her heel and marched back along the carpeted corridor. "Acting like you're one of us when you're really one of them!"

Arabella frowned. "I have no idea what you are even talking about."

"Really? And here I thought you Fortunes were all supposed to be so brilliant."

Fortunes.

It dawned on Arabella then. She'd completely forgotten about her last name. "Hallie, I'm not one of *those* Fortunes." Hearing it, she couldn't help but cringe. "I mean, I'm no different than you! I have to work for a living. Criminy, I can't even afford to move out of the twin bedroom I'm living in at my brother's yet because I'm so broke!"

But Hallie was obviously unconvinced. "I'd say *whatever*," she drawled, "except I wouldn't want to lose my job for being disrespectful."

Arabella let out an impatient snort. "I'm not—"

"I'll check back in an hour." Hallie cut her off. "Front desk needs these rooms available. They've all been blocked for a wedding tomorrow." Then she spun on her heel again and walked away.

Arabella flopped her arms at her sides. "What's a name matter, anyway?"

But Hallie wasn't listening and with a sigh, Arabella reentered the room. She stuffed her squishy headphones into her ears.

"...all up and gonna be someone new..."

The familiar words snuck into her head and she cursed. "I'd like to be someone new, too, buddy," she told the deep voice singing in her ear. "Someone without the last name of Fortune!"

Then she attacked the dusting with renewed vengeance.

She was finally pushing her cart back into the floor pantry nearly an hour later when an alarm suddenly sounded and she nearly jumped out of her skin.

She'd never heard that specific noise at the hotel be-

fore, but that didn't mean she didn't recognize a fire
alarm when she heard one.

She slammed the pantry door closed on the cart and
darted around the corner to the service elevator, only
to remember that the elevators automatically shut down
and returned to the first floor when the fire alarms ac-
tivated. She'd polished the signs affixed to the backs
of the room doors that explained that very point often
enough by now to be able to quote the entire list of
safety rules.

She hit the stairwell, where footsteps were already
echoing throughout the cement tower and started down,
hurrying even faster to help the woman ahead of her
who was trying to manage a toddler and a baby and not
get trampled by the people coming down behind them.

"Let me help," she said and swept the wailing toddler up in her arms.

The mother's eyes were wide and tearful and they
took in Arabella's T-shirt with the hotel logo. "There's
not *really* a fire is there?"

"Even if there is, it's all going to be fine." She spoke
with a calmness she didn't really feel. "I'm Arabella."
Her voice vibrated from the impact of her shoes hitting
the steps. "What's your name?"

"Sierra." The mother clasped her baby closer as they
reached the second-floor landing and started down the
last stretch. "That's Mia you're carrying."

At the sound of her name, Mia wailed even harder,
and knocked her elbow hard into Arabella's face as she
strained to reach her mommy.

Pain exploded in her face and Arabella yanked her head back.

Blinking hard, she slowed only slightly, using the railing to help guide her while she blinked the stars from her vision.

In seconds, they'd reached the bottom of the stairs and they darted out into the corridor where Brady stood. His tie was loosened and it was only because Arabella knew him so well that she could see the agitation in his eyes despite the calm way he was directing people toward the exits.

"There's no need to run," he said in a loud voice. "Please proceed calmly to the exit—" He broke off for a moment, his expression tightening when he spotted Arabella carrying the little girl past him.

But she didn't slow. Her face was throbbing from the impact of Mia's elbow and she nearly ran right into Petunia in the lobby. The florist was carting a box of bouquets as if her life depended on it. An older man with gray hair was with her, carrying a second box.

"Leave the flowers," Arabella said sharply and pushed them both to the front door.

As soon as they were through, Arabella chased after Mia's mother. The young woman had broken into a trot right along with the dozens of other guests who were also more than a little anxious to get away from the building.

Finally, Sierra stopped, though, and sank down onto the grass and Arabella caught up to her. She gratefully surrendered the wailing toddler to her mama's arms and gingerly cupped her hand over her aching face.

Sierra was looking at her oddly. "Are you all right?"

She nodded. "I'll come back and check on you as soon as I can."

"You don't have to—"

"I want to." She cleared her throat and channeling Mariana a bit, gave Mia a quick wink before she turned to work her way back to the front entrance.

It felt oddly similar to the day the balcony collapsed, only this time Arabella didn't have her dad dragging her away. This time there was no ominous cloud of debris wafting through the air. Her nose was stuffy but not from the smell of smoke. She knew better than to trust that meant there wasn't any fire somewhere.

Alarms didn't go off all on their own, did they?

Not unless it was another one of those glitches that Mariana mentioned.

Gingerly pressing her fingertips against the pain beneath both of her eyes, Arabella looked around, wondering how best she could help. She spotted Grace Williams talking to Sybil and Beulah. They were obviously taking count of guests.

Hallie and a few of the other room attendants were pacing around with servers from Roja. They were handing out water bottles to guests and staff alike.

The three-person film crew who'd been taking footage all over the hotel were panning their cameras over the melee as three fire engines turned in to the property.

If this was all just a glitch, it was turning out to be a whopper of one.

"There you are." Jay suddenly appeared next to her. He was breathing hard, as if he'd just run a half-marathon. "I've been looking every—" He broke off with an oath and caught her face between his hands. "You're hurt!"

Before she had time to blink, he lifted her right off her feet.

Chapter Nine

"Jay!" Arabella's hands were patting his chest, but Jay barely noticed. He was too busy looking for a safe place to take her until he could get her some medical attention.

There were people everywhere and the hotel alarm was still blaring.

"Maybe this place *is* cursed," he muttered, finally stepping right over a retaining wall so he could get to the chaises surrounding the pool.

"It's not cursed," she said thickly. "Oh, criminy—" She was holding up her bloody hand as if she'd never seen it before.

"You're going to be fine," he promised even though he had a pit in the bottom of his stomach that made him want to punch something. Instead, he kicked the corner of one of the chaises and it spun on its legs so that he could lower Arabella onto it. His hand shook as he carefully brushed her hair out of her blue eyes. "I'm going to get some help and you're going to be just fine."

"I *am* fine," she insisted. Her voice sounded thick and she kept trying to sit up despite his efforts to keep her still. "I got elbowed in the face is all." She looked annoyed. "I didn't know my nose was bleeding."

"Someone elbowed you?" There were no pool towels conveniently stacked next to the vacant bar now and Jay yanked his shirt over his head and tried staunching the flow of blood with it.

"Not intentionally!" She scrabbled at his hand and the bunched shirt. "Jay, I can hardly breathe here."

He swore and moved his shirt away.

She inhaled through her mouth with obvious relief and closed her eyes for a moment. "I used to get bloody noses all the time when I was a kid. You'd think I'd remember how they felt." She looked at the shirt, stained crimson. "Oh, geez. That's going to be hard to wash out."

Half a choked laugh escaped. He sank down on his knees beside the chaise. "The last thing I'm worried about is a stained shirt." He unwound the bundle enough to find a shirttail and used it to gently dab her cheek. "I never thought the sight of blood bothered me until I saw it covering half your face."

"Half my—" She groaned, then winced sharply and yanked back when his careful dabbing got too close to her nose. "What does a broken nose feel like?"

"Don't know. I've never had one. Who elbowed you?"

"Just a scared liddle girl. She didn' know." She gave a cautious sniff, only to lean over with a choked cough which sent droplets of blood spattering everywhere. "Ohmigod," she groaned.

"We'll get it cleaned up."

"Yeah, by someone who'll have to wear a hazmat suit or something." She raised the back of the chaise, grimaced when she saw the smear she left, and then leaned back against it. She took the bundled shirt from him and held it beneath her nose as she tilted her head back. Her eyes were blue crescents beneath her lashes. "Where'd you cubb frob, anyway?"

They both went still when the strident fire alarm cut off midwail.

"Texas," he said a moment later.

She raised an eyebrow.

"It's where I come from."

She gave a groaning sort of laugh. "Keep your day job," she advised. She slid her fingers through his. "Stadd-up comedy may nod be in your future."

He smiled and kissed her knuckles.

She made a soft sound that finished the job of melting the remnants of panic inside his gut.

"Reminds me of January," she murmured.

"Me, too." Even though there really wasn't room, he slid onto the chaise beside her, careful not to tip it onto its side before he could get his weight centered with hers. "Are you going to disappear on me this time, too?"

She nuzzled her head against his chest. "I didn't want to disappear. You were the best thing about that trip."

He pressed his lips to her temple. "Not the bread?"

He felt her soft laugh. "Nod the bread."

The alarm might have been shut off, but that hadn't stopped any of the emergency responders.

Fire engines were in position, parked strategically around the hotel entrance. Police cruisers had arrived, too, and several officers were busy pushing the crowds back even farther while two more stretched caution tape across the divide.

"What were you going to tell me that night?"

"When?"

Her palm flattened against his abdomen and she pushed herself up a little so she could look at him.

"In January. At the birthday party." Her eyes shied away from his. "You were going to tell me something, but then we heard the balcony start to go and—" She sat up even more, which—unfortunately—was enough to upset the chaise and it tipped them right over the side.

They landed in a heap barely a foot from the edge of the pool. Jay's shoulder hit hard, but at least he reacted quickly enough to turn so that Arabella landed on him versus the unforgiving travertine.

Her shoulders were shaking. "What else?" She lifted her head and he realized she was laughing. "What else can possibly happen?"

He ran his hand up her slender back as they both sat and disentangled the legs of the chaise from their own. "What else?" he echoed, watching Detective Teas duck beneath the caution tape and head toward the hotel.

* * *

It took two hours before the fire chief announced that the alarm was false. Word spread through the crowd waiting outside a lot faster.

There wasn't a single guest remaining in the hot afternoon sun by the time the police cars departed. The fire crews were slower to leave. Before they left, one of the EMTs mopped up Arabella's face and taped her nose. "Looks like a simple break," he told her. "Check with your doctor, though, if it starts bleeding again or the pain gets worse instead of better."

Nicole and Mariana opened the doors of Roja, offering complimentary meals. Standard rooms were upgraded. Additional free nights were doled out.

In short, Hotel Fortune did everything it could to appease their guests who'd been so inconvenienced by the false alarm.

They still lost half of them before morning.

Arabella learned that from Beulah when she checked in the next day for her room assignments.

"Broken?" Beulah peered over her half glasses at Arabella's face.

She nodded. Just as the EMT the day before had warned, she'd woken up with bruises beneath both eyes.

"You look like you've done a round with my ex-husband." It was the first time Arabella had heard anything approaching compassion in the other woman's voice. "Had my share of black eyes just like those."

"That's horrible. I'm so sorry, Beulah."

"So's he." Her tone went right back to its usual terseness. "Pig's still doing time for it." She pulled something from her drawer and tossed it on the counter. "Shake it up and it'll stay cold for a couple hours. It'll help the swelling."

Arabella's eyes suddenly stung. "Thanks, Beulah."

As if she regretted her momentary lapse, Beulah's lips pinched together and she turned back to her computer.

Arabella pocketed the thin pack and left the office to start her day.

Fortunately, it progressed better than the day before. Hallie still wasn't the chatty, friendly soul she'd been initially, but at least she was satisfied enough with Arabella's work to release her rooms the first time around. By the time her lunch break rolled around, she was actually on schedule with the rooms. Which was amazing, because she'd even taken a few minutes in between them to press the cold pack against her tender face.

She knew Jay was working the wedding—that, at least hadn't been canceled—so she wasn't surprised when the whole day passed without running into him even once. Nor did she see his truck in the parking lot when she clocked out at the end of the day.

It was Friday. She wasn't scheduled to work again until Monday. The time until she might see him again stretched out disappointingly.

Until she got home and Harper handed her a jar of brilliant red jam. A small note had been taped to the top of it. "Found it on the front porch after the boys and I got back from taking Murphy for a walk."

Feeling weak inside, Arabella unfolded the note.

Mariana's Market. Tomorrow. Six a.m.

He'd included a simple sketched map as well.

She clasped the note to her breast and practically floated up the stairs.

"I know that look," Harper called after her.

But Arabella didn't respond. She was hearing another voice in her head.

I think you should know that...

...you're the only girl for me.

By morning, the bruises under Arabella's eyes were nearly purple. No amount of cosmetics could disguise them so she gave up trying. She wove her hair into a long braid, pulled on her favorite ball cap that matched her short denim sundress and followed Jay's map to Mariana's Market.

She got there well before 6:00 a.m., but even at the early hour, there were already dozens of vehicles parked in the big lot where venders had set up shop. There didn't seem to be a particular order to the way they were arranged and Jay's map hadn't gone beyond how to get to the location of the market itself, so she just began wandering up and down the nearest rows.

She hadn't really had any expectations about the market. She knew about the jams, of course. Louella's and Mabel's. Knew, too, that Petunia had a booth there at least once a month.

She was nevertheless surprised by the variety of wares that were on display.

She bought a hand-sewn scarf to send to her mother, knowing she'd love it, a vintage record album for her father and a jaunty doggie sweater for Murphy. Admittedly, the dog wouldn't need it for months and months, but how could she resist when "nothing but a hound dog" was embroidered across the back?

Humming under her breath along with the tinny sound of music coming from nowhere in particular, she reached the row of food trucks and spotted Mariana's right away. She wasn't all that surprised that there was a line of people standing outside the window and she couldn't help but wonder how Mariana managed to keep up with all of this as well as help run Roja. But there she was, her bright blond head visible from inside the truck.

Close by the truck a row of tables shaded by green-and-white market umbrellas marched up the center of the aisle. One table was already occupied by a group of old men playing cards.

When she reached the center of the market she noticed an orderliness to the booths that had been absent on the outer rows and after buying a coffee from one of them, she browsed happily among the bins of shining red tomatoes and melons as big as basketballs. She added a basket of deep red cherries to the mesh bag she'd gotten along with the doggie sweater and turned up the next row. A sign for Lou's Luscious Jams hung at the top of an empty booth straight ahead of her. It was more than a tent. Less than a shack. And the long table in front of it was nearly covered with the jars of jam that Jay was unpacking from a big crate.

She hesitated there because watching him stack his grandmother's wares felt so very sweet. He was wearing faded blue jeans, a plain blue shirt and an off-white cowboy hat. The only other time she'd seen him wear the hat was the day she'd run into him at the police station.

It was only a few weeks ago but it felt so much longer.

Then, as if he'd sensed her, his head lifted and his green eyes met hers. A slow smile crossed his face.

I think you should know that...

"I want to see your smile for the rest of my days," she murmured.

He straightened and thumbed his hat back an inch before gesturing at the table. "You just going to stand there talking to yourself, or come and help me?"

She raised her voice. "Maybe I'm enjoying the scenery." She took a sip of coffee. It really was an excellent cup. Almost as excellent as the view of him.

He craned his head, looking behind him, then along the row of booths. "What scenery?"

She laughed and walked the rest of the way to the booth. "False modesty, Jet-pack."

He shot her a close look. "Who told you about that?"

"Mariana."

He seemed to relax. "What else has she been telling you?"

"That you used to steal her lemon tarts."

"I swept in exchange for every single one," he defended. He lifted the coffee out of her hand and set it on the table behind him. "I do have a serious question for you, though."

"I don't know how to make lemon tarts."

His dimple deepened and he slid his hands around

her waist, linking them behind her. "That's not the question."

She couldn't help leaning into him. "Oh?"

"How's your nose feel?"

She groaned a little. "Thank you for the reminder. I'd almost forgotten that I look like a raccoon."

"Yeah, but you're a cute raccoon. The nose?"

She wrinkled it. "Honestly, it doesn't even hurt anymore."

"Good. That means I can do this." He leaned down and brushed his mouth slowly, gently across hers. "All mornings should start with a kiss from a beautiful raccoon," he murmured and kissed her again.

And she fell a little more in love with him.

"You going to stand there kissing the lady or set up shop?"

Jay finally lifted his head. "How you doin', Norman?"

"Fair." A tall, spare man with gray hair and a tanned face stopped in front of the table and though Arabella recognized him from the day before at the hotel when he'd been with Petunia carrying flowers, he obviously did not recognize Arabella. Not if the polite nod he gave her was any indication. "Lou's not sick or something, I hope. Can count on one hand the number of times she hasn't been out here bright and early on Saturday morning."

"She's fine," Jay assured him. "Offered to let me take over this morning so I'd have a chance to impress my girl."

He spoke lightly, but Arabella's heart still swelled.

"Women'll do that to ya," Norman agreed.

Arabella stuck out her hand. "Arabella Fortune, Mr. ah—"

"Just Norman," he said and shook her hand with all the enthusiasm of her nephews when they were afraid of getting cooties. "One of those Fortunes, you say."

Norman's smile was nonexistent but Arabella managed to keep hers in place. "*A* Fortune. I just moved here from New York."

He looked like he thought she ought to have stayed there.

He turned his back on her and gestured at the array of jam jars. "I'll take five jars."

Jay bagged up the jars and gave them to Norman in exchange for the cash that Norman passed over.

Norman didn't spare Arabella so much as a glance when he walked away a minute later.

"Friendly guy," she murmured under her breath.

"He usually is." Jay watched the departing man. "According to my grandmother, he's been having some trouble keeping his medicine straight. Gets forgetful. But he's still a staple out here at the market. Every weekend. Either playing chess near Mariana's truck or helping out at Petunia's flower stand when she's here."

"Selling flowers?"

"He's her dad."

"Ah. Okay." The missing dots connected. "Petunia mentioned him when I was working at her shop. No wonder he was helping with the flowers yesterday. Where's her stand?"

"Doesn't look like she's going to be there today." He

pointed down the row. "Her space is empty. It's next to the yellow tent with the striped awning. That one's Mabel's."

As the minutes had been passing, more and more vendors had been showing up. Rolling up the sides of vinyl tents. Trotting out portable tables. Unloading carts of bric-a-brac and setting out handmade crafts and every other imaginable item. The booth with the striped awning, however, sat empty.

She dumped her purchases and her bag on the square of fake grass covering the dirt ground inside their booth and plucked several jars out of Jay's box. "You just stack these things around?"

"Yep. On the shelves, too."

Since Jay had the table itself well in hand, she began adding jars here and there on the milk-crate shelves in what she figured were artful sort of displays. "How *is* your grandmother?"

"Nursing her aggravation where Mabel's concerned."

"I still can't believe they were brawling over her jam recipe."

"Tell me about it," he muttered. "Gran and Mabel go way back."

"But that's why you're here? To work her booth because of the hundred-yard thing?" She knew the judge had ordered both women to keep away from each other by at least that much distance.

"You heard what I told Norm. I'm trying to impress my girl."

She bobbled the jars and barely managed to catch one before it rolled off the shelf.

"And because my grandmother didn't want to chance running into Mabel," he went on humorously.

It was no less than she'd expected, but her balloon of joy over the "my girl" term deflated slightly. "Considering how desolate Mabel's booth looks, I'm not sure she needed to worry about it. But I guess if one of them doesn't work, it's fair for the other one not to as well."

"Yeah, except Gran's jams are going to sell, anyway, thanks to us." He cupped his hand behind her neck. "So why are you looking sad?"

She looked toward the yellow booth again. "Mabel's booth just looks forlorn to me. Nobody is helping her out like you're helping your grandmother."

He smiled and dropped a quick kiss on the tip of her nose.

"What was that for?"

"Because not everyone has a heart as sweet as yours."

She couldn't manage to form a word. Not with the way her chest felt all full up and her face felt all stretched in a smile.

She hadn't finished stacking the shelves when another customer came by the booth, quickly followed by two more. As the sun climbed higher in the sky, the aisles among the booths became more congested with shoppers and the supply of Louella's jams dwindled.

It wasn't even close to noon when they were gone completely and Arabella gathered up her purchases and slung the strap of her bag over her shoulder.

"Where do you think you're going so fast?"

"What else is there to do?" She swept her arm out, encompassing the empty table and shelves. He could say that she had a sweet heart, but working alongside him all morning had been sheer delight. He had a way with people that was entirely captivating. Male, female, young, old. Didn't matter. They all walked away with smiles on their faces as well as jars of jam in their hands. "Everything's sold."

He closed his hands around hers. "Yeah, but that doesn't mean the fun's over, does it? Come on." He drew her around the empty table that he pushed back onto the fake turf so that it no longer protruded out into the aisle where the shoppers walked. "You haven't lived until you've had one of Mariana's fry bread tacos."

He seemed to take it for granted that she would agree, and since she was more than happy to prolong the pleasure, she did.

Her book bag bounced between them as they wandered through the rest of the market and Jay took it from her to sling over his own shoulder. "This thing gets heavier every time I see you. What're you doing? Collecting rocks?"

"I told you." She poked her hand down into the depths and blindly pulled out a binder with a bright orange cover. "My notebooks." She let it fall back into the bag.

Instead of taking her hand, he dropped his arm around her shoulder and fresh heat flowed through her veins. "How many journals does a girl need?" He angled around a young couple pushing a baby stroller. "And why carry them with you all the time?"

"They're not really journals," she admitted. "They're… stories. Like…novels. Sort of. And I carry 'em around with me because I can't help myself. I had five nosy big brothers. If I didn't want them making fun of me, I learned not to leave them lying around. It's a habit I can't break." And then she braced herself.

But he didn't mock. Didn't laugh. "What are sort-of novels?"

She made a face. "Ones that I start but never finish?"

He lifted the bag as if judging its weight. "How many?"

"Six."

"That was a loose-leaf binder. You write in long-hand?"

"Yes."

"Why not a computer? A laptop or a tablet? Would weigh a lot less than all those binders."

"Yeah, but there's something satisfying about a pen on paper."

He grinned. "What do you do when you want to change what you've written? Wouldn't pencil be better?"

"Probably, but I think better with a pen." She shrugged self-consciously. "It's just my thing."

He squeezed her shoulders. "Your process is your process. What do you write about? What kind of novels?"

"Just…stuff." She could feel the look he gave her and stopped to examine a table filled with screen-printed T-shirts as if they were positively fascinating.

"Stuff, she says cagily," he said. "Now you've really got me curious." He leaned down until he was looking over her shoulder, his chin touching her shoulder. "What secrets are you keeping, Arabella Fortune?" His deep voice caressed her ear.

Her knees went to mush. "A couple mysteries," she admitted faintly. "Fantasies. A bunch of children's stories. And—" She slid a look toward him, feeling engulfed by the warmth in his green gaze so close to her own.

"And?"

"And a romance," she finished in a rush.

But again, he didn't laugh. Instead he just straightened with a smile. "That's quite a variety. Are those the genres you also like to read?"

"I like to read everything," she admitted.

"Looks like they do, too." He picked up one of the shirts so the printed front was visible. Two skeletons wearing sunglasses and holding books in their hands reclined on chaise lounges in the shade of a cactus. *It's a dry heat* was printed below them.

"We're having a special on tees today." A bubbly girl quickly moved from her chair deep in the shade of a market umbrella. "Buy one, get two free." She tugged proudly at the white T-shirt she was wearing that had the words *I'd give it all up for Jett Carr* splashed across her breasts. "Have a whole new batch of these in. We sold out of them last weekend." She turned around briefly to show them the back, which had a black-and-white image of the bearded singer's profile, and smiled brightly over her shoulder at Arabella. "What do you think?"

Arabella smiled ruefully and shook her head. "Pass."

Jay made a sound that sounded vaguely choked. "Not even cactus and bony readers?"

She gave them both an apologetic shrug. "Not in the market for T-shirts today, I'm afraid." She folded the skeleton shirt and placed it neatly atop the small stack of them. "Good luck with your sale, though."

Even before they moved away from the booth, they'd been replaced by two other shoppers—both women—who screeched a little excitedly over the Jett Carr shirt the seller was wearing.

Arabella shook her head. "I don't know what they find so exciting about that singer."

Jay laughed and kissed her on the head. "Me, either." He dropped his arm over her shoulder again and they fell into step once more. "How often do you write?"

He was still talking about her books. As if they were actually something to be taken seriously. "Most every night. Sometimes it's only a paragraph or two."

"Isn't that how books get written? A paragraph or two at a time?" He squeezed her shoulder. "Why d'you suppose you haven't finished any of them?"

"I guess because I get another idea that I think'll be better, and so I abandon what I'm doing and start all over again." The latest were the children's stories that she'd started working on when Brady had become guardian to Toby and Tyler.

"Do you have a favorite?"

"I've never thought about it." She did then, briefly, and shrugged. "I don't have one."

"Is that why you keep toting around even the ones that you abandoned in favor of the next greatest idea?"

"No, I keep toting them around because one day, maybe I'll finish one of them."

"Then they're not really abandoned, are they? They're just hanging out, waiting for some sunshine to start growing again."

He stopped and she realized they'd reached Mariana's food truck. The picnic tables that had been vacant earlier were all now occupied and the line at the window was even longer than it had been earlier. The tinny music that had been playing before was still going strong, though the volume had been turned up.

"Waiting for some sunshine." She looked up at him. "That sounds a lot better than that I can't bring myself to throw them away because it feels like admitting failure."

"Nothing creative is a failure."

A short laugh escaped. "Says the insurance actuary."

He grinned. "Former insurance actuary. I didn't last long."

"I thought you went into that straight out of college."

"I did." They'd reached the end of the line at Mariana's truck.

"What'd you do after that?"

He didn't answer and she looked up and followed his gaze toward the quaint carts filled with fruits and vegetables where Mariana was holding court, talking to a young woman with a mic while a brawny guy nearby wielded a television camera. "Looks to me like she's too busy to be making fry bread tacos."

"Looks that way to me, too." Jay turned to face her and settled his hat more firmly as he studied the line they'd joined. "No wonder it's not moving. What say

we take a rain check on the fry bread until next weekend and raid my grandmother's kitchen instead? Sound
good?"

So he expected to see her next weekend.

She beamed. "Sounds perfect."

Chapter Ten

Louella was not home when they arrived at her house.

Arabella had followed Jay in her car and when they walked in without even knocking, she could read his surprise when they found the place empty.

"Did she leave a note?" Her mother always left a note for her dad whenever she went out.

He glanced around, presumably at the obvious places. "Not that I can see." He dropped the fat envelope filled with the cash they'd taken in at the market into a kitchen drawer and pushed it shut again before opening the refrigerator door.

"Jay!" She couldn't help a protesting laugh. "We're not really going to raid her fridge when she's not even here, are we?"

He gave her a look as if she'd grown a second head.

"You think she makes all of this because she wants to eat all of it herself?" He removed a platter wrapped in plastic wrap and set it on the counter. "Cold fried chicken." He followed it up with another covered bowl. "Potato salad." Then a tall glass pitcher. "Fresh lemonade." He added it to the collection on the counter and then leaned over to open a lower cupboard. "She's been trying to put meat on my skinny ass my entire life."

"Please. You're perfect." The words escaped without thought and she flushed when he shot her a look over his shoulder, catching her right in the act of ogling his butt.

His smile turned wicked as he straightened with the wicker picnic basket he'd pulled out of the cupboard. "We could always compare yours and mine."

She flushed even more and injected some bravado into her eye roll. "How suave you are."

He chuckled soundlessly as he stacked the food inside the basket. Then he grabbed the lemonade pitcher and headed toward the rear door. "Come on."

She hurried around him to open the door since his hands were full and they went outside. She half expected him to stop and set everything on the patio table that overlooked the garden, but he kept walking. Around the beds of strawberries, past the shed and around through the peach orchard.

She saw the big tub of his grandmother's, nestled in a shaft of sunlight beaming through the trees, and her heart began skittering around inside her chest as they neared his stone barn and her feet dragged a little.

He noticed and gave her a curious look. "Something wrong?"

"Not…uh, not at all. I just, I just didn't realize you had a water wheel," she said quickly. Not entirely untruthfully. Because she *hadn't* realized it until now. Hadn't seen it, because she hadn't gotten so close to the barn the last time she'd been there.

But there it was. Positioned closely against the far side of the stone barn, dipping into the stream and producing a soothing, distinctly rhythmic creak as it turned.

But her sudden shot of nerves was caused only because it had dawned on her that she was finally seeing his place. That they were alone.

That *anything* could happen.

She wasn't a virgin. Before Tammy Jo had landed Ham, Arabella had been involved with him first. But that had still been a while ago. Was she really ready to take that step with Jay?

He was still waiting for her to catch up to him. "Barn used to be a flour mill."

She blinked. "Seriously? I was only joking when I asked if your grandmother milled her own flour for her chocolate chip cookies."

"She's probably capable, but she couldn't do it here. Not anymore. The mill was dismantled a long time ago. My grandfather was a farrier. He did a lot of his work here." He aimed toward a rough-looking door positioned closer to the short side of the barn and she was surprised that he stopped to pull a key out of his pocket to unlock it.

"Get a lot of break-ins out here in the middle of nowhere?"

He pocketed the key again. "You'd be surprised." He pushed open the door and waited for her to enter first.

She did, and what she saw inside made her jaw drop.

Whatever the stone building's previous uses had been, the interior now was plainly meant as living quarters for humans. The stone walls on the outside were the same on the inside, but the floors were gleaming wood. A galley-style kitchen was located on one narrow end. At the other side of the room, a couple of rough-hewn posts anchored a staircase leading to a loft area that filled only a limited portion of the magnificent space soaring up to the crisscrossing barn rafters.

She assumed the bedroom was upstairs, because between kitchen and stairs, it was all living space downstairs. A small dining table that looked like it was made of the same kind of wood as the posts sat behind a long leather couch that anchored one end of a large rectangular rug woven in mottled shades of gray. Opposite the couch were a wooden trunk serving as a coffee table and two chairs. Most surprising of all, though, was a gleaming black grand piano that stood near the stairs. It ought to have looked out of place, but it didn't.

In fact, everything looked magazine perfect in one of those modern-yet-rustic ways. Perfect, yet totally impersonal. There wasn't a single personal item in sight.

She turned in a circle, taking it all in. "Your grandmother must have spent a fortune doing all of this."

He set the pitcher and the picnic basket on the concrete kitchen island.

"Was she hoping to rent it out or something?" Arabella wandered nearer, stepping around the buttery-soft-looking couch. There were only a few narrow windows, but they spanned nearly the entire length of the space. Hung horizontally as they were, one above the other, they afforded a view of the horses and the pasture from every position within the barn.

"Or something." Jay opened a cupboard and pulled out a sleeve of red cups that he tossed onto the island. He followed it up with a package of paper plates. "Nothing but the finest china here. Makes doing the dishes a breeze."

She laughed as she undid the twist-tie and removed two plastic cups while he did the same with the plates. She filled them with ice from the dispenser in the door of the refrigerator.

The sound of the ice maker reminded her of the towel that Brady had found. "My brother knows I was in the fitness center the other night," she admitted abruptly.

His eyebrows rose. "How? I know we weren't caught on the security camera."

She told him about the towel as she reached for the pitcher of lemonade and began pouring. "And he knows I wasn't alone. Because not only was my towel there, but your tennis shoes were as well."

"You told him they were mine?"

"Of course not, but he's not an idiot. He knows I'm—" She took a long drink of the cold lemonade, swallowing it along with the rest of her sentence. "I mean he suspects there's something…you know. Going on. Between you and me." Why on earth couldn't she seem to stop her tongue?

A small smile flirted around the edges of Jay's lips. "Does that bother you?"

"No!"

"So then what's the problem?"

"The problem is that he knows we were there when we shouldn't have been. We broke the rules. I never break the rules," she muttered. "I should have known we'd get caught."

He pulled off the plastic wrap from the plate of fried chicken and set it in front of her. "The hotel would have to fire me before they could fire you, so I wouldn't sweat too much over it."

"I don't know how you can sound so calm."

He uncovered the bowl of potato salad and stuck a big mixing spoon into it. "I've weathered worse."

She wanted to ask him more, but instead, followed him to the table, where he set the food in the middle. Then, when he pulled out a chair for her, she forgot to be curious in favor of being quietly charmed. The only other time a man had done that had been with Ham.

Just once.

"What's so funny?"

Arabella looked at Jay. "Sorry?"

"You were smiling to yourself."

She chuckled. "It's nothing. Just remembering the last time someone pulled out my chair."

"A guy?" He eyed her over the rim of his red cup. "Do I need to be jealous?"

She'd always thought jealousy was an unattractive trait. Yet the notion that she could even inspire him to such an emotion was entirely novel. "You be the judge. He took me to the fanciest restaurant in town."

"Any guy can do that. Now this?" He gestured with a fried chicken drumstick. "Raiding grandma's fridge? Takes real thought. So what happened after the restaurant?"

She bit the inside of her lip, but there was no real way to keep her smile from growing. "He dumped me during the soup course."

For once, she was pretty sure she was the one to surprise *him*. "Were the two of you serious?"

"I thought so at the time." She picked a drumstick of her own and took a bite. Even cold, it was delicious. "He's getting married soon. Well, actually, maybe it's this weekend. Or last?" She shrugged. "I can't remember. Far as I'm concerned, he and Tammy Jo deserve each other." She took another bite. "Is *everything* your grandmother makes delicious?"

"Yeah. Tammy Jo the reason he ended things with you?"

"Is that the polite term for getting dumped?" She grinned. "And no. There were a few other girls before Tammy Jo. Knowing Ham, she'll be lucky if there aren't a few other girls once they're married, too."

"Doesn't sound like he left you with a broken heart."

"Mildly bruised." Another bite and her drumstick was demolished. She set the bone on the side of her plate and scooped up some potato salad. "What about you?"

"Mildly bruised."

If jealousy was unattractive, she was looking as pretty as a toad, right about now. "Long time ago?"

His dimple appeared and he lightly tapped the edge of his red cup against hers. "The present company I'm keeping makes it hard to remember."

"Better be careful," she warned with a lightness she didn't exactly feel. "Saying things like that, I might start to believe you."

His gaze held hers. "Would that be so bad?"

Her throat suddenly felt too tight for words. She pressed her lips together and shook her head.

He set down his cup and rose from his chair enough to lean across the table. "Come here."

She swallowed hard and just like he had, set down her cup. She rose and leaned toward him over the chicken and the salad until they were mere inches apart.

His voice was low. "Can I call you Bella yet?"

The sweet heat that had slid into her veins slipped into her heart. "Yes."

He leaned two inches closer.

So did she.

Then his lips touched hers and the knowledge was suddenly just there.

Filling her.

I could love this man.

Not just a crush. Not just infatuation.

Seriously love him. As in good times and bad. As in now and forever.

He pulled back slightly then. His eyes searched hers.

Even though she'd been certain she hadn't said the words aloud, she felt her cheeks warm. "What?"

"I'm really glad your battery died that day."

She smiled. "So am I."

"But—" His gaze dropped. "You're smashing the grub."

She looked down, too, then and realized she'd planted her hand right in the middle of the bowl of potato salad. "Oh, for crying out loud!"

He gave a bark of laughter and kissed her again. "Bathroom's upstairs."

Even though she had mayonnaise and bits of potato stuck beneath her fingernails, she was pretty sure she floated up the stairs.

The bathroom was as lovely as the rest of the place, with a separate tub and shower that both looked out over the top of the water wheel. She washed her hands and controlled the urge to peek into the medicine cabinet behind the mirror. Her dress had a gold zipper from the top of its scooped neckline to the hem that hit her midthigh. Feeling breathless, she lowered the zip a few inches. Then looked at her raccoon-reflection and yanked it back up where it belonged and left the room.

The wide bed occupying most of the loft was covered in a deep blue spread. A chest of drawers was situated beneath another one of the horizontal-style windows. A pair of cowboy boots lay haphazardly on a rug similar to the one downstairs and a guitar was propped in a corner with a couple shirts tossed carelessly across it.

At least there were signs of his occupancy. As well as the fact that he didn't put his clothes away any better than she did.

She was still smiling when she went back downstairs. He'd cleared the table. "Honey, I did the dishes."

She laughed. "What a hero."

"I try." His eyes crinkled. "What do you want to do now?"

Muss up your neatly made bed?

The words only sounded inside her head, though. "Show me the horses?"

He smiled slowly. "As much as I appreciate the outfit, you're not exactly dressed for riding."

"That's okay. I don't know how to ride, anyway."

He pressed his palm to his chest. "You're killing me. You're in Texas, sweetheart. That's something we'll have to rectify as soon as possible."

Any reason to spend time with him was okay with her. "That doesn't mean we can't go look at them now, does it?"

In answer, he took her hand in his and he led her back outside where it was even more hot and humid thanks to the clouds that had rolled in. They crossed the short bridge that arched over the stream and ducked between the rails of the white fence to cross the pasture toward the three light brown horses standing still on the far side of the field. They would have looked identical if not for the white markings on their faces.

Jay gave a soft whistle and the one with the smallest mark flicked its dark tail jauntily and trotted toward them, not stopping until it butted its head against Jay's upraised palm. "This is Loretta. Looking good for a thirty-year-old lady."

"Thirty!"

"Year older 'n me. I learned to ride on her. Almost before I could walk." He tugged Arabella closer and guided her fingers to the white mark. "She likes her star rubbed. Right there."

Arabella rubbed her fingertips against the smooth white hair and Loretta's liquid brown eyes turned in her direction. She felt strangely moved knowing that the old horse had borne a small, young Jay on her back. "I didn't realize horses lived so long."

"Some do." Jay ran his hand down the horse's gleaming shoulder. "She's pampered and healthy. Hopefully she's got a lot more years left in her."

As if in answer, Loretta butted her nose against his shoulder.

He laughed and stuck his hand in the pocket of his shirt and pulled out a peppermint. He barely managed to unwrap it before the horse nipped it out of his fingers.

By then, the other two horses had plodded forward, too. "Waylon," Jay said as he pointed out the one with a long narrow stripe down his nose, "and Willie." He dropped another candy in Arabella's hand. "Unwrap it and hold it flat in your palm."

She did as instructed and Willie's velvety lips rubbed against her palm as he took the peppermint. She giggled and scrubbed her palm down her side. "Tickles."

Jay chuckled. "Here." He unwrapped the third peppermint and handed it to her. "Waylon isn't quite as polite as Willie," he warned.

She eagerly presented her palm with the candy in the center and Waylon butted against Willie to get to it, and left a slobbery smear behind once he did.

"Definitely not as polite." Arabella wrinkled her

nose, laughing. "Your grandmother must really like country music. Considering their names, I mean."

Jay pulled out his shirttail and wiped her hand dry. "She's more of a Sinatra fan. My grandfather was the one who named them. They got Willie and Waylon as foals not long before he died." He patted his empty pocket for the benefit of the horses. "All gone, my friends."

Waylon and Willie bobbed their heads and plodded away.

Loretta remained, though, seeming content with the brush of Jay's hand on her back.

Arabella slowly stroked the horse's back, her hand following Jay's. "It's no wonder your grandmother doesn't want to give them up."

"She never will as long as I have something to say about it."

Her heart squeezed. "You're a good grandson."

His lips twisted slightly. "Not as good as I should have been." He looked over her head toward the barn but Arabella had the sense he was focused elsewhere.

She held her hand still on Loretta's back, knowing his hand would bump into hers. "Why?"

She wasn't sure he'd answer at first. But then his gaze shifted to her face. "I was so focused on my own life I couldn't even make time to get back to celebrate holidays. Birthdays. Then when everything went to hell—" He glanced up when thunder rumbled softly overhead.

She slid her fingers through his, keeping his hand on Loretta's back when he would have pulled away. "What went to hell?"

He frowned. "Arabella."

She winced, wishing for Bella again. "Does it have to do with Detective Teas?"

"Teas?" He frowned even more and his lips thinned. "He thinks I had something to do with the balcony collapse at the hotel."

It took a moment for his abrupt words to sink in. To make sense. "That's ridiculous!"

"I know it is, but why do you think so?"

She turned toward him and settled her palms on his chest. Even through his shirt, she could feel the solid warmth of him. "Because I know you."

He gathered her hands beneath his. His eyes searched hers with a sudden urgency that pulled at her. "What do you know?"

"I know you put your family first."

He started to shake his head and she curled her fingertips into his chest. Even Loretta cooperated, conveniently shifting her considerable size behind him so that he couldn't back away from Arabella. "Maybe you didn't always, but you do now. And now is what I know. I know you're a hard worker. You're loyal to the hotel." She took a step closer until their hands were caught between their bodies. "And I know how you make me feel."

Something else entered his green eyes. Something warm. Something heady. "And how is that?"

She stood on her toes and pulled his head down close enough to press her mouth to his. She put everything she had into that kiss. All of her emotion. All of her yearning. And when she finally went down off her toes again, her heart was hammering so hard inside her chest he couldn't fail to feel it. "Like that," she whispered huskily.

He drew a finger down her cheek. "You're too good for me."

She shook her head. Reached up and kissed him a second time. Went back down on her heels and had to hold on to him just to keep her legs from collapsing beneath her. "I've never wanted anyone the way I want you."

His jaw flexed. She knew he wanted her, too. She could feel it. Not just in the hardness of his body but in the heat of his eyes. In the tension of his hands as they roved down her back.

But still, he was holding back and her frustration rose in her throat.

She went up on her toes a third time. She stopped shy of kissing him, though. Need was a hot hollow cramping inside her. "Do I need to strip off my dress right here, Jay? I'm on the Pill. Perfectly safe, I promise you."

He groaned slightly. "Bella."

"I will," she warned—promised—huskily. "One zip is all it takes." To prove it, she reached between them to tug at the zipper.

"No." His hand caught hers, stopping her.

Her dismay never had a chance to get off the ground, though, because he suddenly reversed their positions until it was her back pressed against Loretta's stalwart side.

"I want to do it," he said gruffly. His fingers brushed against hers as he took over.

Her breath came hard in her chest as she stared up at him. Every nerve ending she possessed stood at high alert, sending frenzied little charges in accompaniment to her pounding heartbeat as he lowered the zipper tab with excruciating slowness. Her dress loosened tooth-by-tooth and she sucked in an aching breath when he took a step back and lowered to one knee as he continued pulling down the zipper. Right to the very bottom of her hem. Then he tugged one last time and the zipper separated altogether.

He exhaled audibly and his hands slid under the denim, settling first on her waist for a long moment before slowly sliding behind her back, drawing her toward him again.

She shuddered, drowning in desire. When he rested his forehead against her belly, she ran her fingers through his thick, dark hair. In that moment, there was something intimate and impossibly vulnerable about him. The slightly sunburned skin at the nape of his neck below his short hair. The long sweep of his spine, just visible beneath the gape of his shirt collar.

Loretta shifted then, pushing so hard against Arabella that she lost her balance and fell forward against Jay, taking him right with her down to the tall, sweet grass.

He caught Arabella against him, his eyes glinting. "Good old Loretta. Always has my back."

Arabella laughed softly as she tried to sit up, but Jay just caught her hips in his hands to keep her in place, sitting right there on top of him.

Then he pressed hard against her and her laughter

died. Her dress had slipped down one arm and was barely hanging on to her other shoulder. And even though she'd been the one threatening to strip, now that she was all but nude in front of him, she was acutely aware of how she must look. No bra. A pair of white bikini panties with pink sunglasses printed all over them.

She started to pull the dress together but he shook his head. "Don't." In fact, he curled his fingers in the dress fabric as if to make sure she couldn't.

Her skin tingled. She didn't think her nipples could get any tighter, but they did. Inside, however, she was simply liquefying.

"Undo your hair."

She moistened her lips and tried not to reveal how shaky she suddenly felt as she raised her hands to her ponytail and worked the thin band free. Her hair fell down around her shoulders.

"Do you know how many times I've thought about you?" His fingers flexed against her hips and his voice deepened even more. "Dreamed about you?"

Thunder murmured again but it didn't matter since she was suddenly incapable of speech, anyway.

"Months." His eyes were almost as green as the grass surrounding him. "And more months. And then there you were. In Rambling Rose. At the police station."

It dawned on her then. She pressed her palm flat against his abdomen and felt his muscles bunch. "Was that why you were so unfriendly? Were you there because of the balcony collapse?"

"I warned you that you're too good for me."

She was shaking her head even before he finished speaking. "I'm perfect for you and you know it."

His dimple appeared suddenly. "Now who's confident?"

She could only attribute her sudden wealth of self-assurance to him. Particularly when she slowly rocked her hips against his. "Does that feel perfect?"

His eyes darkened and the edge of his white teeth showed as he inhaled audibly. "Getting close to it." He deftly slid his hand between them, fingers curling unerringly beneath her panties to find her.

Then she was the one to catch her breath.

"Even closer," he murmured.

And then she couldn't think anything at all. All she could do was feel. His fingers on her. In her. Driving her right to the edge of insanity only to pull back and taunt her even more until she was so desperate that she mindlessly caught his hand in hers, pressing his fingers against her until finally, finally, the pressure inside her escaped.

His exultant groan worked through her as she collapsed in a heap against his chest. But even then there was little rest because he rolled until it was her back cradled in the lush grass. Her eyes staring up at the clouds overhead. He kissed her again. And again. On her lips. On her breasts. On her navel and her big toe and every point in between.

She wasn't even sure how he'd gotten rid of her panties, much less his own clothes, but it didn't matter because he was there, pressing inside her, filling her more perfectly than she could have ever imagined.

She wrapped her legs around him. Her arms around him. Took him into every cell of her soul, and when the ecstasy was almost more than she could withstand, his eyes met hers.

"Now." His voice was breathless. Raw. Beautiful. "Now, we're perfect."

She threw back her head, and together, they flew.

Chapter Eleven

The sweat on their bodies didn't even have a chance to cool when the sky suddenly opened.

Arabella jerked when the first big raindrop plopped squarely between her eyes. "What?"

Jay jerked and swore, too, because that first big plop was immediately followed by a couple million more.

Arabella could only sit there and giggle as he darted around, trying to gather up their bits of clothing that had decided to take flight thanks to the wind that sprang up as unexpectedly as the rain.

"Big help you are." He was laughing too as he hitched up his jeans and swiped his face at the same time.

She giggled even harder, trying vainly to rezip her dress.

"Oh, hell." He grabbed her hand. "Just come on."

And so they ran, half dressed, half not, back to his barn, where they left their clothes in a wet heap on the floor inside the door before chasing up the stairs, where Arabella was all too happy to muss up his neatly made bed but good.

After, they slept for a while. Then Jay brought up the rest of his grandmother's fried chicken and they polished it off lying right there on the bed as they watched the rain pour and pour and pour outside the horizontal windows.

He was facedown, stretched out diagonally across the wide bed. She was stretched out atop him and she idly traced the tattoo on his shoulder blade. She was no musician, but even she recognized the stylized image as intertwined music clefs. She reached out to point at the laundry-laden guitar in the corner and rather less-than-absently enjoyed the feel of his spine against her breast. So much so, that she wriggled slightly again, just to repeat the pleasure. "Do you play that?"

He didn't even bother to look where she was pointing. "Not anymore." He folded his arms beneath his cheek and closed his eyes.

She slid along his back, enjoying the feel of that, too, until she could hook her chin over his shoulder. His lashes were so long she was a little jealous. "Why not?"

His lips curved. He didn't open his eyes. "I'm not very good at it."

"What about the piano downstairs?"

"My mom was a teacher, remember?"

She kissed a bony protrusion in his shoulder. "Doesn't mean that she taught you how to play."

"She did."

"Is that what the tattoo is about? Ode to your mother?"

Jay glanced at the guitar. It was an old one. Back from the days when he'd first started out. "Isn't that what good Texan sons do? Get tats in honor of their mamas?" He reached his hand behind him and closed it unerringly over her thigh. It was warm. Sleek. And he recalled the sprinkle of freckles just above her knee. "Keep rubbing against me like you're doing and neither one of us is going to be able to walk for a week."

She, though, slid her hands over him as if she were luxuriating in the feel of his hairy arms as much as he luxuriated in the feel of her smooth, strong thighs. "Would that be so bad?"

His laugh was a little choked. "I'm a man, honey. What do you think?"

In answer, she slowly slid back down him again, the hard points of her nipples like points of fire every inch of the way.

Then her toes tickled the arches of his feet and he grunted, yanking them away.

"Ticklish, are you?"

He felt her lips on the small of his back. Then the nip of her teeth on his butt.

He shifted slightly, groaning a little. "Playing with fire, honey."

He felt her silent laughter work through him, and then she was slithering again, upward this time, and he was pretty sure his eyes were rolling back in his head at the sensations. She finally stopped sliding again when her breasts reached his shoulder blades and her arms came under his in a backward sort of hug. She kissed the nape of his neck and her breath was warm and sweet against his flesh. "Will you play something for me?"

He could hardly think straight for the feel of her body plastered against his. He exhaled slowly. Carefully. "Will you let me read one of your sort-of novels?"

"Touché." She moved her thigh a few inches along his, then back again. "If you promise not to laugh when you do."

"I promise not to laugh."

She slid her arms out again from beneath him and started to roll off him but he reached behind and caught her leg again. This time it was her knee.

"First you can finish having your fun back there," he said huskily.

"I don't know what you mean," she said in a prim little voice.

"Liar." He laughed softly. "You're as turned on as I am." He lifted his head and looked back at her. "How wet are you?"

Her cheeks were red. The bruised circles under her eyes were almost purple. But her aquamarine eyes met his with that combination of boldness and innocence that was proving to be his undoing.

"Very," she said.

He hardened even more and turned onto his back. "Show me."

Her pupils dilated a little. Then she slid her thigh over his and wrapped her hand around him.

He saw stars.

Then balancing on her knees, she slowly took him in. To all that heat. To all that sweet, wet heat that encompassed him so flawlessly.

The moan she gave then was the sweetest note he'd ever heard. It went on and on, singing inside his head, even long after he'd emptied everything that he was inside of her.

The story was about two penguins named Oscar and Aaron and the mischief they got into whenever Mama and Papa Penguin weren't looking.

"They're Toby and Tyler," he said after he closed the orange-colored binder. "You need to finish this." He handed it to her. "It's really sweet."

She took the binder and clutched it to her midriff. Her dress was still clanging around inside his dryer and after they'd showered together, she'd pulled on a shirt from his closet. She'd rolled up the too-long sleeves and the tails practically reached her knees.

As far as Jay was concerned, it would be his favorite way of seeing her dressed from here on out.

"You're just saying that because we've been playing doctor all afternoon."

"I'm saying it because you have a way with words," he corrected and went to reach for another binder from inside her bag.

But she pulled it away. "Not so fast, Mr. Cross." She waved her fingers at the piano behind the couch where they were sitting. "Your turn first."

He pulled a face. "I haven't played in a while." That much was true.

"I don't care." She dropped her binder in her bag and moved around to sit on the edge of the piano bench. She patted the space beside her. "Make your mama proud."

He chuckled, some of the odd tension that had been building inside him beginning to lessen again. He sat down beside her. "Don't remember ever playing piano wearing nothing but my boxers."

Her eyes sparkled. "Is it giving away too much if I admit I'm relieved to hear it?" She tapped two of the keys, discordantly. "Do you need sheet music or something?"

He shook his head and flexed his fingers comically before settling his index fingers on the keyboard.

He tapped out a fine rendition of "Chopsticks."

She laughed and bumped her shoulder against his. "Even *I* can play that."

The rest of his fingers joined in and "Chopsticks" morphed into the dramatic strains of Grieg's Piano Concerto in A minor.

He made it through the first couple dozen bars, which was a feat in itself since he hadn't played it since he was a kid.

But it was enough to leave Arabella staring at him slack-jawed. "That's not 'Chopsticks.'"

"Edvard Grieg." He gave her a quick kiss and got up from the bench. "Norwegian composer. Only piano concerto he ever wrote. I had to learn it for a recital back in school. I don't even remember the rest of it."

"If you can play like that, why did you ever go into *actuarial science*?" She followed him into the kitchen.

"Music might have been my first love, but I was way

better at math than I ever was in music theory and it paid for college." He kissed her nose. "We ate all the fried chicken. All I've got in the cupboard are boxes of cereal." He opened one to show her the truth of it. "And thanks to the workout you've put me through, I'm starving."

She smirked. "My dress is still in the dryer. So I guess you're stuck with—" She pulled out the nearest box. "Frosted Fruity Flakes. Seriously?"

"Don't make fun. Man's choice of breakfast cereals is sacred." He took the box from her and shoved it back on the shelf. "And your dress ought to be dry by now. We can go have dinner at Provisions." He went through the door that led to a powder room that was so small it always made him feel claustrophobic and into the slightly larger laundry room. When he went back out to her, he was holding her dress. "It's wrinkled but it's dry."

Even though they'd just spent hours discovering every cell on each other's bodies, she closed herself in the powder room to change.

"Not only wrinkled and dry," she said when she emerged a few minutes later, "but about a size and a half smaller." She twitched at the hem that was no longer midthigh but a good two inches higher. And while the zipper was done up, the denim hugged her figure in a snug way that it hadn't before.

It wasn't quite indecent, but he didn't want anyone else seeing her wear it now but him. "I'll buy you a new dress."

She laughed and waved off the offer. "I can buy my

own dresses, thank you very much. But," she said, as she twitched again at the barely-butt-covering hem, "if we're going to Provisions, I'd better stop off at Brady's and change first." She cast him a look. "Not that I'm protesting, but you might need a little more coverage in the clothing department, too."

He struck a pose. "Plaid boxers don't do it?"

"Anything about you does it for me. But the health code probably says otherwise." She leaned over to pick up her book bag and showed off a peek of her sunglass-strewn underwear. Then, as if she felt his gaze, she shot him a look over her shoulder and yanked on the hem again.

He spread his palms. "Only human, honey."

Her cheeks colored. Despite her bruised eyes, she was still the prettiest woman he'd ever known. From the outside to the inside, everything about Arabella Fortune was beautiful.

And now she'd narrowed her eyes to blue slits. "Why are you looking at me like that?"

Like he'd seen his future and didn't want to face what it would be if it didn't contain her?

"Just thinking about the next time Mariana sneaks us in to use the hotel's hot tub."

She made a stern face and pointed her finger at him. "We're not doing *that* again. Brady's already furious with me as it is." She dropped her hand to delve into her bag again. "But that reminds me. Your shoes are still in my housekeeping cart. And if I don't set a reminder for myself, I'm going to forget them yet again." When she pulled her hand back out, she had her cell phone in it. But instead of typing in her little reminder, she just stared at the screen. The color drained from her cheeks, leaving her bruises even more purplish.

"What's wrong?"

She turned the screen to show him. "Fifteen messages. The last time I had fifteen messages, it was after my mom found out Adam had a baby."

"Seems like Adam should have been the one getting the messages."

She sank onto the arm of the couch as her fingertip began swiping her phone screen. "You don't understand. Larkin was really sick for a while. Aplastic anemia. He might not have made it if Adam hadn't been a bone marrow match." She held the phone to her ear as she listened to a voice message.

Color reentered her cheeks as fast as it had fled, though, and she hopped off the couch arm. "There's been a flood at the hotel."

He frowned. "From the rain?"

"I don't know. I guess?" She was hunting in her bag again. "Where are my keys?"

"I'll drive." He bolted up the stairs and yanked on the first pair of jeans he came to. He pulled on socks and his boots, grabbed a shirt and hustled back down the stairs again. "We'll run by your brother's place on the way."

They left the barn at a jog, bypassing his grandmother's house altogether to go straight for the truck. He'd pulled on his shirt by then and she tossed her bag onto the floor, not even noticing this time the way she flashed her sunglass panties at him as she climbed up inside.

There was never any traffic on the road out to his grandmother's place, so he pushed the speed without regret. Not even thirty minutes had passed when he pulled up at the curb outside her brother's house.

Arabella's heart was hammering as she ran inside. Harper and the boys were sitting in the living room playing Candy Land and she hopped up, scattering the pieces when Arabella rushed inside.

"Bella! Brady's been looking—"

"I know." She tugged self-consciously at her dress. "I just found out." She headed up the stairs. "Just going to change," she called down as she went.

She replaced her shrunken dress with black leggings and a loose T-shirt, pushed her feet into her tennis shoes and pounded back down the stairs again. Naturally, Harper hadn't gone to the hotel because she was taking care of the twins.

"You were with Jay?"

"Yes." Arabella reached down and hurriedly provided the hugs that both boys were squawking for. "I just listened to the most recent message. How bad's the flood?"

"Really bad. Brady says he's not sure how much more the hotel can take."

Arabella scrubbed her fingers over Murphy's head when he jumped against her leg, then she hugged Harper as well. "It's going to be okay. It has to be."

She was still repeating those words inside her head when Jay pulled into the hotel parking lot a short while later.

Unlike the last emergency that had turned out to be a false alarm, there were no fire trucks this time. No police cruisers. No flashing lights, no people swarming around.

The parking lot was mostly empty, in fact, which for a Saturday evening wasn't exactly the best thing to see, either.

Jay parked near the entrance and they started to go inside. But even before they made it to the wide, shallow steps of the entrance, they could see the water flowing over them, pooling at the base and running off to the side in the general direction of the pool.

"Good grief," Arabella muttered, stepping more carefully because her tennis shoes were proving to be as useful as water skis. She looked upward. "Do you think it rained here harder than it did out at your place?"

"It's possible, I guess." Jay had closed his hand protectively around her elbow when he'd seen her slip the first time. "Careful."

They went up two more steps and when she slid yet again, she muttered an oath and pulled the shoes off altogether. Her bare feet had better traction but when they entered the lobby, the water was even deeper, covering her feet right over her toes. The water was bad enough. But there were brochures and reams of papers floating about in the mess. Flowers from the arrangement that always took center stage in the lobby drifted along with them.

It seemed like a dozen people were hustling around with big buckets while a dozen more swept at the water with everything from wide brooms to mops to other buckets.

Nobody was above pitching in. Mariana. Grace Williams. Callum and his brothers. Kane and Brady, who greeted her and Jay's arrival with a narrow-eyed glare. Even Beulah was there, her sour face tight with concentration as she mopped water into the bucket that Hallie was holding.

Arabella stopped next to Jason, whose trousers were wet up to his knees while he dragged a trash barrel around in an attempt to capture some of the non-liquid debris. "Here. Let me help." The poor kid looked about ready to bawl.

He gladly surrendered the plastic bin.

"I'm going to check in at security," Jay said grimly.

She nodded and watched him work his way through the mess before turning back to the task at hand. "Jason, what happened here?"

"Sprinkler system went haywire." He pointed to the ceiling. "Went off out of the clear blue sky and then nobody seemed able to shut it off again."

She shook her head, trying to adjust her thinking from a rain flood to a sprinkler system malfunction. "The fire department was just here two days ago because of the alarm going off! Shouldn't they have noticed then if something was wrong with the system?"

"There's no way this was an accident," Brady said, wielding a push broom nearby to send a wave of water hurtling toward the open front doors.

Grace Williams had tears in her eyes as she followed behind Brady with a broom of her own.

Just seeing the woman who was always the epit-
ome of her name in tears was enough to make Arabella
feel weepy herself. "What about the guest rooms?" She
looked over her shoulder in the general direction of the
restaurant. "Roja?"

"The restaurant's okay," Mariana said gruffly. She
was out of breath and had wet splotches all over her
pants and chef's coat. "Miracle of miracles."

"The guest rooms on the third and fourth floor were
spared. But on the second?" Hallie shook her head. She
was on her elbows and knees now, wielding a twisted
towel like a squeegee to push water ahead of her, aiming, too, for the entrance. "They were evacuated as soon
as the sprinklers went off." Her eyes rested on Arabella's
face for a moment. "Maybe it's a good thing the vacan-
cies have gotten as high as they have."

"What I'd like to know is why the police haven't been
able to figure out who the hell has it in for the hotel." Beulah dumped a wad of soaking papers into Arabella's trash
bin. "But then that's the police for you," she groused and
sloshed her way across the lobby again.

Arabella nudged Mariana toward the leather chairs
nearby. "I know they're wet, but go sit down," she urged.
"Take a breather."

The fact that the older woman didn't argue spoke vol-
umes. Arabella took over the broom that Mariana had
been wielding and, leaving the trash bin to Jason once
more, added her efforts alongside Grace.

She knew it was too much to hope that Brady
wouldn't return to the topic of Jay, though she wished

he could have waited until they weren't surrounded by a dozen other people.

"I've been leaving you messages for hours."

"My phone was in my bag." She pushed ahead of him, following her own personal wave of water right outside the doors. She watched the water flow down the terra-cotta steps. "I wasn't trying to avoid you."

"You were with Cross."

"All day." She gave him a tight smile. "So if you're thinking about trying to lay all this—" she swept out her arm "—at his doorstep, think again."

He frowned. "I don't think Jay did this."

"Don't you? Detective Teas seems to think he had something to do with the balcony collapse. Are you saying you didn't know about *that*?"

His expression told her well enough that he had. "I'm not saying I agree," he defended, following her back inside again. "But the guy's got too many blank spots in his background."

"So what if he does? Does anyone's background hold up perfectly under a microscope? Does *yours*?" Her annoyance with Brady was well placed in her broad sweeping against the water. No matter how much they pushed out of the building, it still seemed to maintain its depth above her toes. "Why doesn't the water go down?" Admittedly, she'd only been at it a short while in comparison to everyone else.

"The worst of it's been here in the lobby," Grace said as she wearily pushed her broom past them again. "It was almost ten inches deep before we were able to get the water cut off."

"Fire suppression system bypasses the regular water system," Jay said, reappearing. "Cutting one off doesn't cut off the other, but in this case, the suppression system's cutoff was bypassed, too." He had two long-handled window-washing squeegees in his hand and he gave one to Hallie. "You're going to ruin your back at that rate."

She sat up on her knees, stretching gratefully before pulling herself up to her feet using the squeegee as a crutch. "You'd think I'd still be used to crawling around cleaning under beds and such."

"Nothing prepares a person for this," Arabella said.

Brady propped his arm on top of his broom. "How did you know the sprinkler system's cutoff had been tampered with?"

"Guys in security told me," Jay said evenly before putting his back into helping sweep the water out of the lobby.

"I told you I've been with him all day," Arabella muttered through her teeth.

"Doesn't mean the damage wasn't planned another time," her brother said under his breath.

She huffed and walked away, moving to the rear of the lobby nearest the elevators. The doors were standing open and she stepped inside the furthest one. Every light on the panel was lit. Lord only knew how badly it would misbehave after this latest calamity.

She swept, swept, swept until she'd managed to push almost all of the water out of the car. Then, before it could flow back inside, she shoved a few of the sopping towels that Hallie had been using into the door track, creating a rough sort of dam. Then she did the same thing with the second elevator. Hallie had noticed and brought her several fresh towels.

"Here." She crouched down and helped wedge them into place.

"Thanks." Arabella watched her from the corner of her eye. "Hallie, I'm really sorry that I didn't mention—"

"Forget it," Hallie said, cutting her off brusquely. "I shouldn't have overreacted like I did."

Arabella turned to face her head-on. "We're okay then?"

Hallie made a face. "How can we not be? Look at you. Black eyes and on your hands and knees mopping up water."

"Oh, God." Arabella covered her face again. "All day long I've been forgetting how awful I look. First Jay and now—"

"Jay?" A smile played around Hallie's lips. "What's going on with Jay?"

Arabella's face went hot and Hallie's lips pursed in a silent whistle.

"Not bad," the other girl said under her breath. "Not bad at all, girlfriend." Then she pushed to her feet and started squeegeeing water out of the corridor and toward the lobby.

It was dark by the time they all successfully conquered the water well enough that there only remained a gloss of moisture on the terra-cotta floor.

All of the area rugs had been pulled out to the parking lot. So had all of the heavy wood furniture and everything else that was even capable of being moved at all.

Someone brought in folding chairs—Arabella thought it might have been Jay, but by that point she was too exhausted to really notice or care.

She was just glad to get off her feet and tuck into one of the sandwiches that Nicole and her sisters produced.

Callum, who'd spent much of that afternoon with his cell phone glued to his ear while he helped out with the cleanup, was sitting on the registration desk. His brothers were huddled nearby. One of them—Wiley— had his arm around Grace's shoulder. She looked as exhausted as Arabella felt.

"Obviously, we'll have to close while the restoration work gets completed," Callum announced to everyone assembled.

"What'd the insurance company say?" That came from Kane.

Nobody could miss the look that passed between Callum and his brothers. "They haven't said they'll deny this latest claim outright, but—" He shook his head and eyed everyone in the room. "I'm not going to lie here. The balcony was tampered with." His gaze fell on Grace and his brother Wiley. "We can just count our blessings that nobody was hurt worse than Grace with her broken leg. The food tampering at the Give Back barbecue was a passel more of bad publicity. We've beefed up security in and around the property. We've been trying to advertise the hell out of this place. The commercial we just filmed hasn't even hit the airwaves yet. We've had more cancellations in the last month than we've had reservations. And now this?" He spread his arms and dropped them wearily.

Wiley stepped forward then. "We're not giving up," he said flatly. "We're Fortunes and we don't give up."

Someone muttered a "hear, hear."

Callum clapped his brother on the shoulder. "Wiley's right. Fortunes don't give up." His lips tilted slightly as if he'd only needed that particular reminder. "But I wouldn't be doing my job right now if I didn't caution everyone here that the future right now as far as the hotel is concerned is anything but certain. So if you want to find a job elsewhere or—"

Brady stood. "I can't speak for anyone else, but I'm not going anywhere."

Arabella popped up. "Neither am I." She lifted her hands. "If I'm not cleaning rooms right now, then I'll help paint walls. Whatever it takes."

"So will I," someone echoed.

"Me, too."

Callum's smile widened slightly. "Well. We won't go down for lack of fight and support," he said huskily. "Now, it's late and you guys have lives to get home to."

"What do we do tomorrow?" That came from Beulah.

Grace stepped forward. "If I may?"

Callum waved his hand in invitation. "Everyone's opinion matters here, Grace. Particularly yours."

"If we could have all of the supervisors and department leads report as usual, we'll have enough staff on hand to deal with anything that crops up in the next week or so. Everybody else—"

"Will still receive your regular pay," Callum inserted. "It's none of your fault this is happening, and we're not going to pull the rug out from under anyone's feet."

"Not without due warning," Wiley inserted cautiously.

Arabella knew he was the family attorney. Naturally he had to add something to that effect.

"We'll have an all-staff meeting here a week from Monday," Callum added without missing a beat. "If you don't hear from Grace personally or one of the other managers here, then check in yourself for more details on the where and when. One way or another, we'll have more news by then." He clapped his hands together once. "Any questions?" He looked over the group, waiting patiently.

"Not a question," Hallie said, looking around rather nervously. "Just something to say." She smiled a little crookedly then punched her hand into the air. "Go Hotel Fortune!"

Arabella's eyes misted. She punched her fist, too, and smiled at Jay, who was leaning against a far wall, his arms crossed over his chest. "Go Hotel Fortune!"

In minutes, the cheer had filled the damp lobby as everyone chanted the phrase over and over and over again.

If a hotel could be saved through sheer enthusiasm, Hotel Fortune would end up being just fine.

Chapter Twelve

Despite the worrisome matter of the hotel's repairs, the days that followed were some of the sweetest days that Arabella had ever known.

Neither she nor Jay were heads of anything, which meant they had a vacation, forced or not.

They helped Louella harvest strawberries for half the day on Monday and spent the rest of the day in his barn loft bedroom making love.

On Tuesday, Jay talked Arabella into climbing inside the woefully tiny cockpit of a plane he rented.

They flew all the way to Houston—which wasn't all that far admittedly—and had lunch with his parents. On the return flight to Rambling Rose, Arabella didn't even remember to clutch her armrests in terror because she was so caught up with teasing Jay over the stories his mother had regaled her with over lunch. "You might have *told* me you were a child prodigy," she said. Loudly, because it was the only way he could hear her over the noise of the engine propeller.

"I wasn't a prodigy," he said dismissively, and just as loudly.

"You won a piano competition when you were nine! Against people who were three times your age! And you graduated from college when you were twenty!"

He rolled his eyes and pointed at the checkerboard landscape beyond the windows. "There's the barn."

She looked out and sure enough, she could see the rooftop of his barn and the water wheel beside it.

"Can we fly over the hotel?"

In answer, the wings of the plane banked slightly.

She whooped nervously and closed her eyes to the sound of his laughter. But only briefly, because it was much too interesting seeing the land below.

On Wednesday, he got her up on Loretta's back and with him on Waylon, they rode all over his grandmother's property. Then he heated the water for the tub in the peach orchard and pretended to wash Arabella's back even though he was a lot more interested in her front.

He admitted that he'd suspected, and now knew for certain, that that tub had always been big enough for two.

That evening, they had dinner at Provisions with Adam and Laurel. Stephanie, who was Callum's sister and had acted as Larkin's foster mom for a brief while, was watching the toddler with her husband for the evening.

By tacit agreement, they stayed away from the subject of the hotel. Instead, Adam and Jay talked beer brewing and Laurel and Arabella gossiped about the rest of her brothers—namely Josh and Brian who'd yet to find the loves of their lives as Kane, Brady and Adam had. The only thing she had a hard time doing was keeping Brady's secret about Harper's pregnancy.

But if he hadn't told the rest of the family, it was obvious that she shouldn't do so for him, no matter how badly she wanted to share that good news.

It was late when they all finally parted and much to Arabella's disappointment, Jay drove her back to Brady's house instead of his place.

She twirled her fingers down the front of his shirt when he walked her to the door. "Sure you don't want to…you know."

He laughed and caught her marauding fingers. "I definitely want to *you kno*w. But Brady already wants to strangle me for sleeping with his baby sister. You spent the night with me last night. And the night before. If he has any more stress about it, I'll feel guilty for causing his stroke."

"He's as bad as our father," she muttered, even though a part of her was charmed by Jay's version of gallantry.

"Besides." Jay kissed her chastely on the forehead. "We had the bathtub earlier today. And you still haven't finished Oscar and Aaron's story. You've left them locked in the back of a moving truck. I need to know that they end up okay."

She caught his hand before he could step off the porch and pressed it to her cheek. "I hope you know

I'm falling in love with you." The words just wouldn't be contained. Any more than the fullness in her heart could be.

The only light shining over them came from the porch light that Brady had left burning just exactly the way her father had always done when they'd been teenagers. It was just bright enough to be sure that any kissing that went on was visible to everyone up and down the block.

And it was also bright enough to see that Jay wasn't returning her sentiment anytime soon. His brows were pulled together and the corners of his lips were turned down. "Bella—"

She steeled herself and kept her smile in place through sheer willpower. "I don't expect you to say ditto, Jay. I just wanted you to know." She braced her hands on his shoulders and went up on her toes to kiss his lips. "Oscar and Aaron are waiting."

Then she quickly slipped inside the door and closed it behind her.

Her heart thudded heavily in her chest and she leaned her head back against the door.

A moment later, she heard the soft rumble of his truck engine as he drove away.

She exhaled and opened her arms for Murphy to jump up into them. The dog slathered her face in kisses. And if he tasted a few salty tears along the way, she knew she could trust him to keep her secret.

Jay stared blearily at the cop sitting across the table from him. He'd left Arabella at her brother's house eight hours earlier and he hadn't slept a wink in the minutes since.

Instead, he'd called Detective Teas and arranged to meet him at the police station at seven that morning.

"You wanted my confession," he told Detective Teas hours later when he'd finished his story. They were sitting in the same interrogation room that Teas had used with Jay weeks ago. "And now you have it."

Jay was pretty sure the cop didn't look stunned very often, but he looked stunned now.

He flopped his chair forward onto all four legs and reached one arm out to flip the lock on the door he'd already closed.

"You're Jett Carr," he repeated. *"The one my daughter's been going around wearing a shirt that says she'd give it all up for Jett Carr. That Jett Carr."*

Jay grimaced. "You don't have to rub it in, Detective."

The cop pushed his chair back again, balancing it once more. Only this time, he lifted his legs and crossed them at the ankle over the corner of the table. He propped his hands behind his neck and a broad grin crossed his face. "Why the hell didn't you just say so? And why now?"

Jay scrubbed his hands down his face. "Because I want to sleep at night without *you* hanging over my head." It wasn't the whole truth, but he didn't figure the officer needed to know it was the trust in Arabella's eyes that was driving him more. He pushed out of his chair. "I never even wanted to be Jett Carr." He paced from one corner to the next. "But everyone insisted I needed a name with more...salability than just Jay Cross."

"It's a name," Teas said on a laugh. "Who cares?"

"Everyone in Los Angeles." Jay rubbed the back of his neck and for some reason, found himself telling the detective all about the ways and means that had gone into turning him from a college student with a side hustle playing piano and writing songs into a full-time guitar-strumming singer. It was as if once he'd started confessing, he couldn't make himself stop. "I grew my hair. Grew a beard." He rubbed his jaw, feeling the prickles of day-old stubble. "Trademark shades. Cowboy hat. And one day I looked in the mirror and didn't even recognize myself. I was involved with a woman my family detested. Had a manager who cared more about booking the next gig than he did about the fact that I was losing my mind. Two record deals that barely made the needle jump. And then—" he spread his fingers "—poof. The label cut me loose. Tina followed the day after. My manager about a week after that."

"But that video of yours is all over creation!"

Jay laughed wearily and paced around the room in the other direction. "And it's ironic as hell, too. That was my sarcastic way of bidding it all adieu. Goodbye, LA. Goodbye, Jett Carr, whose skin I'd never fit, anyway. I recorded it on my damn phone for God's sake. Never intended to even upload it, but you know cell phones these days. Once it's got a setting, it's got it forever, and the next thing I knew 'Giving It All Up' was all over the airwaves. Everybody and their mother's brother suddenly wanted a piece of Jett Carr again and—" He shook his head. "I couldn't take it. I escaped home to Texas but the only place that people *really* didn't connect me to music at all was here in Rambling Rose."

"Living in a barn out back of your grandma's farmhouse."

"It might've been a barn," Jay muttered, "but I've put a little money into it over the years."

"Because you knew you'd need an escape hatch sooner or later?"

He exhaled. "Maybe. Jett Carr did earn me money over time. I worked my ass off for it, too. But I never really cracked the ice until that video."

"Well, hiding out after the fact seems like it was the best way you could have found to ensure even more interest in it. If you'd have just told me all this from the start, it would've saved the department a lot of time and money."

Jay threw himself down on the chair he'd vacated. "If I make a donation to the policeman's fund will that help?"

Teas smiled slightly. "How big a donation?"

Jay pulled out the checkbook he'd brought with him, because he'd figured one way or another he would be paying for the visit. He wrote out several digits and signed his name. His real name. He tore out the check and slid it across to the detective. "Will that do?"

Teas gave it a considering look and then nodded. "So if it's not you tinkering with things over at Hotel Fortune, who do you think it is?"

Jay grimaced. "Who the hell knows? Someone who's got a gripe against the Fortunes. The ones who built the place, I mean." He couldn't stand the thought that the vengeance might extend to Arabella.

"Yeah." Teas scratched his chin. "Only thing is, we can't seem to find anyone with a real gripe. That Callum fella and his brothers have done a lot of good things here in town. First they built that pediatric center. The veterinary clinic. Provisions has the best food in town. Took my wife to Roja and that's gonna be just as good. Retail shops. A fancy spa where my wife is constantly begging me to send her. They've brought in new money. Created jobs." He drummed his fingers against the table. "Even checked into that lady who went off the deep end a few years ago. Charlotte Robinson? Ex-wife of that Robinson Tech guy? Her permanent address is still the fancy sanitarium place she got checked into after she tried her hand and failed at kidnapping."

Jay vaguely remembered his mother recounting the sensationalistic story several years back. But he'd been in California then and couldn't have cared less about a bunch of people he'd never met, much less heard of.

"It's gotta be an inside job. But the only one who didn't have a good alibi has been you."

"I still don't have a good alibi," he pointed out. "You just know now what I was doing in the years between insurance and showing up here."

"You saying you tampered with the balcony?"

His lips thinned. "To what end?"

"Exactly." Teas slapped his hand down on the table. "I just need one thing from you." He flipped the pages on his yellow pad to one that was empty and sent it skidding across the surface toward Jay. He followed it with a pen from his lapel pocket. "Sign an autograph for my daughter. Her name is Keisha."

Feeling relieved, bemused and pretty much spent, Jay picked up the pen and scrawled out his autograph.

To Keisha.

All the best.

Jett Carr.

Then he set down the pen and pushed to his feet.

Teas stood as well. He carefully pulled off the sheet of paper and folded it in fourths to tuck into his pocket. "What're you going to do now?"

"About what?"

"Half the world's still looking for you, bud."

Jay unlocked the door and pulled it open. "Long as I can trust you not to out me now, they'll just have to keep looking. Far as I'm concerned, Jett Carr's dead and gone."

"And Jay Cross is happy being a hotel trainee in small-town Texas?"

Arabella's image danced in Jay's mind. Without Teas in his rearview mirror, looking into her beautiful eyes would be a lot easier. "Happier than he's got a right to be."

Teas clapped him on the shoulder. "Good luck with that, then. Just have t'say that I've learned one thing in all my years of police work. Secrets tend to come out."

Another thing on which the detective and Jay's grandmother would agree.

He pulled his hat down over his eyes as he walked out into the morning sunshine.

He was surprised at how much time had passed with

the detective. But then he hadn't intended to treat the meeting like the confessional it had become. He'd just planned to tell the cop the basics about his history in California, buy his silence if it became necessary and get on with his day.

Petunia's flower shop was down the street and on the spur of the moment, Jay pulled over and parked in front. Inside, he picked a pot of geraniums off the shelf only because the small clay pot wore a pair of pink sunglasses above a pair of equally pink painted lips. Then he added another fern to his choice because he couldn't seem to pass one without feeling he ought to buy it for his grandmother.

He'd inherited the habit from Herb. Because as many times as Jay had come to town with his grandfather to pay those parking tickets, when they drove back out to the farm, Jay had invariably been holding a potted fern on his lap.

He carried the pots over to Petunia where she was talking with her dad and set them on the counter. She gave him a smile, though she looked as if she'd had about as much sleep as he had. She rang up his selections on an old-fashioned cash register. "Heard about the trouble over at the hotel. How're things coming along?"

He pulled several bills from his wallet and handed them to her. "As well as they can, from what I know." Which, admittedly, wasn't all that much. "Figured I'd drop by on my way back to my grandmother's place just to check in."

"Give them all my best. They sure could stand a bit of good luck, couldn't they?"

Truer words. Jay looked at Norman. "Going to see you out at Mariana's this Saturday, Norm?"

"What business is it of yours?" The old man nearly barked the words.

"My grandmother's gonna have the last of her strawberry jam for the summer out there." He smiled cautiously. "Figure the way you go through it, you'll want to stock up while you can."

The old man blinked. Then as if a lightbulb had come on, he nodded. "You tell Louella I'll be there."

Jay wished he could say that his grandmother would be there, too, but since she was still prohibited from getting anywhere near Mabel, he was already planning on manning the booth for her. He was also counting on Arabella to keep him company.

He pocketed the change that Petunia gave him and with the box she'd settled the plants into in hand, went out to his truck.

He'd just placed the box on the passenger-side floor when Petunia knocked on his window. He rolled it down. "Did I forget something?"

She shook her head. "No, I just wanted to explain about Dad. He hasn't really been himself these days."

Jay nodded, not really sure how to respond. "My grandmother's already told me about the problem he has with his meds."

She looked relieved. "I'm trying to find a solution for him, but he's a determined old guy, you know? Independent as hell and the idea of having someone monitor anything he does is hard for him to swallow. The only person he tolerates these days is my nephew. I'm sorry if he sounded rude."

"No worries."

She reached in and squeezed his arm. "Louella's always said what a good boy you are and she's right."

He actually felt his neck get hot. "Um—"

She laughed slightly. "Now I've gone and embarrassed you, which wasn't my intention at all." She stepped back onto the curb. "One of these days, buy Louella something besides a fern!" Then she disappeared inside her shop.

He looked down at the plant. "What's wrong with a fern?"

It took only a few minutes to get to the hotel.

There was a sign posted on the front door that it was temporarily closed, but when he pulled it open, it wasn't locked.

He went inside.

The lobby smelled vaguely musty but there were big fans positioned in every corner blowing air noisily across the floor. Baseboards were gone, and the lower portions of drywall had been cut away from the walls, leaving the studs exposed. Whatever repairs were going to be needed, they couldn't even get started until everything was fully dried out.

The fans seemed to be the only occupants, though.

He looked into the office behind the registration desk but it was empty. So was the security office.

The elevators were locked on the first floor and he wandered past them, sticking his head around the door to Roja.

He earned a look from the group of Fortunes sitting at one of the tables.

Brady's eyes narrowed when he spotted Jay. "What do you want, Cross?"

To marry your sister.

The words popped into his head, making Jay forget for a moment why he'd even walked in there in the first place.

Callum rose and walked toward him. "Something on your mind?"

Jay swallowed and focused on the older man's face. It was a lot easier than the glaring one that Brady possessed. "I was just checking on how things were going. Insurance and all that."

Callum's brows rose. "You know about insurance?"

"I used to." He looked past Callum to Wiley. He was a lawyer. Nothing showed in his expression. But Steven and his brother Dillon were contractors. Easier to read. "They're denying the claim?"

Arabella's other brother Kane, who'd been involved with the hotel from the start, was the only one who nodded. "Wiley's been talking about filing a suit."

"They'll pay it if you'll agree to a higher premium," Jay said. "It'd be quicker and less expensive in the long run than a lawsuit."

"That's not news," Brady snapped. "You know how much of a higher premium?"

Jay calculated a moment, then named a figure that had all of the men sitting back with surprise. He figured he was at least within a few thousand dollars of being on target.

"That's oddly accurate," Callum admitted. "Problem is, coming up with that much is a bit of a problem. It's not as if it's a onetime investment. Collectively, we can pitch in from our own pockets but—"

Wiley's hands were fisted on top of the table. "But considering we don't know who's trying to sabotage the hotel in the first place, maybe it's safer for everyone if we just cut our losses now. Nobody wants to throw good money after bad."

No matter how many golden eggs *those* Fortunes had, Jay knew it couldn't be all that easy increasing their investments to such a degree.

"The town needs this hotel," Steven said quietly. Jay knew he was married to the mayor. "It's coming to stand for everything that Rambling Rose is. Embraces the past. Welcomes the future."

"Sounds straight from Ellie's lips," Dillon muttered.

"So what if it is?" Steven countered. "She's right."

Callum dropped his arm over Jay's shoulder and showed him right back to the door. "I'll trust you not to say anything about this before our staff meeting on Monday," he said quietly.

Jay nodded and felt Brady Fortune's eyes burning a hole into his spine as he left.

"Where's Brady?" Arabella slid into her seat at the breakfast table and reached for the stack of toast in the center.

"Went to the hotel again." Harper was nursing a cup of tea, looking vaguely green around the gills.

"You feeling okay?"

"Morning sickness," she admitted. "Why does it have to hit now when Brady's so worried about the hotel?"

"Maybe stress makes it worse." Arabella could see the twins through the doorway to the living area. They were bouncing recklessly on the couch and the fact that Harper didn't even seem to notice was enough to call for action. "Go back up to bed," she urged. "Sleep as long as you want. I'll keep the boys occupied today."

"I was going to take them out to ride again with Laurel."

"I'll take them," she promised.

"But you don't know how to ride at all."

"I know a little bit," she assured primly. "Jay showed me. And I'm sure he'd be willing to come with us, anyway, if you're so worried about my ability."

"I know you'll take care of the boys," Harper said quickly, looking horrified that she might have implied otherwise.

Arabella reached over and gave her a quick squeeze. "Go back to bed. Or take a bath. Whatever."

"Maybe I'll just hug the porcelain goddess," Harper muttered, but she got up looking grateful and left the room.

Arabella finished slathering Lou's jam on her toast and shoved half of it in her mouth as she went into the living room. She snapped her fingers at Murphy who obediently slunk off the couch where he wasn't allowed and then caught Toby around the waist mid-jump. She swallowed her mouthful and set him on the ground. "You know you're not supposed to bounce on the couch." She grabbed Tyler, too, and set him on the floor next to his brother.

"But—"

"No jumping on the couch!"

There were blocks scattered all over the floor. The Candy Land game they usually loved was upended in the corner, little pieces strewn about. Just looking at the mess made her actually long for the simplicity of cleaning a hotel room.

"Come on, guys. Let's clean up and later after you're dressed, I'll take you out to see Auntie Laurel and her horses."

"I want to watch TV," Tyler groused.

"Yeah, and I want a million dollars," she grumbled. Then she smiled and scrubbed her hand over his tousled hair. "Come on. Clean up and we'll negotiate the matter of TV." She knew that negotiating was something the boys were well-acquainted with, thanks to Harper.

Tyler halfheartedly tossed a block into the bucket where they belonged. "Harper's sneaky. She gives us five minutes before bed, but we gotta only read together."

Arabella laughed and went down onto her hands and knees alongside them. "The horror. Come on, we'll all do it together." Roving around, she gathered up a handful of blocks but before long, she was the only one cleaning up the mess on the floor, which proved her negotiating skills weren't up to Harper's level at all. Instead, Arabella was just a sucker for the boys.

At least the two eventually went upstairs and returned, suitably attired in mismatched shorts and T-shirts. Toby's hair was damp so she was fairly certain he'd washed his face and Tyler had a smear of toothpaste on his shirt, so she felt confident he'd brushed his teeth.

Considering all of that to be ticks in the win column, she handed them the television remote. "Your channels only," she warned. Brady had locked down their ability to unintentionally tune in to something too mature for them.

It usually meant that when Arabella actually felt like watching something on television, she was reduced to watching classic cartoons or kid-friendly videos on YouTube.

After a brief tussle for control of the remote, Tyler won and Arabella went back into the kitchen to have another piece of toast. It was cold by now, but the strawberry jam made up for it. She cleaned up the kitchen and realized she was humming along with the dreaded earworm song when it sounded from the other room.

She stuck her head into the living room, prepared to tell the kids to find another channel.

But they were standing there giggling and dancing the floss and she didn't have the heart. Instead, she pulled her own cell phone out of her back pocket and without their knowledge started filming them.

She'd send it to her parents later. They'd love it.

The song had a heavy beat. Oddly gut-wrenching really in comparison to the lively steps the boys were doing. She glanced at the TV screen above the boys' head.

The video was deliberately blurry in the way that some were. Sort of jerky, even. Focusing on the singer's long fingers as he strummed his gleaming guitar while his unbuttoned shirt fluttered from an unseen breeze. Then on his bearded profile as he crooned to some invisible lover. "Giving it all up. Gonna be someone new." His dark head dipped again, giving little more than a flash of dark sunglasses and a dip of his cowboy hat. "Never gonna trust again." His deep voice curled over the words and despite herself, Arabella felt a tingle down her spine.

Hallie wasn't exactly off-track, she decided. Jett Carr did have a sexy demeanor.

"Never gonna find someone like you."

He strummed harder, his fingers working the strings faster, and without volition, Arabella's feet carried her back into the living room. Closer to the television screen.

"You're not s'posed to stand so close." Tyler grabbed her hand and dragged her back two steps.

"Never gonna trust again, never gonna love again, never gonna find someone like you." After the buildup, the singer trailed off, though the music continued on. He stood up from the stool where he'd been sitting and set his guitar down. Then he walked away, the wind fluttering the tails of his shirt madly around his shoulders. She saw a flash of a tattoo and then Jett Carr looked over his shoulder straight at the camera.

He pulled his glasses down his nose, and Jay's distinctive green eyes stared straight at her. "Never find someone like you."

His husky words trailed off and the video went black before switching to a violently colorful commercial for Frosted Fruity Flakes.

I think you should know that...

"You're a liar, Jay Cross," she said thickly.

Because there was no question in her mind that he and the singer were one and the same.

She'd know those green eyes anywhere.

"Why's Jay a liar?" Tyler bounced onto the couch beside her, and then nearly fell over himself getting back off again when she looked at him.

"Here." She handed him the remote control again. Tyler hooted and quickly punched buttons but she barely noticed. She was too busy punching buttons on her own phone.

Only as soon as Jay's line started to ring, she chickened out and hung up again.

She was *such* a monumental fool.

How many times had she mentioned how much she detested that darned song? And he'd just...gone along!

Squelching a moan, she sank down onto the couch and didn't even protest when Murphy jumped onto her lap. She held her phone above the dog's head and opened a browser. She didn't even have to finish typing in the words *Jett Carr* before the video she'd just watched popped to the top of her list on her phone.

She turned down the volume and watched the video all the way through.

Even though she knew.

"Never gonna trust again," she whispered soundlessly. "Not even you."

Chapter Thirteen

Jay drove from the flower shop back to his grandmother's and carried the fern inside. She was in the kitchen, nursing the big metal pot she used to cook down her strawberries.

He set the plant on the table. "Are you tired of ferns, Gran?"

She glanced around the veritable jungle growing inside her house. "It's what your grandpa always gave me. How could I get tired of them?"

He leaned his hip against the table. "I told Detective Teas who I was."

She gave him a sidelong look. "Thought you were just Jay Cross."

"You know what I mean."

"Do *you* know what you mean?"

He muttered an oath and rubbed his forehead. "I'm too tired for your cryptic comments. Jett Carr's a stage persona. That's it."

She turned and gently drew her fingers along the fern's feathery edges. "Jet-pack. Your grandpa loved you more'n anything on this earth. And I loved him more'n anything on this earth. That's why I took on O'Brien when he asked young Louella *Carr* to marry him." She poked him once in the chest with a finger that was definitely not gentle. "Jett Carr isn't just some name you plucked outta thin air. Your problem with Jett Carr was that you were letting other people control who he was. Instead of being who *you* wanted to be."

"Some things aren't that easy."

She made a disgusted sound and returned to her pot.

He dropped it. "Was there ever something between him and Mabel?"

She threw back her head and laughed. "Lord no."

"And I know you didn't steal her jam recipe."

She snorted, still laughing. "No, sir, I did not."

"Then what the hell happened between the two of you?"

She gave him a look over her shoulder. "You really want to know?"

He spread his hands helplessly. "I'm asking, aren't I?" He'd been asking for days now.

She gave a huge sigh. "Shop-World wants to pay me a boatload of money to put my jam in all their stores. From California to Wyoming to Texas."

Jay was glad he was leaning against the counter, because he probably would have fallen on his butt otherwise. *"What?"*

She gave him an annoyed look. "You heard me." She tapped her long wooden spoon against the side of the pot. "My mistake was telling Mabel about it. She's always had a pea-green streak about her. She'll get over it in time."

"Why didn't you tell me about it? Does Mom know?"

"What good would that do?" She looked even more annoyed. "Wouldn't make your mama stop trying to get me to give up my home and move into a dinky bedroom at that house she shares with your dad. Nothing wrong with that house, mind you, but it isn't mine."

"Are you going to take the offer?"

"Would've done it already if it weren't for you."

"What have I got to do with it? Gran, you'll make a fortune."

"Never wanted a fortune," she muttered. "Just wanted my home and my family." She stuck her spoon back into her pot. "And soon as I take it, word is going to spread around this town like wildfire. Shop-World wants to do a whole advertising thing about me growing my strawberries and all that. How's that gonna play when my grandson's famous and afraid to get his face seen on some newscaster's camera?"

"I'm not famous."

"Jett Carr damn sure is now whether you like it or not." She gave him a fierce look. "I know you've been spending time with Arabella. *Quality* time."

"I'm not having a discussion about my love life with

you, Gran." He wanted to dunk his head in the stream
outside his barn just thinking about it.

"There's nothing new under the sun," she told him
tartly. "Why d'you think Herb and I had such a quick
wedding? That's the problem with all you young people.
Thinking you're the only ones who ever invented sex."

He covered his eyes and wanted to be anywhere other
than there.

"You want to keep having your way with that young
lady, you'd better do more than 'fess up to that detective person. Arabella's the one who matters, isn't she?"

He dropped his hand. "Yes."

She gave him a narrow-eyed glare. Then after a moment nodded decisively and pointed the end of her dripping red spoon at a drawer. "There's a metal box in
there. Get it for me."

He pulled open the junk-filled drawer and managed to extract the flattish, rectangular box. He started
to hand it to her but she just waved with her spoon.
"Open it." He did so, expecting the deck of cards that
he vaguely remembered it once contained.

Instead, sitting on a folded yellowed hankie were
two delicate, glittering necklaces and one small diamond ring.

"I had t'stop wearing the ring when my arthritis got
too bad." She waggled her slightly bent fingers. "But
it's yours if you want it."

His gut tightened. "Granny—"

"Just take it." She sniffed slightly and focused on her
bubbling jam concoction. "Give it to that girl. Pretty
sure you love her just like Herb loved me. Or buy your-

self something fancy and modern to give her. I don't much care so long as you get your head on straight and do what's right."

He slid the ring over the tip of his pinky finger. It was as far as it would go. She knew he'd never want modern and fancy. Then he kissed her lined cheek. "You're a helluva woman, you know."

She snorted. "Of course I know." But she patted his cheek the same way she'd done when he was five. "Now get on with you. I don't want to see your face until you've come clean with Arabella once and for all."

He hadn't slept. Hadn't showered.

He knew he probably ought to at least do one of those things before he went down on bended knee, but he did neither. Just got in his truck and drove back into town.

It was a sign of his own stupidity that he had to spend an extra hour getting gas when he ran out of it halfway there.

But finally he was standing on Brady's front porch step. The afternoon sun was high in the sky above him and he squinted against the glare because he'd also forgotten his hat back at his grandmother's place.

"You're falling apart, man," he muttered to himself before reaching out to knock on the door.

He heard the squeals of little boys laughing before the door opened up and he looked down to see Toby—or was it Tyler?—looking up at him. "Hey there. I'm here to see your auntie Bella."

"She's in the backyard," the boy said artlessly. "How come you made her cry?"

He frowned. "She's crying?"

The twin's twin popped his head into the doorway. "'Cause you're a liar," he said seriously. "We gotta get time out when we lie. Are you gonna get time out?"

The only thing Jay had lied about to Arabella was his past. "Can I come in?"

The two boys shook their heads. "We're not supposed to open the door."

"But you did."

They gave each other looks and promptly shut the door right in his face.

Jay started to knock again, but thought better of it.

Instead, he left the geranium on the porch and walked around to the back of the house. It was protected by a tall wooden fence all the way around the yard. Logically, he knew there had to be a gate somewhere, but he was way too impatient just then to try to find it.

Feeling like the biggest louse on the planet, he stretched up and caught the top of the fence, then grunting slightly, managed to heave himself up and over.

He landed in a pile of dog poop, which should have been his biggest warning to date that things were not going to go as he planned. He scraped his boot as well as he could against the grass and walked farther into the backyard, turning around the corner of the house.

And there she sat. Her flaming hair was spread around her shoulders. The temper in Arabella's blue eyes when she spotted him made them almost as black as the bruises that had faded over the last several days. She didn't even seem all that surprised to see him. "What're *you* doing here?"

He took a few cautious steps closer. She was holding

a baseball in her hands and the way she kept turning it between her palms was a little alarming. Particularly when she'd told his mother just two days earlier how she'd played softball in high school.

"I came to tell you something I should have told you a long time ago."

She tossed the ball lightly from one hand to the other. "I think you should know that—" She broke off, seeming to be waiting for some response.

"That I'm—" His voice came out croaky and hoarse. He cleared his throat. "I'm in love with you," he finished more clearly.

She made a harsh, buzzing sound. "Wrong."

"What?"

"Before the balcony collapse. You were going to tell me something. Remember?"

Time had been so full in the last several weeks that in comparison, the balcony collapse felt like it had happened years ago, rather than just six months. "I remember I wanted to tell you everything about me."

"Like the fact that you're a liar?"

Regret sank hard inside his gut. "Bella."

"Don't call me that."

"You know. Don't you?"

Her lips twisted. "That you're Jett Carr?" She bounced the ball twice in her palm. "And I'm the biggest fool on the planet?"

"You're not a fool."

She sent the ball whizzing two inches from his head. It bounced hard on the fence beyond him. "You should have told me," she said flatly and marched inside the house.

She slammed the door behind her.

Jay went over to it and tried the knob. No shock that she'd locked it.

He pressed his forehead against the warm wood. "I should have told you," he said loudly enough that if, by some miracle, she was still standing close to the door she'd be able to hear. "People used to only like me because I was Jett. And the longer things went on with you, the more I was afraid you'd like me only if I'd never been him at all. Bella, I'm sorry. I warned you that I wasn't good enough for you but I fell in love with you, anyway. You're everything that's right in this freaking world."

The door yanked open and he nearly stumbled inside. Tears glittered in her eyes, making them even more sharply blue. "I don't know why I didn't figure it out before I saw your damn video. You gave it all up. Became someone new. Never gonna trust again. Certainly not *me*. Not enough to tell me the truth. Was she the complication in California, Jay? The woman who broke your heart?"

His voice rose. "It wasn't a woman who broke my heart! It was the music that did that!"

She'd paled and taken a step back as he shouted the words, and he felt even worse.

"I would never hurt you," he said roughly.

"Bzzz," she said thickly. "Too late."

And she closed the door in his face yet again.

He sighed wearily. "Bella, please. There's no other woman. There's only you."

"Maybe you should go." He jerked his head back, looking up at the voice from above. Harper was leaning out an opened window. "Brady's going to be home soon and once he sees the state Bella's in—" She looked almost sympathetic. "Give her—give them—a little time, Jay."

He squinted up at her. The sunlight was creating a halo around her dark head. "You overheard, I guess."

"That you're the sexy missing Jett?"

He grimaced, feeling his neck get hot. He'd blushed more in the last twenty-four hours than he had in his entire adult life and he didn't much like it. "Just Jett," he muttered.

She propped her head on her hand. "I overheard."

He spread his hands and his grandmother's diamond ring on his pinky winked in the sunlight. "I should have told her. I know that. But I can't undo the past. So what am I supposed to do now?"

"Undo the future?"

"There *is* no future. Not without her in it."

She smiled slightly. "Find a way to make her listen," she suggested, and then disappeared back inside the window.

Jay blinked against the sun again. He looked around the yard. Spotted the gate finally, as well as the sturdy metal lock on its latch.

Resigned, he climbed back over the gate, this time at least managing to miss the dog crap.

He walked back to his truck, feeling the itch on his

spine of several pairs of eyes, but when he looked back at the house again, he saw nothing but the twitch of curtains in the windows.

He got behind the wheel and started the engine.

As if the fates were mocking him, the radio came on to his own voice singing back at him. He spun the dial and a droning voice reciting farm futures replaced his song.

Harper's words echoed in his head. *Find a way to make her listen.*

"How in the hell am I supposed to find a way to do that?"

He made it all the way back to his grandmother's place before the obvious hit him.

He drove around the house—something he never did—and parked next to the stone barn. Inside, he flipped up the piano bench and shuffled through the music books until he found a couple sheets of staff paper.

He flipped down the lid of the grand piano with shocking disregard for its value and dropped the paper on top of the gleaming black wood. He located a stub of a pencil and then he sat down at the keyboard and got to work.

"Ohmigod, have you heard it?" Hallie squeezed a folding chair in between the ones Arabella and Beulah were occupying.

It was Monday morning and even though Arabella would have preferred to be anywhere else, family loyalty had made her show up at the hotel for Callum's big staff meeting.

"Heard what?"

"Jett Carr's new song. It dropped just last night and every music station's been playing it practically non-stop. There's a rumor he was even spotted right here in Texas. Can you believe it?"

Arabella closed her eyes. "Hallie, I don't—"

It was too late. Hallie had already started the video playing on her phone. This time there was no shot of Jay. Or Jett. Or whatever he was calling himself.

Just hands on a piano keyboard. One raised scar on a long, tanned finger against ivory and black.

The melody was simple but haunting.

"Your love healed me," he sang softly. Much like the way he'd sung that shoe-tying song to her nephews that day that felt so long ago. "Your love revealed me—"

"Thanks to everyone for coming today." Callum's voice cut over the soft music from Hallie's phone that she quickly turned off and tucked away.

Healed me. Revealed me.

Try as she might, Arabella couldn't keep the words from circling inside her mind. To such an extent that she missed almost everything that Callum was announcing.

She'd been so afraid that Jay would also show his face at the staff meeting, but he was nowhere to be seen. More proof that he wasn't the man she'd believed him to be. Jett Carr might have been spotted and now it was Jay Cross who'd disappeared.

She ducked her head, surreptitiously swiping at the tears that kept leaking out.

She wasn't the only one who was crying, though that was more caused by the announcement Callum was making.

"This Friday night," he was saying. "That's just four days. So spread the word. The more people who turn out, the better off we'll all be."

Brady hadn't told her they'd be having a final party. But that was what it sounded like Callum was talking about.

Then the meeting broke up again and Arabella filed out miserably behind the others.

Hallie's car was parked next to Arabella's. "Think you'll go back to Austin?"

"You mean if this doesn't work?" Hallie shrugged. "How could it not?" Considering the situation, Hallie looked quite cheerful.

Arabella got into her car and drove back to Brady's. She went inside and her energy took her as far as the narrow twin bed in her bedroom. She threw herself down on it, staring blindly at the geranium plant sitting on the windowsill. She could hear the muffled sounds of Harper and the boys from the backyard accompanied by Murphy's excited yips.

She could sell her car. Maybe she'd get enough to pay for a one-way flight back to New York.

At least her dad would be happy.

She swiped her cheeks and pulled out her cell phone. She had two text messages, both from Tammy Jo Pendleton, containing photos of her and Ham wearing their wedding finery.

Arabella was so miserable she couldn't even summon a speck of annoyance. She texted back a polite congratulations and then dropped the phone like a hot potato when it vibrated and Jay's name popped up on the screen.

But he wasn't calling her. Just sending a text message. Even though she wished she had enough willpower to delete it unseen, she swiped her screen again and the new message appeared.

You don't have any reason to forgive me, but I still hope you'll come.

Below the message was a small image and she frowned at her own inability to just let it go.

She tapped the image and it blew up, the headlines filling the screen.

Jett Carr
One Night Only

She slowly sat on the side of the bed, expanding the image even more to read the smaller print.

And when she had, she bolted down the stairs, nearly plowing right into Brady as he came in through the front door.

Even though he had his own phone at his ear, she waved hers in his face. "Do you believe his *gall*?"

He pointed to his own phone as he brushed past her, dropping his tie on the couch as he passed it. "That's all it took?" he said to whomever was on the other end of his call. "Fifteen minutes?"

She followed him through the kitchen. "I should've listened to you all along. You said he was hiding something and—"

Brady turned on his heel and held up a silencing hand. "That's good news, Kane. Thanks." He ended the call and waved his hand in front of her. "What's got you so wound up? As if I don't already know."

"He's having a concert! Right here in Rambling Rose. It wasn't bad enough that he lied, but now he has to rub our faces in it?"

"I wouldn't exactly put it that way." Looking entirely too calm about it, he picked up Murphy, who'd been dancing around his legs, and headed out the back door. Boyish squeals greeted him and he was kissing Harper when Arabella stomped out after him.

She propped her fists on her hips. "What way *would* you put it?" The wary looks she earned from both her brother and Harper annoyed her even more. "Why am I the only one who's upset here? Jay—" She shook her phone in the air. "*Jett* is having a concert. Right under our noses!"

Harper disentangled herself from Brady's arms. "Do you know why?"

"Because he's a deceitful—"

"Generous," Harper said firmly, as if Arabella were no older than Toby and Tyler.

"Generous!" Arabella snorted. "He's—"

"Donating his ticket sales to Hotel Fortune," Brady said. "Callum announced it at the staff meeting."

She felt poleaxed. "What?"

"You were there. What the hell did you think he was talking about?"

She blindly felt for a patio chair. "I wasn't listening," she mumbled.

Brady poked his finger at her nose. "For whatever reason, your crush is throwing us a lifesaving buoy and I don't want—"

"Brady." Harper closed her hands around his arm. "Arabella *is* the reason," she said gently. "And it's way more than a crush. Jay is in love with her."

"She's too young."

"I *am* not!" Arabella's ire instantly refocused on Brady as she shot to her feet.

"She's only a year younger than me," Harper added.

Brady frowned. "That's different."

Harper's amused eyes met Arabella's for a moment. "You think Jay—who has managed to keep his alter identity a secret all of these months—revealed himself to the public by volunteering his concert proceeds to Hotel Fortune because he's been so thrilled working there as a *management trainee*?"

Arabella sank right back down into the chair she'd just vacated. "He volunteered?"

"Criminy, Bella. Have you been listening at all?"

She shook her head, ignoring her brother in favor of Harper. There was a gnawing hole in the pit of her stomach, outsized only by the ache growing inside her heart. "Why would he do that?"

Harper smiled. "I think he found a way to be heard."

* * *

The days leading up to Friday were the longest days of Arabella's life.

She couldn't turn on the news without seeing some mention of Jett Carr. His mysterious disappearance from the public eye, now ended just as abruptly and just as inexplicably. There was speculation that he'd gone into hiding over a woman. That he'd been recording a new album for which his latest song was just a teaser. That he'd been abducted by aliens.

There seemed to be no end to it, and it wasn't helped by the fact that the singer, himself, was refusing all interviews until after the concert.

Posters of Jett Carr—bearded, sunglasses-wearing Jett Carr—cropped up all around town. They were in the grocery store. In the flower shop. At Provisions. Everywhere Arabella turned, there were people talking about the coming event. The motels miles outside of town were full.

Mariana's Market was supposedly even transforming itself into a campground of sorts for the weekend.

Meanwhile, aside from that one text message that Jay had sent her, Arabella didn't hear another word from him.

Not even when she went out to his grandmother's place—bearing the linen napkin that he'd wrapped Louella's chocolate chip cookies inside that very first time she'd been there with him—did she see him. Instead, Arabella had been stunned silly to see Louella and Mabel sitting together on her porch as if their brouhaha had never occurred at all.

When she'd finally just asked if Jay was there, Louella had shaken her head. "Gone to California."

Arabella's heart had fallen through the floor. "Is he coming back?"

His grandmother had merely peered cagily from beneath her shady hat. "Got a concert tomorrow night, doesn't he?"

Arabella hadn't had the guts to tell her she'd meant was he coming back to *her*.

By the next afternoon, the traffic lining up for the concert stretched all the way from the blocks surrounding the hotel that had been cordoned off by the police to the other side of town.

As she sat in the rear of the air-conditioned black SUV that had been sent for her and Brady, Harper and the kids, Arabella felt twisted tighter and tighter into a knot of nerves. If the ticket she had wasn't hanging around her neck inside a plastic lanyard, she would have twisted it, too, into a sweaty, pulpy mess.

"What're they doing?" Tyler poked his finger against the tinted window beside him. They were still several blocks away from the hotel but there were tables set up at irregular intervals along the curb and lines of people were already congregating around them.

"Selling concert merchandise," Brady said. He sounded almost as stressed out as Arabella felt.

She wondered what rabbit hole she'd fallen down and restlessly pulled the small mirror out from the purse she'd borrowed from Harper. Her black eyes had mercifully faded. But that was about all she could say about her reflection and she pocketed the mirror once again.

After another thirty minutes of crawling along in traffic, the driver—an amiable guy named Ted—pulled to a stop in front of a mass of yellow caution tape stretching across the main parking lot entrance of the hotel. "Okay, folks. This is where I drop you." He got out and opened the door for them. The sun was just starting to dip to the horizon and lights blazed across the parking lot, focused on the complicated metal framework that was nearly as tall as the four-story hotel behind it.

The stage was at the center of the framework with the hotel entrance immediately behind it. On either side, massive screens hung from the metal bars.

The first few dozen rows of chairs were also positioned beneath the soaring metal framework and Arabella was shocked to see several people moving about in the heights, anchored by safety belts.

"Holy cow." Harper murmured what Arabella couldn't manage to put into words. "Brady, are those cameras or lights up there?"

"Both. A crew came in yesterday and started building the staging. Callum's been working with some guy named Devane on security. The last thing anyone wants is some snafu tonight. That's why there are so many cops and security guards around." They joined the line of people waiting to pass through a metal detector.

In front of them, two teenage girls wearing headphones were dancing together. In back of them, two middle-aged couples were laughing and showing off the T-shirts they'd purchased outside the concert "gates."

Arabella felt dizzy. "I didn't know Jett Carr was so... big."

"Not sure Jett Carr knew it either," the woman behind Arabella stuck her head forward to say. She had a gleam of excitement on her face. "We used to see him once a month at a club he played at all the time in Los Angeles."

"You came from Los Angeles?"

The other woman with her leaned forward, too. "Plane tickets on such short notice were too expensive, so we drove. Took three days."

The line moved and feeling numb, Arabella opened the purse for a security guard to poke a flashlight into before waving her through the arch of the metal detector. She could only imagine how long it would have taken if she'd brought her usual bag.

A vaguely hysterical giggle rose in her throat as she left the metal detector and yet another guard shone a device over her plastic-encased ticket.

Then the lot of them were through and they started up the center aisle between two sections of chairs.

Each row was numbered and Arabella felt even dizzier when she realized there had to be at least a thousand chairs and their row—number 5—was actually the very first row. It was empty, except for Jay's parents and his grandmother, sitting in the very center. Louella saw Arabella and held out her hand.

With a knot in her throat, Arabella took it and sat beside her. She looked over her shoulder at the sea of chairs. Beyond the seats there was even more standing room.

"Exciting day," Louella said.

Turning back around, Arabella could only nod. She was too busy trying to keep her sudden tears at bay.

All too quickly, the seats around them began filling. When she saw Detective Teas and a pretty teenaged girl sit in the two seats at the end of their row next to Mariana, Arabella was even more disconcerted.

Music had been playing on the loudspeakers all along. But until it suddenly went up a notch in volume, Arabella hadn't even realized that none of the songs were Jay's.

The sky was nearly dark and the lights from the steel rafters overhead began swirling around. Shots of Jay playing guitar were spilling over the projector screens overlaid with horses running wild and waves crashing on a beach.

Jay's grandmother suddenly leaned toward her. "Breathe," she advised.

Arabella exhaled on a rush and laughed shakily.

Louella took her hand in hers and squeezed. She didn't let go.

Tyler and Toby were standing in front of Harper and Brady, dancing around with little Erin McCarthy. Kane's future stepdaughter was doing her level best to keep up with the boys even though she was half their age. A chant had risen in the crowd, getting louder and louder as people stamped their feet and clapped their hands. Their chant got even louder, almost drowning out the loudspeakers when a trio of men stepped out onto the dim stage. One went to the big drum set and the two others went to the standing mics and picked up guitars that Arabella hadn't even realized were there. The drummer suddenly rolled out a solo in perfect timing to the music on the loudspeaker and the chanting got even louder when the two guitar players started strumming. Then another trio—women this time—danced out onto the stage and took position to one side, where they started swaying and singing.

Arabella didn't even know the song and she suddenly wished she hadn't spent the past four days dithering over the fact that Jay hadn't called her when she ought to have been listening to every single piece of music he'd ever made.

Then the energy climbed to an even higher pitch and the lights that had been dancing over the skyline suddenly centered on the stage, beams crisscrossing.

Jay stood in the center.

His hat was pulled low over his face. A pair of sunglasses shielded his eyes and a guitar hung down his back. He wore black jeans and a plain white shirt with the sleeves rolled up his forearms and the buttons unfastened halfway down his chest.

Arabella had no way of knowing whether he knew she was there. Whether he was looking straight at her or at any of the people crowding into the parking lot and the street beyond as he pulled the guitar over his shoulder and launched into a hard-beating song that had everyone around her jumping to their feet.

Jay's grandmother pulled Arabella to her feet, too, and she pulled her close, an arm over her shoulder. "Jay's first song," she said into her ear, loud enough that she could hear. It was followed by three more equally fast and rowdy and wonderful tunes, and when the last notes trailed away and Jay lifted his guitar high above his head, Arabella was stomping her feet and clapping as loudly as everyone else.

Then Jay stepped close to the mic again and the crowd abruptly quieted. "It's good to see y'all here." His deep voice rumbled over them.

"It's good to see you," someone yelled from deep in the crowd. "Where've you been?"

"Been around." Jay's smile flashed and he chuckled, which set off another flurry of excitement. "Never had quite a turnout like this before," he drawled.

"We'll go anywhere you go, Jett," a woman screamed.

His smile flashed again. "That's real sweet of you, darlin'." He started strumming again, picking the rec- ognizable notes that had been playing so incessantly on the radio for the last year. "Last year, I thought this was going to be the last song I ever wrote," he admit- ted and with the band and backup singers along with him, he sang it as he walked back and forth across the stage. When he finished and returned to center stage, a grand piano had been rolled into view. Its lid was lifted and the image of the strings and black-and-white keys filled the video screens.

"Wouldn't ever know they only had a few days to pull this all together," Louella commented in Arabella's ear. But she was barely listening because she was raptly watching every movement Jay made as he handed off his guitar and sat down at the piano.

He set his fingers on the keys and the crowd went quiet again as he slowly ran them up and down in a simple scale. "We spend so much of our lives pretending. I'm a piano player," he said quietly. His fingers danced again up and down the keyboard in a melancholy way. "There's only a handful of people here tonight who even know that."

"Play for me, Jett," someone cried out.

His dimple flashed. "And I can't help but think how much better off we would be if we could all just be who we really are. Folks want to know where I've been all this time." He swept out an encompassing arm. "And I've been right here all along. Just me. Figuring out who I really am." He banged out a couple chords that earned another burst of applause, and just as deftly returned to the haunting notes up and down the keyboard. "I play piano. I love my family. I ride horses. I write songs and I make more mistakes than I can count." He pulled off his sunglasses and tossed them into the blackness outside the lights focused over him. "And I've realized how badly everyone wants to be loved exactly the way we are. Even me." He cleared his throat softly. "So I wrote a little song about that. This song."

Then he looked straight at Arabella.

His long, strong fingers picked out the notes with impossible delicacy as he sang right to her.

Even though they were surrounded by hundreds and hundreds of strangers, even though he was helping to save the hotel from financial ruin, she knew in that moment that this song, this moment, was the real reason for it all.

For her.

"I think you should know that your love healed me,"

he sang, his voice turning gruffer. Huskier. "Your love revealed me. You're my Bella. And I never want to let you go. My Bella, please don't go."

By the time the final notes of the hauntingly beautiful piano notes faded into the night, Arabella didn't even care anymore that tears were sliding down her face. Nor did she need the little nudge that Jay's grandmother gave her as she stood and walked to the corner of the stage where a slim man dressed all in black helped her up the steps.

At the top, she turned and was shocked at the way the lights blurred out everything beyond their glare. But at the center of it all was Jay.

Her Jay, standing next to the piano and watching her oh-so-closely with those green eyes. The same green eyes that she'd fallen headlong into on a January night.

A pin drop could have been heard as she slowly crossed the stage, not stopping until she stood toe to toe with him.

"I think you should know that I could never stop loving you." She didn't care that the mic picked up her words. She reached up and slowly pulled off his cowboy hat. "Not even if I tried."

When his arms swept her tight against him, she heard only his whispered words. "I love you—"

But suddenly a spotlight swerved and Arabella felt a sudden *whoosh* of heat.

She didn't even understand that it wasn't normal until Jay swore and shoved her down. Her knees hit the stage and she cried out, blinded by light and Jay's body covering hers, flattening her right down.

She heard shouts. The sound of cymbals crashing. A discordant guitar twang. The stage beneath them vibrated with running footsteps.

"What's happening? What's wrong?"

He raised his head and she could finally see the wall of orange flames licking at the edge of the stage.

She gasped.

Beyond the flames, beyond the spotlights, she could hear but not see the people who were yelling. Then Jay, on his knees, pulled Arabella farther away from the flames. They knocked into one of the standing mics and it toppled, adding yet another screech to the cacophony.

Hands grabbed at them and in a panic, she hit back with all the ferocity her brothers had ever taught her. "Leave him alone!"

But Jay caught her flailing fists. "They're security, Bella. It's okay."

"Nothing about this is okay." She wrapped her arms around him, glaring at the guards who seemed perfectly useless considering the state of things. "We need to get you somewhere safe." They were farther away from the flames now, but the heat was still searing.

"Ah, Bella." She felt his lips against her ear. "You're my somewhere safe. Come on. We're almost at the steps." His lips moved away. "Devane," he yelled. "Where's the crew?"

"Safe." The slim man in black appeared, the sweat on his face shining. "Everyone's off the stage except you. Nobody's been hurt. The audience is being pushed back." He was shining a flashlight on the stage floor. Arabella barely spotted the steep steps before the security guards surrounding them hustled them down them and well away from the stage.

From the other side—the audience side—Arabella could only stare in horror at the tableau.

The images of horses and rolling waves on the big screens were still playing, accompanied now by the sounds of the retreating crowd and the hungry flames hissing and popping.

Jay's arm kept her close to his side. "I told you no pyrotechnics."

Devane lifted his hands. "And there weren't any. This isn't our doing. I already told the cop there, that."

Arabella realized he meant Detective Teas, who was pacing back and forth some distance away, a cell phone at his ear.

Several guards were wielding fire extinguishers which didn't seem to be having any effect. The wall of flames just kept flowing up and over the metal framework of the stage, long fingers flicking back and forth into the sky, neither growing nor shrinking.

If it weren't so shocking and horrible, it would have been almost mesmerizing.

She obviously wasn't the only one who thought so, Arabella realized when she spotted Jason on the other side of the chairs. He was staring at the fire in much the same way she'd been.

She squeezed Jay's hand. "I'll be right back."

He frowned slightly, but when he followed her gaze toward the young man, he nodded and let go of her.

Giving the first dozen rows of chairs a wide berth, she crossed over to him and realized his shoulders were shaking from sobs even before she reached him. "Jason." She slid her arm around him. "It's okay. Nobody's hurt. Listen. You can hear the sirens already. The fire department will put out the fire."

His shoulders heaved even harder. "My grandpa's under the stage."

She stiffened. "Norman? Your grandpa Norman?" She looked back toward Jay and as if he sensed it, he separated from the cluster of people around him. Dragging Jason with her, she dashed toward him and met him halfway. "Jason says that Norman is under the stage."

He swore and gestured to the guards. In seconds, they'd fanned out and were approaching the stage once again from the sides not engulfed in flame.

"It's my fault," Jason was moaning where he'd collapsed in a chair.

She sat beside him and covered his fisted hands with hers. "Of course it isn't," she soothed the same way she would have soothed Tyler or Toby. She knew the young man was close to his grandfather.

"He said he just wanted to see how it was all set up. He's always interested in how things are built. How they work. So I got him backstage."

"Backstage doesn't mean under it," Jay reasoned.

Arabella nodded. "Jay's right." Despite the height of the stage, it was still difficult imagining the gray-haired man clambering beneath the metal framework. But even if he had, the flames hadn't gotten beneath the stage. Hadn't surrounded it or engulfed it. She was nevertheless grateful to see the fire engine creeping through the congested parking lot. "I'm sure your grandpa's fine. There're a lot of people here for the concert. He'll turn up."

"You don't understand. When he was in the army, he used to blow things up."

Her mouth dried and her eyes met Jay's. Because she suddenly realized that Jason wasn't concerned because his grandfather was a curious man in danger. "You think he has something to do *with* the fire? Why would he want to hurt Jay?"

"I don't think it's him he wants to hurt." Jason swiped his face with his arm and held out his hand, opening his fist to reveal his hotel name badge. "I found this in my grandpa's car tonight."

Jay plucked the badge from the young man's palm. "Did you forget it there?"

The firelight danced over Jason's pale face. "I lost that one the first week I started working at the hotel. Before they even opened up in January." He turned slightly and she saw an identical badge already pinned to his chest. "He's had it and he never told me. He could get anywhere in the hotel."

Because the badge was an access key.

Jay grabbed Jason's arm and hauled him to his feet. "You need to tell this to the police."

"Aunt Petunia's gonna lock him away if she finds out."

"He'll be lucky if that's all that happens," Jay muttered. He was aiming toward Teas but Devane caught up to them first.

"Nobody's under the stage," he reported.

Feeling shaky, Arabella didn't know whether to be relieved or not.

"Find Callum and fill him in," Jay told him and the man set off again.

The fire engine had made it through the parking lot, and in practiced choreography, firefighters in full gear began dragging hoses from the truck.

Jason had barely finished stammering out his story for Detective Teas when the crews conquered the fire. The cessation of heat was immediate.

"Jason." Arabella suddenly turned back to him. "You said before that you didn't think it was Jay your grandpa wants to hurt. Why?"

Jason looked more miserable than ever. "When I first started working at the hotel, I was on the cleaning crew at night. I found him sleeping inside the kitchen at Roja. It was locked up tight." His gaze flicked over the name badge that Jay had handed over to the detective.

"Just sleeping," Teas repeated.

"Yeah. When I woke him up to get him outta there, he was all confused. Talking about my grandma and how he—"

"How he *what*?" Teas asked flatly when Jason broke off.

Arabella sat beside him again and squeezed his hand.

He swiped his cheeks again. "He was talking about how he was gonna get her back from the Fortunes and—" his voice dropped to a hoarse whisper "—and make them pay."

Detective Teas swiped his hand down his face. "Is

there anything *else*? Any other details you should have shared before now?"

"He's been in Roja after it's closed more than once," Jason admitted, slumping in his chair.

Jay leaned his head closer to the detective and Arabella knew he was telling the man about Norman's problem with his meds.

Teas lifted his cell phone again to his ear. "Get someone over to Roja now. And I want an all-points on Norm—" she heard him saying as he paced away from them.

Jason's eyes sought Arabella's. "I told you he's just confused. My grandma hasn't lived in Rambling Rose since before I was born. I doubt she's ever even met anyone named Fortune."

A confused man—for whatever reason—with a grudge and unfettered access to a hotel that had been besieged with one inexplicable challenge after another.

Arabella looked over her shoulder at the rows of chairs. What had been neat and orderly when they'd arrived had been knocked askew by the vacating audience.

Only they hadn't really vacated at all, she realized. The outer edges of the parking lot were crammed with faces. The streets beyond, equally packed.

They'd all come for a show, and they'd gotten one none of them could have expected.

"Norman or not, we need to finish the concert," Jay said, as if he were reading her mind. "People paid good money that the hotel still needs."

She looked at the stage. The fire was out, but the foamy substance used to douse the flames flowed over the stage, dripping off the sides while the firehoses still snaked all over the ground. "How?"

"He's how." Jay nodded toward Devane who was jogging their way again, this time with Callum Fortune keeping pace with him. "If there's one thing Michael Devane is good at, it's turning a situation right-side up."

And he did.

In thirty minutes, they had a plan. And while Devane went off to address the crowd, everyone else set to work. The fire chief said that even though the fire appeared to have been set more as a distraction than to cause damage, nothing from the original staging could be used until it was inspected for damage. But there was backup equipment that was pulled off trucks and repositioned squarely in the center of the parking lot. Chairs were repositioned. And before another thirty minutes had passed, the crowd was chanting Jett's name again and when a spotlight suddenly came on, picking out Callum Fortune standing in the center of the impromptu "stage," the chanting got even louder.

"Let's give it up for Jett Carr," Callum shouted and his voice rang out from the speakers. "Thanks to his generosity, Hotel Fortune's gonna be here for Rambling Rose for a long time to come." He stretched his arms, clapping his hands rhythmically over his head and the backup band started playing again and the women were singing something that had the crowd singing along, too.

Arabella looked up into Jay's eyes. "That's your call, Jet-pack. Your fans are waiting. Tonight. Tomorrow."

"Give me my Jett!"

She smiled as the piercing yell was swallowed in the night and the music. "From the sounds of it, every day from here on out."

She felt the fine tremor in his fingers as he stroked her cheek. "None of that out there counts for anything if you're not a part of it."

"Jay."

"I'm serious, Bella. I walked away once but it wasn't for the right reason. Once these shows are done, I could walk away happy. Because *you* would be the right reason. Music's my first love." He kissed her fingertips and pressed them against his chest. "But you're the very heart of me. And if you want to raise strawberries and babies with me, then I'll spend the rest of my life doing just that."

Sudden tears sprang to her eyes. "Babies? You want babies with me?"

He reached in his pocket and pulled out a small ring. A diamond ring. "I want everything with you," he said huskily. "Laughter. Tears. Triumphs. Fears. And babies who'll have all of their mother's beauty and hopefully none of their father's failings. And I'll read them bedtime stories about Oscar and Aaron. If you'll have me."

She laughed through her tears. If she hadn't already fallen so far in love with him, she would have tumbled for good right then and there. "And you'll teach them piano," she added huskily, holding out her hand.

He slid the small ring into place. "Of course it would fit perfectly." He sounded a little choked. "Trust my grandmother. It's her ring."

Arabella's tears spilled over as she pressed her lips to his.

Then she pulled back and gave him a little shove. "Now go make your music, Jay. And I'll be right here waiting."

His eyes glittered. "You're absolutely sure?"

She took the guitar that Devane was holding nearby and held it out to Jay. "I told you. I couldn't stop loving you even if I tried."

His fingers caressed hers as he took the guitar. Then he turned and jogged into the spotlight, holding it high above his head.

The cheer that went up could have probably been heard all the way to Houston.

And even though his smile was directed at the crowd beyond the spotlight, Arabella knew it belonged, most of all, to her.

Epilogue

He sang straight for the next three hours. Then, while the fireworks that shot off into the night sky during the finale were still flickering into nothing, everyone involved in the show gathered inside Roja where, they all learned, Norman had been found and taken unresistingly into custody.

There was coffee. Champagne. There was toast and jars of strawberry jam and fried chicken Arabella knew could only have been prepared by Louella herself.

Mostly, there were kisses and lots and lots of hugs as Jay officially introduced her to Michael Devane. "He's the one who managed to pull together this whole show in a matter of days," Jay explained. "Found the guys in the band. The singers. All of it."

Even as tired as she was, Arabella couldn't help staring. "You'd never performed together before?"

Devane clapped Jay on the shoulders. "Started rehearsals two days ago in a sound studio in California. And we did pretty damn well, considering everything." He looked at his watch. "But now I'd better check on things for tomorrow's show."

"That'd be *today's* show," Brady said, throwing himself down into a chair nearby. "At least we can count on it being less exciting than this one was." He rubbed his fingers through his hair. "God knows how much worse it could have been if Norman had been really trying to burn things down."

Arabella pressed her head against Jay's shoulder as she glanced across the restaurant to where Mariana— her blond bun atypically askew—sat at a table with Jason and his aunt Petunia. "There won't be any charges against Jason, will there? He was genuinely shocked that his grandfather had his badge."

"I doubt there will be charges." That came from Kane, who looked as tired as Brady when he joined their table. "I can't speak for everyone, but I know I'm not interested in hanging the kid on a peg because his grandpa's got it in for the Fortunes."

"From everything Brady said, it sounds like he blames them—us—for losing his wife," Arabella said.

Nicole set down the coffeepot she'd been carrying around to refill cups and perched on the edge of the booth next to her sister Megan. Both Nicole and Mariana had been in the restaurant when the police apprehended Norman. "He kept calling Mariana his wife when Detective Teas took him away. He's always liked hanging around her, but obviously he'd become fixated."

"His meds." Jay shook his head. "Now we all can see why Petunia was so worried about him and his meds."

"He'll get the help he needs with that now," Callum said, sliding onto the table, because that was the only place left. He stuck out his hand toward Jay. "And thanks to you, we've got the help we need now, too."

Jay smiled faintly and shook the man's hand. "It was nothing."

Callum snorted and so did a lot of others. "The revenue from tonight alone should put us back in the black. In fact, it was so successful they're going to play two more shows over the weekend, so what happens tomorrow and Sunday needs to stay in your pock—"

But Jay was already shaking his head. "Now you know that Norman's been behind all of the mishaps around the hotel, you'll have bargaining power again with the insurance company, too. But after making sure the crew's paid, the Rambling Rose concert revenue is all yours." He smiled down at Arabella. "I'm already getting everything I need out of the deal."

"I've got just one question for you," Brady said, sounding pugnacious. "When's the wedding?"

Arabella raised her eyebrows at him and waggled her finger with the ring on it. "When's yours, Brady," she shot right back at him.

"That's actually a good question." Megan bumped her sister's shoulder. "You and Collin are the only ones who've made it legal. But you've still got a honeymoon to take. When's he getting his next leave of service?"

Nicole smiled brilliantly. "He's getting transferred stateside. Should be here in the next several weeks."

Kane sat forward and held up his fingers and started ticking them off. "So who've we got? Grace and Wiley. Me and Layla. Megan and Mark." He nodded at Brady. "You and Harper. Even Dillon and Hailey need to get the deed done. S'pose there's a discount wedding service to get us all hitched at once?"

None of them even noticed when Arabella and Jay started creeping out of the restaurant.

"There you go," Megan said on a laugh. "Always looking for efficiency. But that would finish us all up in the marital department, wouldn't it?"

"Not if you count Josh and Brian—"

The restaurant door closed on Kane's voice and Arabella looked up at Jay. "Now what do we do?"

"We're in a hotel with a couple floors of empty rooms that were never even touched by water damage and that group in there will never find us. What do you think?"

She was tired right down to her bones but she laughed delightedly and wound her arms around his shoulders. "I think I'm very glad we know where the master keys are kept."

I think you should know that...

...the future is ours.

And it was.

* * * * *

COMING SOON!

We really hope you enjoyed reading this book.
If you're looking for more romance, be sure to
head to the shops when new books are
available on

Thursday 10th
June

MILLS & BOON

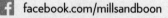

MILLS & BOON

THE HEART OF ROMANCE

A ROMANCE FOR EVERY READER

MODERN

Prepare to be swept off your feet by sophisticated, sexy and seductive heroes, in some of the world's most glamourous and romantic locations, where power and passion collide.

HISTORICAL

Escape with historical heroes from time gone by. Whether your passion is for wicked Regency Rakes, muscled Vikings or rugged Highlanders, awaken the romance of the past.

MEDICAL

Set your pulse racing with dedicated, delectable doctors in the high-pressure world of medicine, where emotions run high and passion, comfort and love are the best medicine.

True Love

Celebrate true love with tender stories of heartfelt romance, from the rush of falling in love to the joy a new baby can bring, and a focus on the emotional heart of a relationship.

Desire

Indulge in secrets and scandal, intense drama and plenty of sizzling hot action with powerful and passionate heroes who have it all: wealth, status, good looks…everything but the right woman.

HEROES

Experience all the excitement of a gripping thriller, with an intense romance at its heart. Resourceful, true-to-life women and strong, fearless men face danger and desire - a killer combination!

To see which titles are coming soon, please visit

millsandboon.co.uk/nextmonth

MILLS & BOON
MEDICAL
Pulse-Racing Passion

Set your pulse racing with dedicated, delectable doctors in the high-pressure world of medicine, where emotions run high and passion, comfort and love are the best medicine.

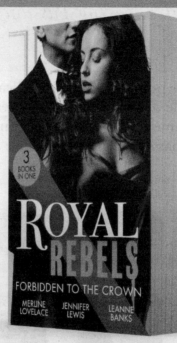